D1385594

BRYANT & MAY ON THE LOOSE

Tracking down a murderer in King's Cross, one of the busiest meeting points in Britain, would be a nightmare for any police force. The discovery of a decapitated body in a shop freezer should be a case for the Peculiar Crimes Unit, but the team has been disbanded, with retirement the only option for its elderly detectives, Bryant and May. When a second headless corpse is found, and a strange half-man, half-beast sporting antlers made of knives begins stalking construction sites at night, the PCU is back in business, searching for body parts and behaving disgracefully as they go in search of London's pagan secrets.

BRYANT & MAY ON THE LOOSE

BRYANT & MAY ON THE LOOSE

by

Christopher Fowler

Magna Large Print Books
Long Preston, North Yorkshire,
BD23 4ND, England.

British Library Cataloguing in Publication Data.

Fowler, Christopher
    Bryant & May on the loose.

    A catalogue record of this book is
    available from the British Library

    ISBN   978-0-7505-3251-8

First published in Great Britain in 2009 by Doubleday
an imprint of Transworld Publishers

Published in Large Print 2010 by arrangement with
Transworld Publishers

Magna Large Print is an imprint of Library Magna Books Ltd.

Printed and bound in Great Britain by
T.J. (International) Ltd., Cornwall, PL28 8RW

To Maggie Armitage,
for her infinite kindness and generosity

ACKNOWLEDGEMENTS

Those who know London well will appreciate that these cases all have their basis in truth. The myths and mysteries of the city are presented as accurately as possible, even though they tend to mutate as frequently as London itself. Here, I was greatly inspired by ideas in Chesca Potter's *Mysterious King's Cross*, and Harold Bailey's *The Lost Language of London*.

My greatest pleasure is knowing that there are others who share the same passions. I'd especially like to thank those who always believed readers would appreciate a modern version of Golden Age mysteries; my agent Mandy Little, who gave me the encouragement and confidence to continue, film agent Meg Davis, for her optimism and insight, Simon Taylor, the best editor I've had the pleasure of working with, Kate Samano, who entirely understands the Bryant & May world, Claire Ward, for her spot-on design, and Simon Moore, for creating such a great website. In the past year I've blogged almost every day, so this is also for everyone who has helped to make the site such a continuing pleasure. A vote of thanks goes to the book groups of Britain, for whom I have the greatest respect. Big love, of course, to Peter Chapman, to Sally, Martin, Ren and the rest of the gang. Writers need feedback, so let's talk at www.christopherfowler.co.uk.

'When house and land are gone and spent,
then learning is most excellent.'
Samuel Foote

'If history is written by the victors, legend
is at the service of the vanquished.'
Steve Roud, *London Lore*

(Note written in crimson felt-tip pen on the back of a flyer for the Tease to Please Burlesque Cabaret, Soho, found pinned to the door of the Peculiar Crimes Unit, 1b Hampstead Road, London NW1 0JP.)

To The Incoming Team Taking Over From Us

Welcome to the former offices of the Peculiar Crimes Unit.

We hope you're as happy here as we once were, and have better luck with your bosses than we ever had.

You may not have heard of us, but we saved London's collective arse on a great many occasions, and for a short but happy time this was our home. We put in a lot of hours here for very little cash. From these rooms the city's longest-serving detectives, Arthur Bryant and John May, controlled an investigation team that handled the stuff you lot couldn't begin to deal with; the cases that caused public panic, the ones that upset the status quo, the unsolved murders that were just too confusing, weird or embarrassing for our mates in the Met.

We were closed down and kicked out because we dared to do what no one else in this fair city would do. We challenged our so-called superiors at the Home Office after the government colluded in the deaths of innocent witnesses involved in a national defence project. So now, we no longer exist.

For anyone taking over Mr Bryant's space (Room 6) – please note that it is dangerous to operate electronic equipment in the area between his desk and the wall. Laptops, mobiles and gadgets containing batteries are all subject to leakage; I don't know why. There's always too much loose electricity knocking around whenever Mr Bryant's in the room. According to him, the old Bakelite radio on the windowsill periodically picks up light-entertainment broadcasts from 1965. On Sunday lunchtimes when the office is quiet you can sometimes hear old episodes of *Round the Horne*. It's quite creepy if you're there by yourself.

Also, please beware of the large jar on top of his cupboard, as it contains a solution produced in the course of our last case at Mornington Crescent and must never be opened. I meant to throw it out before we left. In the event of a spillage, you'll find the number of a good epidemiologist pasted to the lid.

We bleached the kitchen refrigerator but still couldn't get rid of the funny smell in the freezer compartment. It's been like that ever since Mr Bryant left a human foot in it.

Do not use the photocopier beside my desk (Room 4) for more than fifty copies at a time. I spilled a full bottle of Max Factor 'Bowanga' Jungle Ruby nail varnish inside it, and the rollers get sticky whenever the machine warms up.

You might also want to avoid the middle floorboard at the end of the hall, which our Mr Banbury sawed through in the course of an experiment and never nailed back properly. If you get on the wrong end of it, it's like stamping on a rake and will have your eye out.

If you find a membership card to the Mount Pleasant Country & Western Barn Dancing Society, please forward it to DC Meera Mangeshkar at the address below.

On second thoughts, don't bother sending anything on. We have no idea where we're going to be. None of us knows where we're heading. We're all out in the cold. I don't know what went wrong. We're good people, we've always done the right thing. That should count for something. We loved this unit, and now it's gone. Damn it all to hell.

Signed, on behalf of the members of London's former Peculiar Crimes Unit:

Janice Longbright – Detective Sergeant
Raymond Land – Acting Temporary Chief
Arthur Bryant & John May – Senior Detectives
Dan Banbury – Crime Scene Management

and Technology
Giles Kershaw – Forensic Pathology
April May – Office Management
Jack Renfield – Sergeant
Meera Mangeshkar – Detective Constable
Colin Bimsley – Detective Constable
Oswald Finch (Deceased)
Liberty DuCaine – (part-time) Police
Constable
Crippen – staff cat.

1

'A BIT OF BAD LUCK'

The sleek metal cylinder was a little over a foot long, snub-nosed and topped with an inverted V of steel. It weighed about a kilogram, and the section with the fin pattern had been painted green. It hung in the air for a moment after being released, almost as if it had become weightless, then began to roll down through the thin low clouds. It had split away from the other incendiary bombs released from their rack, and now that its carrier had already droned past it fell silently, accompanied only by the soft whispering of the wind.

Below, the clouds parted and the brown curves of the terraced streets came into focus. Grey slate roofs, orange chimney pots, scruffy little back gardens, a child playing on the pavement with a red toy car – the details stood out in sharp relief. It all seemed so silent and undisturbed; there had been no warning siren.

The mundane urban topography came clearer and closer, houses on wide cobbled streets that curved in arching paisley patterns beside the shining stripe of the canal. Makeshift shelters, chicken sheds, lines full of washing, outside toilets – the distance between the bomb and the ground closed fast as the cylinder spiralled down towards the crowded houses of King's Cross.

A sudden wind buffeted it and shifted its direction a little to the right. There were two terraced homes just below it now. The nose of the bomb swung first over one, then the other, as if trying to decide which it would hit.

'I'll have to be getting back, Mrs B,' said Ethel, drying her hands and replacing the tea towel on its rod. 'My Alf creates merry hell if he don't get his tea on time, and I'm late as it is.'

'Do tell him it was my fault,' urged Bea. 'It was kind of you to help out today.'

Ethel wiped her nose and returned her handkerchief to her sleeve. 'You do what you can. I'll just be glad when everything settles back to normal.' She unknotted her apron, folded it neatly, then yanked a grey felt hat over her hair and stabbed it into place with a pin.

'Could you take these back as you go?' Bea handed Ethel a pair of empty bottles, cod-liver oil and concentrated orange juice. 'And you'd better pick up some more soap flakes at Lynch's.' She glanced over at her husband, who was half asleep in front of the fire, his chair tipped back at a precarious angle. 'Harold, Eth's off now.'

'Oh, don't wake him up, Mrs B. He's like Alf, dead to the world when he's not up and about, but it's a good thing. Since we lost Bert it's been hard for any of us to get a good night's sleep.' Ethel's oldest son had been killed at sea. She slipped the bottles into her bicycle basket. 'I'll collect the linens from Wallace's and be back in the morning around half past ten.'

'I shall be here,' Bea promised. 'I agreed to let the Services Comfort Committee have the piano, and they're coming to collect it. I warned them it will need tuning. Mrs Porter is donating all her sheet music.'

'I don't know what you're going to do for a sing-song now, I'm sure.'

Bea was about to tell Ethel that the National Gallery's lunch-hour concerts would be a preferable alternative to Harold hammering out 'Whispering Grass' on the upright, but she didn't get a chance to speak. Nor did Ethel manage to get her bicycle out of the scullery doorway, because the room shook and all the crockery on the dresser was thrown forward, smashing to pieces on the stone floor.

'What the bloody hell–?' Harold's chair fell forward and he found himself sprawled across the rug.

'Lord, not again,' complained Ethel, quickly closing the door to the street and retreating inside. 'Second time this week without a warning.'

Their ears were ringing painfully. From somewhere above them came the clunking sound of falling bricks. They barely had time to gather their wits before a louder blast pulsed the air from the room and shattered one of the taped kitchen windows. Harold had been building an Anderson shelter in the garden, but it still wasn't finished because the Council hadn't delivered enough corrugated iron, so they usually stayed in the cupboard under the stairs until the all-clear sounded.

'Eth, you'd best stay with us for a while,' said Bea. 'That was too close for comfort.' She noticed that the cleaning lady's face was bleeding from a dozen tiny cuts. 'You've got some glass in you, love, just a little. Harold, give me a hand, don't sit there like an article.' She grabbed a flannel from the draining board, dipped it in the washing-up water and gingerly dabbed Ethel's face, removing as many splinters as she could find, but daylight was fading and she could not turn on the lamp because the blackout curtain had been blown from the window.

'Like the world's coming to an end,' said Ethel mournfully. Her face was a crimson mask, but if the process of retrieving the shards from her skin hurt, she made no complaint. The third detonation was further away, somewhere over in the next street, nearer to the station by the sound of it. The Jerries were trying to knock out the railway terminals, and anyone who lived near one was in danger.

Harold looked out through the shattered window frame and saw a great mound of bricks. The house beside it looked like a cutaway model, its private interior shamefully revealed to the world. A pair of slender yellow vases on its front room mantelpiece were still in place. Some pictures on the remaining wall had not even been knocked crooked, although the lace curtains had been torn to tatters. As always, it was the arbitrariness of it all that shocked most. This time nothing seemed to be burning and there was no smoke, but the air was dry and there were effusions of dense brown dust. Several people were wandering in the road, lost to the shock of the blast.

'Blimey. The Porters' house has taken a hit. That's a bit of bad luck. Put Eth in the back room, Bea, and get the kettle on. Buck her up with a glass of something. We should have a drop of whisky in the sideboard. I'm going to see what I can do.'

'Be careful, Harold,' called his wife. 'I didn't hear an all-clear. I didn't hear any sirens at all.'

'I've got to go to Alf, he'll be frantic,' said Ethel.

'You're not going anywhere just yet.' Bea took the cleaning lady's arm and led her into the passage. The bombs were falling further away now, sounding like a thunderstorm in retreat. It was Tuesday 12 November, 1940, the ninth week of the event that became known as The Blitz, and London's populace was getting used to the continual threat of air attack. When the sirens sounded, those caught outside often ignored official advice to file into sanctioned public shelters, and instead formed orderly queues into the city's Underground stations. The ones who stayed at home ducked into shelters, crammed themselves into coal holes and cupboards or hid under the stairs. The government wanted everyone to sleep at ground level, but many refused to give up their beds for a patch of cold linoleum in the kitchen. The war had forced an intimacy on people that made them uncomfortable. It wasn't nice to have everyone knowing your business.

Bea boiled a kettle while Ethel attended to her face and tidied her hair. They were better when they had things to do. The problem, said Bea, was the lack of information. The papers told them nothing, and not knowing got on your nerves. What a Christmas they could look forward to! Then she realized what she had said, and looked back at Ethel, who would be spending her first Christmas without her son.

Harold picked his way between the stacks of fallen masonry, crumpled chunks of an internal lath-and-plaster wall and an entire fireplace surround that had landed perfectly upright in the road, as if it had been placed there by a giant hand. A confused-looking air-raid warden was trying to direct people away.

'Mrs Porter,' Harold called. 'Stay right there. I wouldn't move, if I were you.' His neighbour was standing dazed on a splintered wooden floorboard that jutted out above her smoking cellar, all that remained of her living-room floor. She was dressed in a torn white blouse and skirt, and bedroom slippers. She had been preparing some supper to eat in front of the radio, which was still playing even though it dangled from the end of an electric cord. A jaunty foxtrot, 'Till the Lights of London Shine Again', played as Harold inched his way on to the creaking platform.

'Give me your hand, love,' he called softly.

Mrs Porter seemed not to have heard him. *'Don't you cry when I'm gone,'* sang the radio. *'Wear a smile and carry on, till the lights of London shine again.'*

'I'm just here in front of you,' said Harold.

'And now Syd Lipton and the Grosvenor House Dance Band play "Blacking Out The

Moon" for every–' The radio spat an electrical pulse and went dead. All that could be heard was the soft suffering of the injured, the chink and tumble of dislodging bricks.

Harold stretched out his hand. 'You can do it, love. Don't look down. Just reach towards me.'

Mrs Porter remained frozen, staring past him to where the wall had been. To where her husband had been sitting, waiting for his dinner.

'He's not there,' Harold explained carefully. 'He's gone, love, and the house has gone.' He had passed the old man's body as he approached the house, crushed beneath a collapsed chimney stack. Nearby, a grandfather clock had landed face-down on the pavement, like a felled parade soldier.

She noticed him for the first time, and fluttered her eyelids as though coming to her senses. For a moment he thought she might faint and fall into darkness. Then she held out her arm, just far enough for him to grab her and haul her back from the edge. 'My name's Irene,' she murmured, and passed out in his arms.

2

MR FOX

What the bombs could not accomplish, the town planners finished off. Any building deemed a danger to public safety could be pulled down, and soon this excuse was used to rid the city of anything staid and dull. So the classic portico of Euston station was torn apart, and the Gothic cathedral of St Pancras would have followed it into the dust but for the protestations of campaigners like Sir John Betjeman. The grand edifice remained intact but derelict, a home to rats and pigeons, awaiting rebirth in the next century.

Now that it was open once more, the cobwebs and pigeons had been banished from its environs, but vermin remained...

Mr Fox was the master of his territory, as sly and adaptable as his namesake. He could vanish and reappear at will. The cheap grey hoodie, chain-store leather jacket and tracksuit bottoms he wore rendered him virtually invisible. He gave the impression of being small and pale, so light that he might not leave footprints in snow, but this was not the case. His limbs were thickly muscled, and his strength could startle.

He plotted a route through the great vaulted station of St Pancras, instinctively looking out for the lost ones. Ridges and furrows of glass rose above him in a matrix of pale-blue ironwork, allowing an immensity of light to fall across the concourse. It was the end of April, and Mr Fox was one day away from becoming a murderer.

As he insinuated himself through the crowds, he imagined his appearance as witnesses might remember it: unfocused, silvery and opaque, a blur on a photograph. He was feral, instinctive, always on the move, always wary of being cornered. If his image could be captured (and it certainly could, given that there were over four million cameras watching London, an astonishing proportion of which were hidden in its stations), he made sure it would only appear as lost pixels on a screen, a time-lapsed smudge without a face. True subversives, he knew, were unnoticeable. Fake subversives (suburban kids and people in dull jobs) dressed to stand out from the crowd. Mr Fox was like the King's Cross lighthouse, the strange tumbledown Victorian monument above the street that went unnoticed because it was always somewhere in the background.

In and out of the shops and bars that occupied the glassed-in areas behind the exposed-brick arches – Foyles bookshop, Neal's Yard, Le Pain Quotidien, Marks & Spencer – he searched for the lonely and the weak. He was drawn towards the lame straggler, the vulnerable visitor, the indecisive commuter. He could not afford to take long because too many watchful lenses assembled in clusters on the surrounding arches. One pass through the main concourse of St Pancras was usually enough. The beauty of operating in a place like this was the sheer number of potential victims.

There were plenty of police strolling about, but the location gave them a disadvantage. So many civilians approached with questions in the course of a shift that their differences were dissolved by sheer weight of numbers. The officers were like keepers in charge of an ever-expanding anthill.

Mr Fox never made contact inside the railway station. He followed his targets at a distance, out to the cab ranks and crammed pavements where they waited to cross the road, distracted by their coats, bags and maps, disoriented by their unfamiliar surroundings. He had been born and raised in these grim streets, knew every alley and shadowed corner, but had not known their tangled history until recently. He listened and learned from others, knowing it would all prove useful to him one day. When he lacked knowledge, he befriended people who had it, absorbing everything he needed before discarding them and moving on.

Knowledge was not the only thing he stole.

Sometimes he would look his prey right in the eye, knowing that after they had discovered their loss they would think back without remembering him. He had the kind of face no one could ever recall. In the legitimate business world it would have been a curse, but for him it was a blessing.

He watched and heard and remembered everything. He soaked up even the most irrelevant information and stored it away: every newspaper headline, every station announcement, every passing scrap of conversation. As yet his territory was small, no more than a few roads, but he was still young, and there was time to grow.

He was filled with a terrible, restless energy.

Mr Fox trusted no one because he knew that trust would make him weak, and he already had one flaw – a temper that could make him forget who he was or what he was doing. There was a fire within him that had to be tamped down, for fear that it would flare up and incinerate the world.

He stood behind a beautiful Spanish girl with the latest Apple laptop sticking out of her rucksack, then waited beside a Chinese man who carelessly returned his wallet to an open pocket in his raincoat. Today he had no need of such easy pickings. That kind of thing was beneath him now, small-time stuff. He was looking for a dupe, a penniless rat-boy with the loyalty of a dog for its master, someone he could use and string along, someone he could blame and dump. He did not have to look hard, because the dupe found him. Mr Fox could not believe it; the little runt was about to try to pick *his* pocket! He turned sharply, catching the boy with his arm poised.

'Hey, I know you!' said the boy, suddenly unfreezing from his guilty pose in a tumble of awkward angles. 'Your name's – hang on – it'll come to me.' He wagged his finger. His face was as pale as neon, bony and spotty with drug abuse. Mr Fox mapped out his life in an instant. An illustrious career that went from stealing on demand to hawking drugs and selling himself. The area's old clubbers had their ugly pasts and their doomed futures etched upon their faces, the nights and fights filled with trash-talk, bravado and petty cruelties.

'You're local, innit, I seen you around here loads of times.'

'I'm Mr Fox.'

'Nah, that's not it. Not Fox, another name, unless you changed it.'

'I think you're mistaken, Mr–'

'Just call me Mac, everyone does. Nah, it's definitely you.' The boy gurgled and slapped

31

at his shaved head as if trying to knock sense into himself. 'I always seen you around, all my life. You was in Camley Street Park one time. I was with my mates havin' a smoke an' that. You was– Ah.' Mac suddenly remembered, and even he knew it was better to quickly forget what he had seen.

'What do you do, Mac?' asked Mr Fox, walking with him, leading him from the station.

'This an' that. I make ends meet, shift a bit of stuff here and there. The usual, you know.'

Mr Fox knew all too well. He moved the boy aside as a pair of armed police constables in acid-yellow jackets walked past. King's Cross had radically changed since becoming the target of terrorist attacks. He checked their epaulettes for area codes and saw that they were locals.

'How long have you been out of Pentonville?'

'How d'you know I was inside?' The boy looked amazed.

Mr Fox had spotted the tattoos that edged out beyond Mac's sleeves. The inmates at Pentonville prison were fond of inking themselves with fake Russian gang symbols, most of them poorly copied and misspelled. The one on Mac's right forearm was actually a produce stamp for a Soviet state farm. If the boy knew he was advertising turnips instead of hanging tough, it might be the end of their association before it began.

'Wait a minute, that's where I seen you,' said Mac. 'You was my English teacher, you used to come and teach at Pentonville.'

Mr Fox studied his prey, deciding whether to let the identification stand.

'One day you just stopped coming. What did you give it up for?'

'The doors,' he admitted.

'What do you mean?'

'The seventeen security doors I had to pass through every morning and evening. They added an hour and a half to my journey.' He did not mention the lockdowns, those days when the alarm rang and no one was allowed in or out. Six or seven hours at a time spent doing nothing, shut in a stale blank room like one of the inmates. He didn't mention the smell that got into your clothes and made you dread each working day. Mr Fox was determined to stay out of prison because he had witnessed its horrors from close quarters.

'How would you like to earn some easy money?' he asked.

Mac's eyes shone, then dimmed. You could see exactly what he was thinking. 'I don't do queer stuff no more. I mean, no offence an' that.'

'Don't worry, it's just some simple errands. To meet someone, relay some messages.

Maybe deliver something back to them.'

'It ain't drugs, is it? 'Cause I'm on probation.'

'Nothing like that. It's completely legitimate, I assure you. Just a local job. I need someone trustworthy.'

'I don't let people down.'

'I'll need you to be around here tomorrow evening. Give me your address and mobile number. I have to be able to get in touch with you easily. Tell me, do you drive?'

'I got a van.'

'Unmarked, is it?'

'Well, it's white.'

'We may need to use it at some point. If you do well with this, there could be more work for you.'

'Yeah, then, I reckon I could do something like that. You know, for the right price.'

The right price, thought Mr Fox. *You were going to steal my wallet a few moments ago, you little tapeworm.* But he saw the desperation in the boy's eyes and knew he had found a born victim, and that was all he needed.

As soon as Mr Fox had received the phone call, he had realized he was about to move into the big time. All he needed to do now was remember his own rules: *Never leave a trace of yourself behind, and if things go wrong make sure someone else takes the blame. Always remember, we do not live in a meritocracy. Nobody gets ahead because they're good. The spoils go to those who build the strongest networks. Everything that happens, happens not because of what you can do, but because of who you know. The whole world is corrupt, and only those who acknowledge its corruption find their true place in it.*

Mr Fox felt sure that, despite his age and background, he was moving up, destined to operate in grander circles.

He did not know it, but within twenty-four hours he would be wiping a dead man's blood from his hands.

3

SHUTDOWN

From the *Police Review:*
END OF THE LINE FOR LONDON'S OLDEST SPECIALIST UNIT

After many threats on its life, London's most notorious and controversial crime unit has finally been shut down.

From this month, the main goal of the National Policing Improvement Agency will be to modernize the British police service, taking on some Home Office and ACPO functions, including officer training, national IT infrastructure, forensics and information sharing. As part of the drive to eliminate duplication, the Home Office has closed London's longstanding Peculiar Crimes Unit, returning its ongoing investigations to the capital's murder and major inquiry teams.

The PCU was created to handle specialized cases and crimes (mostly murders) which could be considered a risk to public order and confidence if left unresolved. The unit survived through the second half of the twentieth century, but found itself increasingly mired in controversy after being placed under the control of the Home Office, who accused its management team of becoming politically partisan and failing to follow accepted procedural guidelines.

Although the PCU's two most senior detectives were never formally charged with misconduct, their reputations were irreparably tarnished by behaviour which many in government circles considered to be anti-establishment and subversive. Police chiefs had long been concerned about the unit's repeated failure to conform to government guidelines. It is understood that the Home Office is considering pursuing a number of allegations against Arthur Bryant and John May, including:

• The unauthorized release of fourteen illegal immigrants, who subsequently evaded detention and deportation from the UK.
• The destruction of government property, including the PCU's own offices in Mornington Crescent.
• The contamination and misuse of evidence in criminal investigations.
• Illegal hiring practices, including the commissioning of freelancers specializing in 'alternative' practices such as psychic investigation, dowsing and (on more than one occasion) witchcraft.
• Blackmailing an unnamed senior employee at the Home Office.
• Interfering with a member of the royal family.
• The premeditated release of potentially hazardous chemicals inside a Ministry of Defence outsource agency, in order to discredit it.

Both senior detectives are to face a disciplinary panel. Meanwhile, the remaining members of the PCU staff have been placed on permanent gardening leave, and their old offices at Mornington Crescent have been turned over to the government's newly formed Electronic Fraud Agency.

'The Home Office seems determined that our unit should not be rehoused,' says the temporary acting chief of the PCU, Raymond Land. 'I have asked for the matter to be urgently resolved, but it seems that no one is willing to discuss the possibility with me, or can even be bothered to return my phone calls.'

When asked to comment on the charge, the HO's Security Supervisor Oskar Kasavian explained, 'The Peculiar Crimes Unit proved useful during its post-war heyday but now it is largely redundant to modern policing needs, which are performance- and data-driven and no longer built on public hearsay and personal opinion. The PCU clearly considers itself to be above the law, and has consistently refused to meet our targets. I hope this sends out a clear message to some of the other divisions which are currently underperforming in the league tables.'

But the message is far from clear. Is the PCU officially disbanded or not? HO officials appear unwilling to admit outright that they have closed the unit permanently, but have been accused of enforcing a hidden agenda. Mr Kasavian clashed with the PCU on several occasions, most notably when the unit revealed that his personal relationship with Janet Ramsey, the editor of the daily magazine *Hard News*, constituted a conflict of interest during an ongoing investigation.

Home Office Police Liaison Officer Leslie Faraday concurred with his department's findings. He told us, 'The PCU was a great

British achievement of which we should all be justly proud. It's high time we closed it down.'

Despite their unorthodox methods, the Peculiar Crimes Unit enjoyed an unusually high success rate on murder cases originating in the Greater London area. Many of their investigations encouraged the press to create colourful personas for the killers they sought, including:

- The Leicester Square Vampire
- The Shoreditch Strangler
- The Water Room Killer
- The Highwayman
- The Deptford Demon
- The Belles of Westminster
- The Palace Theatre Phantom

Arthur Bryant and John May, the capital's most highly experienced detective team, helmed the PCU through its most productive decades, but both are now beyond the official retirement age. Neither was available for comment.

Detective Sergeant Janice Longbright confirmed that the unit was closed down with immediate effect after the staff resigned in solidarity with Mr Bryant and Mr May, who may have their pensions revoked pending investigation into issues of alleged misconduct. Despite the fact that a record number of retired detectives posted messages of support for the PCU and have set up a legal fund, the Home Office today issued a statement suggesting that the unit would not be reopened under any circumstances.

As the officers of the Peculiar Crimes Unit now search for new jobs in the private-security sector, it seems that a piece of London police history has been lost for ever.

4

MOVING ON

The alarm clock's mechanism pinged inside its tin case. He listened to the spring slowly unwinding, waiting for the catch to be released and the bell to ring. He was always awake before the clock went off. There was a pause, a dull click, and the ticking continued as before. There was no jarring call to force him from his bed.

Of course. He had unscrewed the clapper and thrown it out of the window.

He settled his weight more deeply into the mattress, sinking into the feather pillows, pulling the eiderdown over his cold ears, ready to return to his dreams. Except that now his brain was awake and he hated just lying here, because memories would rise in his unclouding brain like road markers appearing out of fog, guiding his way back to vivid moments of triumph and regret. Back to times when he wished he had done things differently.

It was better to get up than to lie here remembering. There was nothing in the past that could be put right from the confines of a bed. Still, there was no reason now to rise. *Better to let tepid sleep fold itself over you*, he thought, *a little more each day, like calibrations of death.* He turned over, fidgeted, tried to settle, but finally pulled back the covers and slowly forced his aged, aching bones to an upright position.

Catching sight of himself in the dressing-table mirror, he was repelled by the scrofulous old hermit he found staring back. *If I get any wrinklier I'll be mistaken for a Shar Pei*, he thought. His eyes were red on the outside, worse on the inside. His white tonsure stuck up around his ears. He looked like a frightened monk.

He peered out at the rough planked floor, the dust meandering in beams of watery sunlight, a petal divorcing itself from the dehydrated roses on the wonky little bedside table. The bare grey day stretched ahead with nothing to mark it from the ones before or after. Inertia drifted on to his numb shoulders like a gathering weight of snow.

There really was nothing to get up for.

'Oh, sod it.' Surrendering to his body's apathy, Arthur Bryant allowed himself to fall back into the enveloping warmth of his bed.

The morning was so sharp with winter sun that the yellow streets were striped with black shadows that looked as if they had been painted into place. Light like this belonged in Paris, not London, John May decided. The masts to Chelsea harbour glittered and rattled, pretending they were in Monaco, but no amount of money could replace sluggish brown Thames water with the raunchy azure of the Mediterranean. The old wharf that had once housed coal for the railway industry had been redeveloped into lofts for the conspicuously wealthy, clinquant shops and blind-eyed offices. At weekends there was more life on the surface of the moon.

May walked through the dock with his granddaughter. April was so translucently pale that she always looked cold. The winds that ruffled the surface of the river caught at their coats as if anxious to detain them. This stroll was a test of April's agoraphobia; it had shown signs of returning in the weeks that had passed since the unit was disbanded. The spaces between walls pressed a sense of panic upon her that she fought to ignore.

'It's going to rain later,' she said. 'You need

a haircut.' Her grandfather's elegant silver mane hung over his collar, but he appeared well. He always knew how to look after himself. John May was private and organized. He filed away his emotions as neatly as he kept his apartment, and considered a bad temper to be a sign of weakness. While this level of control was generally thought to be a good thing, it also meant that you could never have a really good fight with him, and sometimes April longed to clear the air between them.

'Property,' he said, pointing at the deserted arcades housing empty shop fronts. 'It's all about who owns the land. I read that London has become the most expensive city in the world. Apparently, even during the economic downturn an apartment in Knightsbridge has still managed to sell for ninety million pounds. Dear God, Knightsbridge, the most dreadful place in the entire city. All those ersatz English houses filled with dodgy millionaires pretending they're in some kind of Edwardian time bubble, assuaging their guilt with bling and bad restaurants. And it's not even near town!'

'You sound just like Uncle Arthur sometimes, you know.'

Whether it was criticism or a compliment, May ignored the remark. 'I suppose the land was simply too valuable to be left in our hands any longer.'

'It wasn't your fault, John.'

'Oh, it was. We extended the lease on Mornington Crescent until 2017 but I didn't check that all the documents had been properly notarized.'

'That was just a technicality. You were tricked by the Home Office. I went through the paperwork myself. The mistake was a small one, little more than a tick in a box and a date stamp. They wanted you out.'

The Peculiar Crimes Unit had been made homeless. The detectives who ran it were the leaseholders of the maroon-tiled building that rose above Mornington Crescent Tube station, but their agreement with the owners, the Crown Estate, had been declared void. Despite pleas and threats the Home Office had stood firm, and the unthinkable had begun to happen: the staff had started to disperse to other forms of employment.

'You knew the HO would put the unit on ice the moment they moved it under their jurisdiction,' said April. 'You embarrassed them. You showed them up at every turn, instead of making them look good. Every case you solved was another slap in the face.'

'I suppose I thought we could eventually win them over. We had public opinion on our side.'

It was true that the PCU had breached behavioural codes of conduct in the course

44

of its duty, but it had always got the job done, and there had been very few complaints from the public registered with the IPCC. For most of its life the unit had operated perhaps not in secrecy, but in an absence of information that had granted it an extraordinary amount of freedom. When civilians finally became aware of the unit they had wholeheartedly endorsed it, but the publicity had brought condemnation from naturally secretive government officials. A new generation of number-crunchers had come forward to insist on regulations being followed to the letter. The concept of an agency run on principles of instinct and experience was anathema to them.

'I know how much professional jealousy you've had to put up with over the years. I saw the files, John. The pair of you managed to upset just about everyone.'

'We resolved most of the major cases we handled. OK, a few got away from us, but our success rate was higher than anyone else's in the force. We're not being judged by our success, but by our failure to conform. Well, you know Arthur – what chance did I have of ever changing his ways? Now Raymond Land can't even get his calls answered.'

'He's the wrong person to change their minds. Only you would be able to do that. They like you, John; they'll hear what you have to say. They won't listen to Uncle

Arthur because they think he's completely loopy.'

'April, we have no equipment, no money, no offices, no status, no technical backup, nothing. How the hell are we supposed to proceed?'

She twisted out of the breeze, pushing back her ash-coloured fringe. The sharp methylene blue of her eyes always came as a surprise to him. 'Why don't you suggest we continue operating from rented accommodation? You can't give up now. Half the staff have relatives who worked in the unit before them. It's a family business.'

May appeared not to hear. 'The Home Office knew it would be better to weaken the unit step by step. I've been to see Raymond four times since the day we were thrown out of our offices, but he can't get an appointment with anyone. Leslie Faraday keeps making the most pathetic excuses not to see him. Any day now our temporary leave will end and our resignations will be officially accepted. There's nothing that anyone can do.'

As part of the closure deal, the staff of the PCU had resigned en masse in order to prevent the blemish of prosecution from appearing on their employment records. The unit was in a limbo created by process and paperwork; neither officially disbanded nor reinstated, but suspended in a state of non-operation. In this fashion, the Home Office could disarm its critics by denying that it had entirely abandoned one of London's most prestigious departments. The official line was that the staff were on temporary hiatus pending investigation, but everyone knew that Faraday and his security supervisor Oskar Kasavian had no intention of allowing them back into the field. Faraday and Kasavian could afford to bide their time and wait while the ties of friendship and loyalty within the team loosened and staff members drifted apart, driven by the need to earn a living wage.

'Why did you bring me here, John?' asked April. 'We already had a farewell drink at the pub. If you're not going to fight for us, what more is there to say? I know we'll always be family but right now I'm still angry, not about the way you've been treated, but by the fact that you're not going to do anything about it.'

'I think growing older affects you in one of two ways,' said May. 'Either you sink into a state of perpetual fury, or you cease to get angry about anyone or anything. You make your peace with the world, and I want some peace. We came here so I could show you this.' He pointed to an empty office unit tucked behind the redbrick arches, all neon panels and lowered ceilings. 'This may become my new home. I've been offered the opportunity of setting up a small private-detective agency. They've really started to take off again in London. A couple of old colleagues from the Met have bought the lease on the ground floor. It's a wealthy area. There are a lot of divorce cases to be had, lawsuits involving private businesses, civil actions worth a lot of money.'

'I don't think Uncle Arthur would approve of that very much.'

'I'm afraid the offer doesn't extend to him,' May admitted uncomfortably. 'The other partners – well, they don't think he'd be insurable.'

'You couldn't possibly go on alone,' said April, shocked. 'Not after all the two of you have been through together.'

'I didn't say I'd definitely take the job, April. I said I'd think about it. The work would be easier. And the change of pace would do me good.'

May's recent cancer scare had caused him to reconsider how he might live the remainder of his life. His emergence from the gloom of University College Hospital into the dazzling daylight of the city streets had wrought a fundamental change in him. Watching commuters, shop assistants, bus drivers and newspaper vendors going about their business without a thought to the battles raging in the great white hospital that towered above them had made him realize how precious each passing day had become. He had been granted a new lease of life. The world was brighter and more colourful than he could ever remember seeing it. The operation had left him sore and scarred, but more alive than he had felt in years, and he needed to make the most of every passing minute.

April was adamant. 'Going private would be a betrayal of everything you both believe.' She shook her head in disbelief.

'Would it? I've seen neither hide nor hair of Arthur since the unit was disbanded,' May replied hotly. 'He's gone to ground. He refuses to speak to anyone. He won't even come to the phone. What am I supposed to do?'

'At least go and talk to him; you owe him that much.'

'It wouldn't do any good. He's a stubborn old mumpsimus.'

'You're the only person he really listens to. You can get through to him.'

'Look, I want to see him – he just doesn't want to see me. I can't wait around for ever.' May felt sure that Arthur would not return to his old position now, even if by some miracle he was offered a chance to do so. The pair had barely spoken since being forced to move out of the building. May had left several messages for his partner, but, uncharacteristically, they had not been returned. Such behaviour usually signified Bryant's descent into black dog days, and when he was in a foul mood he was impossible to talk to.

'So that's it; we all just walk away from each other?' April tried to control her rising anger. With the stress of the unit's closure her moodiness was starting to return, and she had reluctantly resorted to taking medication. 'We agreed to hand in our resignations for Uncle Arthur to show him our support. You always said we were a team.'

'For God's sake, April, be realistic. How can we remain a team when we have no support and no work? It's over. We have to move on.'

'Why?'

'Because that's what you do when there's nothing else left.'

'If Arthur stops now, he'll die. You know that. If he stops using his brain he'll age overnight and simply go to sleep, like a tortoise. Except he won't be hibernating, he'll never wake up, and it will be your fault.'

'You can't lay the blame for this on me, April. That's not fair. Believe me, if I could think of a way of getting us back together, I would. I'm sure the others are out there looking for jobs. They're all talented. Something will come along, and if it doesn't I'll help them find employment, OK? I swear it. I'll take care of you, too. Then I'll go into private practice for myself. You think I want to handle divorce cases and office lawsuits after wading through the sewers with Arthur in search of a murderer?'

'I don't understand how you can just give up. I know you've been ill and probably feel differently about things now, but you came through it. You survived. You've been given another chance.'

'That's right. I have to be prepared to make a new life for myself, form new friendships. Without police work taking up my time, I can start planning a future. I'd like to travel. I've hardly seen anything of the world.'

The truth dawned on April. 'You've met someone,' she said.

'As it happens, I have. Her name is Brigitte. She's French and completely impossible, and I can't imagine that we would ever be good for each other, but I want to spend some time with her, just to see if it's possible for me to let go. Work imprisons us, April; we only do it because we have to. I see that now. I have some savings, enough to enjoy a little time off. I want to travel home with Brigitte to Nice. I'm fed up with always doing the right thing and being broke.'

'And I don't suppose the fact that she's a sexy French divorcée has clouded your judgement in any way?'

'How did you know she's a divorcée?'

'Oh, come on, they always are. When it

comes to women, you reveal a painful flair for the obvious. Most men do. Where did you meet – in some dimly lit Soho dive?'

'No, at the wet-fish counter in Waitrose. She was having a fight with the fishmonger over scallops. She only wanted the ones with their orange tails on, and started shouting at him in French. I helped her out, then we went for coffee. I knew a little about her home town because of that business Arthur keeps referring to as the White Corridor case. She poured cognac into her café au lait from a hip flask. It was ten thirty in the morning.'

'So she's an alcoholic, too.'

They walked on in silence. If a woman came between Bryant and May, April doubted that her grandfather's partnership could ever be restored.

5

CAREER OPPORTUNITIES

The first punch sent the postman slamming into the oak table behind him. The second knocked him over the bench and on to the floor. Glasses from the tipped table rolled and smashed about him. Colin Bimsley had barely wiped the blood from his grazed fist when the other postmen jumped on his back and dragged him towards the door. One of them punched him in the kidneys while another planted a boot on his coccyx, propelling him outside and sprawling into the street. They swore and spat on him, emptying packets of crisps over his head, before returning to their fallen mate and their waiting pints.

Bimsley had not expected postmen to be so ready for a punch-up, but they had not taken kindly to being described as a bunch of useless work-shy tossers. Contrary to popular belief, Londoners are generally hard to entice into a scrap. Usually they'll settle for a sarcastic remark and a withering look before walking away, but the postmen of the Pakenham Arms, the pub nearest to North London's Mount Pleasant Royal Mail Sorting Office, were clearly made of sterner stuff.

Bimsley dusted himself down and examined the torn sleeve of his jacket. This had been his third fight in as many days, and none of them had proved really satisfying. Anger and alcohol were a lousy combination, he told himself, but for now they suited his mood. He felt betrayed, not by Bryant and May, who had done everything within their power to keep the unit open, but by their cowardly bosses, men who hid behind their computer terminals as they totted up the savings to be made on each closed department.

Bimsley had no job to go to. The Met would never take him back, because he had repeatedly failed his medical. Only the unit had agreed to overlook his condition, which was brave of them considering that Diminished Spatial Awareness, an inability to judge distances, was a pretty serious drawback in a job that required him to chase criminals down alleyways and over rooftops. He had hoped to make Detective Inspector, but was now considering taking a position as a private security guard. As his self-respect faded he had started hitting the pubs, and then their patrons. Bimsley had trained for three years at Repton Amateur Boxing Club in the East End, but the fact that a bunch of postmen could whip him suggested it might not be worthwhile pursuing a career as a pugilist.

Meera Mangeshkar had stopped returning his slurred late-night phone calls. Bimsley's hopes of winning her respect and her love had vanished along with his ambitions. Tucking his ripped shirt back into his jeans, he headed off towards the next pub in the street. He was vaguely aware that he smelled of sweat, spilled beer and crisps. *So much for the innate dignity of the unemployed,* he thought with a grimace.

'Hello? Are you open?' Dan Banbury, the late unit's Crime Scene Manager and IT expert, pushed back the door of the little red-painted shop in Camden High Street. 'Yield to the Night' was named after a noir film starring buxom British sex-bomb Diana Dors, and sold clothes from the 1950s and '60s. Its windows displayed the kind of sequined battle-dresses that could transform a shy, slightly overweight woman into a hard-bitten, sexy nightclub hostess.

'Hello, Dan, what are you doing here?' Detective Sergeant Janice Longbright made a magnificent entrance through a shimmering curtain of rose-coloured beads. She had pinned back her newly auburn hair with tortoiseshell combs and was wearing a curvaceous Dorothy Lamour sarong, one of the shop's best-sellers and a masterpiece of intelligent engineering. Her maquillage was a theatrical mask of exaggerated sensuality. Her lipstick was bright enough to warn ships away from rocks.

'Blimey,' said Dan.

Thick, sweet incense smouldered in the air. The crimson-draped counters were stacked with pink suspender belts, patent-leather stilettos and long-forgotten cosmetics. Longbright gave her old colleague a kiss that marked his cheek like a cattle brand.

'I thought you were going away on holiday,' she said, releasing him.

'We were, until I lost my job,' Banbury explained, wiping his face and looking around. 'I decided we couldn't afford it. My nipper was well put out. How are you doing?'

'All right, I suppose. I'm helping an old friend, just to tide me over.'

'You enjoying it?'

'Yeah, I'm on commission. The money's better than I was getting at the unit. Want to pick up something for your wife?'

'You're joking. This stuff's a bit too risqué for her; she's more the jeans and T-shirt type.'

'We can soon change that. We run pole-dancing courses every Wednesday and Friday.'

'I'm not having my missus sliding her gusset down a length of cold steel when she should be defrosting my dinner, thank you. I just wondered if you'd spoken to anyone.'

'I've talked to John a few times. I left a message for Mr Bryant on the old work number but he hasn't called back.'

As Banbury was surrounded by pointy-busted mannequins sporting wired cutaway brassieres, he elected to stare down at his shoes. 'So, no news from anyone? About the unit, I mean.'

'Not a sausage. I had a spot of lunch with Meera the other day. She says Colin's drinking too much. He's been making booty calls at two in the morning, begging to come round. But she hasn't heard anything about the unit. According to John, the Home Office isn't prepared to discuss the matter with us, so I wouldn't keep your hopes up. I'm beginning to think that too much time has passed now.'

'Oh.' Banbury was never the most voluble of men, but he seemed even more tongue-tied than usual. 'I just thought – you know the Met has frozen us out as well?'

'What do you mean?'

'I thought there was a chance that we might get our old jobs back, so I made a few calls. None of them want to know.'

'You can't be surprised about that, Dan. They barely tolerated us at the best of times. The only one who's likely to be offered his old job is Jack Renfield, and that's because he'd only just joined the PCU when it was closed down. They'll probably feel sorry for him, and he was on their football team.'

'Even so... I keep thinking if I just wait for a while, Mr Bryant will somehow persuade them to re-form the unit.'

'I did, too, at first. I think when something gets this badly broken, it's pretty tough to fix. We went down upsetting a hell of a lot of people.'

'We got letters of support.'

'Yeah, but more were glad to be rid of us. I was sent a black wreath from some joker at Albany Street nick.'

'I thought the old man had some well-placed government pals. I was hoping he'd pull in a few favours. That's what he's done in the past.'

'I don't suppose Arthur's in the right frame of mind to whip up fresh support in Whitehall.'

'You've known Bryant and May longer than anyone, Janice. Why did they never accept promotion?'

'Because they knew most investigations would go to DCs, TDCs and PCs. They didn't want desk jobs, and they didn't want to end up in something specialist like working with Tactical Support Groups.' Riot police needed their senior ranks to be involved on the ground, but it was a general rule of thumb that the higher you went in the police force, the less chance you had of regaining the excitement of your early days.

'Hang on, why did you call Bryant's old work number?'

'Because he's not answering his mobile, and there's something wrong with his house line. I'm worried about him. I went round there and knocked the other day but there was no answer. The only other way of getting in touch is through Alma's church.'

'The thing is, I've got an interview with a software development company in Manchester and they seem pretty keen to get me in. The work's not very interesting but the pay's good, and it could tide me over until something better comes along. I just feel so bloody disloyal.'

'You have to go for it, Dan. We all need to find a way through this, and you've got a family to take care of. No one's going to think any less of you. I've spoken to Giles, and he's been going for interviews, reckons there's a couple of good jobs around. Raymond was relieved to be able to take early retirement. He's been wanting to do that for a long time. April's pretty devastated, though. I think she feels let down by her grandfather.'

'It's so bloody unfair. You work for years honing your skills, thinking you're going to end up using your experience and making a difference–'

'You're still young, Dan.' Longbright laid a gentle hand on Banbury's arm. 'You'll find something to inspire you. Do you want to have a cup of tea? I'm just brewing up.'

'No, I can't stop. Well, give my regards to the others when you speak to them.'

'I will. Here, take these home to the missus. You might start something.' She handed him a packet of ruby-sequined nipple tassels.

Banbury pocketed them and was about to leave but stopped in the doorway, rubbing his hair, suddenly as lost as a child on a beach. 'Tell them to stay in touch. I mean, I don't suppose they will, but...' At a loss for anything further to say, he turned and left.

As Longbright watched Banbury go, she wondered if she would ever see him again. She had come to regard the PCU staff as the closest members of her family. *This is how mothers feel when their kids leave home*, she thought, folding an embroidered satin girdle and snapping it smartly into a drawer.

6

TROUBLE IN STORE

Rafi Abd al-Qaadir looked around the filthy shop and wondered if he had made a mistake. Buckled metal sheeting marked the spot where the shawarma spits had turned, spattering grease on to the walls and ceiling, and there had clearly been a fire at some point in the past. The meat counters and the bolted-down tables had been left behind, but the ovens and the refrigerator had been ripped out, leaving ragged holes in the plaster.

Rafi had borrowed money from his brothers to buy the lease of the Paradise Chip Shop, Caledonian Road, and knew that he would have to carry out most of the conversion work himself. The first consignment of pottery and rugs was already on its way, and the task before him was daunting because he could not afford to hire a team of professional builders. Even though the lease he had purchased would soon need to be renewed, the handsome young Arab felt sure he could use his charm and wits to turn a profit. The site was good, a corner store in an up-and-coming area with plenty of passing foot traffic.

As he walked through the empty room, his boots crunching on scattered debris, he studied the task ahead. The trickiest part would be the removal of the enormous ventilation system that wound across the ceiling before punching its way out on to the roof. He could get hold of the right equipment easily enough, but the physical element of the job was beyond him. Rafi's left leg had always been weak, and would not support him if he tried to carry anything too heavy. What he needed to find was a strong labourer who would work cheaply and quickly.

When the man with the cropped head and shoulders like an upended bed appeared in the doorway asking if he needed any work done, Rafi knew that fate had smiled upon him.

Former Detective Constable Colin Bimsley needed to make some fast money. He had already drunk his way through the pitiful payment granted to him by the Home Office. He was now broke. Walking back towards

King's Cross Tube station, he had passed the derelict takeaway outlet and watched the guy inside measuring up.

'Do you know how to take one of these out?' Rafi asked, pointing up at the cylindrical ventilation shaft.

'Easy,' said Bimsley. 'I can get that down for you, and put in new electrics. I can handle just about anything except plumbing.'

'That's fine, I've already got someone for that.'

Bimsley walked over to the far wall and gave it an experimental slap. Dirt showered down. Lath and plasterboard – it would come apart easily enough. He could render and cement the outer wall, re-board the interior, sand and paint, put in new electrical sockets – it wouldn't take long. 'So you're not going to be cooking in here?'

'No, I'm going to be selling homewares.'

'You could apply for a grant from the local council.'

'I don't understand. Why would they give me a grant?'

'You're going to be improving the area, mate. This road has too many junk-food outlets attracting trouble. You'll be doing everyone a favour. I could probably help you with that as well.'

'I'm Rafi,' said the young man, smiling broadly as he shook Bimsley's heavy hand. 'Let's talk about the money over tea.'

They agreed upon a fair price, and Bimsley offered to start at once. After making a trip to B&Q in Rafi's van, they borrowed an industrial vacuum cleaner, a crowbar, a drill and a box of tools from the mosque across the road, and set to work. Clouds of plaster dust billowed through the shop as Bimsley hammered through the partitions, tearing out the ventilation tubes to emerge looking like a desert warrior caught in a sandstorm.

'Hey, Rafi, the power's still live in the back room.' Bimsley lowered his paper mask and pointed his thumb back through the white fog. 'It must be on a separate circuit. I need to turn it off.'

Rafi headed down to the basement, found the breaker box beside the meters and killed the power. Upstairs, Bimsley checked the light and assured himself that it was safe to proceed. Ripping down the last of the wall with the end of the crowbar, he waited for the dust to settle. Something smelled bad. A broken drain? He dragged a stepladder beneath a small, high window, chiselled through the crusted paintwork and forced it open.

As the air became more breathable, he shifted a stack of folding chairs, empty ghee drums and flattened cardboard boxes away from a large white metal object as long as a coffin.

'Hey, did you know you've got a freezer back here?' he called.

'I thought they'd thrown everything out,' said Rafi as Bimsley tried the lid.

'It's got a padlock.'

'Why would they lock it?'

'Allow me. This is a job for a skilled professional.' Bimsley eased his new friend aside and pulled out a set of slender keys, a memento of his days at the PCU. Deftly popping the padlock in a matter of seconds – an old party trick Arthur Bryant had taught him – he unstuck the lid.

'Whoa.' Bimsley backed away as the sour-sweet smell of putrefying meat filled the room, making them retch. 'They must have left food in it.'

Rafi took a look inside. When he did not speak but merely covered his mouth and stared back into the freezer, Bimsley came and followed his gaze.

'Blimey, no wonder they kept it padlocked.'

The body was that of a naked male in a bad state, knees bent to fit into the freezer. His hairless stomach was bloated by expanding intestinal gases, ruptured and blistered from attacking bacteria. Bimsley had seen plenty of frozen turkeys stacked in supermarket freezers, but the sight of a human being similarly arranged was made more grotesque by a further detail. The body was missing its head. The white knobble of the exposed spinal stump was as neatly carved through as any pork or poultry joint, even if the skin was marbled green and purple.

The freezer had not been airtight. Bimsley could see that insects had already burrowed deep into the decaying flesh, and hastily closed the freezer lid before any more could be attracted. At this time of the year swarms of flies appeared because the shop was near the canal, and he was aware of the dangers of further contaminating the corpse.

'Who had this place before you?'

'This is nothing to do with me, I swear–'

'All right, calm down, nobody's saying it is, OK? Who had the place?'

'I don't know, some Nigerian guy. I didn't deal with him, just the agent. Then it was empty for a while.'

'So when did you first see it?'

'About a month ago. I came here with my brother a few times, but I couldn't always lock it up behind me. There's something wrong with the door. I figured there wasn't anything worth stealing.'

'Does the agent know about the problem with the door?'

'I don't know – I just said I'd rent it, it was cheap, I don't know anything about the building or who had it before.' Rafi's cheerful confidence had vanished. Now he was sweating and fearful.

'This is going to put back the opening of

your store a little,' said Bimsley, digging for his mobile and punching in John May's number. 'It looks like you've got yourself a murder site.'

'Oh, no.' Rafi covered his eyes with his hands. 'I'll lose all my money. Couldn't we just get rid of him? Who would know? I could call my brothers—'

'No, mate, we can't do that. I'm a copper. I have to call it in.'

'I thought you were a casual labourer. You're with the *police?*' Rafi looked betrayed.

'Well, I was until recently. I'm sorry.'

'What will happen now?'

'Someone from the Coroner's Office will come and take the body away. Then I think the investigation team will want to find out what happened to the most important part of him.'

7

SHRINKAGE

Alma Sorrowbridge longed for the clear skies, white beaches and warm salty sea breezes of her homeland, Antigua. Instead, all she saw when she looked out of the window in Chalk Farm on Thursday afternoon was a man trying to shove a sodden mattress into a van. In her garden, sooty rain pattered on a sprawling bush of half-dead rhododendron, underneath which a stray ginger cat sat with trembling haunches, trying to pass a stool. Alma pulled her cardigan over her immense bosom and sighed. If there was one thing more depressing than waiting for spring to arrive in London, it lay in her view in the other direction, sitting by the gas fire in a ridiculously long scarf and a ratty quilted crimson dressing gown, moaning about everything and everyone. And when he wasn't complaining, he was expatiating on subjects of no interest to anyone but himself.

'...looking for a lost Roman city full of treasure somewhere under Watling Street,' Arthur Bryant was explaining to no one in particular. 'There's still a place called Caesar's Pond on Stanmore Common where Boudicca's final defeat took place. It seems absurd to celebrate Boudicca as a rebel leader, considering she lost most of her battles, her troops were barbarians, she slaughtered her own people and she burned down half of London.' When Alma next tuned in, Bryant's topic had changed. 'The Shoreditch Strangler took his last victim home in a taxi, and was almost caught by passing constables because the bollards in Boot Street prevented him from parking near the disposal site. Traditional street bollards were fashioned from French cannons captured at Trafalgar, but now – do you know what I'm talking about?'

'Bollards,' said Alma, who was only listening to one word in ten. Living with Mr Bryant, you soon learned to tune out most of his rambling diatribes and concentrate on something more important, like unclogging the sink. She turned to him in annoyance. 'Why don't you get out of the house for a while? Go on, go for a walk or something. It would do you good.'

'I can be just as miserable here as in a park, thank you.'

'For heaven's sake, will you just go *somewhere?* You can't just sit around all day. Sometimes I can't tell where you end and the sofa begins.'

Bryant set aside his copy of *British Boundary Lines: 1066–1700* and turned his attention on her. 'What's the matter with you?' he asked. 'You've been acting strangely all morning.'

'It's you, stuck here at home with no office to go to, just plonked in front of the fire feeling sorry for yourself, reading out loud from all those dusty old books. Look at these things.' She picked up several at random from the sideboard. '*Intestinal Parasites, Volume Two; A Guide to the Cumberland Pencil Museum; Greek Rural Postmen and their*

Cancellation Numbers; The Pictorial Dictionary of Barbed Wire. And why are you learning Hungarian? Filling your head up with all this rubbish – and the mess you make with those chemical concoctions in your bedroom, and the language! I don't mind a bit of swearing, it's only natural, but I draw the line when you involve Jesus.'

'Oh, please spare me the sanctimony. The Christian legend is an embarrassingly childish reiteration of hoary old vegetation myths, the simple impregnation-and-resurrection cycle of pagan tree gods. You should try one of the more complex, grown-up religions from the Far East for a while, rather than worrying over a bunch of ghost stories concocted by bored shepherds in tents. Wait until they confirm life on other planets, that'll mess up Christianity for you.'

'Shame on you, you wicked old man! Every time you blaspheme, an angel is stripped of its wings.'

'A good job too. Sanctimonious bloody things drifting about with their harps, ticking people off all the time like feathered traffic wardens.'

'I don't think you'll ever get into heaven.'

'The only reason why people need to believe in an afterlife is because they're fed up with this one.'

Alma tried to deflect his remarks by busying herself with the pile of washing stacked on the dining-room table. She loved her old friend dearly but he was an affront to her sense of order. Bryant was not a private person. The details of his life were not kept under lock and key, but messily spread about him for everyone to see. Any door he passed through was left open, any chair he inhabited slowly filled with books, magazines, scraps of paper, pens and envelopes containing everything from seeds to microscope slides. He invited everyone into his world, the better to embroil them. 'I don't know why I should have to spend my day repairing your trousers while you sit there having a go at me,' she told him. 'I'm not a wife. I tried that with Mr Sorrowbridge and look where it got me. Go on, sling your hook and give me some room to breathe.'

'And where would you have me go, pray tell? My unit has been turned into some kind of electronic-fraud investigation agency and I have been put out to pasture, sent off to the knacker's yard to await execution.'

'There's no need to talk like that. What about your guided walking tours? I thought you were going to introduce a new one.'

'I was planning to cover London's forgotten burial grounds in a walk entitled "Whose Head Are You Standing On?", but the response was so abysmal that I decided not to bother. You'd think people would be interested in what they're walking over, but no, they're too busy messing about on the interweb, indulging their infantile preoccupation with bosoms by perusing photographs of actresses falling out of nightclubs.'

'Well, you could still go for a walk. I'll get your hat and coat; just half an hour will do you the world of good.'

'I am not creeping about Primrose Hill in the pouring rain, peering into shop windows and frightening small children. Or am I supposed to take myself off to the pictures and sit through some appalling Hollywood adventure about people who can turn themselves into giant ants?'

'I just think a change of scenery–'

'What are you up to?' asked Bryant suspiciously. 'And what have you got in your pocket? Not that one – the other one. Come on, I can see a letter poking out.'

'You don't want to hear about this right now,' said Alma, suddenly solicitous. 'It can wait until later.'

Bryant attempted to lever himself out of his cracked leather armchair, but had trouble getting upright. Since the PCU had closed down and he had nothing to do any more, he seemed to be ageing with undignified celerity. In the last few days he had even taken to staying in bed in the morning, and Alma could do nothing to make him get up. She had heard of people who simply lost the will to live, and was beginning to fear for him. Mr Bryant had no faith with which to protect himself.

'I'm not a child, Alma. If it's bad news I might as well have it now. Come on, hand it over.'

'I don't know why you should want to read this particular letter,' she huffed. 'Look at that great pile of mail sitting over there. You haven't opened anything in weeks. If I hadn't fished out the electricity bill and paid it, you'd be sitting in complete darkness right now.'

'Just give it to me.'

She knew he would worry at her until he had discovered the truth. Reluctantly, she pulled out the letter and passed it to him. 'You won't like it,' she warned. 'We're going to be made homeless.'

Bryant extracted a pair of smeary reading glasses and found himself looking at a compulsory purchase order for their house. 'Public meeting?' he exclaimed. 'What public meeting?'

'It was last night, at the town hall. The letter only arrived this morning.'

'The law says there has to be a notice posted on a public highway for at least a month. I didn't see one.'

'They stuck it on a section of pavement that's been closed to pedestrians,' Alma explained. 'Nobody saw it. Besides, you haven't been out of the front door.'

'Why, this is absurd.' He read on. 'New retail development ... adequate compensation at market rates ... a lot of old blather about shops and offices. Property developers, a bunch of sleazy sybarites with the morals of praying mantises – how dare they try to sell the ground from right under our feet?'

'You put the property in my name, remember, so it's my responsibility to sort it out. You'll help me fight it, won't you?' Alma's determined tone was a call to action, but the brief flare of energy was already fading from Bryant's eyes.

'Oh, I can try. But frankly, what's the use?' he said, lowering himself back into his chair with a grimace. 'First the unit, and now our home. Nowhere to go and nothing to live for. I've not got the energy to fight any more. Let them do their worst. I'm sure they can find us a flat you hate just as much as this place.'

Alma had never expected to find herself living in a semi-derelict toothbrush factory at her time of life. The tumbledown building gave the rest of the neighbourhood a bad name. Last weekend several slates had come loose in high winds, and an upper corner of Alma's bedroom now boasted a water feature, but neither she nor Bryant was in any fit state to get up a ladder and repair the damage. Perhaps a modern flat with easy access would be better, after all.

With the ironing balanced in one broad hand, she took stock of her old friend. He looked smaller somehow, as if he had started shrinking on the day the unit closed down. His world was diminishing, too. She wanted to take his hand and softly stroke it, to tell him that everything would be all right, but found herself wondering if he had reached that stage of his life where there was no going back. Bryant had always been a noisy fidget, pulling down books, setting up experiments, fiddling and whistling and interfering with things that didn't concern him, but this new placidity was the most disturbing change of all.

'Why won't you let John come and see you?' she asked gently. 'You know he wants to.'

'He'll try to convince me to go to Whitehall with a begging bowl,' Bryant complained. 'He's an eternal optimist; he thinks we'll survive by calling in a few old debts, but we've used up all our favours. Our work together is over and there's no point in pretending it isn't. I don't want to end my days arguing with my oldest friend.'

For once, Alma was stumped for an answer. Her mouth opened, then shut again.

'I think I'll have a sleep now, if you don't mind,' he said, lowering his head on to a cushion and closing his eyes. 'Leave me alone. I feel tremendously weary.'

He had taken the news that they were to be thrown out on the street with alarming equanimity. She needed to shock him out of his complacent attitude, but could not imagine anything working, short of attaching her van's jump leads to him. His fire was fading, like a setting sun. She resolved to summon John May against his partner's wishes, even though Bryant had expressly forbidden her from inviting him over.

'Suit yourself,' she told him finally. 'Do as you wish. But you can get rid of that skull on the mantelpiece. It stinks.'

'That, Madame, is a religious artifact. It was smuggled out of Tibet.'

'Yes, and it's going to be smuggled into the dustbin. If you need me, I shall be upstairs. I have some urgent ironing to attend to.' Slipping the telephone into her pocket, she beat a hasty retreat to the kitchen, wondering what on earth she could do to save her old friend from himself.

8

STALEMATE

Colin Bimsley was smudged with thick white dust. It was matted in his cropped fair hair and even falling out of his ears as he hopped about on the kerb outside the derelict take-away at the end of the Caledonian Road. He seemed inordinately excited about something.

'I wasn't sure if you'd got my message,' he called to the approaching detective. 'I tried Mr Bryant but his phone was switched off.'

'Yes, it would be,' agreed John May. 'The last time we spoke, Arthur told me he was getting too many phone calls from the dead. Apparently he subscribed to a psychics' hot-line and is now being pestered by people wanting him to avenge their murders. It's a scam to make him use premium phone lines, but he doesn't realize that. What are you doing around here?'

'This is Rafi.' Bimsley introduced his new friend. 'I called you first. Rafi's got a serious problem, and I thought he'd be better off talking to you.'

'Let's go inside.' The dark flat-bottomed

clouds above their heads were threatening a deluge. Bimsley led the way through the shop to the cluttered back room and opened the lid of the freezer. May peered in. The body was virtually hairless, Caucasian, ordinary, mid-thirties at a guess.

'Rafi bought himself the lease on this shop and found he'd already got his first customer. The freezer had been hidden behind some boxes.'

'You didn't know this was here?' May asked Rafi.

'I swear. I don't want no trouble. I just want to get my shop open.'

'Who had the place before you?'

'An African guy.'

'But Rafi got it through an agent,' Bimsley explained. He felt the need to protect this man, who had given him a job without knowing anything about him. 'He didn't meet the former owner, and the place was left empty for a month with the door unlocked, so anyone could have come in. We've got a white male with his head removed; the only noticeable identifying mark is a tattoo around the left upper arm. And you're going to find my dabs all over the lid.'

'Let's have a look at the tattoo,' said May, gingerly raising a swollen limb to examine the wreath of entwined ivy branches. 'It goes all the way around.'

'Armbands were popular in the 1990s:

Buddhist mantras, twisted ivy, roses and thorns – a lot of clubbers had them, and this is a big clubbing area.'

'It doesn't make sense. If someone's gone to the trouble of cutting off the head, they'd also remove the tattoo and the hands to prevent the body from being easily recognized. He's done a lot of manual labour; the fingers are pretty callused.' May examined the edges of the freezer. 'No blood? Seen any on the floor?'

'Look at the state of this place, John. Builders' rubble everywhere. We'll have to strip it.'

We won't have to strip it, they will, thought John May, knowing that the case would go to either Camden or Islington Met, depending on whose jurisdiction the shop fell under. The dividing line between the boroughs ran somewhere around here. He dropped to his haunches and looked about. 'You're right. I'm dying to have a look, but we'd create problems moving anything right now.'

'The front of the shop is all glass, so the counter and eating area are exposed to the street.'

'No.' May pointed up at several pairs of hooks in the corner of the ceiling. 'They've taken blinds down. A lot of the shops and pubs around here have wooden shutters.'

'There's a pile of strong plastic sacks in the back that look like they might have been used for something.'

'What makes you think that?'

Bimsley scratched his snub nose. 'Dunno. They're in the wrong place. Like someone's shifted them around to kneel on.'

'It would have made a mess, taking off the body identification.'

'You reckon he was murdered off-site, and this place was convenient?'

'I didn't say he was murdered. He could have died, and it's in the interest of someone to keep his identity a secret, at least for a few days. I'd have thought he died here. You don't drag a body to a place like this in a busy high street when there's a huge deserted industrial site just up the road.'

'The Met won't give us this, will they?' asked Colin.

'No, why should they? We're nobody any more. You'd better take your friend outside, he doesn't look very well.'

May was itching to disturb the site and make a careful examination of the space, but he no longer had authority to call in a forensic team. Besides, who would he be able to summon? As soon as they found out he was interfering on their patch, the Met would kick him out and take Mr Abd al-Qaadir into custody.

He looked back at the freezer. The lid had provided a partial seal, so the decay would have been created largely by internal bacteria. How would that affect pinpointing an accurate time of death? The previous tenants had known there was a freezer sitting here. Either it had been empty when they left, or they had hoped that the discovery of its contents would occur long after they had gone. At least he had a starting point.

May swung the front door back and forth, trying out the lock. It looked shut from outside, but you could pop it with a little pressure. If it was someone who knew the area, they'd know that the shop was vacant, even if it had its blinds down – except...

Except it wasn't his case. In fact, if Bimsley had stumbled across a pile of corpses thirty feet high, it would have nothing to do with any of them. He opened the lid once more and studied the blue-red-grey neck, the stump so neatly cut around the bone that he could have been looking at a surgical amputation. Finding a body in an area like this was not exactly a rare event: King's Cross was a confluence of five railway stations and as many major roads, where thousands of commuters, students and tourists daily crossed paths. There was always something bad happening nearby...

Slowly, a plan began to form in May's mind. He called Bimsley back in. 'Colin, I need you to hang on here,' he explained. 'Keep the doors shut and don't admit anyone until I return. And don't let Mr Abd al-

Qaadir out of your sight.'

'Do you want me to start searching for the head? I could have a look around–'

'And fall over something. No, don't disturb anything. Try to get hold of Dan Banbury; have him come over if you can. You'd better stress that this is entirely unofficial – make sure he doesn't say anything to anyone about where he's going. I doubt you'll find the head on the premises. There wouldn't be much point in removing the victim's most visible feature then leaving his face in a cupboard.'

'Maybe he was wearing an unusual hat,' said Bimsley. 'What are you going to do?'

'I have to take someone to afternoon tea,' May replied.

Leslie Faraday enjoyed the rituals of his working day, starting with a cup of Earl Grey and some biscuits, preferably Lincolns, Garibaldis or Ginger Nuts, as he thumbed through his correspondence; café au lait mid-morning as he broke down his departmental expenditure into the kind of detail that could make the collected works of Anthony Trollope look like a fast read; then a nice carb-heavy luncheon in the office canteen, preferably the kind of pudding or pie that would take him back to his days at boarding school; and a nice mug of builder's tea mid-afternoon, served with a slice of

Battenberg cake or Black Forest Gateau. He was pear-shaped by habit, physically and mentally. His brain operated like a traction engine, slowly but with an inexorable progress that flattened everything in its path. No detail, however small, escaped his attention, and as the budget overseer of London's specialist police units he was fully entitled to poke his nose into everything.

After questioning costs, trimming sails and cutting corners, he would annotate and parenthesize his documents, aware of every grammatical nuance, never stopping to consider the bigger ethical and moral dilemmas posed by his job. He kept his pens tidy and his head below the parapet and worked all the hours God sent, never thinking that one day someone might fire him just to wipe the smug look from his face. In this sense Faraday was the perfect civil servant, remembering everything and understanding nothing. He toiled on the accumulation and expedition of data, not in the hope of advancement, but in the resigned expectation that one day it would require him to betray his superiors.

Faraday would not be drawn into a meeting with Raymond Land, the ineffectual temporary acting head of the PCU, because he knew that Land would want to complain about his retirement package. He was quite happy to return John May's call, however, because the detective had always treated him with equanimity, no matter how petty the official's requests sometimes seemed. So it was that he made himself available at short notice and appeared at Fortnum & Mason for afternoon tea on the dot of four, to be met by a phalanx of sycophantic waiters armed with very tiny, very expensive sandwiches. Faraday appeared to be unaware that this kind of afternoon tea was an elaborate ritualistic parody provided for tourists who wanted to believe that the London of 1880 still existed. The frou-frou pink and cream décor, the tea-strainers and doilies and cake stands, were the trappings of a cheap seaside boarding-house elevated to absurdist theatre props, but all that shot over his balding head.

'Well, this is a nice surprise,' Faraday lied, leaning back while a member of staff draped a bleached-linen square across his lap. 'I heard about your unfortunate mishap with the lease at Mornington Crescent.'

'A technical formality, I'm sure,' May lied back, accepting tea as pale as urine, piddled from a great height by a constricted silver spout. 'It's simply a matter of finding new premises.'

'Not so simple, sadly.' Faraday offered up a look of pantomimed injury. 'Mr Kasavian, our security supervisor, doesn't feel there's really a pressing need for operational units like the PCU any more.'

'One of the unit's main remits has always been to prevent loss of public faith in law and order,' said May.

'A rather nebulous concept, one feels,' said Faraday, lasciviously eyeing the sandwiches.

'Not when it involves the potential loss of millions, perhaps even billions, of pounds.'

Faraday's fingers had been straying waywardly towards a Bath bun, but now he was brought up short. 'What do you mean?' he asked.

May knew he had to build his case carefully. 'London is a major global crossing point, and King's Cross is now the hub of London. As the home of the largest and most complex regeneration project in Europe, it's undergoing the biggest upheaval in its millennia-old history. It's where the Eurostar arrives, and is set to act as the main terminus for the Olympics. The government is hoping to attract billions in overseas investment to the area, and the building schedule must be strictly maintained if contracts are to be honoured. Of course, you know all of this.'

'Oh, indeed. Of course. Understood.' Faraday looked blankly at May as he struggled to puzzle out the connection with the Peculiar Crimes Unit.

'In fact, the area of wasteland between Euston and St Pancras is set to become an entirely new London district, with new policing requirements. It represents a potentially phenomenal contribution to the national economy. I'm sure you were copied in on the estimates, Leslie. By 2020 there will be around sixty-five million passengers a year passing through the King's Cross Interchange. That's more than the number of passengers currently passing through Heathrow Airport. It's a tricky balance – preventing the area from descending into chaos while so much planning and building takes place. The number of undercover police officers operating in the King's Cross area has recently been tripled. The crack-dealers and con-men who used to hang about in the streets have all been moved on. And of course, after 7/7 there's always the threat of terrorism to deal with.'

'What about the more domestic problems? Sex workers and teenage gangs are still an issue, I believe.'

'True, they keep trying to come back. The gangs are based in the big housing estates that border the area, but there are special units tackling those, and they're having considerable success. Sex workers will always appear at points where so many journeys start and end, but the clip joints are closing, which means that they don't have anywhere to take the punters. MAGPI – the Multi-Agency Geographical Panel – meets regularly with the Safer Neighbourhood Team to discuss harm-reduction strategies, and the Met uses outreach services to conduct Environmental Visual Audits to reduce anti-social behaviour. King's Cross will never again be as run-down as it once was. Teams of architects and construction engineers have already moved into key properties bordering the site. So it's essential not to return to the bad old days of organized crime. But there are bound to be new territorial battles in the area. As it becomes more prosperous, hard-line criminals will be trying to move back in.'

Even someone as obtuse as Faraday could sense that May was getting at something. The civil servant realized there would be no easy enjoyment of the sandwiches. He raised an enquiring eyebrow.

'I mention this,' said May casually, 'because it looks as if organized crime has already returned to the area. Today one of my men found a headless body in a shop on Caledonian Road, right near the mainline station.'

Faraday's eyes widened imperceptibly. He could see himself missing the 17.45 train home from Charing Cross. 'Your men?' he said. 'You don't have any men any more.'

'It looks to me like a professional execution, because the head has been expertly removed. The odd part is that other identifying marks remain. There are no further injuries, so I think there's a reasonable chance that if we find his head there'll be a single bullet wound in it.'

'You know that Operation Trident was set up to combat gun-related activity–'

'Within London's young black communities, yes, but this is different. The victim is a white man in his early to mid-thirties.'

'What were you doing there in the first place? You have no authority–'

'It was a coincidence. One of my detective constables happened to be working on the site.'

'I assume you've turned the case straight over to Islington?' The London Metropolitan Police did not come under Faraday's control, and out of sight was out of mind.

'I'm not sure whose jurisdiction the case falls under. The boundary line between the policing areas lies somewhere along the Caledonian Road. Besides, a crime like this should fall exclusively under our old remit, Leslie, you know that.'

'Your remit died with the closure of the division.'

'If organized crime returns to the area, public confidence will be undermined and overseas investors will start to pull out. There are literally hundreds of buyers waiting to see how the regeneration is handled before they commit, and something like this could do a lot of damage. It's a contract killing; the head has been cut off with the kind of professionalism you usually only get from a surgeon – or maybe the butchers in Smithfield Market. We'll be lucky if it turns up at all. Maybe the killer was intending to remove the hands but was disturbed before he could do so. The case requires special attention and the Met is simply not equipped–'

'Neither are you,' Faraday interrupted. 'The unit would have to be rehoused and staff and facilities reassembled before you could touch this. No, I'm sorry, John, it's impossible, there's no way I can sanction it. I wouldn't be able to without Mr Kasavian's approval anyway, and you know how he feels about the unit. You really should never have crossed him. When you leave here, you need to report your findings to Islington, who'll probably pass it on to SOCA. Give their officers everything you know and take them to the site at once; otherwise, I'm afraid it will be my sad duty to report you for obstruction. Pass me one of those salmon fingers, would you?'

John sank back in his chair, defeated. He knew that the only person who might be able to change the situation now was Arthur Bryant, because he had old friends in the Home Office who operated on levels above Faraday and Kasavian. He had spoken to Alma Sorrowbridge a few minutes earlier, but she had warned him that any visit would be met with a rebuff. When Bryant made up his mind, it stayed that way.

Late that afternoon, members of Islington's Operational Command Unit turned up at number 73 Caledonian Road to remove the freezer and its grisly contents. They also took Rafi Abd al-Qaadir into custody for questioning. Despite May's best efforts the case was lost to the Met and divisions beyond, and the PCU remained in a state of limbo.

Leslie Faraday went home with a guilty weight on his mind and chronic indigestion in his gut.

9

STAG NIGHT

The sifting silver rain had not managed to dampen anyone's spirits. Most of the party-goers had made their way along the broad, empty road to the club as if taking a stroll on a summer's night. Certainly many seemed dressed for hiking, in boots and jeans, browns and greys, baggy woollen sweaters and padded jackets. The idea of donning outrageous outfits at the start of the weekend was losing its appeal in the capital, as if the young were too worried about their place in the world to appear frivolous. Besides, it was considered provincial to be seen wandering about in white-feathered angel wings and bare midriffs, which belonged on teenagers from unfashionable towns. London's night-club denizens associated dourness with sophistication, although they still bellowed into the dawn sky and woke whole neighbourhoods after a night of dancing and a few happy pills.

Among the drifting clusters, a small handful were fancy-dressed: a droopy-looking chicken, some Playboy-bunny types and cavemen, groups on obligatory hen and stag nights determined to see out their last moments of unmarried freedom in feats of alcoholic endurance. As the two women left, they passed a girl dressed in a St Trinian's outfit sitting on the kerb, oblivious to the rain, trying to heave up the last of her fried chicken while her friends held her hair out of her face.

Sometimes Meera Mangeshkar studied her peers and regarded them as an alien race. She felt no connection to other women of her age. Meera had not marked her teenage birthdays by hiring a white stretch limo and driving around the West End screaming from the windows. A third-generation Asian Londoner, she often felt stranded between cultures, too sensible for England, too eccentric for India. She had agreed to come out with Sashi to prove that she could still have fun.

The Keys club hosted Friday-night specials in a Victorian train shed at the rear of King's Cross station. Those who left it on foot were forced to walk back along the desolate S-bend of York Way to one of the termini, but the route had been further twisted by on-going construction work, taking them on to a makeshift tarmac path that curved over a field of churned earth. On either side, yellow earth-movers stood beneath tall spotlights with rain sparkling on their steel canopies. A thin river of brown mud was creeping across the path as if trying to obscure it.

'I can't see where I'm going,' said Sashi, staring down at her shoes. 'My feet are soaked. Couldn't we have got a minicab?'

'This evening has already cost a bloody fortune,' Meera replied. 'I won't be going back there in a hurry. Twenty quid entrance fee, just to have the bouncer run a light hand over my arse and joke about me with his mates.'

'Did he do that?' asked Sashi. 'You should have told me; I'd have threatened him with harassment.'

'I think that's my job,' said Meera. 'I've still got the badge, if nothing else.' The young detective constable had come clubbing with her old schoolfriend, but had hated every minute of the evening, which had mainly consisted of queuing for the entry stamp, the cloakroom, the toilets and the bar. She had forced herself to come out and be sociable, if only to prevent herself from thinking about the PCU and how it had screwed up her career. Her sister had called to suggest a part-time job in her coffee shop, but Meera had so rudely refused the offer that she had upset both of them. If things got bad she would have to sell her Kawasaki, but for now she was determined to hold on to the motor-bike until something decent came along.

'It's only half past one,' said Sashi. 'They don't shut until six a.m. Everyone else is still inside. Look, there's no one around now.' She was right; the streets outside the club were suddenly deserted.

'You could have stayed. You didn't have to come with me.' Meera sulkily stomped around a water-filled ditch. 'I'm capable of seeing myself home.' She suspected that Sashi had taken something earlier, because she hadn't stopped talking for the past half-hour. Meera enjoyed a few beers but drew the line at taking recreational drugs, which meant that she gained no pleasure from watching those around her jabber into each other's ears while their limbs tightened and their pupils dilated. She knew Sashi thought she was no fun, but Meera cared too much about her career to risk it for so little.

She wanted to hate the PCU, but never thought she would miss it so much. She had spent the week hanging out with old friends with whom she now had nothing in common. Watching Sashi cut loose on the dance-floor tonight, flirting with guys who stared at her breasts as if they were fillet steaks, she felt like she had turned the clock back five years. She tried to understand how she had come to leave so much of her former life behind. Bryant and May had encouraged her to observe the world with a kind of detached amusement. In doing so, they had shown her another way of living. The unit had changed her; she had gone too far now to change back.

'Damn, I've broken my heel. Hold on, I can't see.' Sashi raised her foot and examined it.

'Don't take your shoe off, there could be glass around.' Practicality came naturally to Meera. She waited while the damage was assessed. Sashi hopped and squinted and complained. They were in the centre of the city, but could have been in the heart of the English countryside. The canal ran nearby, and a gaggle of ungainly Canada geese shook themselves as they passed, making her start.

'Come on, Sashi, I'm getting drenched here.' She set off again, moving from the circle of dim light that fell across her path.

Sashi hobbled up behind her. 'There was this guy, right, the tall one with the tied-back blond hair? He wanted to tell my fortune.'

'It looked like he was trying to do it by staring down the inside of your shirt.'

'What's wrong with that? Honestly, Meera, ever since you joined the police you've become so boring about men.'

'Maybe that's because most of the ones I see are drunk, abusive, vomiting and in handcuffs.'

'That's exactly what I mean. Don't take this the wrong way, but maybe you're a lesbian. Hey!' Meera looked back. Sashi had come to a sudden halt. 'What's he doing?' She pointed to a low ridge of turned earth on her right. About fifty feet away a man stood beneath a spotlight in the drifting rain, his head down, his legs braced. 'Is that a sculpture or something?'

'No,' said Meera, 'that's a guy.'

He seemed abnormally tall and thick-legged. There was something odd about his legs; the trousers were low-slung and made from a strange kind of furry brown material. Something on his head glittered in the overhead light. For a moment she was reminded of the Highwayman, the murderous figure they had tracked across London, because this man, too, was dressed up in some kind of weird outfit. Not a historical costume filched from a fancy-dress shop, though, but something rough and hairy, so that he looked oddly mythical, like a large animal standing on its back legs.

Slowly he raised his head and studied them. He was wearing a black mask like a bandanna across his eyes. Long metallic branches sprouted from above his ears, catching the light. 'Oh, I get it,' said Meera. 'He's dressed as a stag. It's his stag night. He looks really drunk.'

'Well, he's creeping me out. Come on.' Sashi grabbed her arm and walked faster, but the path took them further towards him, and the two young women were not pre-pared to scrabble up the muddy bank that now rose at the sides.

He turned his head to watch them. His muscular arms were bare, his chest and thighs covered in some kind of coarse fur. They had almost passed him when he abruptly dropped from the ridge and loped towards them. Sashi screamed.

Meera turned as the stag-man came alongside, reaching down and looping his arm around Sashi's waist to lift her easily off the ground. The detective constable was about to kick out at his knees when she saw that he was playing with Sashi, swinging her from side to side. Sashi's shrieks were fear-ful but flirtatious, like those of a girl at a funfair.

The stag-man swung her on to his hip and

Sashi started to laugh. His shining eyes were deep-set above a short-haired snout. In the lamplight Meera could see that the brown and white fur on his chest and shoulders rose seamlessly to his thick neck and headpiece, on top of which was a magnificent pair of glittering steel antlers. *They must be heavy,* Meera thought vaguely as she stood by, miserable in the rain. 'Come on, Sashi, stop—'

But then the stag-man swung his captive high above his right shoulder and let her go, so that she tipped and fell into the surrounding vale of mud, landing heavily on her side. Sashi's yelp of laughter turned to anger and confusion as Meera ran forward, first pulling her friend to her feet, then slamming into the stag-man. *He's stoned, he'll go down,* she thought as she struck out, kicking him in the stomach, but it was like hitting rock. As that didn't work her next kick aimed lower. This time he cried out. As he dropped his head at her, she saw that the steel antlers were made not of sticks and tinfoil, but the blades of dozens of kitchen knives bolted together. *That's why the headpiece is so light,* she remembered thinking, *that's how he can keep his head up,* but by that time he had slashed at her, slicing open the material of her leather sleeve and cutting through to the skin of her right arm.

By the time she looked back he had disappeared over the ridge, and Sashi was left kneeling in the mud, crying.

Meera sat on an orange plastic chair in a cubicle of the A&E department at University College Hospital, watching dispassionately as a nurse placed sutures across the cleaned wound.

'You were lucky,' said the nurse, tapping her forearm. 'He just missed the artery here.' She had a strong Irish lilt in her voice that most patients would have found comforting.

'Yeah, right, lucky me,' said Meera, who was not comforted. She had sent her mud-spattered friend outside for a smoke. Sashi was probably on the phone by now, telling everyone what had happened. Meera was surprised she hadn't managed to film the attack for her web page.

'Why did you have a go at him, love?' asked the constable who had accompanied her to UCH.

'You mean apart from the fact that he was assaulting my friend?' She found it hard to keep the sarcasm from her voice.

'You said he was on his stag night, so he was probably a bit drunk.'

'No, I said he was dressed as a stag – there's a difference.'

'So why did you have a go at him?'

'Because I'm trained to react like that,' she told him, reaching across into her jacket with her free hand and flipping open her badge wallet.

'Bloody hell,' complained the constable. 'Peculiar Crimes Unit? You lot have given us some grief in the past, you know.'

'Don't start with me, PC – what's your name?'

'Purviance, Darren.'

'You're from Camden nick, Purviance Darren.'

He wasn't wearing his jacket, with its identifying epaulettes. 'How d'you know?' he asked.

'You've got the look.' She didn't mean it nicely.

'Hasn't your unit just been disbanded?'

'Placed on hiatus,' Meera corrected. 'Don't you want a description of the bloke who attacked me?'

'I thought you attacked him. You didn't go after him, then?'

'It was dark and muddy, I couldn't see where he went. There'll be plenty of prints, though. He was holding on to the spotlight pole.'

PC Purviance seemed less interested in the culprit than the victim. He'd heard a lot of wild stuff about the PCU, how they looked down on the Met and behaved like a law to themselves. 'So, what's your official status then?' he asked.

'I was off duty, OK?'

'What's happened to old Bryant and May?

Finally been made to retire, have they? They were a right pain in the arse, both of them. Drove the lads down at the station mad. We always said they should leave police work to the professionals.'

'That'd be you then, would it?' Meera winced as the last suture was put in place. 'So what are you going to do about catching this guy?'

'Come on, Mangeshkar, be realistic. You know how it works. The bloke was obviously out of order, but look at the situation. You were outside a nightclub in a dodgy neighbourhood, he was on the sauce and having a bit of fun before the old ball and chain gets clamped on him. You two overreacted, that's all.'

'I thought attempting to stab someone might fall under your initiative to prevent knife crimes in the area.'

'He wasn't carrying a knife, he was wearing them on his head, according to you.'

'What do you mean, according to me? Sashi saw him too – she was right there.'

'Yeah, well, your mate's dropped a couple of pills, by the look of it, so who knows what she saw? Don't get smart with me, love. Just file your report and leave it alone, OK?' Purviance took a call on his radio and rose to leave.

'Don't take no notice of him,' said the nurse wearily. 'It's already been a long night.'

'Do you get a lot of trouble in this area?' asked Meera, rolling down her sleeve.

'You're joking, aren't you? We've had a dozen Cat As in since my shift started and God knows how many Ambers – mostly hypervents, overheats and panic attacks. Not bad for a Friday, considering the EOC's main computer is playing up again.' The Emergency Operations Centre dispatched London's ambulances, assigning each job a number. Yesterday, there had been over 3,600 calls logged to the emergency service; a fairly typical figure.

The nurse threw away the anti-tetanus needle and snapped her opaque white gloves into the disposal bin. 'There are at least a couple of dozen nightclubs within a quarter-mile of here and we're not even in the West End. Half the kids in them seem incapable of enjoying themselves without ingesting some kind of stimulant. There are fifteen-year-olds out there tonight sucking low-coke wraps up their nostrils without the faintest idea of what they're ingesting.'

'Low-coke? What's that?'

'Oh, haven't you heard? The dealers are expanding their markets by creating a two-tier price structure for their drugs: thirty-pound rubbish quality for the kids, purer fifty-pound stuff for the white-collar workers. Thoughtful of them. Low-coke is cut with anything the dealer can find in the cupboard under his sink. Funny, when you think kids are so picky about what they eat.'

'And I thought I had a tough job. Why do you do it?'

'Honestly? I heard doctors were really good kissers.'

Meera found herself laughing.

The nurse rose. 'Go on, off with yourself. You're good to go, but don't put any pressure on that arm for a few days. The sutures will get itchy before they dissolve, but don't pick them off. And don't forget to do us all a favour and file a report on the gentleman who did this. Bollocks to what your man over there says.'

Meera had already decided that it was pointless going back to PC Purviance. Instead she decided on more direct action.

10

CONVINCING ARTHUR

'I really don't think this is a good idea,' said John May as he and Meera stood on the doorstep of Bryant's chaotic home. 'You two always end up arguing, and he can be – well, difficult – when he's feeling down.'

'You should have brought DS Longbright

along for company, then.'

'I tried, but I couldn't get hold of her. She's working in some kind of women's undergarment shop. You're here by default, so watch it, all right?'

'I'll behave myself, I promise.' Meera pressed the doorbell. Somewhere deep inside the converted toothbrush factory there was a noise like someone dropping a stone into a bucket. After about a minute, they heard the door being unlocked.

Alma Sorrowbridge's features were inclined towards a receptive smile on most days, but she was clearly alarmed to find visitors on her doorstep this early. Saturday was her morning for spraying everything in lavender polish and baking, and she didn't like to have her routine disturbed, but more to the point she did not wish to referee a fight between her oldest friend and his partner. 'He's still in his room,' she informed May, 'and with all due respect I don't think he'll be wanting you here.'

'I'm not his enemy, Alma. Anyway, who said I came to see him? Are you making cornbread today?'

'Cassava and ginger bake, and cinnamon buns. And I'm doing a pineapple cherry cake.' She wiped her hands on her apron and opened the door wider. 'I suppose you can come in, but I have to be at the church before nine. You know I do my rounds on

102

Saturday. The first batch is just cooling.' Alma would have been capable of single-handedly supplying the British Army with all of its pastry requirements. She cooked with evangelical zeal, arranging vast batches of cakes and filling her van with trays that she would take around to old people who couldn't get to the shops.

The old industrial unit in which Arthur Bryant had made his home was so bizarrely arranged that the contrast between the inside and the outside required mental adjustment. May and Mangeshkar made their way into a huge room that looked like a cross between a seventy-year-old furniture repository and a Moroccan rubbish dump. Around the walls were tottering piles of encyclopaedias, a moulting championship perch in a glass case, a great many post-war lampshades, sextants, telescopes and outdated opticians' equipment, several late-Victorian seaside dioramas, including one scene of drunken Jack Tars swinging from lampposts and another featuring a family of dancing weasels, some large drippy brown canvases that provided more clues to the artist's disturbed frame of mind than pleasure to the viewer, and a miniature model of the port at Gdansk made entirely out of painted bread.

'I try to get the place clean but he keeps bringing back more of these things,' Alma complained. 'What am I supposed to do? I have no idea where he finds it all. It's not like they're even antiques.'

May eyed an ancient bear's head that someone had seen fit to make into a lamp. One of its eyes had fallen out and was lying on the table. 'Obviously,' he said.

'At least he's stopped doing that now.'

'What do you mean?'

'He's stopped going out at all.'

'Oh, that's a bad sign.'

'You should see his bedroom; it's a thousand times worse than this. If I wasn't a good Christian, I would walk right out of here and never come back.'

'So that's what you think of me, you gargantuan quisling.' Arthur Bryant stood propped in the doorway in a Victorian nightcap and a purple quilted dressing gown. His snowy hair stuck up around the cap like a row of alfalfa sprouts. He appeared smaller and more wrinkled than ever. 'I gave strict instructions that I was to receive no visitors until further notice.'

'We're not visitors, we're your friends,' said May indignantly.

'We've all been worried about you, sir,' interposed Meera, who was determined to sound less blunt than usual and show the caring side she was fairly sure she must possess. 'You can't just hide away like this.'

'I'm hardly hiding away, am I?' As Bryant

104

made his way over to the armchair by the fireplace, the others noted how slowly he was moving but kept the thought to themselves. 'I'm at home, that's all. I feel tired and ancient. My back is playing up. I need new knees. All I ask is that I am left alone. And now this ... this Antiguan termagant has denied me even that basic right.'

'Hmm. You've become a stranger to the badger's brush.' May indicated the bristles on his partner's cheeks.

'I have no good reason to shave. Men only shave for other people. If left to themselves they'd all grow beards like Robinson Crusoe. And they probably wouldn't wash, either. I choose not to go out. I've seen all the world I need to see.' His voice grew softer. 'I don't want you to see me like this.'

'So you've elected to become the god of this reduced realm,' said May, displeased.

'I have all the home comforts I need, my books, my notes, Alma to cook for me.'

'I've seen this sort of behaviour before. When great teachers retire they lose the will to live. Soon you'll start regressing into another childhood. You'll be asking Alma to leave your bedroom door ajar at night, and telling her you don't eat sprouts.'

'I don't eat her sprouts now.'

'So this is what it's come to, has it? Our friendship means nothing to you. I always knew you were selfish, Arthur, but your behaviour surpasses even my expectations. I should have known. Right from the moment I first met you, when you had me deciphering naval flag codes before I'd even got my coat off, all you ever cared about was yourself.'

'That's not entirely true,' retorted Bryant indignantly. 'There have been times – not lately, perhaps – when my generosity has known no bounds. I gave you all the credit when my efforts brought about the capture of the Little Italy whelk-smugglers.'

'An action which resulted in me having to hide several dozen drums of black-market treacle from the police, I remember. You always give me the credit when you're about to get caught for something.'

'Excuse me,' intervened Meera, whose brief attempt at patience had already evaporated. 'This is, like, an ancient-history lesson or something. Can we get back to the real world? Tell him, Mr May.'

'There's been a murder in King's Cross,' said May, duly prompted.

'Hardly headline news.' Bryant slouched further into his dressing gown. 'I'd be more surprised if there hadn't been.'

'It's a professional job.'

'One for the Met, then. They have all the right contacts in that area. There are eleven recognized gangs in the borough of Camden alone.'

'Except that in this case no one has a clue who's behind it. The victim's remains haven't been identified because his head was cut off and we don't yet know if his fingerprints are on file. He's been dead for a few days. I thought it might pique your interest.'

'Well, you thought wrong,' snapped Bryant. 'You think every time someone dies my heart quickens? It doesn't.'

'You're being so unfair, Mr Bryant,' said Meera. 'Why don't you just get dressed and come and visit the crime scene?'

'You come any nearer, young lady, and you shall get the benefit of my toasting fork where you least expect it.' He turned back to his old partner. 'I was looking through my casebook over the weekend, and realized that once you get beneath the unique circumstances of a crime, the perpetrators are depressingly similar. They're selfish, blind, unpleasant people, and worst of all, they no longer have the ability to surprise me in any way.'

'Perhaps not,' said May, 'but there's a very good reason why you should be interested. It's a case that could bring down the government.'

'This kind of crime creates a potentially disastrous situation in the area,' said Leslie Faraday. 'King's Cross – of all places – the PM's flagship development – you understand the implications.'

Faraday had taken to coming in on Saturday mornings because his supervisor did, and he was anxious to have his diligence noted. He ventured into Kasavian's office with the trepidation of Van Helsing entering the lair of the undead. The room of casket-coloured oak had absorbed a hundred years of tobacco smoke before the banning of cigarettes, and somehow the very air seemed to be stained sepia. There were patches on the carpet where no light had ever fallen.

Oskar Kasavian winced at the pallid morning sunlight and turned away from the window, slipping back into shadow. With his sharply hooked nose and pale, elongated features he reminded Faraday of Nosferatu in the 1922 German film version he had seen on a drizzly evening in November 1979 at the East Finchley Rex, an event he had never forgotten, because he never forgot anything. He had been on a date with a girl called Deirdre Fairburn who went out for a choc-ice halfway through the film and never came back. Faraday had remained in his seat to watch the end of the film because it was not the first time a girl had given him the slip.

'Of course I understand. Do you know how much money the government is spending on security resources to convince investors that the area has been cleaned up?

The return of organized crime is unthinkable. Have you spoken to Islington? I heard they had a suspect in custody.'

'They seem to think the crime didn't occur on their turf, but yes, they were holding a man called Rafi Abd al-Qaadir. They had no evidence and were forced to let him go, thanks to our Mr Bimsley, who brought in a lawyer to argue on his behalf. Now they're trying to track down the Nigerian businessman who sold the lease of the shop where the body was found. Trouble is, the place was open and empty for a month. They're checking their usual contacts, but I can tell they don't know what to make of the death. I'm waiting for a pathology report.'

'Have you at least managed to keep this away from the press?'

'For the moment, but there's no way of stopping information from getting out so long as it's a publicly registered CID case. I've already warned APPRO not to issue any kind of statement.'

'St Pancras International is right next door, and it's the terminal for the next Olympics. They're about to open a luxury hotel that will house senior members of the Olympic Committee not five hundred yards from where this corpse was found. If anyone at the PM's office gets wind of this we will be crucified.' Kasavian looked like a man who was no stranger to crucifixion, or subsequent resurrection.

'There may be one solution,' Faraday ventured, 'but I don't think you're going to like it.'

Back in Chalk Farm it was like old times, insofar as the detectives were arguing. 'All you have to do is talk to Leslie Faraday,' said John May. 'He owes you several favours. If he can be persuaded–'

'You're forgetting one thing.' Bryant leaned forward, his blue eyes widening. 'I am not interested.'

'Come on, we're wasting our time here,' said Meera, grabbing May's arm. 'I'm disappointed in you, Mr Bryant, after all your lectures about looking for the unexpected in everyday crimes.'

'That's because I've finally realized there's nothing unexpected any more,' Bryant replied, slumping back.

'That's not true and you know it. Unexpected things happen all the time. I was coming out of a nightclub on Friday night when some bloke dressed as a bloody stag attacked me in the street, slashed my arm and ran off.'

Bryant was brought up short. 'A stag?' he repeated.

'Yeah, you know, big animal, they have them in the countryside or in zoos or something. Furry coat, antlers, the lot.'

'Where was this?'

'Right in the middle of King's Cross, the bit behind the cross-Channel railway line that's a dug-up field.'

'You're talking about the triangular piece of land between the Battlebridge Basin and the Eurostar terminal?'

'Yeah, I suppose so.' Meera looked puzzled.

'You have to show me exactly where this happened, right now. Find my shoes, someone.' Moments later Bryant had shucked off his dressing gown and was scrabbling to get into a grubby old herringbone overcoat, still clutching his walking stick, which became accidentally threaded through one of the sleeves, so that as he floundered about he resembled a particularly disreputable scarecrow coming to life.

'For God's sake, don't just stand there, woman, help me get this blasted thing on properly!' he shouted. Then he fell over.

'Oh, Mr Bryant, you're back!' cried Alma Sorrowbridge, pulling him out of the fireplace and patting him down before anything could burst into flames.

11

TREMORS

'You know, I always felt that the Peculiar Crimes Unit might finally find its spiritual home in a railway-terminus district like King's Cross,' said Bryant as the trio marched along York Way in blustery squalls of rain. He spoke above the ever-present bourdon of taxi engines, a low thrum that underscored life in the area from dawn to midnight.

The road behind the railway yards turned into the kind of strange no man's land Bryant had often seen in London after the War. These urban limbos had been created by bomb damage and government indecision. With a nation to rebuild and decades of punitive reparations to pay, cash for housing was in short supply. After the rubble from fractured terraces had been cleared away, the scarred earth remained as a slow-healing memory of the wounds inflicted by war. Children turned the chaotic rockeries of brick and plaster into fantasy lands, exploring for buried treasure. Dandelions sprang up between chunks of brickwork and rusting iron. If they were lucky, children might gleefully discover a live, undetonated bomb. Occasionally someone was blown sky-high. *Those were the days*, thought Bryant.

'I don't understand,' May admitted. 'You're not interested in a mutilated corpse found in a derelict chip shop, but a drunk in fancy dress annoying a couple of girls immediately gets your attention.'

'That's the difference between us,' said Bryant, tapping the side of his head. 'I always see the bigger picture.'

'What bigger picture? What do you see that I've missed?'

'Let's find out if he's left any tracks first. Meera, you lead the way. My energy's coming back, but my legs don't seem to have got the message yet.' They picked a path through the geometry of scaffolding that had sprouted from the walls of King's Cross station. The signs of construction and renewal were everywhere. Roads were closed; pipes were being lowered into trenches; a hundred canary-jacketed labourers crossed the roofs of half-renovated warehouses, bellowing to each other.

'I remember when there were only fields and factories behind the station.' Bryant waved his walking stick at a vast wall of blue-tinted wavy glass, the first of the new buildings to be completed. 'Wild horses, barges and gypsies. The ladies of the night brought so many punters to the grassy area beside the canal basin that it was nicknamed Pleasure Field.'

'Must have been a long time ago,' grunted Meera.

'Not at all. Twelve, maybe fifteen years at the most. It's changing fast now. Nearly all of the traditional gasholders have been dismantled, the old tenement buildings torn down. It was never pretty around here in my lifetime, but it had a rugged, dirty charm. My old man had many professions; one of them was as a street photographer. He showed me the pictures he took. There was a garden of rose bushes in front of the station. A liquorice factory. An old theatre called the Regent, pulled down to make way for the town hall. And there was a wooden roller-coaster.'

'It's got a Starbucks now.'

Bryant gave a shrug. 'It won't be there for long. Nothing ever stays around here. To my mind the symbol of King's Cross is a sturdy drain-fed weed sticking out of a sheer brick archway, something that can survive in the most inhospitable circumstances. An honest area, in the sense of being without hypocrisy, and a true test for the urbanite. The buildings will rise and crumble to dust, but the people won't change.'

From the corner of Wharf Road they could see a group of low brown buildings, Victorian warehouses that had somehow been spared the wrath of bombs and town planners. The structures huddled alone in a field of tractor-churned mud, bordered by railway embankments, the canal and the bare brick wall of the road that passed between them and the Eurostar railway terminal. The area roughly formed a great triangle, upon which was soon to rise a new town of glass and steel. The project was vast in scope and barely possible to imagine completed, even with the help of the computer-rendered images in its publicity brochures. Colleges and offices, shopping malls, social housing and luxury apartment blocks were to appear on a blighted site that had been alternately ignored and fought over for decades.

'I wonder what they'll find under all this soil.' Bryant stopped to get his breath and tapped the muddy road with his walking stick. 'In the Middle Ages this was part of the Great Forest of Middlesex, although it was inhabited in prehistoric times, of course. The first Paleolithic axe ever recognized in England was discovered near King's Cross Road – in 1680, if memory serves.'

'You were there, I suppose,' said Meera. 'The club's this way.'

The Keys club was living on borrowed time. Having survived the death of the super-clubs and the return of acoustic music, it had remained true to its hard house and electro roots, only to face annihilation at the hands of property developers. It had received a stay of execution when Camden Council rejected a plan which would have required the demolition of the listed building it inhabited, but construction had started all around. Each day, the earth-movers came a little closer. The new town would spread out from its nexus at the shoreline of the Regent's Canal. The first building, a shopping arcade, was nearing completion. The site even had its own concrete plant; such was the quantity required to pave over so many acres of earth and landfill.

'Meera, you were walking between the club and the road when you saw him, is that right?' May was forced to shout above the roar of the industrial equipment as they approached.

'See the tall spotlight, over there? I borrowed Dan's fingerprint kit and came up here first thing this morning, before it started raining. I tried to lift prints from the pole but they were too badly damaged. He'd swung around and smudged them.' She pointed to one of a dozen tall steel lampposts that kept the landscape illuminated at night.

The slippery mud made walking treacherous. May and Mangeshkar were forced to take Bryant's arms to keep him upright.

'I shouldn't have worn Prada shoes,' said

May, watching as liquefied clay closed over his toe caps.

'Not at your age, no,' agreed Bryant. 'You've always been a bit of a clothes horse, haven't you? Heaven knows how many people tramped across here on their way home after your scare, Meera.'

'I wasn't scared. The odd thing is I don't think he meant to slash my arm. He sort of fell into me because I kicked him.'

'You said he was wearing knives on his head. He'd already broken the law, albeit in a preposterous way.'

'Yeah, but I was thinking... It takes a certain type of mind to come up with antlers made out of knife blades. It was right here.' She pointed to the chewed-up earth around the base of the anodized post.

'Help me down,' said May.

'Ha!' Bryant was triumphant. 'It's usually me who needs a hand down.'

'I've only just recovered from an operation.' May was indignant. 'What's that?' He pointed to some matted strands of brown fur embedded in the mud. 'Something from your stag-man?'

'Probably hair from a passing rat,' answered Bryant gloomily. 'The canal system is besieged by them. They live off discarded chicken bones and grow to the size of Alsatians.' He dug a small clear plastic bag from his overcoat pocket and passed it to his part-

ner before creeping off in search of footprints.

The wind was sweeping across the great
churned field, thumping against pallets and
stacks of steel plate. Meera squinted at the
dark tumble of the sky. 'There's something
weird about this place,' she muttered. 'I
don't like it here.'

Bryant was interested. 'Oh, why not?'

'I don't know. It doesn't look right. Too
bare.'

'You don't have the comfort of surrounding
buildings. That's because we're on a hill. You
don't notice the gradient as you walk here.
King's Cross has a strange and convoluted
history. There are spirits, of course – there
always are near water and the poor. But
there's something else besides.' He sniffed
noisily. 'An unrest. A disquietude. Even on a
day of clear skies there's something turbulent
here that comes up through the soil. You can
smell it in the stormy air, can't you?'

Meera found herself nodding in agreement,
against her better judgement. She gave an
involuntary shiver. Bryant patted her arm in
understanding. 'Someone just walked over
your grave. I'll have to tell you all about the
area some time and I guarantee you'll feel
even stranger. Every act of kindness or violence, every deed of benevolence or cruelty,
leaves its mark on the land. Those marks
resurface in tiny tremors. And the ground

here holds a great many dark secrets.' A sheet of corrugated metal blew over, making Meera jump. Bryant smiled suddenly. 'I wonder, can you get Dan Banbury up here? We could use his plastic-mould kit for this – look.' He pointed to a pair of semi-circular shapes embedded deeply in the mud. 'They look like hoofprints to me.'

'They're very big.'

'Presumably they had to be large enough to fit over regular shoes, like pattens. This gentleman took his outfit seriously. There are a couple of costume shops near here. You'd better check them out.'

'Are you going to explain why you're so interested?' asked May.

Bryant cupped his hands, blew into them and thought for a moment. 'No, I'm not. Let's see your freezer body now.'

'We can't,' said May. 'It went to the Upper Street Morgue, which is under Islington's jurisdiction.'

'You're telling me we can't get at it?' Bryant's watery blue eyes widened in surprise.

'Ah, you finally understand! No, Arthur, we're not allowed.'

'You mean we're *persona au gratin?*'

'Yes. Perhaps now you could go and see your pals at the Home Office and try to pull a few strings for us.'

'Indeed. I exerted a great influence over the last Senior Commissioner. He still owes

119

me a huge favour because I saved his son's reputation.'

'How?'

'Well, you know the sauna on the corner of Camden Road–'

'No, I mean how did you exert influence over him?'

'Oh, well, basically I told him what to do. Except I can't any more.'

'Why not?'

'Well, for a start he's dead. Coronary embolism, about two months ago. A damned nuisance. I never liked him much, but I felt sorry for the passengers in his car.'

'Now what do we do?'

'I suppose we'll have to break the law again. I mean, there's something wrong here and the Met won't be able to do anything, so it's down to us. Meanwhile, strong tea, lots of it. There's a café on York Way that does bacon sandwiches you'll be pulling out of your teeth for days. I won't be, of course, because I take mine out and give them a rinse. If you can't get hold of Dan, put in a call to Jack Renfield and tell him to meet us there; we're going to need his help. But first let's get out of this mud.'

As they headed towards the café, the trio tried to stamp the dark earth from their shoes, but it remained stuck fast, as if the very ground was determined to leave its mark upon them.

12

RE-FORMATION

The Café Montmartre ('Open 24hrs For Hot Snacks') was the second most inappropriately named retail outlet ever to appear in central London (the first was the Beverly Hills Nail Salon, Whitechapel). The owner, a former nightclub promoter called Alfie Frommidge, had changed the name from Alf's Café in order to attract a new up-market clientele, but all he had succeeded in doing was to annoy the builders who had been using the place for cheap lunches, and who did not take kindly to paying double for the same menu just because it had been rewritten in bad French. Alfie's plan had been to appeal to Parisians arriving on the Eurostar, but they never ventured this far along the road, and if they did, one look at the first item on the menu – *'Saucisses et frites avec un oeuf et Baked Beans'* – would have seen them off.

DS Jack Renfield found the three ex-members of the Peculiar Crimes Unit seated in a row behind a wall of dusty plastic ferns. Alfie dropped an absurdly elaborate menu in front of him and continued to address Arthur Bryant.

'Since we got an alcohol licence we get your so-called professionals in the evenings now,' the restaurant owner explained, 'all the staff from the new offices next door, the branding company for the new King's Cross. A million quid for a logo that's a coloured squiggle my old gran could have knocked out in ten minutes, and she's only got one eye.'

'I know,' said Bryant. 'I've seen them in here, braying halfwits and drunk PR girls shrieking like demented chickens. I think I preferred the place when it was a dump with empty scallop shells on the tables for ashtrays.'

'Me too, but you can't halt progress, Mr Bryant. People want something classier.' Alfie wiped his hands on his apron and headed back to the kitchen to throw a fistful of parmesan shavings on to his instant mash.

'Ah, Renfield.' Bryant turned to his former detective sergeant. 'You've got good pals in the Met. Most of my influential friends are either dead or not feeling very well. I've put a couple of calls out, but no one's come back to me yet. Anyone at Islington nick who could smuggle one of us into the mortuary?'

'If you're talking about Bimsley's corpse, Islington reckons the south side of the Caledonian Road falls under Camden Council, so they've now taken it to the coroner's office at Camley Street, just round the corner.'

'You don't know anyone there, do you?'

'I used to go out with a really weird Greek bird called Rosa Lysandrou who worked there as a receptionist. This was a few years back, but I think she's still there. I could give her a call.'

'Kindly do so, would you? Have we heard from Dan yet? And where's Longbright?'

'Wait a minute,' May interrupted. 'You can't just go assembling the old crowd again. This isn't *The Blues Brothers*, we're not getting the band back together.'

'Why ever not?' asked Bryant, genuinely puzzled. 'Even Kasavian will see the financial sense in reopening the unit. I'll talk to him and persuade him to recommission us.'

'And what if he won't do it?'

'We'll hardly be any worse off than we are now.' On some subconscious level, Bryant knew that the only way to pull himself out of his self-pitying nosedive was to try and solve a murder that no one else in the Central London area was equipped to handle. The effort of succeeding was possibly the one thing that could restore his self-esteem.

Alfie returned with teas the colour of Thames mud. 'Are you going to be using this place as your office?' he asked. 'I could rent you a table.'

'Yes, and I could call a health inspector,' Bryant told him. 'It's just until we get sorted out. Tell me, do you get many customers from the nightclub over the road?'

'They come in here off their faces and order big breakfasts, then can't eat them,' said Alfie.

'Ever get anyone in fancy-dress outfits?'

'At the weekends sometimes. Nurses, schoolgirls, vampires, blokes in gorilla suits – we had a bunch of people done up as a bathroom once. Pipes, a bidet, the lot.'

'Anyone dressed as a stag?'

'Stag? Oh, I get it, stag night. No. Hang on a minute.' He went back to the kitchen and returned a minute later. 'Yeah, the sous-chef saw some guy dressed as a stag a couple of weeks back. Furry coat, antlers, the works. Just stood outside here having a smoke.'

'A bit of a nuisance, was he?'

'Doesn't sound like it. Why?'

Renfield snapped his phone shut. 'You're on. Rosa says she can get you into Camley Street right now for a few minutes because the office is closed, but she'll only take one of you.'

'That had better be me,' said May. 'Arthur, wait here. Perhaps you're interested enough to put in that call to Faraday now. Sound him out about reopening the unit.'

'What do you want me to do?' asked Meera.

'If Arthur really can persuade the Home Office to back us, perhaps you should find out about the current availability of our former staff. Just refer them to me if they want to know about salaries. Start with Colin Bimsley.'

Meera grimaced. 'Don't make me call Colin, chief. He doesn't need the encouragement.'

'Meera, you're not asking him on a date; this is business. Get cracking. Then round up Raymond Land and the others.' May turned back to find Bryant staring happily at him. 'What?'

'Nothing,' said Bryant, but he couldn't stop smiling.

'Ah, Mr Bryant, I was rather expecting you to call,' said Leslie Faraday, who wasn't thrilled about being disturbed at lunch, halfway through a bowl of canteen macaroni cheese. 'There's been some movement on your situation. After my conversation with your partner, I talked with Mr Kasavian. He's not at all happy about the idea of reforming the PCU.'

'I imagine he's even less happy about the idea of criminal gangs returning to an area that will become one of the main arrival points for the 2012 Olympics,' said Bryant. 'King's Cross isn't the only place undergoing a transformation. After the games, the Lower Lea Valley will become the largest urban park created in Europe for 150 years.'

'So I am led to believe. The government expects international traffic through King's Cross to become permanent, and that means even more overseas investment, public–private partnerships, that sort of thing. The Prime Minister is anxious to maximize the business opportunities afforded by the new Eurostar link, and as you know, it only takes one incident to swing the British press in the wrong direction, so–'

'For God's sake, Leslie, do stop waffling,' cried Bryant, exasperated. 'Is he going to bring us back or not?'

Faraday looked back at the phone and scowled. He had dropped macaroni cheese down his trousers. 'Well, I don't think we have any choice in the matter.'

'Does that mean you are?'

'There's good and bad news. You can reform the PCU as long as it's on the strict understanding that this case is resolved very quickly and very quietly. No later than the end of next week. After that, it returns to Islington CID.'

'I take it that's the good news.'

'Correct. The bad is that we won't be able to officially recognize you.'

'What does *that* mean?'

'It means no one can know of your existence. You won't have access to police information or technology. No identity intelligence, file sharing, fingerprint databases or forensic utilities of any kind. We simply can't afford to let them know about you.'

'You mean we'd have to operate with fewer tools than Sherlock Holmes had at his disposal, and he was fictional! How are we supposed to do that? This is the twenty-first century.'

'I'm sorry, that's the best I can do.'

'Can we at least get our old building back?'

'I'm afraid not. There will have to be some kind of temporary arrangement–'

'Then we'll take out a rental agreement on a cheap office in King's Cross and send the bill over to you.'

'I don't know about that–'

'I'm a pensioner, Leslie; I've got no money. What am I supposed to do, bung the expense on my Sainsbury's card?'

'Well, I'll have to clear it–'

'Fine, you do that and I'll get started at once.' Bryant could hear the sweat breaking out on Faraday's forehead; he decided to ring off before the civil servant changed his mind.

'Meera? Is that you?' Colin Bimsley was still in bed when the phone rang. He could scarcely believe that the diminutive Indian DC was actually calling him.

'Don't get your hopes up. The old man's trying to get the unit back on its feet. I think you'd better come over here as soon as you can.'

'Do you want me for my body? I mean, the body I found in the shop?'

'I'm not sure what Bryant's up to. I've tried working out how he thinks, but it's like trying to reset the clock on my oven without the manual.'

'I didn't know you cooked.'

'I can heat up take-out. Are you coming or what?'

'Where are you?'

'In some horrible fake-French café at the back of King's Cross station, just past the junction of York Way and Wharf Road.' Meera gave him the address. 'Don't say–'

'So is this, like, a date?'

'You had to say it, didn't you?' She cut the connection, then called Janice Longbright.

'Come back to the unit?' Longbright wedged the heavy Bakelite telephone receiver under her ear while she folded a pair of 1950s crimson silk broderie anglaise knickers into a ribboned box. Saturday was a busy shopping day in Camden Town. 'To be honest, I'm quite enjoying myself here. Why would I want to come back?'

'I could say we'll be performing a service by taking on the case,' said Meera, 'but the truth is I think old Bryant will peg it if we don't.'

'He's not ill, is he?'

'Not yet, but he's been going downhill. Let's just say he doesn't have a lot to live for without you and John beside him.'

Longbright sighed and looked around the sumptuous lingerie store, already knowing she would have to bid farewell to it. 'When does he want me?'

'Right now.'

'Then I guess I'll be there,' she promised, trying to keep the regret from her voice.

Raymond Land was at his club, waiting for the bar to open. He missed his shot when the phone rang.

'Buggeration!' He rose from the billiard table with a wince. Flipping open his phone, he tried to recognize the number. It couldn't be Leanne, his wife; she was having a lesson with her Latin American dance instructor. Apparently the man was teaching her to rhumba.

'Mr Land, it's Meera.'

'Hello, Mangeshkar, how are you?'

'Very well, thanks. How's Crippen?'

'I'm not very good with cats.' Land still had a bandage on his hand. He had been stuck with the PCU's mascot ever since the unit shut, and the damned thing kept trying to bite him whenever he picked it up. 'Do you want it back?' he asked hopefully.

'I have some wonderful news for you.'

Land's heart sank. He set down his billiard

cue reverently, sensing that something was about to die, probably his long-term retirement plan.

'The Peculiar Crimes Unit is going to be reopened.'

No, thought Land. *I'm out. I earned it, all those years of being made to look stupid while Bryant and May took all the glory. I can't do it. I won't do it.*

'I won't do it.' He realized he had spoken the last part of his thoughts aloud.

'I'm afraid you have to, sir,' said Mangeshkar. 'I just had a call from Mr Leslie Faraday at the Home Office. His orders come from Mr Kasavian, and *his* orders come directly from the Prime Minister. They want you to start work immediately. A matter of priority.'

'But I thought the team had split up.'

'No sir. I've located all of them except one.'

'Why, who's missing?' asked Land.

13

IDENTITY

The steep-roofed Gothic building at the back of Camley Street had a melancholy air, even for a coroner's office. The wet green banks of the St Pancras Old Church graveyard sloped down on either side of the walls, as if threatening to inundate the little house with the cascading tombs of the dead. Even a modern extension could not erase the sense of desolation that enveloped it. Tall black iron railings, each spear topped with a gold-painted fleur-de-lis, surrounded the doorway. Beneath a rowan tree, a muscular gravedigger stood motionless, looking down at them with feigned disinterest. He was young, but it seemed to May that the mournful atmosphere had stained his features with sorrow.

King's Cross was increasingly becoming an area of paradox; the more its pavements filled with commuters dashing between the stations, the less travelled were its backstreets. The morgue was only a few hundred yards from the huge international terminus that linked England to Europe, yet it was bordered by plane trees and beeches, waterways where herons stalked the reed beds and a nature reserve so quiet that often the only sound to be heard was the bleating of geese. Apart from the grave-digger, there was not a soul to be seen.

'What a bloody miserable place,' muttered Renfield, glancing up at the swaying branches that scraped against the building's low roof.

'You haven't been here before?' asked May.

'No, I always met Rosa at the pub around the corner. I dumped her.'

'Why?'

'She gave me the willies. She's got a funny attitude to the dead. A bit like old Bryant. Believes in spirits and all that malarkey.'

'Why is she doing this for you if you broke up with her?'

'I don't know. I was a bit surprised myself.'

Renfield thumbed the door buzzer. A slender olive-skinned woman with centre-parted black hair and dark, haunted eyes opened the door. She had an air of recent bereavement about her, which was at least appropriate considering where she worked. 'Come in,' said Rosa Lysandrou, checking the empty street behind them. 'There's someone here who wants to see you.'

May shot Renfield a look as they passed into the gloomy nicotine-brown interior. Rosa was dressed in mourning black, an outfit she regarded as respectful and proper for processing the dead. She looked like a woman who had lost any reason to smile soon after her teenage years. It seemed entirely natural for her to be in such a solemn place as this, although she did come over a bit like a character from a Daphne du Maurier novel.

'Hello there, Giles, what are you doing here?' asked May, shaking Giles Kershaw's hand as he stepped into the corridor.

'I applied for this position as soon as I heard about the vacancy,' replied Kershaw, unzipping the top of his green disposable suit. 'St Pancras Coroner – it's a huge step up for me. Come on, I'll show you around.' He led them into the building.

'I must say I feel bad about what happened, the unit closing just after we recommended you for the position at Bayham Street mortuary. We put in a good word for you. I'm glad you landed on your feet.'

'Well, I owe you a favour. Perhaps I can find a way to pay it back. Here, take a look at this.' Giles opened a carved church door that led into the Chapel of Rest. Usually such places were bare white cells adorned with a single plain oak cross and a bench or two, but this one was elaborately Gothic, a proper Victorian chapel with brass candlesticks and a life-sized painted statue of Christ crucified. His anguished eyes were turned heavenwards and were weeping tears of blood. Livid wounds in His side gushed crimson rivers. Was this a deliberate psychological ploy, May wondered, that after relatives had identified the bodies of their loved ones in the morgue they should come in here and see how Christ suffered? Was the idea to place their own grief in perspective and bring them to a better understanding of their religious beliefs? Or had it simply been done to creep them out with guilt?

'A bit over the top, isn't it?' observed May.

'Constructed by the architect of the church behind us. There was never a shortage of money for its upkeep, because of the fine residents in the graveyard.'

Kershaw took them along the passage to the autopsy room, and turned on the overhead lights, green tin circles that dated from the 1940s. 'Come on in. Sorry about the smell of damp. I asked Rosa about it, and she said, "What smell?" I think she's been here too long.'

'Renfield used to go out with her,' May whispered.

'Oh, no offence meant. She's very nice in her own way.' Kershaw flicked the lank blond hair from his eyes. 'Anyway, now I'm the new St Pancras Coroner. Rather an honour.'

'You always had ambition,' said May, following him.

'I'm sure Mr Bryant would appreciate the

circumstances surrounding my employment.'

'What do you mean?'

'Didn't you hear? The old coroner, Professor Marshall, apparently had some kind of nervous breakdown last October and vanished. Rosa knows all about it. She's still very loyal to him. Gets a bit Mrs Danvers-ish if you ask too many questions. They couldn't keep his job open any longer.'

'Death doesn't wait. I imagine you've stepped into a bit of a backlog.'

'They had someone covering, but he rubbed Rosa up the wrong way and was forced to move on pretty sharpish. I couldn't have taken on the position without you and Mr Bryant showing so much faith in me. Sadly, I don't think I can repay that faith today. I'm afraid I've no ID on your freezer man. I can't access any of the old PCU databases. It's annoying because I wanted to check his fingerprints through IDENT1, but we're not allowed to use the system. Fifty identification agencies in Great Britain, and we're locked out of all of them.'

'Islington CID are trying – his prints haven't come up yet.'

Kershaw led the way to the drawer cabinet, pumped up a trolley and slid out a body covered in a white plastic sheet. Transferring the remains to the table, he folded down the top half of the sheet. 'I've conducted an internal examination but the results won't be very reliable without deeper analysis. Although the freezer was fairly airtight, I'm told the unit backed on to a warm ventilation shaft from the building next door, which raised his body temperature.'

'Do you have anything at all?'

'I can't tell you exactly when he died because the crew from Islington had to pass the investigation over to their opposite numbers at Camden, and they didn't maintain the body at the temperature in which it was found. By the time he got here he'd been placed in a variety of different atmospheres. As you can see, he's a white male, roughly thirty-three years of age, outwardly healthy if a bit overweight. He's worked outdoors; there are tan lines on his upper arms, hard skin on the thumbs, a few cuts and nicks. The amputation was made with sharp, slim blades. Two distinct types of cut here, a series of small strokes to cut through the skin and flesh, and a second with stronger pressure to sever the cartilage in the neck. Two knives, one for the heavy cutting, the second smaller and finer. It's a professional job all right. I'm surprised the tattoo and the hands are intact. Unfortunately the ivy wreath is straight out of the book, a standard design, and one of the most common available. The cutting could have been done with surgical equipment, or the type of vegetable knife you can buy in any decent kitchenware shop. He was beheaded after death. The cuts are uniform and smooth, nothing to make the killer's handiwork recognizable. We have microtomic equipment here, which has proved useful. I took a thin slice of tissue from the throat and another one from the gut to compare the effects of decomposition in an airless atmosphere. It's not my field, so I had to use one of Professor Marshall's contacts. Luckily Rosa kept his address book.'

May walked slowly around the body, studying it. Putrefaction had been halted in its advance, but the corpse's skin had turned green and black, producing an acrid odour. He found it hard to imagine that this man had recently been walking around, eating in restaurants, watching TV. He was someone's lover, someone's son, but there was almost nothing human left. Without a head his trunk bore an unsettling similarity to something you would find in a meat locker. How would his loved ones feel if they could see him like this? 'Get anything else?'

'It's tricky because the usual decay process has been interrupted by the relatively sterile storage of the body. Usually, after two to three days you get staining on the abdomen. The discoloration spreads, veins grow dark, the skin blisters after a week, tissue starts softening and nails fall off at around the three-week stage, and finally the face becomes unrecognizable as the skin liquefies—'

'We don't need a lecture about decomposition,' interrupted Renfield impatiently. 'Have you got a date of death or not?'

'Four or five days ago,' Kershaw replied, rattled. 'The victim's blood hadn't had time to pool. He was dead when he was cut up, so it's possible the attacker struck while he was in the shop. Either that, or he was killed very close by. In that case you'll be looking for a van, because he was laid out flat; there were no blood creases behind the legs or in the elbows. I made a couple of calls; Islington CID have a record of gangs who have removed identification from their victims in the past, but there's no obvious MO match with any of them, and none are currently active in the area where the victim was found. Whoever killed him was a bit careless about washing the body. There's a streak of mud here, on his right shoulder blade. Looks like London clay. I'd like to get a sample off for analysis, but I don't have a case number.'

'Any idea how he died?'

'There are no entry wounds on the body so it must be on the missing part. Possibly head trauma, although we'll have to find it first.'

'We haven't found anything on the premises yet,' said May. 'Not that we expected to. I'll have Dan Banbury make a thorough search, but the property has been used as a dumping ground for builders' materials, so we won't have time to get to it today.'

Kershaw looked down at the corpse and ran a forefinger around the neatly severed neck with tenderness. 'I guess he'll yield his secrets when the last piece turns up.'

'We don't have the time to wait for that,' said May. 'We have to establish an identity fast.'

'There was one peculiar thing,' said Giles, uncovering the corpse's pale feet. 'What do you make of this?'

Renfield and May leaned forward. Just below both ankles, there were dozens of tiny black specks.

'Scratches?' May asked.

'Burns,' replied Kershaw. 'Hot metal filings. He didn't wear proper work boots. They're in different stages of healing, so they didn't all happen at the same time. It's an occupational hazard. He's done some welding.'

14

RATS

And so it was that late on Saturday afternoon, the Peculiar Crimes Unit made arrangements for an invisible return to the streets of London. Bryant frightened the life out of a local estate agent by threatening to requisition property on behalf of the government, and instantly acquired the keys to a partially furnished building that had been sitting empty on the agent's books for almost a year. The gimlet-eyed agent, Mr Hawker, a man who would have sold his grandmother's bed with her in it if he thought he could turn a profit, had been unable to shift the property because prospective tenants complained that there was something unsavoury and bothersome about the maze of interconnected dust-grey rooms, and indeed, Hawker possessed a secret file on the building that he was careful to hide from his new client. His desperation to offload this millstone was almost as urgent as Bryant's desire to occupy it, and so a deal was struck to the immediate satisfaction of both parties.

In this latest incarnation of the PCU, much

had changed. Instead of decently equipped offices in Mornington Crescent, they found themselves on the first and second floors of an unrenovated warehouse on the corner of Balfe Street and Caledonian Road, a property standing on the boundary between respectability and knife fights. On one side were green-footprint restaurants, cappuccino bars and glass cliffs of offices packed with time-strapped executives. On the other were run-down pubs, sex shops and dazed gangs of visiting drunks in football strips.

Arthur Bryant did not see it like that, of course. He stood on the roof sucking Liquorice Allsorts with his trilby pulled over his ears and his scarf knotted tightly around his neck, and watched the dying sunlight whiten the dome of St Paul's Cathedral. *Life is a very beautiful dream*, he thought. *I'm so glad I chose not to wake up from it just yet.* He had almost forgotten how lovely the city could appear to the right eye at the end of the day, when the shining yellow buildings of every shape, age and size radiated light beneath a panorama of blue-grey cumulus.

Below him was the most connected part of the city. It operated like a gigantic wall socket overloaded with too many crackling plugs. Above, behind and underneath the roads ran the railways: GNER, First Capital Connect, Midland, East Coast, Hull, Grand Central, Virgin, Silverlink and Scotrail.

Beneath these were the Underground lines: the Northern, the Victoria, the Piccadilly, the Metropolitan, the Circle, the Hammersmith & City; and across them all ran a dozen bewildering bus routes.

Most of the time, the thousands of men, women and children who rushed past each other to their transport links managed to do so without ever colliding or uttering a sentence longer than 'Sorry' or 'Excuse me,' but occasionally the system momentarily fractured and something terrible happened. Here, in 1987, a fire in the Tube station had killed thirty-one people. In 2005, terrorists had murdered fifty-six. Yet this was merely the most recent twist in the area's knotted history, for the scruffy, unassuming site had reflected the rise and fall of empires.

It was perhaps appropriate, then, that the Peculiar Crimes Unit should find its spiritual home here, among the debris of the past and the construction of the future. Early on Monday morning, Raymond Land placed Crippen in a box and reluctantly left his pleasant house in Putney to trudge his way across London. In truth, he was happy to be getting out from under his wife's feet. Leanne found him more annoying than ever since he had been at home, which was odd because she was hardly ever at home herself. She was forever disappearing for one-on-one tuition with fitness trainers, makeover

142

artists, yoga gurus and dance instructors, all of whom seemed to be suntanned males half her age. The fact that she needed to have her hair done before attending a pottery class mystified Land.

The acting temporary head of the PCU had been wooed with a promise of promotion; if this case was resolved quickly and quietly, he would finally be bumped up to Superintendent, a job title he would have been granted long ago if Bryant and May had not upset so many important people. Still, the thought of coming back to work was undignified. It was like making tearful farewells at a leaving party, only to have to come back and collect your scarf. Perhaps the investigation would fail and he would once more be released. Perhaps he could borrow some of Bryant's little blue pills to get him through the week. That Monday morning, Land stood before the black-painted door of Number 231 Caledonian Road, drew in a great lungful of traffic fumes, then rang the bell.

Janice Longbright dragged chairs along the warped corridors of the musty warehouse, trying to ignore the smell of old oysters, cloves and candlewax. She had spent Sunday arranging empty packing crates into makeshift desks, and trying to find places for everyone to sit. At least the electricity had been left on; the building had little natural light, and the agent had no desire to be sued by anyone taking a tumble in the gloom. April had already prepared a briefing room, and had arranged for some second-hand computers to be delivered from Mornington Crescent later in the day, but the place was still a shambles. Bryant had demanded that the office be ready for immediate operation after the weekend, but there was too much to do.

'What's this I hear about you going on a date with Jack Renfield?' April asked Longbright as they shook open dust-crusted curtains to allow dirty sunlight into the room. 'I thought nobody liked him.'

'Nobody did, and I still don't like the way he behaves, but I think working at the PCU is changing him for the better. Anyway, it wasn't a proper date. We just went up Brick Lane for a curry. He's still got a bloody great chip on his shoulder, but I can deal with that.'

'I wouldn't have thought he was your type.'

'These days my type is any type who still likes my type,' said Longbright, slamming down the chairs. 'It's been a while since I even bothered to look at a man. Jack hasn't got a clue how to treat women. He hasn't got an ounce of imagination. He's more like an Alsatian than a human being.'

'Then his ears have probably pricked up,'

said April, 'because you're talking about him enough.'

'God, I am, aren't I? I must be getting desperate.'

'If you don't mind me asking, how old are you?' asked April, who thought she was young enough to get away with asking such things.

'I'm old enough to have to memorize a date before which I'm not supposed to be able to remember anything. Let's get on before I change my mind about coming back. You've got your grandfather's impertinence.' She glanced around the chaotic room. 'We should give this space to John and Mr Bryant. It would be a good idea to have them working in the same room again. I wonder where Jack is. He's supposed to be here giving us a hand this morning.'

'There are rat droppings everywhere. And what is that revolting smell?' April sniffed the stale air.

'I dread to think,' replied Longbright. 'Something's probably dead in here. I'm going to risk opening some windows. It feels like the place has been sealed for years.'

They set about making the warehouse fit for human habitation.

Leslie Faraday always looked forward to the end of his working week. By lunchtime on Saturday he had expected to have an empty inbox and a desk swept clean of paperwork. Then his superior had called with instructions for handling the newly risen PCU, and the happy harmony of his weekend had collapsed abruptly. Now he found himself wrangling over an alarming number of expenditure requests from the very detectives he had thought he would never have to deal with again. Plus, Renfield was proving obstreperous.

'You're trained in surveillance,' Faraday told the telephone wearily. '*Surveillance* is the continual observation of a person or a group. *Spying* is the gathering of clandestine intelligence. So don't think of it as spying; think of it as surveillance.'

'I know the difference between them, Mr Faraday. I'm not an idiot.'

From what he had heard about the detective sergeant, Faraday thought he would have jumped at the chance, but Jack Renfield was audibly uncomfortable with his proposition. 'All I'm asking you to do is keep a diary for the duration of the investigation, Sergeant Renfield. At the end of each day, starting today, you will call me on this line, which is direct and secure, and inform me of anything out of the ordinary. This way, we can call a halt to any unauthorized procedures before they get out of hand.'

'You're asking me to rat on my colleagues?'

146

'That's a rather old-fashioned way of thinking. We're all being monitored these days. If I wanted to, I could have CCTV cameras installed in the PCU's offices.' *But you're cheaper*, Faraday thought.

There was a time when Jack Renfield would have been happy to obey the instructions of the Home Office to the letter, but he had recently undergone a change of heart. He had only just gained the trust of the others in the unit. Now he would be risking his new career to please this porcine paper-shuffler. Renfield could be an obstinate man when he chose, and he chose to be so now.

'What if I tell you I'm not prepared to do it?' he asked, already sensing the answer.

'Then we will have to question your suitability for the PCU, and return you to the Met.'

'You know I can't go back there. I guess you're also aware that the CID turned me down.'

'Yes, I heard you rather burned your bridges when you joined the Peculiar Crimes Unit. So I take it you'll accept this task?'

'You're not leaving me much choice,' snapped Renfield, hanging up. *But I'll do it in my own way*, he decided, astonished by his new allegiance to the unit.

15

VENGEANCE MADE MANIFEST

'He never puts his bloody tools away,' Clive the chief electrician complained as he rolled up the heavy red plastic cables and kicked them across the floor. He checked his watch: 7.45 p.m. The place had been deserted since one minute past six. *They couldn't have cleared the decks of the* Titanic *this quickly,* he thought. That was the trouble with the lazy sods that management was hiring these days. No pride in their workmanship. It was a bloody disgrace. It was a matter of principle in Clive's family to work hard and joylessly until the day you dropped dead.

'From Essex, isn't he, your friend?' said Constantin, his trainee.

'What's that got to bloody do with it?'

'They are all cowboys, the ones from Essex.'

'What do you know? You're from bloody Romania.'

'We are a hardworking people. When you have so little, it makes you work. Your friend has too much, I think.'

'Can you stop calling him my bloody

friend?'The two electricians were clearing up for the night. The central block of the building that would eventually become the shopping mall now had power. Three of the floors were temporarily lit, dimmed at night for the sake of the council flats opposite. Constantin unplugged the extension cards and carefully set them aside. Clive cut the remaining spotlights, and the floor was suddenly darker than the surrounding land, so that they had to be careful reaching the open staircase to the site exit.

Two hundred and seventy men and women were currently working full-time on the Royal Midland Quadrangle, a retail complex being constructed around a raised concrete platform that would form the centrepiece of the new town to the north of King's Cross station. Tonight, apart from two security guards, Clive and Constantin were the only workers still left on site.

When Constantin stepped outside and found himself facing the railway embankment, he was aware of another human presence standing nearby. He could feel someone watching him. He scanned the dug-up fields, the park for the earth-movers, the construction-site cabins, but nothing stirred in them.

When he turned back to the embankment, it seemed that his worst childhood fear had sprung to life. A great half-human creature rose on its spread haunches against the deepening orange skyline. It slowly raised its glinting antlered head until it seemed to be staring directly at him. The electrician let out a groan of fear and backed away.

'Hey, Dinu,' Clive called, using the diminutive version of Constantin's name. 'Look where you're going.' But it was too late. The Romanian boy was so entranced by the creature standing on the ridge of earth before him that he did not remember the newly dug basement at his back, and fell into darkness.

Ten thirty-five p.m. Another night, another party.

Izabella and Piotr had been going out for over three months, and had never slept together. Izabella had no idea what had gone wrong, but they had passed the point where they might have fallen into bed, and had now drifted into a limbo world of friendship. She still fancied him, craved him even, but it was difficult to bring the subject back now that it had gone. She was Polish and smart and thought too much about what boys wanted. He was a dirt-common Russian from the suburbs, weighed down with his father's new money, and he enjoyed playing the field.

On that night, they, too, saw the horned man. He was draped in deerskins and wearing metallic stag antlers that shone in the streetlamps. He stood against the low wall of the bridge across the canal, sometimes moving out of sight when a car pulled up at the traffic lights.

They were picking their way over the field from Battlebridge Road to York Way, going for a drink before heading for the Keys club, and the stag-man was handing out flyers; several had been tossed aside and were tumbling away towards the embankment. Izabella had thought nothing of it. So many flyers were handed out, usually at the end of the night. She picked one up and tried to read it in the dim light: a horned skull and some kind of poem. The printing was poor and she could only catch the last four lines.

Long have two springs in dull stagnation slept,
But taught at length by subtle art to flow,
They rise; forth – from oblivion's bed they rise;
And manifest their vengeance to mankind.

What was it advertising, a Goth pub? There was nothing printed on the back. The stag-man was still there when they left the Keys several hours later, and this time his appearance was more memorable, perhaps because he stood out in stark silhouette against the electric darkness. From the way he was weaving about beside the bridge, he appeared to have been drinking.

She recalled thinking that the sky was strange, a sickly ochre reflection of the radiant city beneath. The air was cold and gritty, and left a cuprous tang in the mouth, like being near a steelworks or in the proximity of blood. The night was not right. They had argued over something ridiculous – a spilled drink – and left. A lone girl was tottering ahead of them, faun-thin legs in a too-short dress. She looked awkward, frozen and friendless, as if, leached of life and colour, she might fall over and expire at any moment.

Izabella was still sniping at Piotr on their way to the night-bus stop, a hectoring banter they had evolved when they were feeling frazzled and fractious. She saw the thin girl approaching the bridge from the corner of her eye, saw her long black hair whip up around her dark eyes, and then the stag-man was there as well, towering over her. Backlit by the canal lamps behind the bridge, Izabella saw his antlers glitter and fracture the light. She heard the girl scream or laugh hysterically, but the sound was snatched away by the wind. She watched in shock as he lifted her up, placing her under one arm, and seemed to drop beneath the bridge.

By the time Izabella reached the spot with Piotr, there was no sign of either of them. No ripple on the petrol-iridescent surface of the canal, only the cold breeze from the tunnel and a fading sigh in the trees, as if the pair had evaporated into the thickening mist like a pair of exorcized ghosts.

16

FIRST DAY

'I spent two hours at something called the King's Cross Police Shop in the early hours of this morning, waiting to be seen, and after I got to make a report they made a phone call and finally sent me to you, only you weren't open,' Izabella told DS Janice Longbright. 'All I wanted to do was explain what I saw, OK?' She took a look around the room and wrinkled her nose, trying to make sense of it. 'This isn't a police station. What is this place?'

'We're in the process of moving in,' said Longbright. 'We're a specialist unit.'

'What do you specialize in, pest control? I just saw something in the hall that looked like a rat.'

Smart mouth, thought Longbright. *She'll make a good witness.* 'Yeah, we have a few of those. Look, I've read your statement and I know you're telling the truth about the man you saw, but are you sure he actually abducted someone?'

'I was with my–' She stopped herself. 'A friend. He saw it, too. The dressed-up guy, he was pretty big...'

'How big?'

'I don't know – he had to reach down to her, he put her under his arm, actually under his arm, although she was a skinny little thing, then when I looked back they were gone.'

'You think they went down on to the canal?'

'No idea. The path to the waterside is further back along the road. I'd have seen them if they'd used it, but I suppose they might have ducked into the tunnel. They disappeared so quickly I thought I must have imagined it.'

'Did you?'

'No, I didn't.'

'This girl, she didn't fight back?'

'I don't know. I guess so – I mean I saw her hands go up in the air and I think I heard her scream.'

'What do you mean, you *think?*'

'At first I thought it was a laugh, like maybe she thought he was joking, but it turned into something that sounded like a scream.'

'What did she look like? If I was trying to recognize her in the street, how would you describe her to me?'

'Skinny, very pale, wearing a short pink skirt with little black ruffles, black high heels, dark hair. Maybe there was more colour – you can't really tell under those yellow street-lights. She was kind of invisible, like everyone else who comes out of a club. I didn't see her face.'

Not much to put out a MisPer for, thought Longbright. 'And no one apart from you saw what happened?'

'No, it gets really quiet around there before the Keys shuts down. I couldn't do anything because they were too far away and it happened so fast, but you hear about bad things happening to girls by themselves, and I hate the idea that she might have been abducted without anyone coming forward.'

'You did the right thing. I'm sorry they made it difficult for you. The problem I have is that your description of this girl doesn't give us much to go on. We can get some leaflets posted around the club, ask around, see if anyone's failed to check in at home, but we can't do much more unless she's reported missing.'

'That reminds me, this guy was handing out flyers. So he's not trying to hide himself away, is he? I thought he was advertising a club, but it was some kind of poem.' She dug in her pocket and produced a crumpled ball of saffron paper.

As Izabella left, she passed Constantin waiting in the corridor. His right leg and ankle were heavily bandaged and he was on painkillers, but he still took a great interest in her backside.

'The guy out there saw him, too,' said

April, dropping a report on the arrangement of tea chests that served as Longbright's desk. 'He was so shocked that he fell down the unlit stairwell behind him and broke his ankle.'

'What was he doing there?' asked Longbright, digging out a pair of mad rhinestone-winged glasses with which to skim the statement.

'He's an electrician working on the site's new mall,' April explained. 'There's a hypermarket going in, and they're running behind schedule. He was terrified. He could have been killed. Luckily they hadn't started pouring concrete, so he landed in dirt. This might have started as someone's idea of a joke, but it's going beyond that.'

'You don't need me to re-interview him, do you?' Longbright asked. 'Nothing's working here, and I could really use some time to get straightened out.'

'Well, he has an interesting twist on what he saw.'

'What do you mean?'

'He's Romanian and very superstitious. He insists he saw – hang on.' She checked her note. 'Veles, the Slavic god of sacred animals. According to this guy, it's a forest creature that has horns like a ram or a stag, and protects hallowed land from enemies. He's refusing to go back to work on the site, and he's told his friends not to go back, either. He insists it's an indication that something evil has been disturbed. That the land wasn't meant to be built on.'

'Hmm. Is he cute?'

'I'd go to a boxing match with him if he promised to touch my breasts afterwards.'

'Fair enough,' said Longbright. 'Send him in.'

'You're enjoying this, aren't you?' said May, narrowing his eyes at his old partner. 'Look at you, sitting there surrounded by dirt and chaos, eating your Liquorice Allsorts and reading witness statements about a character from Eastern European mythology. You think you're back on track. This is not an office, Arthur, it's a chamber of horrors. We've got bare bulbs in the ceiling, no phones, no computer network, no authorization, no legal existence at all, a broken toilet and hardly any floorboards. By comparison, Mornington Crescent was Versailles. I should never have let you pick a rented property without consulting me.'

'It was cheap,' said Bryant, happily patting the arms of his new chair, a studded green-leather number on broken castors that exuded horsehair stuffing like a disembowelled corpse. 'Besides, I knew you had your hands full getting the team back together. We'll manage somehow.'

May looked up at the blackened ceiling

and wrinkled his nose. 'I'm wondering what was here before; I keep finding joss sticks and pots of strange-smelling incense behind the doors. Poor Raymond nearly had a conniption fit when he saw the place. I think he actually started pining for his old office.'

'Raymond's only happy when he's got something to complain about.'

'Chief, how's your knowledge of local poetry?' asked Longbright, sticking her head around the place where the door should have been. 'Message from the stag-man.' She threw the balled-up flyer on to the arrangement of crates that constituted a pair of makeshift desks.

Bryant hooked up his reading glasses and unfurled the page. The silence that followed was broken by a piece of ceiling falling down.

'I know this; it's part of a long chunk of doggerel written when Battlebridge was still a spa town of royal patronage. It's always quoted in books about the actress Nell Gwynne. The last line has been altered: ...*from oblivion's bed they rise, and manifest their vengeance to mankind*. But it's not supposed to be "vengeance", it should be "virtues".'

'Amazing,' May exclaimed. 'When I went to pick him up this morning, I had to wait twenty minutes while he remembered where he'd left his shoes, but he can recall a one-word mistake in a two-and-a-half-century-old poem.'

'It's not a mistake,' Bryant explained, 'it's a threat. Janice, get everyone together, will you? I think we should talk to them in our new briefing room.'

'And where might that be?' asked Long-bright.

'The big black-painted room opposite. They can sit on the floor and take notes.'

'I'm not one to make a fuss, but there are rats.'

'Let Crippen out. He'll take care of them. I'll be there in a minute.' Bryant tore open a cardboard box and dragged out a stack of books. As May watched, his partner seemed to be reversing the ageing process, becoming visibly younger and happier before his eyes.

It had taken only one working day for the team to recreate a semblance of their old offices. Now they had time to reacquaint themselves with each other. 'Hey, Jack.' Dan Banbury held out his hand to Renfield. 'How have you been coping for the last month?'

'Just been getting on with it,' replied the taciturn sergeant.

'Raymond, I thought you were determined to stay retired,' said May.

'Yes, I thought so, too,' Land admitted despondently.

'Come on, everyone, this is great, we're all here again, feel the love, group hug,' said Bimsley. Someone threw a piece of wood at him.

Giles Kershaw had popped in from the coroner's office in Camley Street to welcome his old friends back and offer them his limited facilities at the morgue. Even Meera accepted a bear hug from Colin Bimsley, telling herself that it would probably never happen again.

When Bryant entered the room he received a round of applause. 'All right, you lot,' he called, 'settle down, we're losing time. John, run through the salient points, will you?'

May stepped forward. 'In order to make this work we have to be very organized,' he told them. 'I know the place is a dump – we won't even have a functioning loo until Friday at the earliest, so you'll have to use the one in the pub opposite – but the freedom we have does give us a few advantages.'

'The Home Office won't be able to find us,' remarked Bimsley, causing laughter.

'That's true, we have a few days in hand before the old restrictions kick in. They want this so-called "gang killing" dealt with before word gets out, and we have to work with them. If they've covered up our existence, the press won't know where to look for us, but even so I reckon we only have two or three days' grace. You'll have read Janice's notes on what we have so far, which isn't much at all – no positive ID on the body, no cause of death, no motive, no suspects.'

'Situation normal, then,' said Meera. There was more laughter.

'We have an approximate date of demise – a week ago, around last Tuesday – we think our victim was a welder, and he probably wasn't killed on site. Islington CID's only suspect has been released on bail. A gentleman named Rafi Abd al-Qaadir – have I pronounced that right? – who purchased the shop's lease. Oh, and the original owner of the property has been traced to Nigeria. We're waiting for the Lagos police to interview him, but you won't be surprised to hear that they're being uncooperative and are refusing to tell us when that will be.'

'So we have no leads at all?' asked Banbury. 'I don't know how we're supposed to work without access to police databases.'

'I found traces of mud that appear to match the construction site up the road,' said Kershaw, 'where they're building the new King's Cross development. But it's all over the area, trodden into the pavements and gutters. It's probably just transferred material.'

'Unfortunately,' said May, 'there are probably more welders and general building workers in King's Cross than anywhere else in London right now, which is going to make your job much harder. Start with all the site foremen, see if they're missing anyone. We need to hit all the shops on the Cally Road and find out if anyone saw the door to number seventy-three being forced. Try the tattoo parlours in Camden, see if there's anything unusual about the ivy-wreath tattoo. And see if anyone noticed a van parked outside the shop at night.'

'Vans park along there all the time after six-thirty p.m,' Banbury pointed out.

'Ask anyway. Janice has a task list, and you'll see that everyone has been assigned a specific set of duties over the next few days. It's by-the-book stuff, and we stick to it until we get a break. Giles, if you could spare the time I'd like you to take a look at the location with Dan. We're treating it as a murder site. The place is full of plaster dust and timber – whoever did this must have left something behind. I'm sorry we haven't got any safety kit or any Airwaves – you'll have to use your mobiles to contact us, but it's not as if you'll be requesting armed back-up. Any questions?'

'Good. Let's move on to the other odd event in the neighbourhood,' said Bryant with relish. 'The sighting of a man dressed as a stag near the Keys nightclub, and the possible abduction of a young female last night.'

Meera blew through her nose and looked

at the ceiling. Bimsley shot her an angry look.

'Arthur has a very good reason for wanting to investigate this second matter,' said May. 'The issue here is that some of the more superstitious workers on the surrounding building sites hail from remote villages in Eastern Europe. Stories about such creatures are apparently still part of their cultural heritage. Since these sightings, some of them have started refusing to operate on buildings nearest this creature's supposed haunts. If the employers can't keep their workers, and at the same time get wind that a gangland killing has occurred in the area, they'll start asking questions the police can't answer. At this point there can be no loss of confidence in the King's Cross project. It requires a gigantic leap of faith in a neighbourhood that has always been associated with poverty and crime.'

'Wait, so which of these are we investigating?' asked Renfield, confused.

'Both,' said Bryant.

'The gang slaying,' said May, glancing over at his partner. 'Arthur will have to take care of the other matter by himself.'

'But if any of you would care to give me a hand, I'd be grateful.' Bryant summoned up his pitifully helpless look, even though it had long since stopped being effective.

'I suppose we're working round the clock

until we get something,' said Meera.

'You're not officially working at all,' May pointed out. 'If you need money we may be able to give you a small cash advance, depending on how much Raymond can draw out on his ATM card.' He looked at Bryant and gave a grim smile. 'Just catch us a murderer before the King's Cross project crashes. That's not so much to ask, is it?'

17

THE HORNED ONE

'What did you mean by that?' asked Bryant angrily, as soon as the meeting had dispersed. 'You tricked me into coming back here by telling me about the stag-man, and now you try to prevent anyone from helping me find him.'

'I didn't trick you,' said May. 'If you remember, Meera volunteered the information quite by chance and you seized upon it. We only have a short time to solve an extremely nasty murder, and we're not equipped to do the job. I can't have you directing the others to go gallivanting off in search of someone who's obsessed with stag nights.'

'A girl may have been abducted.'

'We don't have proof of that. This witness, Izabella what's-her-name – her boyfriend wouldn't back her up so we only have her opinion about what she saw, and no one has reported a missing girl. I'm not saying you can't investigate it, just that you can't use the others until we get a grip on the case we've been hired to crack. This is another chance, Arthur – no, another last chance. Have you got your mobile?'

'Of course, and it's charged up, although I miss my old Storno, don't you? Fine piece of equipment, never went wrong.'

'Well, we're in the twenty-first century now, and stop changing the subject.'

'All right, I can see I'm going to have to explain why I'm so interested in our antlered abductor. Come to my office.'

'You haven't got an office. None of us has.'

'Don't be pedantic. Come back to the space which I plan to turn into our centre of operations.'

They walked together into a dingy, cob-webbed front room overlooking the Caledonian Road. 'Pull up a crate,' said Bryant magnanimously. He seated himself in his cracked leather chair and lifted a yellowed scroll of paper from the floor, wiping dust from it. 'Right, this is King's Cross during Mesolithic times.'

'Dear Lord, do we have to go back that far?' asked May, fearing the meeting would be a long one. He knew that the disturbing myths and mysteries of old London were Bryant's obsession. Besides, it was getting towards lunchtime and he'd had no breakfast.

'Now, we know there was a Mesolithic settlement just up the road from here, on Hampstead Heath, but most pre-Christian tribal activity was in the district we now call King's Cross, near the Battlebridge Basin. The area was still unspoilt countryside a couple of centuries ago, filled with meadows, streams and wells. Water drained from Hampstead Heath down to King's Cross, which was then the Bagnigge Wells, then to Sadler's Wells and Clerkenwell – all wells, you see, and very healthful because they contained so much sodium, iron and magnesium sulphate, although they can't have tasted very nice.'

'I get the idea. You've told me all this before.'

'Just checking that you were paying attention.' He threw open a filthy, dog-eared book and stabbed at a lithograph. 'In the Middle Ages, the area of St Pancras was part of the great forest of Middlesex. The last remaining piece of that is Caenwood – what we now call Kenwood – in Hampstead. Where you get water, you get villages, crops – and fertility rites. Now, around 1550 a fable resurfaced about the Pindar of Wakefield. The pindar warns that no one may trespass upon his land, is challenged, and acquits himself by winning a sword fight. He appears in folk songs and his story forms the basis for part of the Robin Hood legend, where he becomes a man named George-a-Green, and his challenger is Little John.'

'I really don't see what on earth this has to do with a bloke abducting girls outside a nightclub.' May was exasperated. 'What is a pindar, anyway?'

'He's a man who keeps the village's stray cattle in a pen, or pinfold. The pindar's story goes back much further, all the way to Paleolithic times, because he's based on a pagan British god, the lord of the forest beasts, the stag-headed "Horned One". This character reappears throughout our history as Herne the Hunter, and represents the fertile male power of nature. In prehistoric times he would be portrayed by a shaman dressed in deerskins and a headpiece decorated with stag horns, a man undergoing transformation into a god.'

'You think we've got someone who knows his history?'

'Or his pubs. After catching our pub killer, you'll agree that I know an awful lot about houses of refreshment. Now until recent times, the inns in Highgate still practised Swearing on the Horns, a debased fertility rite for visiting strangers who were required to worship the god and kiss a maiden. The

Pindar of Wakefield pub nearby in Gray's Inn Road only changed its historic name in 1986, to The Water Rats. But here's a strange thing. In 1517 when it was built, the landlord's name was George Green. The whole area is associated with the most ancient pagan god in British folklore. There was even a pub called The Horns right on the site where this stag-man has been spotted.'

'What on earth can he want?'

'Well, there's a sinister side to all of this.' Bryant's blue eyes glittered as he found another lithograph. 'George-a-Green, or Herne, the Horned One, is also Jack in the Green or the Green Man, the spirit of vegetation. The Green Man is a story that predates Christ. Uniquely, it has its roots in both pagan and Christian history. The legend tells how the dead Adam had the seeds of the tree of knowledge planted in his mouth. From this mix of fertility and soil grew a sinister god, the Oak King, the Holly King, the Green Man – the symbol of death in life. The Green Man is found in a great many English churches. I understand that there are over sixty green men in Exeter Cathedral alone. He appears both in church carvings and at May Day celebrations, as a sort of primeval trickster, a symbol of spiritual rebirth, but also as a vengeful rapist and bloodsucker. Look at this.' Another etching, this more disturbing than the last. 'The Green Man is a forest creature with the power to wipe out cities and return them to nature. He destroys men by unleashing natural forces upon them, and reappears when the earth is threatened. He can be benign and healing, but there's a wildness about him, a dangerous cruelty – and a terrible madness.'

May studied the pictures. He opened his mouth and shut it again. 'No,' he said firmly, 'I'm not going to buy into this, Arthur. You always do this to me, you sidetrack me from the business at hand. The sighting and the killing are not connected. We're after someone who has been punished for flogging dodgy drugs or black-market fruit machines, not some – vengeful god.'

Bryant wasn't listening. His face was transformed with youthful excitement. 'Don't you see? The stag-man is being perfectly clear about his intentions. It's all in the flyer he's been handing out. The rivers will rise forth from oblivion's bed and manifest their vengeance to mankind. He wants to reclaim the ancient woodlands.'

'But it hasn't been woodland for two hundred years.'

'Hasn't it? Take a look at the area between St Pancras Old Church and the new rail link. Apart from the odd warehouse and a few streets that were knocked down during the War, there's nothing there.' He thrust his hand in the direction of the window. 'The land behind King's Cross is finally about to be concreted over and densely populated. For the first time in two and a half million years – humankind's entire time on earth – the forest will become a town. Someone is trying to stop that. And they're prepared to kill in order to do so.'

18

THE WATCHER

It was safe to say that things had not gone according to plan.

Standing beside the green park bench beneath the rustling beech trees, Mr Fox tried to understand how it had gone so badly wrong. He had painstakingly followed his own rules. He should have been prepared for anything. Instead, his anger had resurfaced at the wrong time, unfolding like a malignant bloom, spreading poison and panic across the situation. No matter how hard he tried to behave like a machine, the dark devil inside him returned to make him human.

In a way, Mr Fox had got his wish. He had moved up, because there was no going back. He had been suddenly thrust into the big league. Now that he was a murderer, the word defined who he had become, and who he would always be. It was the ultimate description of a human being, how the rest of the world would see him if they ever found out. The term overrode any other that could be applied. What he needed to do was stay calm and find a way to turn the situation to his advantage.

Murderer. He actually felt different. The word freed him. He had nothing more to lose. If he could guarantee that no trace of his path was left behind, the way ahead was clear. He could kill again, and again. His new life required no great change in the patterns of his behaviour. It was merely an adjustment. He had always known how to make himself invisible. His unique skill had always been to absorb the talents and knowledge of others, use what he needed and discard the rest. He never allowed anyone to get too close. He kept the world at arm's length in order to look down on it.

Checking across the road he saw three women standing beside their prams in the forecourt of a block of flats. Jasmine Wincott, whose husband had left her for a girl half his age; Paula Trainer, whose teenaged son was now mainlining heroin; and Sylvia Crane, whose oldest boy had been stabbed to death in a territorial fight between two gangs that had been disbanded by the time the case went to trial. In the road, working on his van, was Casey Potter, who'd done time for B&E, and was now studying chemistry at UCL. Mr Fox looked at the rows of boxy windows above them and knew who stood in every room. He had made it his business to know.

He watched as the shabby old detective marched past on the other side of the road, his walking stick held jauntily at his shoulder. That was Arthur St John Bryant; the middle name was not pronounced '*sin*jon' in the traditional way. He had been given the name because his mother had been delivered to hospital in a St John's ambulance. Not even his partner knew of this, but Mr Fox had been determined to find out as much as possible. Bryant was formerly of Bow Street, Savile Row and the North London Serious Crimes Division. Although he had been born in the East End, the old man had lived in Hampstead and Battersea, and was now residing in Chalk Farm. His parents came from Bethnal Green, and his brother had died after suffering an accident on a Thames barge. He had never remarried after his wife's death. He was a rebel and a nuisance, but not someone to be dismissed lightly.

Mr Fox made it his business to know everything about everyone. The price of freedom was eternal vigilance. This was his area. He had learned the history of the Bagnigge Wells, with its lake of swans, peacocks and seashell grottos. He had been to the British Library and studied an online copy of the Domesday Book in order to learn about the four ancient prebendal manors in his parish – Pancras, Cantlowes, Tothill and Ruggemure. He knew how the bucolic village of Battle Bridge had become the sprawling chaos of King's Cross, how the vast piles of ashes from Harrison's Brickworks that had accumulated in Battle Bridge Field were eventually sold to the Russians, to help rebuild Moscow after Napoleon's invasion.

He had discovered that the name King's Cross came from the unpopular octagonal monument to George IV that once stood at the junction of four roads, less than half a kilometre from where he now stood. The building had been used as a police station and then a tavern before being torn down. Every time he walked through the station, he was aware that he was walking upon the site of a smallpox hospital, and that the Centre for Tropical Diseases still stood nearby. So much had been demolished around here in the last three years, so many road names changed, that it was already becoming hard to recall the streets of his childhood. He had watched the old buildings fall. Only the Coal and Fish Offices and the Granary had been spared the rapacious bulldozers. The Grade II-listed Stanley Buildings had been torn down, and all but one of the famous gasholders had been dismantled. But he knew that no matter how hard you tried to change a place, it would find a way of reverting to its historical character. The only way he could stay here was by recording people and events even more carefully than the CCTV lenses that covered the stations. *I am the future,* he thought. *One day all people will be like me. Not because they want to, but because it will be the only way they can prove they are still free.*

And I will be free, thought Mr Fox as he watched the elderly detective head off in the distance. *No matter how many I have to kill to remain so.*

19

UNBURIED

'I'm only coming along to make sure you don't say anything inflammatory,' warned John May as he and Arthur Bryant picked their way across the torn landscape of the building site. Around them, Caterpillar trucks burrowed and strained beneath a mean-spirited sky. 'But it's as far as I'm prepared to go on your stag-man. After this I'll be helping the others, so you'll be on your own. OK, what are we looking at?'

'This is the head office of the Albert Dock Architectural Partnership Trust,' Bryant explained, checking the brochure April had given him. 'ADAPT is in charge of planning the entire area. The contract was awarded to a single company so that the new town would "observe a single cohesive vision of design", it says here. I imagine they want to avoid any more ghastly balls-ups like the Paddington Basin.' Paddington, another derelict area bordered by canals and railways, had been filled with a mixture of offices, retail outlets and community housing, but the resulting confusion of styles had ended up satisfying no one.

Bryant leaned back and looked up, holding on to his hat. 'Nice building,' he said. 'It's a pity they pulled down all the others like this.'

They had reached the doors of a huge two-floor warehouse restored in reclaimed yellow brick. The former jam factory was one of the few surviving industrial units left in an area that had once been filled with foundries, flour and timber mills, varnishers, laundries, hat manufacturers and beer-bottle washing plants. Cobbled courtyards had been sand-blasted, interior walls removed, roofs renovated and steel walkways added to create a modern version of Victorian architecture, lighter and airier than anything imagined by their ancestral counterparts.

'Who are we seeing?' May asked.

'A woman called Marianne Waters. She's one of the senior partners, certainly the one with the highest visibility. She made a fortune in the City during the eighties, set up this company, the ADAPT Group, with her two former bosses, and became one of the biggest property developers in the city. She's leading the way towards more ecologically responsible building, and has the ear of the environment minister. Their children go to the same school. She wrote a self-help book about running companies while being a single mother.'

'Now give me the bad stuff.'

'Well, ecologically sound architecture comes at a price, and Marianne Waters has a habit of running behind on her projects. This one is no different. They've been slipping back their deadlines; the new shopping mall in the centre of the development was supposed to be finished by now. Before she saw the green light Waters was a great pal of Maggie Thatcher's and, unfortunately, London's arch-villainess, Lady Porter. There are stories about her that she doesn't enjoy seeing repeated in print. They mostly involve persistent rumours about her involvement in the "Building Stable Communities" scheme.'

Councillor Dame Shirley Porter's infamous secret policy was the stuff of London legend. She sold off Westminster Council properties and shifted homeless voters from marginal wards because they were less likely to vote Conservative. Despite being described as the most corrupt British political figure in living memory, the disgraced Council leader still protested her innocence. 'There's also been talk about the strong-arm tactics being used by property developers like ADAPT to seize the leases of buildings that stand in their way. Critics say that Madame Waters's concern for the environment is just PR spin. This is ADAPT's biggest project, and any negative reaction to the company's plans, mainly posted by community groups, is usually met with a barrage of lawsuits. So if you're asking me whether she belongs to the forces of good or the powers of darkness, I'd have to say that the jury is still out.'

'It's not our job to make a judgement call,' said May, 'but a little background material is always helpful.'

The detectives were greeted by two security guards, a receptionist, a personal assistant, a group organizer and finally the lady herself. Marianne Waters was in her late forties, with the strong features of a county-bred woman and a cropped coiffure in a thoroughbred shade of chestnut. She looked as though she had what it took to survive in the modern business world. Encased in an open-collared black dress that reset her body to a younger age, she wore surprisingly tall heels for a woman who regularly crossed muddy cobblestones.

'Mr May.' She greeted him with a stern voice and a firm, dry handshake. She looked puzzled by Bryant's presence, as if Harold Steptoe had brought his father along to the meeting.

'Arthur Bryant, John's partner,' said Bryant, unhappy with having to explain who he was. She shook his hand with noted reluctance. It didn't help that Bryant had massaged Vicks Vapor Rub into his neck earlier and now smelled pungent.

'You work together at the local crime unit?'

'The PCU handles specialist cases,' May pointed out. 'We deal with particular issues not covered by the local police or the CID.' He was determined not to go into the details of their situation.

'We could do with more community officers,' Marianne Waters said crisply. 'We've had some security issues with undesirable types hanging around the compound at night.'

'That's a matter of local policing policy. Technically speaking, I'm a civil servant and therefore required to be non-partisan,' Bryant assured her, pulling a face at May that said, *See? I can be diplomatic.*

'Fine. Shall we walk?' Waters led the way

between the renovated buildings. Trestles had been laid through the vast steel framework of the shopping mall. It felt like walking through a three-dimensional blueprint of the new town. Waters navigated the duckboards which lay across the final few metres of mud with an ease that suggested she spent much of her time on-site. 'We've had over a dozen sightings, reliable accounts posted by two or more members of our workforce, but there are supposed to have been countless others. Unfounded rumours have a habit of running around building sites. The men gossip much more than women. We do what we can to limit the rumours.'

'When did the sightings start?' asked May.

'The first verified sighting we had was about a month ago.'

'Always the same figure, doing the same thing?'

'That's right, just standing there watching. He only ever appears at dusk or shortly after. Many of the witnesses are young, but they're as superstitious as their grandfathers. They're in a strange land, struggling with the language and customs, susceptible to their own imaginations. In their culture, a man dressed as a stag is a malevolent spirit.'

'Have you actually lost any staff over this?' asked May.

'The walkouts started right after the first sighting. They're more serious now. After all, Constantin could have been killed.' *She remembers his first name*, Bryant thought. *A nice touch.*

'And you have no idea what this – creature – wants?'

'I didn't take it seriously at first. The nearby nightclub attracts all types. I assumed the man had mental-health issues, a tendency towards exhibitionism.'

'But now?'

'Now I think he's clearly trying to attract attention to something, but I've no idea what that might be.' She pointed beyond the framework of the mall. Against a green and orange sky, the industrial vista was a Dante's Inferno of steel and concrete, the guts and skeleton of a great body being constructed across the razed land. 'All the sightings have been up there, along that ridge. Somehow he gets inside the perimeter fence.'

'How can he do that?' Bryant asked.

'He only needs a pair of bolt-cutters to get in. The grounds are frequently patrolled, but we've had trouble with some of the night security. We think he must have friends on the inside.'

Bryant's forehead wrinkled. It didn't make sense. Why cultivate friendships within the very workforce you were hoping to disturb? 'When building first started here, did any of your employees leave with unresolved grievances?'

'I imagine there were quite a few,' Ms Waters replied, 'but I deal with government ministers and planning advisers, not staffing issues.'

'Then why didn't you send your personnel officer to see us?'

'Because yesterday morning our electricians voted to go on strike. They stay later on the site than anyone else except management, and most of the reliable eyewitness reports have come from their sector. I need to get this matter sorted out quickly. If you want a job done properly – well, you know how that goes.'

'You say he gets inside the perimeter fence. Has he been picked up on your CCTV monitors?'

'It's a huge site and we only keep recorded images for two weeks. Unfortunately, unless he passes right beneath the spotlights we can't read the images clearly. We have an IT team looking at the problem.' She had been joined by a small, balding young man with a stressed, purposeful air. 'I'm sorry. This is Maddox Cavendish; he's been here since the project began, one of the original architects.' The two spoke quietly for a moment. Cavendish broke off to study the group of labourers who had clustered around a mechanical digger.

'Excuse me, gentlemen.' Waters left with her architect. As soon as they saw her coming, the workers quickly found their boss a hardhat and overshoes.

'Well, what do you make of her?' asked May as he watched Waters speaking with the foreman.

'She's getting the job done. It can't be easy. But I wonder why she's taking such a personal interest in such a relatively inconsequential problem.'

'You heard what she said; she may have a strike on her hands.'

'Very small beer on a project like this. They must have thousands of employees.'

'Mr May, I wonder if you could help us?' she called back suddenly.

'See, she's calling for you. Women always do that. Why not me?' grumbled Bryant. 'Why do they always ask you first? I look older. It's ageism, pure and simple.'

May made his way across the mud with Bryant following warily at his heels. The knot of workmen untied itself and parted, revealing a mound of clay-streaked earth that the digger had pushed aside.

The pale, naked body reminded Bryant of wartime photographs he had seen, the disinterred victims of concentration camps, except that this one was missing its head.

20

HALLOWED GROUND

It was dark by the time Dan Banbury emerged from the white forensic tent carrying something heavy in a plastic bag. 'I've got a little present for you, Mr Bryant,' he said cheerfully, wiping his forehead and leaving behind a streak of dark clay. 'Take a look in here. It got pretty mashed up by the diggers, but still...'

Banbury was always cheerful when he faced a challenge, which suggested that the contents of the bag were likely to be unpalatable. Bryant allowed his scarf to ride further over his chin, peering in as the Crime Scene Manager carefully revealed his find. Inside was the crushed and mud-smeared head of an adult male, one swollen eye open, the other squeezed so tightly shut that the dead man appeared to be winking lasciviously.

Giles Kershaw pointed back at the tent. 'It looks like your killer was interrupted before he could complete his task. He made the amputation but dropped the head near the body. Perhaps he was disturbed by one of the workmen.'

'Got anything to connect this to the first victim?'

'You mean beyond the location?' ADAPT's construction site was only two streets away from where the other body had been found. 'The MO looks exactly the same: neat single striations from more than one knife, professional stuff, a definite scalpel-blade mark, no other signs of violence on the torso. I'd say without doubt that this is the same chap at work.'

'Did he kill his victim here, then behead him on-site?'

'Hard to tell, old thing. If you're going to leave the body in a different place, why not dismember it first? Even if the killer knew exactly what he was doing, it would take a few minutes of hard work. Then again, he's done it once before so he's probably getting better at it.'

'There's no blood visible in the surrounding earth,' said Banbury, 'but it's clay, and there's been a lot of rain lately. Giles is going to run some tests for us.'

'If he did cut up the body here, why would he run the risk of being discovered in the time it took?'

'Your job to find that out, squire.' Kershaw nodded at Banbury for support.

Bryant hitched up his scarf, thinking. 'He doesn't want to leave the body where he's committed the crime because it's not safe to remain in the location, so he takes it somewhere, removes the head and dumps the remains here. This is a man with a plan. The killer's male, because both bodies are heavy to lift and women rarely mutilate. He could have backed a van right up to the perimeter fence and cut his way in. We'll never sort out his tyre tracks from everything else that's been churning around in the field.'

'The head's putrefying,' said Banbury, sticking his own head in the bag and sniffing. 'The body's in really bad shape. Probably because the mound it was concealed in has been driven over by plant vehicles quite a few times, and there are plenty of insects in the ground.'

Bryant cocked his head back at the partially exposed corpse. It had taken on the texture of the earth in which it had been lying. The dead always seemed to absorb their surroundings, as if trying to rush the process of returning to the soil.

'One useful thing.' Kershaw took the bag from Banbury and turned the bald head around in its bag, pointing to a small blackened puncture below its ear. 'See? A single tiny stab wound to the side of the throat, punched upwards. The angle and depth suggest something like a thin sharpened screwdriver. According to Dan here, they're very popular in professional circles these days. It would explain why we didn't find any damage on the first victim's body, and wouldn't necessarily spill a lot of blood. The perpetrator is right-handed, shorter than the victim, strong. No throat, chest or arm bruises, no defence cuts on the hands. I'd say this fellow was surprised without much of a struggle. I need to run tests on some decent equipment.'

'How are his fingers?'

'Pretty torn up, but there'll be prints if they're on the system. As for the time of death, we'll have the entomological track. We'll take some temperature readings and see if any insects have been attracted to his fluid leakage, find out what stage they've reached. If the body was moved, we might be lucky enough to get different bug sets.'

'Could you give me a very rough PMI?'

Banbury sucked his teeth in thought. 'I'd guess about seven or eight days ago, something like that. Giles will be able to give us a more accurate time of death.'

'What's the chance of getting an ID on him quickly?'

'You mean without going through AMIP or any officially sanctioned database? I'll have to pull in a favour. We could really use a fast-track.'

'Raymond can't get us authorization, you know that.' Bryant shoved his hands deep in his pockets, pacing around the site. 'Any contact you use will have to be kept off the records. I want every inch of this ground photographed within a twenty-metre radius. You're looking for a large shoe-print in the shape of a deer hoof.' Kershaw and Banbury tried not to look surprised.

May made his way over to join his partner. 'Come out of there, Arthur. You're sinking into the mud.'

Gripping Bryant's hand, he pulled him up on to the duckboards. 'The Lagos police couldn't be bothered to search for our shop owner, but lucky for us he got into a fight a couple of days ago and the cops were called. They say he has all the papers for the sale of the shop lease and everything's legit. The freezer and other bits of equipment came with the property. He's been out of the country since April the seventh, before Rafi Abd al-Qaadir took over the lease, and the estate agent says that he remembers the freezer being empty then.'

'So it looks like he's in the clear.'

'I know what you're thinking,' said May. 'The only other suspect is your stag-man because he's carrying knives, and Waters says he cut open the perimeter fence.'

'Something like that, yes.'

'Which would mean you were right to trust your instincts and go after the stag-man. It also suggests we can reasonably expect the girl he abducted to turn up next without her head.'

'It's possible.' Bryant unwrapped a boiled sweet and popped it in his mouth.

'Now you don't sound convinced.'

'I think it's odd she hasn't been reported missing. A phantom girl, no real description beyond "short skirt", and no one who cares enough about her to go to the police.'

'Suppose gangs have decided to use the area as a dumping ground? They could be coming in from Essex or even the coast.'

'No, no. There's something far stranger than just the dumping of bodies going on here.' Bryant had a disconcerting look in his eye. 'This is an area where death is used to walking among the living.'

May clapped his hands together, dispelling the sinister mood. 'OK, let's fix this chap with an ID and we might start to discover a motive. Giles, get the body over to your place, and we'll have the rest of the shops on both sides of the Caledonian Road searched. I'm going to try to interview everyone who's seen our furry friend before the end of the day. Raymond has been asked to provide the Home Office with an update tonight.' He gave Bryant a look of gentle concern. 'Are you up to all this?'

'I'm as fit as a fiddle if you don't count my knees,' Bryant snapped. 'They packed up shortly after my legendary tango performance at the Queen's Silver Jubilee. Nobody told me that Princess Margaret's table wouldn't take my weight.' May gave his partner a sceptical look. Lately he had become convinced that Bryant was manufacturing his memories. 'Besides, you're the one who's had the operation. You should be resting up and taking it easy.'

'How could I, with everyone so worried about you?'

'Well, you did a good thing, taking me out of myself. I only hope I can do the case justice. It's difficult understanding the mind of a man who is prepared to dress as a stag to issue an ecological warning to the world.'

'You think he trotted out in fancy dress trying to scare the natives, didn't see much of a result and upped his game to include kidnap and murder?'

'Even I wouldn't be that presumptuous, John. Besides, it doesn't give us a feasible MO. Think about it.'

'Seems perfectly straightforward to me.' May spoke with more than a hint of sarcasm. 'He puts on an outfit that must radically restrict his movement, hunts down his victims in another part of town, kills them, drags them back to his place and dismembers them before driving here, through the most heavily policed part of the entire city.'

'He dumps them at this spot because it's his hallowed ground,' said Bryant. 'Then he dresses up and appears immediately afterwards. It's a pagan ritual of appeasement

189

and celebration. Meera said she was reminded of the Highwayman, but our chap's driven by indifference, a blankness of character. This man is a vanguard of Europe's oldest religion. I'll be a little presumptuous and suggest that we're looking for a neo-hippie, a tree-hugger, a modern-day shaman who probably smokes too much weed and believes he can impede the onward trundle of progress. He sees the big bad corporations moving into King's Cross and wants to show them that the old ways still prevail. We should find out who's been attending the local protest groups, who's been taking pagan volumes out of the local library and attending alternative-religion societies, check the notice boards in Camden's head shops.'

'But these are your kind of people, Arthur, the ones you usually regard as allies.'

'Murder makes enemies of us all,' said Bryant, pulling on his hat and staggering back to the dry firmness of the road.

21

THE QUIET ONES

The following morning, Raymond Land sat down tentatively on the leather swivel chair Longbright had found for him and looked out of the filthy window. Below, traffic on the Caledonian Road had choked itself to a standstill. He should have been at home in bed, reading the papers.

He turned back to study the dingy brown room and realized with a sinking sensation that he was now worse off than he had been before. His fate was once more tied to the unit, his dreams of retirement had retreated even further and his new surroundings were positively Dickensian. Creaking forward in his chair, he peered into a cobwebbed corner of the room, then rose to examine it. A patch of stained wallpaper had divorced itself from the grey plaster, as if the room had died and was sloughing its skin. Something was revealed underneath, part of a design. Reaching on tiptoe, he brushed aside the spiders and seized the edge, gently pulling. A metre of damp paper rolled slowly down, tore and fell on the floor in a cloud of mildew spores.

Land found himself looking at a drawing of a naked man poised between two tall iron braziers. He appeared to be having intimate congress with a goat that was standing on its hind legs and wearing black leather thigh-boots. Shocked, Land attempted to cover over the drawing, but the paper would no longer stick to the wall.

In his own room, Arthur Bryant was seated on top of some packing boxes, non-chalantly swinging his legs back and forth as he thumbed through a reference book.

'What the hell was this place?' Land demanded to know, storming into the detective's office. 'There's something really unpleasant and unwholesome about it. There's a very bad feeling here. You told me it was a ware-house.'

'No, *mon vieux fromage*, I said it was a whorehouse,' replied Bryant, not bothering to look up. 'Later it reverted to its original use as a warehouse.'

'That doesn't entirely explain why there is a picture of a man passionately embracing a farmyard animal on my wall.'

'Show me.' Bryant climbed down from his packing crate and led the way.

They examined the picture together. 'That's a puzzler,' Bryant agreed. 'It's rather too well sketched to be the work of a bored workman. Look at those flesh tones. And the perspective is most convincing, don't you think?'

'I don't give a stuff about its artistic merit, I want to know what it's doing here. Look.' Land pointed across to the corners of the room, where two blackened iron braziers stood. 'They're the ones in the drawing. Does that mean there's been a goat up here too?'

'Oh, it's probably some bored packing clerk's idea of a joke,' said Bryant unconvincingly. 'How are you settling in?'

'I can't do any work without at least some rudimentary equipment. I thought we had it bad at Mornington Crescent but this is infinitely worse. Look at this.' He indicated a dark gap beside the ratty armchair he had placed in the corner. 'There's a hole that goes all the way down to the basement. The floor's rotten. Suppose I fell through it? The place isn't fit for habitation.'

'We needed something near the site that was instantly available, and this was all I could find,' Bryant explained. 'I'll tell you what – why don't you work from home for a few days?'

'Oh no, I'm not falling for that old trick. I need to be here, where I can keep an eye on you. God knows what you'll get up to otherwise.'

'Then I guess you'll have to make the best of it.' Bryant dragged out the pieces of his pipe and began to fit the bowl to the stem.

'You are not going to smoke that in here!'

'Actually, I thought the scent of my Aromatic Rough Cut Full Strength Navy Shag might dispel the smell of damp. I'm glad you popped by, Raymond. I was about to come in and see you. I am the bearer of good news. We have an identity for the body in the freezer. His name's Terry Delaney and he lived just a couple of streets away, in Wharfdale Road. He was arrested on a D&D some years back, but no charges were pressed. He listed his profession as a builder. There's nothing else on file, but that's enough.'

'So they did have his prints, after all. How did you get hold of them?'

'Oh, I didn't. Kershaw used the St Pancras office to request them. Longbright and Renfield are on their way right now. I'm not sending anyone in alone where there may be organized crime involved.'

Land was relieved. 'Then all we need to do is round up his mates. He probably crossed his drug-dealer. We could get a lock on a couple of suspects by nightfall.'

'Let's not jump the gun, Raymond.' Bryant tamped his pipe and lit it. 'I have a feeling things aren't going to be quite so simple as you'd like.' Bryant held in his head the image of a murderer dressed in the skin of a stag, but decided not to share it with the Detective Inspector for now.

Jack Renfield's shoulder did the trick. Terry Delaney's landlord lived in Holland, and the woman downstairs had no spare key, so there was no choice but to break down Delaney's door. Renfield had played rugby until a back injury had put him out of the game, and was easily able to smash the lock apart.

'Blimey.' Longbright stepped into the hallway and tried the overhead light, but the bulb was broken. 'Someone's had a real go at this place.'

The apartment had been ransacked. Progressing from room to room, the detectives were shocked by the scale of the destruction. Every sofa cushion, mattress and seat had been slashed open and picked apart, every cupboard emptied and its shelves removed, every stick of furniture disjointed. A shelf had contained books on the history of King's Cross, but every copy had been tipped down and torn apart. The carpets had been prised up and the floorboards examined, and some of the bathroom tiles had been removed. In the main bedroom the radiator had even been taken off the wall, and yet there was order here. The dissection had been carried out with elaborate care; the component parts were laid in careful rows as if they were all to be reassembled.

'Whoever did this expected Delaney to have hidden something well,' said Longbright.

'What did they expect to find inside a chair, for God's sake?'

'Drugs? High-denomination banknotes?' Longbright suggested.

They tried the bathroom. Longbright watched as the sergeant removed the side panel of the bath and rolled under it with a torch. 'No blood on any of the surfaces, but I think Delaney was murdered here.'

'Why do you say that?'

'The bath's been cleaned by an expert, but he forgot to empty the U-bend trap. Hang on.' Renfield rooted about. 'There's a piece of shredded paper towel inside, looks like it's absorbed blood. I can't see it clearly but I can smell it.'

He slid back out covered in dust balls, and tapped the side of his thick nose. 'Never lets me down, this. Banbury might be able to fish whatever it is out without it breaking apart, but I shouldn't think he'll be able to perform much useful analysis on it.' He set the drain trap to one side for bagging. 'The killer didn't cut Delaney's head off here. That would have emptied blood all over the apartment. This is just a small amount.'

In the kitchen, Longbright pulled a folded newspaper from under the cascaded spice pots and sugar bags on the counter. It was a copy of the *Daily Mirror*, dated 25 April. She needed to check Delaney's clothes for anything that could give her a later date. It would be useful to turn up a photo.

She went through the ransacked jackets and jeans in the bedroom wardrobe, and found an Oyster Tube pass tucked inside a plastic sleeve. 'Hey, technology we can deal with,' said Renfield, bagging it. The card would show when and at which station it was last used. 'There's more.' He dug into the jacket and produced an employee photocard.

'You sure this bloke's involved with organized crime?' asked Longbright.

'Why?'

She examined the laminated square. The head shot showed an innocuous, pleasant-faced, shaven-headed man in his early thirties. There was a softness in his eyes that somehow suggested he was a husband and father. 'Delaney just doesn't look the type to me. He's got a kid, a little girl. There's a picture of her in the bedroom.'

Renfield snorted. 'You can't be sure who's a villain these days. Says he works at a painting and decorating company in Highbury.'

'Let's go and talk to the downstairs neighbour,' Longbright suggested.

'I can't tell you anything about him because I don't know anything,' said Mrs Mbele as she tried to claw her young son back from the precipitous drop of the stairs. 'He was here before me, friendly enough but silent as the grave. You're lucky to get two words out of him. A bit of a loner. Divorced.'

'Did you ever see him throw a moody, keep bad company, get drunk?' asked Longbright, thinking of the D&D charge.

'No, a bit wobbly a couple of times coming up the front steps late but nothing to give you trouble. These floorboards creak and you can hear everything that goes on overhead, so it's good to have someone nice and quiet here. Why? Has something happened?'

'When did you last see him?' asked Renfield.

'About two weeks ago.'

'Exactly two weeks? Morning or afternoon? Think for a moment, please. This is important.'

'I think it was the Monday morning before last.'

'Coming in or going out?'

'Going out. I suppose he was going to work, 'cause he always left early during the week. We stayed at my sister's that night so I didn't see him again.'

'How was he?'

'Same as always. Smiled and gave my boy a little wave, went out the front door. I never encouraged him to be friendly.'

'Any particular reason why not?'

'He's a bit rough, you know? What you call salt of the earth. I once heard him swearing on the phone to a mate. I didn't want my boy picking anything up. Don't get me wrong, he's a very nice man, works long hours, always pleasant.'

'Ever have any mates around here, did he?'

'No, I don't think so.' Mrs Mbele picked up her scrambling son and threw him on to her shoulder like a cat. 'Sorry, I'm not being very helpful, am I?'

'Any women?'

'One, quite young – not his wife, 'cause he showed me a photo of her.'

'What did she look like?'

Mrs Mbele thought for a moment. 'Ordinary,' she said finally.

'Amazing how people share the same house for years and know nothing about each other,' said Renfield as he called the PCU's Crime Scene Manager with their location. 'What the hell could he have done to make someone want to saw his head off? It's the quiet ones you have to watch out for.'

'He might have surprised a burglary in progress,' suggested Longbright.

'You're joking, aren't you? Take a look at this place, Janice.' He pointed up at the peeling stucco and dirt-crusted windows. 'Can you see the signs of wealth that would attract a burglar to a dump like this? Besides, what kind of burglar arranges everything on the floor in neat little piles?'

'Maybe he did that because he didn't want to make a noise. You heard what she said about the floorboards.'

'You're not suggesting Delaney did it himself?'

'Perhaps he lost something and was desperate to find it.'

'So he slashes open his own sofa cushions and even empties out the kitchen flour jar? I thought you PCUers were supposed to come up with stuff that would never cross the minds of us lowly Metropolitan plods.'

Janice smiled. 'You're PCU too now, remember.'

'Yeah, and you were Met once. You know what we're like. Fair-minded, decent, but not always the sharpest knives in the drawer. And rough as guts, as you're so fond of reminding us.'

Longbright remembered. If the Met coppers were blunt-edged it was because they had to be. You could only clean vomit off your trousers and return a runaway kid to its drugged-up parents so many times before you started wanting to smack someone or throw them in prison. And when you found yourself arresting the grandchildren of the men and women you were arresting at the start of your career, it was time to get out.

Renfield shot her a sly look. 'Of course, I only switched sides because I thought it might give me a chance with you.'

'Yeah, right.'

'Don't use a double positive to suggest a negative – it makes you sound like a teenager.'

Longbright raised an eyebrow. If there was one thing everyone knew about Renfield, it was that he had no sense of humour. Had he just made a joke? Wonders would never cease. 'If you're going to keep flirting with me, Jack,' she cautioned him, 'you'd damn well better mean it.'

'Oh, I mean it all right.' He caught her gaze and held it until she broke away.

'We used to make fun of you all the time. I mean, when you were with the Met.' She always felt it was best to be honest. 'We thought being a desk sergeant all those years had got to you. We knew we could tease you about your name, because you'd never read Bram Stoker's *Dracula*.'

'Yeah, well, I've read it now. I don't think I'm quite the same bloke any more. The Met feels a long way behind me.'

'I know what you mean.' Longbright smiled at the thought. 'I think of those long nights collating records, avoiding male attention, doing my fitness training for postings on the Territorial Support Group, then drinking bottles of whisky left in the CID offices. I did a lot of ops for TSG, surveillance jobs lying on my stomach among the corpses of pigeons on the flat roof of some windy council block, peeping over the side of what seemed be a cliff, looking down on some estate agent about to be robbed or watching some dozy drug-dealer do business from his house. Not the best way to spend your life. The smell of bird shit cleared my sinuses, though. I never had a problem staying detached – I think we all had a good sense of black humour – but the work got to me at times. Don't get me wrong; I enjoyed being operational. I still love pulling down a long shift. But John and Mr Bryant were my salvation.'

'Some of the riots were bad,' said Renfield. 'I remember a lot of West End officers got hurt after an anti-capitalist clash in Oxford Street – they were sitting around the yard in bloody bandages, deathly quiet; it was like a field hospital. And the commissioner came round in plainclothes with his Personal Protection Officers, like some general inspecting the troops. I think one of the PPOs told him they wouldn't be able to protect him, 'cause they all turned tail and walked out in the street. The Met took the blame for that particular outbreak of civil unrest, but it was really the economy that was the cause. I don't want to see that happen again.'

It was the longest speech she had ever heard from Renfield. The sergeant had made an error of judgement in the course of his duty that had ultimately cost a life, and knew he would have to live with the mistake for ever. He had been appointed a therapist, and although he had only recently started attending sessions, Longbright could see he was already changing.

'Anyway, we talked about you as well,' he told Longbright. 'We had a nickname for you at the station.'

'You did? What was it?'

'Frostyknickers.'

'Oh, cheers.'

'But I always liked you.'

'I can't think why.'

'You're strong. There's something real about you, sort of sturdy–' Renfield broke off.

'*Sturdy* is not a word women long to hear used to describe them, Jack.'

'Solid, then.'

'You're digging a hole for yourself.'

'You know – *womanly,* only more of a...' At the point where he enlisted the help of his hands in trying to describe her, she stopped him.

'If you're going to call me a rough diamond I'll clout you.'

'No. You're more of a pearl than a diamond.' Renfield did not realize that he was almost endearing when he was being honest. 'There's a soft lustre about you.' He looked embarrassed now.

Longbright broke the awkwardness between them. 'Jack, listen, one of us should stay here and wait for Dan.'

'Why, where's the other one going?'

Longbright held up the laminated ID card. 'Highbury. Got a coin?'

Renfield flicked a ten-pence piece and slapped it on his wrist. 'You call.'

'Tails.'

'Tails it is.'

'I'll go. I could do with the exercise.' Longbright turned up her collar and stepped out into gently sifting rain.

22

GHOSTS OF VIOLENCE

As soon as Longbright was on her way, Renfield called Leslie Faraday to inform him of the day's events. He was ashamed about having to sneak behind the detective sergeant's back, and wondered how many days he would manage to avoid giving the Home Office any useful information.

Faraday: You were supposed to call me last night, Renfield.

Renfield: I couldn't get away, everyone was still in the office.

Faraday: Couldn't you have slipped out for five minutes? What have you got for me?

Have there been any irregularities so far?

Renfield: We've got an identity on the first body. The one in the freezer.

Faraday: I'm not interested in the victim, I just need to know that you've caught someone. Have you?

Renfield: No.

Faraday: But you at least know who you're looking for, yes?

Renfield: Not exactly.

Faraday: What do you mean, not exactly? Policing should be considered an exact science. Either you're close to making an arrest, or you haven't the faintest idea what you're doing. Which is it?

Renfield: We're…

Renfield struggled with his conscience. He knew how much trouble he could make for the PCU, but was suddenly loath to do so. They had offered him unexpected support at a time when his career could have been destroyed.

Renfield: …very close to making an arrest.

Faraday: Oh. Well, then. Good. But you must let me know if anything goes wrong. I have to make reports too, you know.

Faraday was clearly disappointed that this was all he could offer, but was forced to accept the meagre information. Renfield signed off wondering how long he could hide the truth.

As the sergeant sat on the corner of Delaney's bed in the gathering gloom, he thought about his hopeless situation. If he lied to Faraday, he would be exposed when the PCU failed to deliver. If he told the truth, news of his secret disclosures would soon reach the unit. If he asked Longbright on a date and she discovered that he was ratting on his colleagues behind her back, she would never talk to him again. *Forget it, Fat Boy*, he told himself. *She's too good for you anyway.*

He had always wanted to do the right thing, but how many times had it placed him in a spot like this? It was the wayward guys who made friends, the womanizers, the hard drinkers, the ones who bent the law around themselves. The officers at his old station had nicknamed him Captain Bringdown because of his determination to play by the rules. The PCU had merely made a harmless literary joke out of his name before accepting him for who he was. Yes, he wanted to do the right thing, but perhaps this time the right thing was something different.

Meanwhile, DS Longbright found herself opposite the great letters sculpted in white concrete that spelled out the team name 'Arsenal'. The new football ground filled the skyline of the street like a great spaceship. Opposite, the remaining rows of shabby Victorian terraces stretched away uphill, from

Drayton Park towards the horrors of North London's crack-addled Blackstock Road.

Longbright checked the ID card, but spotted the builders' outlet before needing to search for street numbers. She could hardly have missed it; picked out in the Gunners' shades of red and white, K&B Decorating stood in homage to the team grounds that had existed in the area since 1913. A muscular boy with strong Grecian features was carrying in a delivery of planks and dropping them noisily inside the store. The ground floor was a confusion of sawdust and shouting.

'It's funny,' the Greek boy told her. 'Terry ain't been in for more than a week, 'as 'e? Nobody knows where he is.'

'Can you give me an exact day when you last saw him?'

'Monday before last, something like that. It'll be on his work sheet.'

'Didn't any of you think to talk to the police?' she asked, already knowing the answer.

'The police?' He almost laughed in her face. 'Listen, love, the blokes here go a bit mad every now and again, then come back and pick up where they left off and nobody mentions it. Not worth going to the police about.'

'They get paid by the number of days they do?'

'Yeah, so if they don't come in, it's up to them, innit.'

'Anyone been round to Delaney's flat to check on him?'

'Terry don't like people going round there. His missus kicked him out of the house and I think he's a bit ashamed of the place he's renting. I told him he wouldn't get back on his feet if he kept taking time off.'

'So he's done it before? Has he been here long?'

'About four years. He had a couple of days off the last week he was here. Is he in trouble or what?'

'You could say that. I need to know everything you know about him. If you can't remember right now, that's fine, call me first thing tomorrow morning.' Longbright gave him one of the cards Bryant had had printed up for everyone at Mornington Crescent, an odd little art-deco number in black and silver that looked more like a calling card for an antiques store. She had crossed out the old address and hand-written the new one.

'He's not been hurt, has he?'

'Why, you think he's done something to deserve it?'

'Terry? You're joking.' The young man called over his shoulder, 'Oi, Jess, tell this lady what Terry's like.'

'One of the nicest blokes I've ever met,' replied Jess. 'If he was a bird I'd marry him.'

They all laughed.

'Keeps his nose clean, does he?' asked Longbright. 'Stays out of trouble?'

'Honest as the day is long. Always helping other people. That's Terry's trouble, if anything. Does charity work in his spare time. One of the best.' It seemed that everyone in the shop agreed with that sentiment.

'What did he do here?'

'Painting, decorating, some building work, welding, a bit of demolition.'

'Do you have a list of his most recent jobs?'

'They'll be in the book,' said Jess. 'Come with me.'

Dan Banbury was in many ways the PCU's least likely member, in that there seemed to be nothing wrong with him. He was the married one who lived with a loving wife and a well-adjusted ten-year-old son in the suburbs of South London. He was the unit's voice of common sense, and had been selected for precisely this reason. However, he possessed a skill that singled him out as unusual: he had an almost preternatural ability to understand what had happened in a vacated room. He followed standard procedures, establishing a three-dimensional grid pattern at a crime scene to mark off prints and collect fibres for analysis, but above this he had an understanding of the way in which frightened humans confronted one another. He saw the shape of their fears and passions, the psychology of their actions, the way in which they translated their emotions into physical movement. The ghosts of violence were visible to him.

The extraordinary thing was that until being asked to join the PCU he had been entirely unconscious of this sensitivity. Bryant had found such a skill present in only a handful of forensic experts, and had campaigned for Banbury's inclusion in the unit. He needed people who saw more deeply than those around them.

When Banbury entered Delaney's flat, he quickly recognized four people: Terry Delaney, his girlfriend, his daughter and a stranger. Terry was the most noticeable. Signs of his occupancy were everywhere, from the newspaper he had folded back to read over breakfast, to the whiskers rinsed from his razor and imperfectly cleaned from the sink, to the toothpaste that had dried on his brush. The bed had been occupied by one, but there were magazines, titles that would be read by a woman in her mid-twenties, thrown on to the bedside table beside a half-emptied tub of make-up remover and a brush containing long hairs. She was a dyed blonde, untidy, and her habits had annoyed Terry. He kept his territory tidy and separate. The little girl had slept on the sofa in the neutral zone of the lounge. A single duvet was stored beneath it, together with her pyjamas, pink slippers, a jewelled hair clip.

But it was the stranger who interested Banbury most. Judging by the faint oily striation on the front door lock he had first tried to use a simple burglar's tool to gain entrance, but had been defeated by the London bolt set in place on the inside of the door. He had gone down the hall and climbed out of the window, reaching around to the apartment's bathroom casement. The carpet tiles at the end of the hall were rarely walked on, but the pile was slightly flattened at their edge, as if someone had reached out on tiptoe.

The conversion of the house into flats had placed the bathroom sill in a shaded corner behind a tree, and had left the second floor vulnerable. The window was awkward to access, but easy to open if you recognized the type of catch. This had been no ordinary burglar. He had not been looking to steal a CD player or a television. Anything heavy or awkwardly shaped would have proved difficult to manhandle across the building's exterior. This thief was after something that he could pocket. He had ransacked the place without bothering to put anything back, but could not avoid precision. He wanted Delaney to know that someone smart was on to him.

But then the householder had unexpectedly returned. He had unlocked the door from the hall, stepped inside, let the door swing shut behind him and stopped, confronted by his dismantled apartment.

And in the next room, the stranger had stopped, too. His search had suddenly ceased at this point. It had not been a good idea to wear workman's boots because they had steel inlays, and were so heavy that their marks were easily discernible from any others on the carpet. Some criminals kept a specific pair of shoes to burgle in. Banbury would have liked to be able to access FIT, the Footwear Intelligence Technology system that catalogued over fourteen thousand images of shoe-print types. He crouched on the floor and looked for pattern, wear, size and damage features, but could not see enough detail with his naked eye.

The prints led to behind the door, where the intruder must have waited – they were heavier here – before attacking Delaney. Now the boot prints danced in a tight circle, to be joined by twin drag marks, Delaney's shoes, the toes rather than the heels, as he was pulled away to the sofa and laid down on his stomach. A single droplet of blood had fallen, and there was a small patch of dried fluid on the carpet that looked like spittle. Banbury sniffed delicately, wondering if he might catch a faint chemical odour in the room, but found none. Yet Delaney had simply fallen to the floor. Not a drug, then; something else with the power to render a man unconscious in a second – or perhaps kill him outright. A thin knife or long needle, through the underside of the jaw or behind the ear, straight up into the base of the brain. The signs were so easy to read that Banbury felt as if he had witnessed the entire scene unfolding before him.

But if Delaney had surprised a burglar, and had been killed while the robbery was in progress, how had he wound up in a shop freezer?

'Everyone says Terry Delaney is one of the good guys,' Longbright told John May, setting a mug of tea on his desk. 'He never touched drugs, had no known connections with anyone dodgy, was working hard to pay his wife money, saw his daughter every other weekend.'

'Why was he divorced?' asked May.

'Nothing unusual there. He and his wife were working all hours and their schedules never matched up. She's a nurse at UCL. Actually, we know her. Niamh Connor takes shifts in A&E. She treated Meera for her cut arm. These are the last jobs Delaney took on.' She dropped an additional page of addresses on the desk.

May studied the sheet and tapped the last

line. 'Allensbury Place – that's near the railway line bordering the King's Cross site. It's within walking distance of where he was found, and where he was living.'

'He mainly worked on local projects. Didn't do the West End because his boss was having some kind of row with him over unpaid parking tickets. He drove a white van, but we didn't find it outside his flat.'

'We need to know who Delaney was working with in the days leading up to the burglary. Get Bimsley over there. And have Meera talk to his ex-wife.'

'Dan's convinced that Delaney didn't know his attacker. He says the footprints in the apartment suggest he surprised a burglar, simple as that.'

'So there's a fight and the burglar kills him, bundles him into his van in a panic, can't think what to do with the body, takes it home and cuts it up, then remembers the empty shop up the road and dumps him in the freezer. Or he takes him straight to the shop, out into the back room, lays him out on the plastic sheets and does his cutting there. It would be ironic if the first straightforward case we've handled in years turns out to be the one that gets us the unit back.'

'What are you going to do, John? Do you want some help?'

'No, just keep an eye on the others for me. Arthur and I will try to have this place running more efficiently by the morning, providing he gets back soon from wherever he's wandered off to. At least we have electricity and the neighbourhood has Wi-Fi, so I can use my laptop.'

'Where did Mr Bryant go?'

'He wrapped that disgusting old scarf around his head and told me he was meeting an old friend in a graveyard. If we keep operating by the book, we might be able to clear this whole thing up in time to satisfy the Home Office. I do hope Arthur isn't going to try and muddy the waters with some unlikely scenario involving, oh, I don't know, resurrectionists or pagan worshippers.'

'I've heard him mention forest gods quite a few times.' May sipped his tea, thinking. 'He sees ghosts, you know.'

Longbright's brow furrowed. 'What do you mean?'

'Not in the conventional way. It's just – I think the past is always there. The ghosts walk beside him. All the things that have happened here in times gone by remain burned into his vision like after-images. It's Arthur's weakness. And, of course, his greatest strength.'

23

A WARNING TO THE CURIOUS

St Pancras station soared up above him, its pink granite columns supported on drums carved with shields and figures in late-Victorian extravagance. The niches had been designed to hold statues, but the Midland Railway had baulked at the extra expense, so they had remained empty. Here, at the hotel which prefaced the station, Venetian High Gothic met the beginnings of the Aesthetic Movement, the whole edifice looking down on the surrounding area as if in command of it.

Bryant rested himself, remembering how King's Cross, Euston and Somers Town had looked when he was a child. He vaguely recalled a Christmas party held at Reggiori's restaurant, a genteelly shabby dining hall with a chipped fountain of turquoise porcelain standing at its centre. A neon amusement arcade now stood upon the site. Further back had been the fragments of Regency terraces that had miraculously survived the wartime bombings; the Rising Sun boxers' pub; the German eating rooms where they sang 'Lili Marlene' as they served boiled sausage; the great gasometers. The peculiar old lighthouse that stood on the roof of the building in the centre of the road had supposedly been built to advertise a long-vanished fish shop. The lighthouse was still there, but had fallen into disrepair. In a way it was a perfect symbol of the area, in such plain view that nobody noticed it.

Bryant turned, trying to conjure the past, but as fast as he dragged one piece from his memory another slipped away. He wondered if the few remaining residents older than he looked down from their windows and saw how it had once been, or whether they could see only what was now before their eyes. Remembering was pointless; but forgetting somehow seemed immoral.

Bryant's right leg was troubling him, so he used his stick as he walked. Although it had rained during the day, the unseasonably warm day had caused a soft mist to rise from the earth and shroud the low buildings behind the station. Across from St Pancras station was Pancras Road, beneath which the Fleet River ran on its way to Blackfriars. The streets to the rear had been built on the banks of the river valley, and were noticeably cooler.

His path took him behind the frenetic theatre of the station, into the dim backstage area of silent roads and empty pavements. He had reached St Pancras Old Church, its graveyard gardens reaching down to the curving edge of the canal. Between the trees he could see ducks and moorhens nesting, and a single heron standing alone in the reeds. The gravedigger was dragging an old-fashioned hand-operated lawnmower across the green, but stopped to watch balefully as Bryant passed.

The church itself suggested a building in repose, weathered by centuries of devout prayer. It was a strange *mélange* of styles: Roman, German and English. Its bell tower was inset with elegant convex clock faces, finished in shiny black lacquer painted with gold numerals. Only these, and the elaborately regilded railings around the graveyard, gave any hint of the structure's true importance to the city.

Austin Potterton was on top of a Gothic monument doing something unsuitable to a sundial. Above him, leathery crows cawed in the claw-like branches of the trees.

'Austin, what on earth are you up to?' asked Bryant, poking him on the boots with his stick.

'Ah, it's you, Arthur. You're early.' The man who clambered down had straggling shoulder-length hair the colour of tobacco ash, but wore a pin-striped suit with a navy tie and matching handkerchief, like an old hippie going for a job interview. He had a filthy toothbrush behind his ear. When he rubbed his nose and shook Bryant's hand he left charcoal on his face and on the detective's sleeve.

'*Tempus Edax Rerum* – a bit gloomy, don't you think? I cleaned it up a bit; somebody has to. The crows have been using it as a toilet for years. Toothbrushes seem to work best. I think this monument was paid for by Baroness Burdett-Coutts. Rather nice mosaic panels. I was just making an impression.'

'Well, you weren't making one on me,' sniffed Bryant, scowling at his sleeve. 'These tombs and monuments aren't meant to be climbed over. It's not an amusement park, you know.'

'I'm doing some research for the diocese. They've hired me to photograph and catalogue everything in the churchyard, because the last time they did it the documents were stored in the undercroft and sustained water damage when it flooded.' Potterton dusted himself down and replaced his materials in his briefcase. 'St Pancras Old Church deserves decent treatment – it's very possibly the oldest Christian site in Europe. And it's finally getting a bit of a makeover now that the rail link has come here.'

'Saint Pancras,' Bryant mused. 'He was fourteen when he died, wasn't he? A Christian martyr, decapitated on the orders of the Emperor Diocletian. I read somewhere that his severed head still exists in the reliquary in the Basilica of San Pancrazio.'

'You're absolutely right, although Heaven alone knows why you'd want to retain such information. His name was anglicized.' Puffing out his cheeks, Potterton leaned back and looked at the old building.

'The place doesn't look like much, does it?' said a new voice. A minuscule vicar appeared from behind the fountain. He gave the impression of warily walking on tiptoe, as if checking for broken glass. He clasped Bryant's hand and gave it a limp shake. 'The Reverend Charles Barton. Welcome to St Pancras Old Church. This is a very well-connected little parish. We'd be terribly proud of it, if pride wasn't a sin, ha-ha.'

Bryant refused to laugh. He rarely chose to make friends with clergymen.

'I'm not, ah, part of the usual ecclesiastical team here. I'm sort of filling in.' Charles Barton was young and untested, of ineffectual appearance and extremely pale, as if he had been washed clean too many times. There were vicars who fought battles for the souls of their parishioners, and vicars who were more interested in pointing out the stained glass. Barton was of the latter sort.

'Are you acquainted with some of the illustrious residents in our little churchyard?' he asked.

'Do introduce me,' Bryant suggested,

offering up a frightening smile.

'Well, Sir John Soane, the architect of the Bank of England, has his tomb here. Charles Dickens makes reference to it in *A Tale of Two Cities*. The shape of the tomb inspired Scott's design for the traditional red telephone kiosk. And I'm sure you know that Mary Shelley was wooed by Percy Bysshe Shelley in the churchyard. It used to be much bigger, but the Midland Railway cut away a great chunk for its sidings. Mary Shelley used to come here because her mother had been laid to rest in these grounds. The family lived nearby, but then the Midland Railway destroyed their house, too. The couple romanced each other on the gravestones, not my idea of an appropriate venue for a date, but I suppose tastes change. Have you seen the Hardy Tree?'

'No,' Bryant lied. In fact he had sat under it when he was a child, before railings had been placed around it. The old ash tree was beset by great grey gravestones, laid end to end against the trunk like a rising tide of stone, so that the wood had grown over them, nature engulfing the remains of man. Hardy was forever linked with Wessex, and it was odd to think of him here in town, fighting with locals over land the railway had usurped.

'Most of the graves – some eight thousand of them – were relocated to Highgate and

Kensal Green,' Barton told them. 'The young Thomas Hardy helped to clear them, and spent many hours in this churchyard. I'm just brewing up. Would you like a cup of tea?'

'Good idea, Rev, I'm spitting feathers.'

Barton led the way to the vestry, where a brown china teapot stood warming on an electric ring. Potterton joined them unasked and squeezed himself into a wicker chair, ready to be served.

'Apparently Thomas Hardy was very upset about the lack of respect shown to the graves when they were moved,' Potterton explained. 'It sounds as if many of the bodies were simply shoved in together.'

'We found this in the sacristy.' The vicar clearly did not like Potterton usurping his position as parish historian, but was not the sort to complain, at least within earshot.

Barton detached a yellowed scrap of lined paper from the stack of documents on his desk and carefully unfurled it. 'Hardy wrote a little poem which he called "The Levelled Churchyard".

We late-lamented, resting here,
Are mixed to human jam,
And each to each exclaims in fear,
"I know not which I am!"'

'Mary Shelley pre-dates Hardy by quite a

bit, doesn't she?' asked Bryant. 'When she walked with her lover through the church-yard it would still have been its original size.'

'Quite so. She often popped in to put flowers on her mother's grave.'

'You don't suppose she first caught a glimmer of the idea that would become *Frankenstein* here?'

'No, she wrote that while summering on Lake Geneva,' Potterton reminded Bryant.

'But imagine how the churchyard would have looked in those days, wild and over-grown. The bodies weren't always buried properly, you know. The trees uprooted cof-fins, thrusting them to the surface. Human remains, bones and skulls would have been found all over the site. The church had a much more cavalier attitude to death in those days. What a ghoulishly picturesque place for inspiration! Of course the story goes that Shelley wrote the tale in Switzerland, but ideas take a long time to come bubbling up through the soul, and this was her spiritual home, after all.'

'Oh, you just like to imagine her sitting under a London plane tree creating mon-sters.'

'I suppose so. Austin, you usually know about these things. Is there any history of strange sightings in the area?'

'Are you being funny?'

'No, why?'

'Arthur, I thought you would know more than anyone. The entire area is rife with them. It's long been associated with pagan hauntings. There's a pre-Christian barrow around here somewhere.'

The vicar harrumphed childishly at the mention of paganism.

'I know a little about the hauntings,' Bryant admitted.

'This area was also known as the Brill, the site of Caesar's camp. The Romans had a colony at nearby Horsfall. They supposedly fought Boudicca, the Queen of the Iceni, and her army of Britons right here – their encampment was literally opposite the church – and most died on this spot, which as a result became known as Battle Bridge. The bridge itself used to cross the River Fleet. The spirits of the dead armies were seen here for centuries after.'

'No, no, no.' Bryant raised a protesting hand. 'That story turned out to be a hoax. Queen Victoria transformed Boudicca into a heroine of Albion because she wanted to be seen as sharing the same qualities. Lewis Spence's book immortalized the legend and wrongly sited Boudicca's death at Battle Bridge. It's just an urban myth that she was buried under a platform at King's Cross station.'

'I know that,' said Potterton, nettled, 'but the general public doesn't. The power of any preacher can only be created by his believers, after all.'

The Reverend Charles Barton appeared uneasy at this turn in the conversation, and went off to annoy the gravedigger.

'This must be one of the most underrated sites of theological importance in the whole of Great Britain,' Potterton continued. 'Not only did the Emperor Constantine found the oldest church in London here; it was the last place in the country where Catholic Mass was spoken before the Reformation.'

'So you have a tangle of paganism, Catholicism and Christianity leaving a trail of spectral figures through the forest, and even though you cut down all the trees and erect factories and office buildings, the ghosts of the past continue to resurface,' said Bryant, pleased at the thought.

'Oh, the diocese is very aware of its religious heritage. That's why the place has been cleaned up. A couple of months ago they employed an archivist to supervise a dig in the vault – Dr Leonid Kareshi, he consults at the Hermitage in St Petersburg and is very highly thought of. Would you like to see what he's found?'

The church was dark, and smelled of damp and disuse. The greenish light gave it the impression of being underwater, but the calm was spoiled by a wonky recording of a choir singing 'Jesu, Joy of Man's Desiring' slightly too loudly from speakers above the pews. At the rear of the building, a stairwell led underneath the floor to a small vaulted area that was formerly part of the crypt. Bryant followed Potterton, carefully picking his way between dislodged piles of bricks. He arrived at a ragged hole in the end wall, around which a rickety trio of arc lights had been erected. A broad-bodied man was bent over a trestle table, and turned to face them. He looked more like a Russian gangster than an archivist. Leonid Kareshi was not a man you'd pick a fight with.

'I am happy to make your acquaintance.' Kareshi made no attempt to shake Bryant's proffered hand. He had a thick Slavic accent.

'Mr Bryant knows a lot about London,' Potterton explained. 'Perhaps he can help you.'

'You have good knowledge of this city?' Kareshi raised a thick eyebrow.

'Oh, he's been here since it was founded,' Potterton joked, but Kareshi did not laugh.

'I have been trying to discover more about the sacred sites of King's Cross and Pentonville, but there is very little reliable reading material available on the subject. These names – Brill, Somers Town, Euston, Agar Town, Pentonville, so many names for one tiny area – it is confusing,' the archivist said.

'Well, Pentonville was founded in the mid-

1770s on the estate of a Member of Parliament called Henry Penton,' said Bryant. 'It's as simple as that.'

'Not so simple, I think. His name has a meaning, no? Mr Potterton tells me that the Penton was at the – how you say – peak? – of Pentonville Road, but nobody knows exactly what it was.'

'Actually, I can help you there.' Bryant was pleased to be able to put his arcane knowledge to use. 'A penton was a head. I mean, a kind of round hill in the shape of a human head, probably designed to point to the sunrise. At least, that's the theory.'

'A sacred stone.'

'That's right. *Pen* is a Celtic word meaning high point. We get the word *pinnacle* from it, and *penny*, so named because the coin has a head on it.'

'Then you should see this,' said Potterton. 'Mr Kareshi uncovered it a few days ago, and the diocese is in a bit of a quandary about reporting the find. I think our reverend feels very uncomfortable about the building's pagan origins. The building is on the heritage register and can't be disassembled, but there's clearly something of major historical importance under here. If it pre-dates the Christian site, it's been buried for something like two thousand years.' Potterton stepped back from the excavation, allowing the lamplight in.

Bryant peered into the hole. He found himself looking at an elongated chunk of pockmarked grey granite. 'What is this?' he asked.

'I know it's difficult to see clearly. Let me adjust the lights.' Kareshi moved the tripods closer. 'How is that?'

The elderly detective could just make out a pair of eye sockets, an aquiline nose, the partial line of a jaw.

'There is no more of him. I mean, we have not found it attached to a body,' said Kareshi.

'This part was just inside the wall?'

'Yes, but there is another, from the main chamber. Come and see.' Kareshi led the way through panels of dusty plastic sheeting, into a wider hole of fractured brickwork. 'There was a spa here that connected to the well behind the church. Such places were constructed like temples. You can see the remains of a main circular chamber with a domed roof. This is why the crypt was built in the same shape.'

A narrow alley of damp brick had been lined with lamps. It opened out into a circular stone room just over three metres high. On the opposite wall was the faint painted outline of a robed woman in a crown. She was holding chains attached to a pair of dogs.

'The spa was opened to the public in 1760 – we have this from parish records – but the wells had already been popular for more than half a century by then. It is recorded as being a fashionable meeting place, with pump rooms and a House of Entertainment, which means skittles and bowling, the drinking of beers and teas. And there was a garden with – how you say? – exotic animals.'

'Funny, isn't it?' said Potterton, 'the church being stuck between the Adam and Eve tavern and the pleasure gardens. The spa had royal patronage but eventually fell into disrepute, although it took forty years to do so. Prostitutes and gangsters moved in, and stayed right up until recent times. Nell Gwynne's house is still clearly marked, you know. There's a stone inscription set into the wall of number sixty-three, King's Cross Road.'

Bryant stared at the greenish-brown spa walls and breathed in the wet air, lost in thought. 'Tell me, Austin, do you believe in evil spirits?'

'Odd question. No, I suppose not. Why?'

'The word "Pentonville" can be interpreted as "Hill of the Head". Many Celts believed that the soul resided behind the eyes. That statue of yours hasn't been broken off from a larger icon. You can just make out the scroll-work on the base. The carving was clearly intended to appear as a severed head.'

'Why would that be?' asked Potterton.

'It's the sign of a sacrificial site. This was

intended as a warning to the curious. What else have they found?'

'Some small iron symbols, very degraded, but they seem to match up to other markings in the undercroft. A face shaped by tree branches, typically Hellenic in appearance.'

'The horned king of the hilltop,' muttered Bryant. 'The great god Pan is back. Perhaps he never really went away. Of course. I'm beginning to see now.'

'See what?' asked Potterton, curious.

'A connection between gods and mortals,' replied Bryant mysteriously. 'Well, I mustn't detain you any longer; I have work to do. But I'll be back, Austin.' He nodded to both, and took his leave.

He wasn't quite ready to return to the temporary residence of the PCU. Bryant stopped outside, looking up at the back of St Pancras station. He tried to find the statue of Boudicca that supposedly looked down on the street, but misty rain was now falling too heavily for him to see.

He turned his mind to a piece of history so distant that no fact could be verified, and myths that were considered ancient a millennium ago. Boudicca, the Queen of the Iceni, had inherited the kingdom after the death of her husband, King Prasutagus. But the Romans, under Suetonius Paulinus, had pillaged their own protectorate, slaughtering over eighty thousand and defeating the

Warrior Queen in battle. Brutalized, defeated, her daughters raped, Boudicca had committed suicide in despair. Some said she had been transformed into a hare, to flee into the thick woodlands surrounding the site of her final battle. But, as Bryant knew, the grimmer historical reality had not survived the burnishing of her legend.

Could such mythologies really maintain their grip on the present? There were those who believed they did. *This is the world of London before history*, he told himself. *It doesn't matter if such things really happened, only that somebody out there still believes in them.*

24

THE TWO DELANEYS

Rosa Lysandrou slowly opened the door of the Camley Street Coroner's Office like Mrs Danvers beckoning a visitor into Manderley. She examined the man standing before her with a glum stare that could have brought a corpse out in a sweat.

'Is Giles in?' asked Dan Banbury, in the manner of a schoolboy asking if a friend could come out to play.

'Can I ask who is calling?'

'I'm Dan. We work together.'

'He already has one visitor. I'll have to see.' Rosa's grey eyes narrowed in faint disapproval. The door closed again. Banbury took a look around. Rain was mizzling lightly against the grassy banks on either side of the entrance. The only sound came from the wind in the reeds that grew beside the canal. It really was the most forlorn, depressing– The door opened again.

'Dan! Hello! Sorry about that – Rosa is insisting on screening my callers. Come in.' Kershaw clapped a hand on the Crime Scene Manager's broad back and drew him into the gloomy corridor. 'Apparently that's what she always did for the Professor, her previous boss. He came here from the Hospital for Tropical Diseases just up the road. Have you heard, some absolute doombrain wants to make the place a containment area for unknown serious infection? The press has been speculating about what would happen if it became a terrorist target. Can you imagine the disaster scenario we'd have on our hands? At present such things are dealt with up near Mill Hill. They have PCs from Haringey and Barnet guarding the place. Anyway, the Disease Centre moved out of that weird old Gothic building you can see from the road in 1999, and the Professor came here. By all accounts Rosa was dedicated to him, but there seems to be some kind of mystery about how and why he left that she won't talk about; disgrace, a nervous breakdown, it's all very– Ah, here we are.'

Bryant was standing in the main room, having just arrived from the church next door. He grinned. 'What do you think of this, then, Dan?'

'What an extraordinary place,' Dan marvelled. He tended to admire buildings from an engineering perspective. A modern extension had added nothing of architectural interest, but the slender vaulted morgue ran deep under the road, cutting through ground that had once been filled with coffins from St Pancras Old Church. It reminded Banbury of a postwar railway station, mainly because of the row of green tin lights hanging low over the pair of dissection tables that occupied the main space in the room. The floor vibrated faintly as a Tube train passed. Glassware pinged in a cabinet.

'Rather atmospheric, isn't it?' Kershaw loved having visitors to whom he could show his new domain. 'It could do with more light, but it's surprisingly big.'

'It would have needed to be when it was built,' said Bryant. 'The parish church was pretty busy, and I imagine there were plenty of violent deaths to deal with. You can blame both the reformers and the property speculators for that.'

'Why so?'

'The fields of Somers Town and Holloway were dug up to build wealthy villas, sub-urban homes and houses for the Irish who came here for the Copenhagen Street cattle market. People were pouring in to work on the new railways. Some houses quickly degenerated into slums, but the land was so valuable that it would change hands five times in as many years, leaving the rich butted up beside the poor. London in microcosm, and a classic recipe for trouble.'

'Yeah, well, shoving the lower-waged into council estates doesn't work, either,' said Banbury, who, like Meera, had been raised on one of the rougher London housing developments.

'No, so now they're planning to mix households with different incomes within individual land plots, to break down social barriers. An old idea whose time has come again. Whatever the result, I'm sure it'll keep Giles busy.'

'How are you getting on, Dan?' asked Kershaw.

'You mean apart from having no officially recognized existence? Mr Bryant has found us a temporary home of sorts, but we're so far off the grid that I can't get access to any data. At the moment I'm using the wife's online account to get into systems.'

'Did you get anything more out of our corpses?' Bryant asked.

'See for yourself,' answered Kershaw, 'although I warn you, they're not pretty. Here you go, body number one.' He rolled out a green steel drawer and unveiled its contents. Without its identifying features, the remaining grey flesh bore little resemblance to anything human.

'There seems to be some confusion here. From the contents of the stomach and the condition of his skin, I've set the time of death for the cadaver that was found in the shop a little earlier than the body found on the building compound–'

'He wasn't killed on the premises,' Banbury interrupted. 'But I think he was beheaded in the shop. Any blood that fell landed on plastic sheeting that was then removed; there are drag marks in the dust consistent with that.'

'OK. I imagine the head was destroyed separately. You've got a pretty good confirmation on Terry Delaney from the prints plus the scar marks caused by the hot iron filings falling on his ankles. I also found a small star-shaped scar on his right calf. Janice gave me the number of his neighbour, Mrs Mbele, who now remembers that Delaney told her he'd been stabbed in the leg with a screwdriver when he was a kid. Best of all, his chums at work remember he had the ivy-wreath band tattooed on his arm. So, that's the ID taken care of, but not much else.'

'What about the other one?'

Kershaw closed the first drawer and opened the second with an eardrum-shredding screech of metal. 'Sorry, I've got to oil the runners. This equipment was installed in the 1930s. OK, this guy is very messed up. He has no identifying marks on his body. We know he was thirty-four years old and has some lung damage from heavy smoking, but that's about it. The arms and legs are badly crushed – obviously from the earth-movers.'

He removed the plastic bag containing the victim's head and tenderly set it down on its left cheek. 'Despite the damage by the site excavators it looks like the same method of evisceration, severing at the exact same points with the same blades. So we have a positive ID for Terry Delaney at the building compound.'

'So what's the confusion?' Banbury asked.

'Well, I managed to get hold of Delaney's dental records, which proved highly distinctive – he'd had some major surgery – and I was looking at the second corpse's head, and suddenly I realized I was seeing Delaney's bridgework. So it seems there are two Terry Delaneys. What I want to know is this: how can the victim be in both places, days apart? And if they're not *both* Terry Delaney, who the hell is the other one? Am I making any sense?'

'Not really, no,' said Bryant.

'Look, maybe I'm overtired. I haven't been sleeping well since I got here. But Delaney's been identified *twice*.'

'Then one of them must be wrong. Or else he had a twin.'

'I thought you might say that, so I checked. Terry Delaney doesn't have a twin.'

'Then perhaps he cloned himself.' Bryant didn't seem too bothered by the problem. 'Tell me, do you think the killer is simply removing signs of identity? Or could there be something more ritualized in his method?'

'You mean is he the kind of serial killer you get in supermarket novels, picking off victims according to the plagues of Egypt or following arcane rules laid down in the Bible? No, I think the neighbourhood has got itself a hit man, taking care of local trouble and sending out a warning to others by looking tough – removing the head. Either that or he's a psycho; sometimes if there's a sexual element to the death the killer can't bear to be watched by the victim.'

'I haven't been able to file a detailed report about Delaney's apartment yet,' said Banbury, 'but it wasn't a simple hit. Delaney kept his place neat and tidy, but everything had been pulled out. Not by him; there were no prints on any of the drawer handles. The intruder was surprised while he was searching for something.'

'So where was Delaney while that was going on? Standing around watching? Having tea with his twin brother, perhaps?' asked Bryant.

'No, at the very least he was knocked out. If the blow was fatal, it certainly didn't cause much external haemorrhaging. The attack happened during daylight hours, because the owner had installed a fancy Lutron lighting system that's operated by a remote. You need to point it at the base controls to turn on the overhead spots, but I found it in a different room to the base, under the contents of ransacked drawers, and the attack was too well placed to have occurred in the dark.'

'What about the time of death?'

'Tricky to ascertain without knowing exactly how airtight the freezer lid was,' said Kershaw, 'but the seal was strong enough to stop the skin from drying out. Clearly there was bacterial activity inside the body for about four days. I was able to access my old PCU insect charts from here when I performed the autopsy. I used that data to compare the life cycles of the mites I found present in the gut. I can take you through the larval stages–'

'Not necessary,' said Bryant. 'Your conclusions will be fine.'

'Let's say he died four or five days before he was found. The trouble is, that date plays

238

havoc with the rest of my calculations. Even allowing for the difference in locations, I'd swear that from the comparable condition of the bodies, the two men were killed with an interval of at least two days between them. It's pretty clear that Terry Delaney died on Monday afternoon, not on Wednesday or Thursday.'

'Wait, I know I'm old and easily bamboozled,' Bryant complained. 'What does this actually mean?'

'Well,' said Kershaw, scratching the side of his head with the pointing-antenna Bryant had given him, 'you've got the same man dying twice in two separate places, days apart. So to answer your question, I'm buggered if I know.'

25

VISIONS AND PORTENTS

Lying on her back only increased the uncomfortable fullness in her stomach. Dragging the duvet over her breasts, Lizzi turned on to her side, wondering how anyone managed to bear a child in the heat of the summer. It was only May. *My child is turning within me, just as I turn*, she thought, as if a secret alliance had already formed between them. Reaching out her arm, she distantly registered the fact that the other side of the bed was empty, but knew that Xander often rose early to work on his computer in the kitchen.

The soft click of the front door told her that he had returned from outside, so she assumed he had been to the Cally Road gym. 'Xander,' she called out, 'where are you?'

'I'm sorry.' His muscular frame appeared in the doorway. He was wearing his ragged brown sweater with the holes in the sleeves. As he tugged off his knitted cap, she saw that his hair had not been combed in days.

'Look at you,' she said sleepily. 'Hope no one's seen you like that.'

'I've been organizing the picket,' he told her. 'Marianne Waters is going to be at the mall for the ground-breaking ceremony, and the press will be in attendance. We're planning to lie down in front of the tractors as they enter the site. I had to meet the others at Ground Zero and it's been raining, so I put on my old clothes.'

She had asked him to attend the Camden antenatal clinic with her on Thursday morning, just as she had done several times before, but he had clearly forgotten again. It was probably for the best, Lizzi decided; he would only get in her way and slow things down. She loved him, but wished he would show as much passion about his unborn child as he did about his protest meetings. Tomorrow morning, as ADAPT announced the next construction phase of their shopping plaza, a long-disputed area would finally be fenced off, and Xander would begin another round of protests.

'Did you remember to ring the *Islington Gazette*?' she asked him.

'Damn, I forgot.'

'You won't get any local coverage unless you remember to tell the media. And you've got to sign on for work.'

'I'm not sure there's going to be time,' he told her, scratching his hair flat. 'I've still got to finish painting the banners.'

She pushed herself up on one arm. 'You have to do it, Xander. We can't live on my salary.'

'I have to prioritize what's important. We want more council housing, not more offices, and we're asking for the area's historic pagan connections to be respected. If we don't picket the offices of ADAPT tomorrow they'll continue to ride roughshod over everyone, tear up the last of the old town boundaries and build another soulless business district that has no respect for the area's original layout. The ancient hedgerows—'

'I know all about the ancient hedgerows,' Lizzi interrupted, climbing out of bed. 'You've told me a thousand times.' Mired in endless controversy, the battle over the sale of the railway's grounds had continued in London courts for nearly three decades. 'The public consultations are all finished, and the appeals have all failed. Ten people lying in a field isn't going to make any difference now. It gives you no credibility, Xander. Worse, it makes you look stupid. Protests are no longer won by tree-huggers; they're established in courts of law along proper legal guidelines.'

'I didn't think you'd give up on me as well. I thought you were on my side.'

'I am, but we've also got to start thinking of ourselves. You're going to be a father soon. I want to be able to rely on you.'

'I can't just suddenly abandon my ideals, Lizzi. What they're doing is illegal, but the police don't care. We have to protect the disputed property twenty-four hours a day.'

'The people you've got in those tents look like tramps!'

'That's because there are no washing facilities. Look, I'll make you some breakfast, but then I have to go. The burial grounds of St Pancras Old Church will be under threat from the new building extension. Somebody has to show these people how to lead a protest. I have to conduct the rehearsal. Somebody has to *care*.' He stormed off into the kitchen to clatter about with breakfast dishes.

Lizzi often thought back to the University of London party where they had first met. Their class differences had been more pronounced in those days. He had introduced himself as Alexander Toth. It seemed that his family owned quite a lot of property in the city, but he had fallen out with them and was living in a squat in Bloomsbury. Gradually his accent had changed until it had become virtually cockney. Lizzi, a genuinely working-class girl born within the sound of Bow bells, had spent her teenage years trying to speak with a more middle-class accent, and at some point they had passed each other, heading in opposite linguistic directions.

Xander's idealism and commitment had excited her at first, but Lizzi could not help wondering if his devotion to a lost cause was a form of autism. He focused on the reclamation of King's Cross to the exclusion of everything else. She had grown jealous of the protestors who shared his days, but she also pitied them, a straggling handful of unemployables, embittered single fathers and disgruntled ex-council workers who devoted their time to the noble art of failure. If they genuinely cared about restoring a healthy environment they would come up with realistic plans, plant trees and flowerbeds, remove graffiti, start youth groups, instead of sitting outside the headquarters of companies with incomprehensible slogans painted on bedsheets and leaflets demanding the return of pagan sun temples.

At first she had listened to Xander's angry rhetoric and offered her help, but at some point the effort of believing in him had exhausted her. He thought he could turn back time to reach an arcadian idyll that had only existed in myths and legends. What he wanted was impossible. The history of King's Cross was murky and violent, a clash of obscene wealth and grotesque poverty, filth and gold, peacocks and coal dust. She accepted that its new incarnation as an upmarket business district was a natural economic progression. She needed the old Xander to return, but to do that he would have to be convinced to let go of his cause.

There are six weeks remaining to the birth of my little boy, she thought. *If I can't change his ways by then, I'll bring my son up on my own.*

At seven thirty on Thursday morning, the detectives met with their team and planned the day's schedule, but within minutes the meeting had fallen into disarray, largely as a result of Raymond Land's foul mood. By agreeing to resolve the case by the end of the week or have the unit removed from the investigation, he had created a painful paradox for his own future. Failure would doom the PCU's plans for reinstatement and finally free him from his loathed position as so-called acting temporary head, but success would enhance his reputation and trap him at the unit. As a consequence Land was behaving like a traffic light with an electrical short circuit, switching plans until everyone was confused.

'Raymond, let me handle this,' said John May finally. 'I'll put in a call to Kasavian's superior and explain that the investigation has expanded. I don't think he'll have much choice but to extend the deadline. Why don't you go and get some air?'

'We're in King's Cross,' said Land despondently. 'There isn't any air.'

'April, you saw Delaney's ex-wife yesterday; what did you get?'

'Not a lot. He'd fallen behind with his child-support payments and the ex was trying to stop him seeing his daughter until he paid up. He was nuts about the kid.'

'That's tragic,' said Banbury, shaking his head in sorrow. 'If he hadn't come back from work early he wouldn't have surprised a burglar. He might still be around for his little girl now.'

'You're convinced this is a burglary that went wrong?' asked May.

'The signs are clear as day, all over the flat. The problem is that it doesn't fit with the beheading. If it was a hit, there's no reason why his killer would turn the place over. But you don't carve someone up like that just because a robbery goes wrong.'

'What about Delaney's girlfriend, have you tracked her down?'

'She's coming in this morning,' replied Longbright.

'Anything else on the first victim? Colin, have you been back over the premises?'

'I've had the floorboards up, boss. Nothing. I'm taking one more look later today.'

'Before you do that, take Meera with you to the site where they found the second body,' said May. 'ADAPT has got some kind of PR announcement happening there at ten this morning. There's a rumour that the event is going to be disrupted by picketers. And Arthur–' He looked around. 'Where the hell is Arthur?'

'He's on his smoking deck,' said Longbright.

'What smoking deck?'

'That's what he calls it. The little iron balcony at the back of the building.'

'Go and get him, will you?' May ran a hand over the nape of his neck. 'Keeping you lot in one room is like herding cats. Who hasn't got anything to do? Renfield, do you feel like doing door-to-door?'

'Not really, no.' Renfield was also in a lousy mood, knowing that he had to sneak behind everyone's backs all week to report to Faraday.

'Fine, then, it falls to you: I want the rest of the statements – anyone who knew Delaney, or saw him, or employed him – on my desk by the end of the day. Come on, ladies and gentlemen, I want you thinking beyond the obvious.'

'You're looking for me?' Bryant sauntered in, his pipe tobacco still smouldering.

'You can't use that platform as a smoking area; it doesn't look safe,' May warned. The balcony had once contained a block-and-tackle for raising cargo into the building, but now the iron framework was rusted through, so that the entire cage shifted when any weight was placed upon it.

'Can I enjoy my pipe in here?'

'Certainly not,' said Land.

'Then I shall continue to indulge this innocent pleasure on my deck. What would you like me to do?'

'I thought you might like to help me find out who is leaving body parts all over the neighbourhood. You could lend a hand, preferably one that's still attached to an arm.'

'Has anyone ever told you you'd make a first-class nightclub comic?'

'No.'

'They never will. I think I can help you with the vexed question of extremities,' said Bryant, tearing open a bag of mints and doling them out. 'I was pondering the problem just now. Did you know that the Celtic area of Penton, part of King's Cross, is directly connected with the severing of human heads?'

Land looked back blankly, as if struggling to decipher what he had just heard.

'It's true. The Celts believed that the spirit dwelt in the head, and built a sacred mound in which they buried the heads of their enemies. This is the mound that was known as the Penton, hence Pentonville, town of the sacrificial mound. It is also in the diocese of St Pancras, who was himself beheaded. It would seem that the sighting of the Horned One, our chap in the stag's outfit, and the headless victims are historically linked. King's Cross is a land of great mystical significance, after all.'

'No, no! I will not go down this route, Bryant.' Land raised his hands in complaint. 'One minute everything is normal, and the next you'll have crackpots with spiritmeters and dowsing rods taking over the place.'

'Look, it's very simple,' Bryant explained patiently. 'St Pancras Church as we know it was founded in the third century, but it's built on the site of a temple to Mithras, and the area has deep connections with the occult. The Horned One is intent on reclaiming his land. I've been working, too, you know, interviewing witnesses and checking through local records, and I think this vision which has been spotted on the King's

Cross construction site is intended to be regarded as an incarnation of the great god Pan himself, Jack in the Green, London's oldest and most enduring myth. Now, I'm not saying it *is* him, of course, merely that it is a representation.'

'Why do you think this mythical creature would leave a body in a freezer? Why are you so sure that the events are connected?' May asked his partner. Sometimes Bryant tried too hard to join facts together.

'If you understand the motivation, everything else follows,' said Bryant, screening out reasonable argument. 'Think it through. Once the bulldozers move in, the battle is lost. There are no valuable buildings to save on the site, no architectural wonders to fight for, just derelict factories and barren wasteground used by prostitutes and drug addicts, so who could possibly raise an objection when companies offer to pump millions into the neighbourhood?' Bryant raised a wrinkled finger. 'Ah, but imagine someone with a different agenda, a plan to restore the area's lost religious significance, someone still intent on disrupting the building schedule. What's the best way to do that? Complain to the board of directors? Forget it; it won't work, because the consultations have all been concluded. Corporations pay huddles of lawyers vast fortunes to crush the Council's paltry opposition teams. So how about simply frightening off the workers, many of whom are migrants with a limited grasp of English who've been plonked down into a strange land? Visions and portents. Evil omens. Simple, cheap and extremely effective.'

'That's the best you can come up with, is it? The Scooby-Doo defence? It was the mill owner dressed as a ghostly stag? Plus, it doesn't give us any clue as to who might be responsible,' said May.

'Oh, I think it does,' Bryant disagreed. 'In fact, we can meet up with him this morning if you like. But I warn you, identifying him and proving his culpability are going to be two entirely separate problems.'

'It sounds to me like he doesn't know what he's doing.'

'That's precisely what makes him so dangerous,' Bryant warned.

26

PROOF OF INNOCENCE

'I want them off the premises right now,' warned Marianne Waters. 'Put them back beyond the perimeter fence.'

'I can't. Mr Toth has somehow got hold of press passes. They're legit, and Toth knows his rights. I can't throw him out without attracting more attention. They're right across the path between our team and the site for the ground-breaking ceremony.'

'Then delay the start until I can get down there.'

'They've already kicked off.'

'Jesus, Cavendish, what do I pay our security team for?' Waters angrily closed her mobile phone and stalked out along the office corridor.

At the front of the fenced-off triangle of land before the railway embankment, Maddox Cavendish watched helplessly as Xander Toth led the picketers in another chant, something about the freedom of the land. There were no more than a dozen of them, but the public was falling into line, singing along. A shout of indignation went up every time the security guards pushed back the advancing picket. Above the bellowed slogans, the architect fought to make himself heard. A handful of police constables were keeping a watchful eye on the wavering line between protestors and guards.

On a raised platform, monitors showed computer-rendered graphics of how the site would look once the building works were completed. Attractive, willowy people meandered robotically over glass bridges and through sculpture parks. From the computer-assisted designs it appeared that the new buildings would not only transform the area, they would change the city's weather patterns as well. The entire landscape appeared to be basking in Mediterranean sunshine. When the picketers suddenly surged forward some of them bumped the edge of the stage, and the screens wobbled alarmingly.

'What are they protesting about?' asked Colin Bimsley as they approached. 'I thought Mr Bryant said that the whole deal was signed off.'

'It's the second phase of construction,' Meera explained. 'The plans got changed: more offices, less affordable housing, more concrete, less parkland – the usual sort of thing. The Council must have signed off on the alterations without public consultation. I don't believe it!'

'What's the matter?'

'Bryant's over there with the bloody protestors!' Meera was right; their superior was wedged into the front of the picket line. They could see Bryant's moth-eaten brown trilby bobbing up and down.

Marianne Waters had arrived and was talking to a member of the PR team. Moments later, she had grabbed a walkie-talkie and was ordering the construction workers to break through the picket line. The noise level welled up as both sides pushed forward and megaphones squealed feedback.

'We have to get Arthur out of there,' said Meera. 'This is going to turn nasty.'

'Leave it to me.' Bimsley charged off into the surging crowd. Meera saw a scaffolding pipe being raised, then suddenly there were bricks and bottles in the air. She ran after Bimsley, shoving her way into the brawling mass. They saw Bryant rise peculiarly above the seething scrum, then slip and sink between a pair of security guards. Diving deeper beneath the collapsing bodies, Bimsley managed to catch his boss's outstretched arm and lift him up, pulling him over his broad shoulder.

'What were you thinking of?' asked Meera as Bimsley laid the elderly detective on the grassy bank of the railway line. 'You could have been badly injured.'

'I wanted to get a closer view,' said Bryant, closing his eyes and drawing a few deep breaths. 'I wanted to see him in action.'

'Who?'

'Xander Toth, the protest leader. I think he's our stag-man. Colin, do me a favour, would you? Go back in there and get him. If he won't come, arrest him.'

They went to the Café Montmartre, where Alfie Frommidge served them sausage rolls and tea while Bryant recovered and studied his quarry at close quarters. In his late twenties, Toth was lean enough to have retained the awkwardness of his teen years, but also appeared to have been working out for some time. He had nervous energy and the kind of charisma that could turn a certain type of lonely student into an acolyte. Bryant was already warming to him, even if he did seem somewhat clueless when it came to expounding a comprehensive worldview.

'The company just announced its intention to build beyond the original boundaries of the site,' Toth told them heatedly. 'They're in violation of their contract, and they know it. We had a tip-off that they were going to do this. The ground has been in dispute for years. Residents are required to register all the property deeds. If registration isn't forthcoming, the Council allows them to build despite local objections. The onus is on the public to prove they have a claim on the land, not the other way around. It's like treating an accused man as guilty until proven innocent. It's wrong.'

'Why do you care so much?' Meera was studying him with ill-disguised contempt.

'The pastor of St Pancras Old Church is a relative of yours, isn't he?' remarked Bryant. 'And the church grounds are now under threat.'

'How do you know that? It's not why I care. ADAPT is run by a bunch of crooks. If they're allowed to get away with this kind of thing, no land is safe from development.

The government is already allowing building to go ahead on the Green Belt.'

'Hmm.' Bryant stared down at his coat buttons, thinking. 'Tell me, did you ever do any work for the company?'

Toth remained silent.

'All we have to do is look at the employment files.'

'That has nothing to do with this.'

'How long were you there?'

'I worked for them for eighteen months, about four years ago.'

'Doing what?'

'I was helping their records office locate property deeds. The land had to be purchased from dozens of separate owners. Some of the property was still tenanted. The company was always looking for ways to get the tenants out. They offered cash payments, new housing, and when the legal routes failed they tried other methods.'

'You mean they broke the law.'

'Yeah, they broke into houses, smashed up cars, frightened residents. I couldn't prove it because no one would speak out. Tenants who told me they would never move, that they were born and would die in the same house, suddenly started leaving. It's obvious what was going on.'

'So you have no proof. We understand you're passionate about this,' said Bimsley. 'Just how strongly do you feel?'

'What do you mean?'

'Strongly enough to commit murder?'

'Who really owns the land, in your opinion?' Bryant asked, disregarding Bimsley's questions.

'It's been public ground for two thousand years.' Toth could see that Bryant was the most sympathetic of the officers, and addressed his comments to him. 'The plots were subdivided and changed hands after the Enclosure Acts. They continued like that until recently, but now ADAPT has the land rights to the entire area. They've been on the site for nine years, preparing themselves for this. They'll be able to dictate where we can and can't go. You can't privatize what belongs to the people.'

'You can,' disagreed Meera, annoyed. 'I'm not saying it's right, but companies do it all the time. They're closing off entire districts. You can't simply take the law into your own hands just because you don't approve.'

'We don't,' said Toth angrily. 'We follow the law and we have the right to protest.'

'Mr Bryant here thinks you like to dress up as a woodland animal and frighten people.' She tried to imagine Toth draped in a deerskin.

'Our objections to the plans were legally registered a long time ago,' said Toth. 'I've done nothing wrong.'

'No, but you could be charged with attempted manslaughter.'

'What are you talking about?'

'One of the workmen was so frightened by what he saw that he fell down a stairwell and nearly died.'

'And you think it was my fault?'

'You admit you know about the stag-man?'

'It's not me you should be trying to arrest.'

'Then give us some proof of your where-abouts on the dates the stag-man was seen.'

'I don't have to do that. Proof is your job, isn't it?' Toth rose to leave. 'It was good to meet you, Mr Bryant.'

'We're going to talk to your girlfriend, you know that.'

'Leave Lizzi out of this. You've no right to involve her.'

'She can eliminate you as a suspect,' said Bryant genially.

Toth looked suddenly defeated. 'Look, we're having difficulties at home. Please don't involve her.'

'Fine, then give us an account of your movements on these dates,' said Bryant, handing him a sheet of paper that looked as if it had been screwed up in his back pocket for a month. 'By three o'clock this after-noon, if you please.'

'I'll see what I can do,' said Toth, but he seemed oddly unsure of himself.

27

THE FIRST MR DELANEY

From the early edition of the *Evening Standard:*

THREE HURT IN PROTEST CLASH WITH POLICE

Protestors demonstrating against the plans of property developers clashed with police in King's Cross today, injuring three bystanders. Fighting broke out after the peaceful picket turned nasty, say local Met officers. This is the third time that protestors have fought with security guards from ADAPT, the property company behind the multi-million-pound project to transform the urban wasteland behind King's Cross station into a new eco-friendly town.

'We are bringing thousands of jobs to a deprived area,' said Head of Development Marianne Waters. 'But a small, vocal minority is still trying to disrupt work.'

Several companies say they have already pulled out of the controversial new plan after being subjected to threats and intimidation by the protestors. Earlier this week a workman was injured in mysterious circumstances, and construction teams have threatened strike action. This latest protest was sparked after confusion arose over the boundary line between picketers and company officials. The police have been criticized for using heavy-handed tactics.

'This is an area of historical importance,' said Xander Toth, the leader of the Battlebridge action committee, 'but ADAPT has no respect for the capital's heritage. Time and time again it has attempted to bypass planning restrictions.'

'The residents were consulted at every stage of the planning process, and their rights are being carefully observed,' the company's senior public relations officer, Chris Lowry, told us. 'Many of these protestors are former offenders and ex-employees with grudges who have nothing better to do with their time.'

The construction area is now being guarded twenty-four hours a day to prevent acts of vandalism. Work to the west of the York Way area is not expected to be completed for another three years.

John May and Janice Longbright met with Terry Delaney's girlfriend, a hard-faced blonde who stood on the street furtively smoking until it was time to be interviewed. Her name was Casey, and Longbright thought she looked like a younger, more feral version of Delaney's wife. She had been informed that Delaney was dead, and was handling the news without emotion.

'I don't know why I was with him,' she told the detectives. 'All he ever did was talk about his ex. I said to him, "There's three of us in this relationship. Someone's got to go," but he never got around to making a choice.'

'Did he have any financial worries?' asked Longbright. 'Was he broke?'

'Terry didn't like talking about money. I got the impression he was behind on his child support, but that's nothing unusual, is it? I mean, with men.'

'What about the evenings when you didn't see him? Where did he go?'

'Down the pub with his mates, the usual stuff.'

'Any problems?' asked Bryant. 'Drink, drugs, gambling? Anything that would get him into debt?'

'Not that I know of. We'd both been through some hard times, but he's a good man.' That phrase again, suggestive of strong morals and respectability but conveying nothing of use.

'What sticks most in your mind when you try to describe him?'

'He's dependable,' said Casey, her face softening. 'He's one of those people who picks up everyone else's rubbish in the street. He'd tell off a kid for putting his feet on a bus seat. He was always trying to help people he hardly knew. Like, there was this woman he was trying to trace.'

Bryant's ears pricked up. 'What kind of woman?'

'Terry had something of hers and wanted to return it, but I have no idea what it was. I suppose I should have asked.'

'Do you know who she was?'

'No idea. But he was very anxious to get it sorted out quickly.'

'Do you know if he succeeded?' To Bryant this was a point of significance.

'I don't know. As I told you, the last time I saw him was on the Sunday night, when I stayed over. He'd already left for work by the time I got up.'

'Can you think of a reason why anyone would want to hurt him?' Longbright asked.

'Not at all,' Casey replied, at a loss. 'As I said, everyone liked him. Terry was the sort of man you would go to if you were in trouble. A good man.'

'You don't murder someone because of their goodness,' said Bryant, disappointed.

Colin Bimsley's doctor said that his lack of spatial awareness had been exacerbated by the misalignment of his spine and the differing optical fields in his left and right eyes.

261

None of which was any consolation when the detective constable fell over the edge of the fire escape at the rear of the Paradise Chip Shop.

'Are you all right?' called Banbury, who heard the crash.

'I'm fine; I landed on my head. The railing was rotten. Give me a hand up, will you?' Scrambling to his feet amidst bags of builders' rubble and shards of rotten timber, Bimsley tried to find a way to climb back out of the stairwell.

He was rubbing his sore pate when Banbury came out on to the fire escape. 'I can't lift you, you're too big,' he called down to the DC. Banbury was trying to work out a method of levering Bimsley up when his nostrils detected a familiar but highly unpleasant smell. He was instantly reminded of the odour that lingered on the lab coat of the PCU's late medical examiner, Oswald Finch.

The dark space between the buildings housed the ventilation shaft of the takeaway, but had been used by builders as a dumping ground for the shop's old interior.

'Can you smell something?' Banbury sniffed and followed his nose, sifting out the musky odours of mildew, moss and London dirt.

'Rotten food,' replied Bimsley.

'Have a poke around down there, would

you?' Banbury indicated a wet, dark corner filled with plastic sacks.

'I've got my good shoes on, Dan. I'm going out tonight.'

'Just do it, would you?'

Pulling aside half a dozen bags stuffed with mortar and plaster, Bimsley dug down into the waste, listening to the scuttle of fleeing rodents.

In a cement bag, he came to the source of the smell.

Gingerly opening the top of the sack, he shone his pencil torch inside.

A single blue eye glittered back at him.

Bimsley yelped in alarm, but was drawn back to the thing in the sack. The skull had been so badly battered that only the eye was left intact. 'Oh, man.' He covered his nose and instinctively released the bag.

'What is it?'

'I think we've located the missing part of the first Mr Delaney.' He took another look. The head was surrounded by pale mounds of spaghetti, giving it a Medusa-like appearance. He realized that he was looking at the remaining piece of the body from the freezer, buried here where only someone with an acute sense of smell and a predilection for digging in rubbish would ever think of looking for it. 'Maybe now we'll find out who he really is. And how many of him there are.'

28

THE LAND DECIDES

Raymond Land shifted about in his chair and rearranged the few items on his desk, then looked for something useful to do. Everyone else was busy, and he had no one to talk to. He wasn't needed here at the office, and he certainly wasn't needed at home. The only person who had come to see him this morning was Crippen, and that was because the cat wanted to be fed.

Life wasn't fair. At least retirement would have allowed him regular games of golf. He had a little money saved, and might have taken a holiday somewhere far away – South America, perhaps. Leanne could have put her rhumba lessons to use. Heaven knows she'd taken enough of them. Instead, he was stuck in this crumbling warehouse, where chill winds crept in through the cracks in the walls, wondering if he would ever get warm again and how on earth he could be of help to anyone other than the cat.

Outside it was just starting to rain again. May in London, a month when nobody talked about anything but the weather. He sharpened a pencil. The bulb on his desk light flickered and went out. His chair had a wobbly leg. Folding a beer mat into quarters he bent down to use it as a makeshift prop, and found himself looking at a painted white line, about an inch wide. The line came to a point under his foot, then set off again beneath his desk.

Puzzled, Land rose and pushed back his chair.

Another point, further to the left, went under the ancient, moth-eaten Persian rug Bryant had thrown down on the floor. Land lifted a corner with his shoe to see where the line went next. It disappeared under the desk, so he moved the desk and rolled the rug back.

'Mr Bryant...' His voice rose and broke. He cleared his throat and tried again. 'Arthur, may I have a word with you?'

After what seemed like an age, Bryant stuck his head around the door. 'What is it? I'm very busy, you know.'

'There's a pentacle under my desk.'

Bryant came into the room and made an elaborate fuss about getting out his spectacles. Fitting the wires firmly behind his ears, he peered at the floor. 'So there is.'

Land was outraged. 'Have there been Satanists up here?'

'I really have no idea.'

'I'm sure you do. You always have an idea.

You pretend you're dotty, but you know a hawk from a handsaw. You've probably got a dossier on this place tucked among those weird books you keep.'

'Is this all you wanted?' asked Bryant irritably. 'You do know we've got a murder investigation on our hands? Perhaps I can be allowed to return to my—'

'No, it's not all,' said Land plaintively. 'I don't know what I'm doing any more. I don't have a purpose. You always know what to do. What should I do?'

'Stop feeling sorry for yourself. Nobody takes any notice of you because you don't do anything. You sit there worrying. People do peculiar things and you can't understand why. Life is short and filled with pain, and just when you start to finally get the hang of it, you drop dead. So pull yourself together and give me a hand. Do something and make a difference. I have over a hundred blurry photocopies of land-purchase agreements to go through, and could really use some help.'

Land should have been annoyed. There was a murderer on the loose, time was running out, and he had no idea what Bryant was doing with property contracts, but as he followed Bryant's instructions he felt strangely elated.

'I was told I'd find Xander Toth here,' said

John May. He had come to the Camley Street Natural Park, an urban nature reserve run by the London Wildlife Trust, to talk to the leader of the Battlebridge Action Group. The small sanctuary consisted of woods and wetlands backing on to the canal, and had been reclaimed from the former red-light district. The site had originally been a coal drop for the railway, but after the discovery of wild orchids growing by the water it had been reborn as a wildlife park. Toth worked here as one of the volunteer gardeners.

'He's planting, over there on the bank,' answered the girl who was refilling the bird-feeders at the entrance. May followed her directions and picked his way across a muddy meadow filled with reedmace, wondering if he was about to meet the abductor who stalked the lonely road leading from the Keys nightclub. He decided to take a soft approach to the subject and let his suspect speak out.

'Xander Toth?' he called.

'You're the other one, aren't you?' Toth set aside his spade and pulled off his gardening gloves, leaning over to shake May's hand. He was standing in a dell filled with evening primrose, hollyhocks and ox-eye daisies.

'Detective John May. You know me?'

'I saw you talking to Marianne Waters the other day. You think I'm a trouble-maker.'

'I didn't say that. I know you want to build

a pagan temple on the site of St Pancras Old Church, but that's about it.'

Toth grinned. 'See, that's the kind of quote that's taken out of context.'

'Maybe you should have thought more carefully before you gave it.'

'People will think I'm crazy whatever I say.'

'Are you? It's the kind of thing that can really damage a good cause.'

'No, I'm not crazy. I'm committed.'

'And you don't believe in compromise.'

'Tell me, Mr May, how would that work? ADAPT gives back a little corner of land so that we can erect a maypole or something, donates a bit of money towards the restoration of the graveyard in return for sticking up some sponsor plaques? And we agree to back off so they can build London's largest shopping mall on public property?'

'That's a very cynical outlook, Mr Toth. The world moves on; you can't go back in time.'

'I don't want to go back. I want people to have what's rightfully theirs. ADAPT has spent years perfecting the art of turning people out on the street and making them feel grateful for it.'

'Help me with something I don't understand. You have fewer than thirty registered members on your side. That's according to your own website. If all these people you say you represent can't even be bothered to stand up for their own land, why should you care?'

Toth looked down at the freshly turned earth and shook his head. 'You know how quickly areas can change? ADAPT demolished all the buildings on the land they bought, and ploughed up the ground. Since then, wildlife has started returning to the region. Geese, herons, foxes, rare flowers, migrating wild birds not seen here for decades. Do you believe that the landscape in which you grow up has the power to shape you?'

'Of course. Inner-city kids are very different from ones who–'

'I'm not talking about demographics. The land on which we build our houses decides who we are. If you thought your environment had become harmful, how would you feel about raising a child in it? I'm about to become a father.'

'How much do you know about the history of this area?'

'Pretty much everything there is to know. It's my specialist subject. I talk to the local people and try to educate them about it.'

May thought back to what his partner had told him about the myths born in the ancient woodlands of Battlebridge. 'Then you know how strongly it's associated with the image of a man in horns. You have the knowledge, Mr Toth. You have the motive. Who else is it more likely to be?'

'You're accusing me, Detective. What are you going to do – apply for a warrant to search my home?'

'You were supposed to provide my partner with details of your whereabouts at certain times and dates. We're still waiting for that list. Several of your members have criminal records for drug offences. Your flat is listed as the registered address of the Battlebridge Action Group. If there are reasonable grounds for me to suspect that there are drugs on your premises, I don't have to apply for a warrant. If I find anything that connects you with the stagman, I'm going to arrest you.'

'Oh, really?' Toth studied him with interest. 'What are you going to charge me with?'

May was suddenly struck by the absurdity of the idea. If Toth was responsible, what had he actually *done?* A few workers had walked out, and one man had broken his ankle in an accident that had arguably been caused by a hallucinated sighting of Veles, a Romanian childhood legend. What about the girl the stag-man had supposedly abducted? She had apparently vanished into the night sky, no name, no identity, no loved ones to even report her missing. May had nothing. He was chasing an invisible man.

'Nice to meet you, Mr May,' Toth shouted

after him. 'I don't want you coming near my house, you hear me? Remember, I know my rights better than anyone. Stay away from me.'

Even as he walked away, May felt sure there was another part of Alexander Toth that remained hidden from view. And until he discovered what it was, he would not be able to put the case to rest.

29

ANCESTRY

If Euston Road is the ugliest street in London (it isn't, quite; City Road can induce such a state of clinical depression that there should be a medical term for it) then the chamber of Camden Council is its Sistine Chapel of human misery. Arthur Bryant was feeling rather buoyant as he approached it, but each step he took into the building drove the sensation from him. He had come to see a town-planning officer named Tremble, formerly a solicitor with Horsley, Dagett & Tremble, who now acted as an adviser to the Council in matters concerning the compulsory purchase of land.

Bryant wanted to be outside digging up

corpses and chasing (as far as his bad leg would allow) unscrupulous but fiendishly brilliant villains through the back alleys of the city. Instead he was meeting a clerk about forgotten bits of paperwork.

And if Camden Council was a boring place to be when there were desperados waiting to be apprehended, Ed Tremble looked like the most boring of Council officials, to be ranked beside Leslie Faraday in the great roll call of grim government time-servers. No man ever seemed riper for retirement. Bryant could almost see the weeks, days and hours counting down on his face. Tremble appeared to be having trouble remaining upright. The solicitor looked as if he was covered in dust: baggy grey suit, thin grey face, thinning grey hair. On closer examination he actually *was* covered in dust, having just returned from the basement archive where he had been digging up information for the insistent detective who had called him (on his mobile phone, a number he was sure he had never given out!) at an unearthly hour on Thursday morning.

Tremble had a secret, however. Underneath his dreary exterior, he was quite interesting. When his penchant for investigating the area's past was indulged, a light shone in his eyes and he became almost passionate, which was why his wife kept a stack of local-history books on his bedside table.

'I'm not entirely sure that some of this information isn't classified,' said Tremble, plonking down a huge stack of filthy green folders and leaving more dust on his jacket in the process. 'The development of the King's Cross site has been under public scrutiny for three decades. Nobody wants to make any more mistakes.'

'What do you mean?' asked Bryant, unwrapping a lemon drop.

'Well, the building of the Regent's Canal and the Great Midland Railway turned a thriving area into an industrial wasteland. The river was filled in and the fields were turned into cheap housing for French immigrant workers. Dickens called the site "a suburban Sahara". So this time the consultation process took in every local group and involved literally hundreds of meetings. Summary reports were produced after every stage. Perhaps you'd rather see those.'

'No, I want to go right back to the beginning,' said Bryant. 'I'm interested in the very first tranche of purchases made by ADAPT.'

'They weren't in the picture back then,' said Tremble. 'It was called the King's Cross Central Development Office in those days. The company became a public–private partnership in the mid-1990s, and finally changed its name to ADAPT in 2003. All the companies have sexier names now. Process, Change, Pulse – I can't keep up. What are you really looking for, Mr Bryant? I mean, what interest could the police have in old land purchases?'

'All wars are fought over territory, Mr Tremble. And this is a fascinating piece of ground. How much do you know about King's Cross?'

'Far too much for my own good,' Tremble admitted. 'What's most striking is the way it has continually switched between rural idyll and urban squalor. One decade you have swans and spa fountains, the next, dust-heaps and decay.'

'What do you know about Xander Toth and the Battlebridge Action Group?'

'He's a pain in the rump, but I suppose he has more reason to be than most.'

'Why is that?'

'The name, Toth. The area around Euston was once the Manor of Tothele, later Totten-ham Court Road. I suspect it derives from a word meaning "the sun". Altars on druid sites are called Heal or Hele stones, because the sun rises over them. *Helios* is Greek for sun. Tot-Helios became Tothele, or Sacred Sun Site. The manor was a royal residence of King John in the thirteenth century. He hunted in the surrounding forest. Very popular with the royals, that area. Edward the Fourth, Elizabeth the First and Charles the Second's mistress Nell Gwynne all lived in the neighbourhood, by which time it had become Tottenham Court. So it was a rare example of a sacred site that became a royalist stronghold. Which means that Mr Toth can trace his ancestry back to the throne of England. That might explain why he feels so strongly about the land.'

'So it would be a prestigious area for ADAPT to own in its entirety, presuming they could purchase back all the separate properties and reunite it into one site?'

'Indeed. I think it even comes with its own sovereign laws, rights to hunt and dig, that sort of thing.'

'That's very useful, Mr Tremble. You're wasted here.'

'Tell me about it,' said Tremble.

Bryant headed for his next stop.

The elderly detective looked hopelessly out of place in the arctic-white reception area of the ADAPT offices. He was rumpled and tired, and very nearly ready to slide off the vast white-leather sofa and fall asleep. He was at the age where he fantasized about having an afternoon nap. Indeed, a nap had been his habit throughout his fifties, but now he was old enough to be constantly aware of his fragile place in the world, and would not allow himself to miss a moment more of his life.

So there he patiently sat with his brown

trilby squashed between his hands, his presence making the place untidy. Bryant's shabby overcoat was so vast that he appeared to be vanishing inside it. His wispy white tonsure was still fanned up around his ears as if he had just risen from bed.

An impossibly slender young woman approached the sofa where he sat, but changed her mind when she saw its occupant. Bryant kept his watery blue eyes locked on the receptionist, daring her to leave him stranded in this snowy wasteland of designer chic for much longer.

After a few minutes, a small boy with a perfect blond designer haircut and an outfit that made him look like a miniaturized member of a boy band sat down next to him and began hammering a hand-held computer game. Electronic explosions and power chords filled the lobby. The boy punched the air, texted his success to a friend, then grew bored. He turned his attention to Bryant, studying him with vague distaste.

'Are you more than a hundred years old?' he demanded, as if interviewing an Egyptian mummy.

'I feel like it most days,' Bryant admitted. He did not like children because he had always been an adult.

'Then how do you stay alive?'

'I eat small boys.'

'Yeah, right.'

'You don't believe me.'

The boy looked disgusted. 'Duh. Get real.'

Bryant removed his false teeth and nipped the child hard on the arm with them. The boy screamed and burst into tears.

'Mr Bryant, you can go up now,' the receptionist called. 'Miss Waters is ready for you.'

As he passed, she whispered urgently at him, 'That's Miss Waters's son.'

'Good. Where is she?'

'Her administrative assistant will meet you on the third floor.'

The closing lift doors snipped off the sound of the wailing child.

Marianne Waters had a floor-to-ceiling-glass corner office overlooking a steam-cleaned courtyard lined with chrome uplighters and silver birches. She was a strong-looking woman, Bryant decided, studying her tight black suit. Hard-bodied and muscular, without a centimetre of body fat. He tried to imagine her saying silly words like 'ping-pong' and 'hippopotamus', but the image wouldn't spring to life.

'Do you ever watch television, Mr Bryant?' she asked, walking to the window. 'I always enjoy the historical adaptations, all those happy street urchins and ladies in bustle skirts worrying about their suitors. The reality was down there.' She tapped a nail against the double-glazing. 'It's hard to imagine how tough urban life used to be. These buildings were blackened with soot and filled with laundresses who were too old and ill to work by their mid-thirties. A woman of twenty-five looked fifty.'

'At least you were able to save some of the original buildings,' said Bryant, dropping on to the nearest seat.

'These factories were left over from the bad old days. Their staff worked with mercury, lead and arsenic. The dyes rotted their nails, and mercuric vapour burned out their bronchial tubes. They suffered from anaemia, blood poisoning, cardiovascular disease, dermatitis, kidney damage. The employment laws favoured management, of course. The rates of pay were whatever you could get away with. Now the offices are air-conditioned and have natural light. We've improved the environment beyond all imagining.'

'I agree that our standards are different now, but the gap between rich and poor remains. It's not your fault. Most of the office workers we interview hate their jobs and are only doing them to pay their bills. They binge-drink and take drugs and go mad with frustration and boredom.'

'You're right. It isn't my job to rebalance the whole of society, Mr Bryant.' Her mood changed as soon as she realized he would not be easily led. 'Why are you here?'

'A rather esoteric subject for an investigation unit, I'm afraid. Land purchases. You made over two hundred and sixty of them in order to secure this land, and it took thirty years. Any problems there?'

'What kind of problems?'

'Well, what do you do about the ones who don't want to sell?'

'You mean do we trick property owners into signing away their homes?'

'Oh, I imagine all the guidelines are carefully followed. At least on paper,' Bryant replied lightly.

'More than that. We have government backing every step of the way, at both local and national level.'

'So you can't really fail, can you?'

'If you're implying something, Detective, it might be better to just come out and say it.'

'Well, you must admit you're having a fairly unusual month. Body parts turning up on your site, some lunatic stalking the workers in fancy dress. At first I thought someone was out to stop you from finishing the project. Silly, of course; an international juggernaut derailed by a worker with a grudge. Then I thought, what if he's just trying to draw attention to the company and its work practices? You don't have a high public profile. You get on with your work and keep your heads down. Suppose someone started to shine a spotlight on you? So, first the culprit dresses as a local hero and marauds around your site, making a mockery of your security system. Perhaps he still has friends inside the company who'll arrange to leave doors unlocked and lights deactivated. And when that has no effect he gets desperate, stepping up his activity until it results in a murder which has to be hidden, which then turns up a second corpse. And he dresses it all up in the myths of local history, just to keep everyone interested. That's why you need to search through your employment records and see if there's someone on your books who's capable of such a thing.'

'We don't have time to do that. We have deadlines to meet.'

'Then we'll do it for you, starting this afternoon.'

'This is a privately owned company, but it's sanctioned by the government,' Waters warned.

'It's publicly accountable. You'd better make sure you have nothing nasty to hide, Miss Waters, because if you do I will find it and I will bring you down to earth.'

'If we wanted to hide something, Mr Bryant, I can guarantee you'd never find it.'

Bryant left in a fury. No one was telling the truth. Everyone had something to conceal. And an ordinary, decent man had been killed in impossible circumstances. Another working day was almost over; there was an ever greater danger that the Met would regain control of the investigation, and the truth remained just beyond his grasp.

Worst of all, he could not shake the strange feeling that he was being watched.

30

PREDATOR

Bryant sat in the Costa coffee shop opposite the station entrance, staring into the falling rain. He was thinking about the Sioux star of Buffalo Bill's Wild West Show. *Chief Long Wolf made it all the way here in 1892*, he thought, *only to die of pneumonia in London's dreadful weather. That says it all. Look at it.*

He had sounded confident in the meeting with Waters, but knew that the case was falling apart around his ears. The first victim was bothering him. At least the head had now been found, and was undergoing tests. Why had it turned up on the same site? If the killer had really wanted to keep his victim's provenance hidden, he would have taken the head far away, or simply weighted it and thrown it into the fast-flowing current of the Thames. The invention of the bin bag had been a boon to murderers everywhere. If the murderer was that much of a professional, it didn't make sense to bury the head in rubble at the back of the shop.

Which meant that their killer was not a hit man at all, but an ordinary fallible human being. No professional would have left the parts where they would be found. But if there was no hit man, where did this leave the investigation? They had no one. A face in the crowd. An invisible man. Ordinary people left spoors, and Banbury had turned up nothing: not a hair, not a thread, not a flake of skin. That in itself was rare enough to suggest they were dealing with someone extraordinary.

The ghosts of Battlebridge obliterated those who would desecrate their land. Veles came storming through the dark-green forest to take his revenge. A supernatural killer had risen out of the torn soil, from an age so long gone that civilization did not even have a trace-memory of it. Time fragmented the past into bright moments, tumbling diurnally until they finally faded from view. The pagan god of all things wild – of woodlands and beasts and storms and rushing rivers – had come back into a world being re-created in concrete, back just in time to restore it to a natural state where faith in the rising sun and the blossoming of plants could reign once more. And he was removing the heads of his victims in rituals of pagan sacrifice.

Preposterous.

If anyone was to be sacrificed, surely it should be Marianne Waters, or the Council members who had approved the desecration of the site, not a workman who had never hurt anyone.

I'm going mad, thought Bryant. *Well, maybe I've always been a little mad. My father warned me about that, God bless his beer-sodden soul. We have to close the investigation fast or I get to go back to my fireside and watch the rain running down the windows until the end of my time. We haven't got the staff to go through all of ADAPT's employment records. We're not being thorough; it feels as though we're missing something blindingly obvious. There must be a simple answer to all this, something that's right in front of me. Come on, Arthur, use that brain of yours.*

He realized he was doing what he always did. John May endlessly accused him of failing to make a stand on the side of rationality. *He's right*, thought Bryant. *I'm always drawn to the other side, the spiritual, the instinctive. If we're to survive this, I need to do something practical and useful. I think I need to see a witch.*

It was dark and still raining. Janice Longbright and Liberty DuCaine sat on the brick wall that crossed the canal, although Liberty's legs were so long that they touched the pavement. Longbright dipped into a white paper bag, sharing DuCaine's chips. Blowing on one, she licked tomato ketchup from her fingertips.

'I'm glad John asked you to come and give us a hand,' she said. 'We need all the help we can get.'

'He heard I was taking a sabbatical,' DuCaine replied. 'I needed a break. I was getting burned out.' PC DuCaine was currently on leave from Camden constabulary, but always enjoyed working with the PCU.

'I love eating hot chips in the rain,' said Longbright. 'It reminds me of being a teenager.'

'I bet you were a terror.'

'I was horrible, running around the streets, charging after the night bus with my mates when the pubs shut. Mum was on nights at the PCU a lot of the time, so I was always on the loose in London. I used to resent her for not spending more time with me. We never went anywhere outside London; none of us had any money. I wish I'd travelled a bit.'

'Yeah, me, too,' said DuCaine. 'I'm third-generation Caribbean, from Tobago, but I've never been back. My gran always wants me to go.' The constable had been angling for full-time work at the unit for several months before its closure, and had volunteered to help with the investigation. Tonight, this meant patrolling King's Cross on the lookout for the stag-man.

Longbright watched DuCaine as he neatly rolled up the empty chip bag and folded it into his pocket. He was the kind of man who never went through a door first, and always carried a handkerchief. The huge, muscular young officer often gravitated towards her. At first she thought he might be attracted to her, despite the difference in their ages, but he had never made a move.

'Liberty, seeing as we'll be spending the rest of the investigation together, can I ask you something?'

'Ask away.'

'Don't be offended. It's just that – well, you dress nicely, you're over-attentive to women...'

'Yes...'

'...and every time I see you my Gaydar goes off.'

DuCaine's laugh was so deep it might have been mistaken for a passing subway train. 'Yeah, I get that a lot. You're thinking of my brother, Fraternity. I guess it's a genetic thing.'

'I hope you didn't mind me saying.'

'My mother's a control freak, my dad was an old hippie, my brother's gay, my sister Equality is a wild child. We're Caribbean, but not at all old school. Anyway, it's about time someone was over-attentive to you. I know how hard you work.'

'That's because I don't have a social life.'

'Maybe it's the other way around.'

A comfortable silence descended between them. 'Ready for another turn?' asked Longbright. They had circumnavigated the perimeter fence bordering ADAPT's second-stage site three times in the past two hours.

'Go on, then, last one,' said DuCaine.

The rain was descending in misty swathes across the ripped-up fields behind the railway line. Dozens of seagulls stood motionless in the rain beside the natural ponds that had formed in the soil dips. The perimeter fence was illuminated by tall neon lamps that created corridors of silver needles. It was still difficult to believe that such a desolate spot had sprung up in the heart of the city.

Longbright pulled her cap down harder, but the rain was running down her neck. 'We could do this faster if we took one side each and met back in the middle,' she said. 'There's no one around.'

DuCaine agreed. They set off in opposite directions. The mud sucked at Longbright's boots as she trudged around the steel fence. In the distance, the clock tower of St Pancras rose in spectral splendour. Soon that Gothic monument would be joined by modern equivalents as a new town rose from the shifting wet clay of the hillside. *It's easy to forget London's on a slope until you have to climb it*, she thought, turning a corner into the next lengthy stretch.

She came to a sudden stop. The stag-man was standing on the path no more than twenty metres away from her.

Although he still wore his leather boots and ragged fur jacket, he was no longer trying to assume the appearance of a wild beast. The headdress of blade-antlers had been replaced with a brown balaclava and cap. His face was smeared with mud. He reminded Longbright of a primitive forest hunter, especially since his right fist contained a large knife with a serrated blade.

Wary of confronting him, she remained calm enough to make a visual analysis. He was muscular, between twenty-five and thirty-two. His boots raised him to an imposing height. His eyes gave less away than she'd expected, but there was something in his posture that recalled John May's description of Xander Toth.

He was waiting for her to make a move.

If she called DuCaine, how long would he take to skirt the perimeter fence and reach her? She pulled out her mobile to make the call, but to make sure she had a record, snapped a quick photograph first. At that instant he lunged at her, lowering his body like a sprinter leaving the starting blocks. She jumped back, then ran.

'Liberty, I'm heading west around the fence, he's right behind me.' The phone crackled and she heard no clear answer. She had already lost ground. The stag-man was close behind and gaining.

Her shoes were slipping in the mud. She grabbed at the security fence and swung around its corner, running hard as he swung out at her arm, the knife reverberating against the wires. There was a feral grunt close behind her, and another, each expulsion of breath matching hers as they pounded beside the fence.

He's within range of the CCTV, she thought. *That's it, keep coming*, and now she saw DuCaine racing towards her. The stag-man suddenly backed off and she heard him springing up against the steel fence, over the razor-wire on top and down the other side, to be lost within seconds among the heavy plant machinery and stacks of building materials. DuCaine started to go after him, but his concern for Longbright held him back.

'You OK?' he asked. 'You've been cut. I saw him swing at you. I'm glad you didn't turn around and see how close he was.'

'He's stuck inside.' Longbright bent down, hands on knees, panting. 'Blimey, he nicked my jacket. If we can get back-up we can keep him in there.'

'No back-up,' DuCaine replied. 'Can't call in the Met.'

'Then how do we stop him from getting out?'

'You know how wide the site is. There must be over a dozen other exits. You think it was Toth?'

'We have no proof. Raymond says we'll need a warrant to search his apartment unless we can prove that we're preventing a breach of the peace, and he doesn't think we have evidence for that. I'm happy to go with a gut feeling, but he's insisting on doing everything by the book. I'm sure he thinks we're being monitored. At least I got a photo of our stag-man.' She held up her mobile.

'That's something. Let's get it to Dan and see what he can find.'

'Damn, if I could have just made an ID, I'd have had him.'

'No,' said DuCaine, 'he nearly had you.'

Rufus Abu was waiting for John May in St Pancras station's champagne bar. He was under the minimum legal age to be served alcohol, so a waitress had given him an orange juice, to which he had added some gin from a small silver flask.

'Hey, my man.' Rufus touched May's fingers in a complex salute and waited for him to sit. It was cold in the station, but the bar seats were heated. Rufus was a computer hacker without a base who did not take kindly to being described as 'homeless', for he regarded the whole of London as his home. He had just entered his teenage years, but showed no sign of growing any taller. With the mind of a university professor and the body of a child, his disconcerting mix of intelligence and innocence gave him an edge no bedroom-bound hacker could beat. He left no signature in the electronic ether and managed to pass beneath the city's surveillance radar. He could usually only be lured into the outside world with gifts of illegal software, but had agreed to answer May's call-sign because he owed the detective a favour. May had cleared him after a breach in CID online security had tagged his name with suspect status, resulting in the police looking for someone they still regarded as a runaway child. But Rufus kept moving on, like the zigzag blur of a night-time tail light, lost in the rainy static of the night.

It comforted May to know he was out there somewhere, watching and listening. Sometimes when he was at his computer at a late hour, he would pick up a faint vapour trail left by Rufus. Other times, odd events revealed the hacker's mark: a flash mob in Liverpool Street station, where six hundred home-going commuters suddenly performed a dance number choreographed via their mobile phones; an ugly Trafalgar Square protest clash that turned instantly docile after the receipt of a single text message. Spontaneity and unpredictability were Rufus's style, but those were the qualities that made him hard to find.

'How are you doing, Rufus?' asked May.

'I'm young, gifted and back.' He held out his arms, indicating his surroundings. Rufus had an IQ of above 170 and a fondness for cheesy old-school slang. 'Not for long, though. With the plurality of CCTV around here I can give you five minutes between sweeps, then I'm ghosted. How's life in the statistic majority?'

'We got disbanded.'

'Yeah, I tracked that. IMHO, you had a good run, man. You're gonna re-boot, right?'

'Well, we have a short lease on new premises, it's pretty much make or break. But I'm sure you're already aware of that.'

'I keep you tagged. We configured a handshake long ago, you and I, so I look out for you.'

'That's comforting to know.'

'Besides, I'm still waiting for you to match.com me with the dominatrix Longbright.'

May was shocked. 'Rufus, she's old enough to be–'

'She appeals to my Oedipal streak. Don't sweat it, I'm hooking you.' Rufus's weak spot was sensitivity about his age. He hated the idea of being mistaken for a child, with a child's mind. 'So, I heard you put out an ICQ. What can I do for the PCU?' He leaned back in his chair and sipped his gin-

and-orange. His super-white trainers did not touch the platform floor.

'There's a company called ADAPT Group. Architectural design, planning and construction. I need a list of employee names from their system.'

'What, you can't get some Trilobite processor to handle that, you need an expert?'

'I'm afraid so, yes,' May admitted. 'ADAPT is very protective about its workforce details, and we currently have no access to programmes that will get us in. I'm assuming it will be a piece of cake for you. I need the information fast. Will you do it?'

'Hell, this doesn't even count as a favour. I'll have something for you tomorrow.' When Rufus laughed it was the only time he sounded his age. He set down his drink.

'Hello, John. Janice said I'd find you here.' Arthur Bryant was standing beside them, jauntily leaning on his walking stick. He reached down and ruffled Rufus's head. 'Hello, little boy, do you want a sweetie?'

'Do you want a smack in the mouth?' retorted Rufus.

'I remember you, Rufus. I've known you since you were so high.' Bryant held out his hand. 'Oh, you still are.'

'Good to see you, too, Mr Bryant,' said Rufus. 'Have you figured out how to open your e-mail yet?'

'Mr May won't let me do it any more, not

since I crashed the interweb. I hope you're taking care of yourself, with so many children carrying knives these days.'

'Don't worry, *senex*, they gotta catch me before they can juke me. I don't want no cellotaph.' He was referring to the plastic-wrapped bundles of flowers that were left tied to railings at murder sites.

A pair of yellow-jacketed station policemen caught May's eye. They were entering the champagne bar and heading in their direction. Rufus sensed them behind him, too. 'Hey, check it, sharks at midnight. You gotta bail me a less readable venue next time, man.'

'Don't worry, Rufus, they're not after you, they're just–'

But when May turned back, he found the seat opposite him empty.

31

MAGNA MATER

The little house on Avenell Road, Finsbury Park, had been painted a hideous shade of mauve since he was last here. The bell didn't work and the knocker seemed to be welded to the door, so Bryant tried to rattle the letterbox, only to find that this too was stuck fast. Looking around the chaotic front garden (home to a mangle, a half-burned chest of drawers, a gigantic dead aspidistra and a table lamp made out of a cow's leg), his gaze alighted on a hanging basket blighted with a single sickly nasturtium. The front-door key was sticking out of the pot, so he let himself in.

'None of your door-furniture works,' he complained to Maggie Armitage, the white witch from the coven of St James the Elder who had helped unit members so many times in the past, although not always in the way they expected or desired.

'Ah, no, it wouldn't,' she called back. 'I hired a Polish gentleman to decorate my hall, and he proved rather over-enthusiastic. He painted over my knocker, the bell, the letterbox and my fanlight.'

'So how do you know when anyone's calling?'

'I always know, you foolish man, I'm a witch. Give me a hand with this.' Maggie appeared, dragging a large fibre-glass model of a child in callipers through her hall. 'Remember these charity boxes? They used to have them outside shops. Collectors' items now, apparently. This is from a grateful client. So I thought until I opened it, anyway. I'd successfully located her lost Yorkshire terrier, but had forgotten to tell her it wasn't alive any more. A technicality, from my point of view, but she wasn't pleased. I gave her a voucher for a free séance.'

'Let me help you with that.'

'Perhaps it's not such a good idea, with your knees. Go and put the kettle on.' Maggie set the collection box aside and patted her fiery red perm back in place. She had chiming incense balls and a necklace of little plastic babies around her neck, pencils and bits of tinsel in her hair, miniature bunches of bananas dangling from her ears and what appeared to be a bell-ringer's cord tied around the waist of her blue and yellow striped skirt. She looked like a deckchair piled with seaside knick-knacks, but Bryant had learned not to be surprised by her sartorial choices.

'Come here,' said Bryant, reaching forward and wiping Maggie's cheek. 'You've got mascara all over you.' He brushed harder. 'And pollen.'

'Maureen and I were conducting a spring spell to bring back the bees,' she explained. 'I did miss you.' The white witch was a source of goodness in a dark world, forever on the move, using positive energy to banish despair. If Bryant could have his way, Maggie's services would be available on the National Health.

'I missed you too,' he said tenderly. 'You've always been there for me, Maggie. I'm not very appreciative, am I? You're always sending me things, thinking of me. I presume it was you who sent me the postcard of Merlin's prophecies with the Get Well Soon message. *London shall mourn for the death of twenty thousand, and the River Thames shall be turned to blood* – cheered me up no end.' She had stapled the card inside the envelope and he had torn it to pieces trying to get it out.

'Yes, that was me. The last of Merlin's edicts, and the only one yet to come true. I thought you should be warned, at least.' She smiled up at him, her eyes diminishing to crescent moons. 'It's good to have you back. Arthur, I felt your aura ebbing.' She clapped her hands together. 'Oh, I meant to tell you: I found something odd in the cellar. Come and look.'

'What do you keep down here?' Bryant followed her down an unstable narrow staircase.

'I'm looking after Maureen's scuba equipment until she's had her operation. She can't risk getting into a wet-suit with her bladder. Look at this.' She pulled out a huge photo album filled with faded Polaroids. 'There seem to be pictures of me in a Playboy Bunny costume. You don't suppose I was a Bunny Girl in a past life, do you?'

'You were a Bunny Girl in this life, you silly woman,' Bryant snapped. 'I know it was a long time ago, but how could you have

296

forgotten?' There were few careers Maggie Armitage had not tried in her life. She had been a nightclub hostess, a teacher, a carnival burlesque dancer and, for a brief period in the 1980s, the astrological adviser to Number 10, Downing Street. Some of her insights had displeased Margaret Thatcher, but it was not the first time the incumbent Prime Minister had been compared to Beelzebub.

'I think you're right, it is me.' Maggie pulled a chopstick out of her hair and scratched her décolletage idly with it. 'I asked Maureen to hypnotize me because there were things I wanted to forget, but I think she overdid it, and now I can't remember the name of my first husband or where I've put the pressure cooker. The line between past and present is so easily erased.' The curse of her unusual talents had not led her to an easy existence. She had often been drawn to harmful people in a desire to save them. 'Let's get that tea, shall we?'

'We've moved into King's Cross now,' Bryant called over his shoulder, heading for the kitchen to search for two vaguely clean cups. 'Two thirty-one Caledonian Road. It's got upright goats on the walls and a pentacle on the floor. Any idea why that might be?'

'Well, of course I have,' said Maggie, appearing in the cluttered kitchen. She shifted a pile of dolls' heads from a chair and sat down. 'Two thirty-one was the address of the Occult Revivalists' Society of Great Britain. They split away from the Hermetic Order of the Golden Dawn in order to write their own magical rituals. The original founders of the Golden Dawn all lived in King's Cross until the members of the Lodge of the Isis-Urania Temple fell out with each other. Self-governing societies are a nightmare when no one can agree on the founding rules.'

'So what happened?'

'The splinter group set up on the Cally Road. They shunned the former Imperator, W.B. Yeats, and ran things on their own for quite a few years, but it eventually collapsed and the rozzers closed the place down. There was a court case, if memory serves. It transpired there was a fair amount of licentiousness going on, quite a few naked ladies happily offering themselves as sacrifices, that sort of thing. The *News of the World* exposed them, and jail sentences were doled out. The building's also on a major confluence of ley lines. There are definitely mystical upheavals associated with it. And some kind of scandal in the fifties that I can't quite recall.'

Bryant considered the information. Yeats, Blake and Hardy, all visitors to St Pancras Old Church, mystics and occultists operating nearby, the seeds of Mary Shelley's modern Prometheus springing up in the local graveyard. Once again he felt himself moving at a tangent, drawn to areas of exploration he knew he should shun. 'Let me get this clear in my head. The town of Battlebridge, later to become King's Cross, is built on a pagan site that's a mound from which the sunrise can be seen. Battlebridge's forests give rise to legends of Jack in the Green and it becomes associated with fertility, hunting and the great god Pan. The surrounding areas become Christian, but the church is built on the pagan site and the neighbourhood remains forever associated with the occult, right up to the present day when our stag-man attempts to turn public attention back to ancient traditions.'

'Common knowledge,' said Maggie, dunking a homemade seaweed biscuit into her tea.

'But there's something else. They've just unearthed pre-Christian carvings of severed heads in the vault of St Pancras Old Church. I suspect it indicates that worshippers of Pan made likenesses of their sacrificial victims. If they did so then, why couldn't someone be doing the same now? Here.' He fiddled with his mobile phone and handed it to Maggie.

The white witch donned her reading glasses and squinted at the screen. 'This is a picture of you in a party hat covered in streamers,' she told him. 'You've got cake all over you.'

'Oh, sorry, that was me at our coroner's wake.' He moved the camera album on a few frames. 'That's better. Janice sent me this picture of the stag-man. The next shot is of the stone head in the crypt.'

'Wait a minute.' Maggie climbed on her chair and dragged down a paving slab of a book that was wedged on top of her fridge. It was entitled *Myths & Legends of Ancient Londinium.* Thumbing through it, she showed Bryant a drawing of a head that was remarkably similar to the one on his phone. 'It's not a victim; it's Bran, the Crow God. That's not a nose, it's a beak.'

'Bran?' said Bryant, disbelieving. 'I thought he was Welsh.'

'Yes, but his head was buried in London, and the story goes that as long as it stayed facing France, Great Britain was safe from invasion. Bran's the model for King Arthur's Fisher King, the keeper of the Holy Grail. His head was kept in the White Tower, which is why the ravens in the Tower of London have their wings clipped, to prevent the fall of London if they should ever leave. When the Grail was sought, it turned into a human head. That's why the primal god Bran is forever associated with the cult of the severed head.' She tapped the page with a wise smile. 'Well done, Arthur, you've hit the big time. You've arrived at the heart of the city's most venerable mystery.'

'John will kill me,' muttered Bryant despondently. 'I can't go back and tell him that we're looking for the seeker of the Holy Grail.'

'Oh, you don't have to do that,' said Maggie. 'The story is a load of old cobblers. These tales share common roots that aren't meant to be taken literally. The French have twelfth-century poems woven from the same source. Bran kept a cauldron that brought the dead back to life. You haven't found that by any chance, have you?'

'Mercifully, no.'

'A pity. We tried to revive Daphne's terrapin once but the spell didn't take.'

'What happened?'

'It exploded. You mustn't get caught up by all this, you know. It's tempting to imagine that everything that happens in London is somehow related to events in the past, but you'll be led into blind alleys. It's happened to you often enough before.'

'You're right, Maggie; I can't afford to do it this time. John is investing a lot of faith in me.'

'Then whatever you may be tempted to believe, you must treat it as a sceptic. I say this because I don't want anyone to make a fool of you. How long have we known each other? One more mistake could destroy you.'

'Even if I'm sure there's a connection?'

'Arthur, there are invisible roads criss-crossing this city, thousands of passageways layered on top of each other so thickly that the bottom ones have been crushed to the tiniest shards. Their power wanes, so they aim to deceive. Follow the wrong one and you become hopelessly lost.'

'You believe this?'

'Absolutely. If you want to see the real nature of things, study them in decline. You say you're seeking a follower of Pan, but you could equally be looking for an acolyte of Merlin. I must have been thinking of him when I sent you the postcard. He has connections to the area, too, because he predicted that Bran's head would be dug up, which it was, by King Arthur. Merlin had a cave in King's Cross. There's still a street named after him. Back when the town was a spa, there was an underground passage leading from the cave – later the site of the Merlin's Cave pub in Margery Street – all the way to the Penton, and to a deep well connected to the river known as Black Mary's Hole. It was supposedly lined with the heads of great leaders, who would guide others between this world and the next.'

Bryant knew that Maggie's belief in the spirit world had the power to infect him like flu germs when he was feeling susceptible. 'Was there really a tunnel?' he asked.

'Oh yes, it was only boarded up a few

years ago. It connects to a second tunnel, leading from St Pancras Old Church to the site of Tothele Manor, but I think that one collapsed in the mid-1800s, killing some anti-royalists.'

Bryant could feel the unseen strands of London gathering about him like a web. 'I think we should stop there,' he said decisively.

'Then let me see if I can help you find a way out of the maze,' said Maggie. 'Let's see what they say about the church.' She ran her finger down the book's index and turned to another page. 'Here we are. "St Pancras Old Church, the Magna Mater, the mother of all Christian churches, founded by the emperor Constantine three hundred years after the birth of Christ. In the seventeenth century it was used for illegal marriages and fighting duels."' She looked up from the page. 'And finally this sacred place was desecrated by something no conqueror could ever envision.'

'What happened?'

'The railway happened, Arthur. Against all the force of public opinion, the railway destroyed the churchyard, which was filled with over thirty thousand graves. Progress arrived in the form of the steam train, and shattered its sacred spirit for ever. Now you understand why someone is fighting back.'

'I understand that there's no vengeful god

at work,' said Bryant, 'but an ordinary human being.'

'I don't know about that,' said Maggie. 'If he's aiming to halt a multi-million-pound development by re-enacting an ancient ritual, I'd hardly call him ordinary. What are you planning to do?'

'I'm not sure yet. I've got my old staff back together.' He checked his watch. 'I have to be off.'

'Including that detective sergeant, the one who looks like Diana Dors?'

'Janice? Yes.'

'Tell me, has she discovered yet that she has the Gift?'

'She hasn't mentioned anything to me.'

'No, she wouldn't. Most people never real-ize until it's too late. I keep seeing her in connection with Merlin, for some peculiar reason. Well, stay in touch and let me know what happens.'

'I thought you'd already know, being a witch.'

'It doesn't make me clairvoyant, although I have my moments.' She slapped him playfully. 'I can't even read your tea leaves today; I've only got bags.'

'Don't worry,' said Bryant. 'If I don't get a break in this case soon, I can tell exactly what's going to happen, and it won't be pleasant.'

32

THE COLLECTOR

The dawn brought heavier rain. The sky was gutter-grey. The downpour seemed to be carrying soot from the sky. Inside the warehouse at 231 Caledonian Road, the staff of the PCU were discovering how badly the roof leaked.

'Rufus has come up with five names,' reported April, looking across her desk at Meera. 'Five cases that went as far as the courts.' She moved the papers to avoid getting them soaked, and shifted a plastic bucket into place with a casual flick of her foot.

'Not bad, considering how many people the ADAPT Group have employed over the years.' The two women had been going through the details of hundreds of staff members considered an employment risk by the company, but the young hacker had cracked their problem in minutes. It appeared that ADAPT had made a lot of enemies over the years.

'They've usually managed to settle out of court.'

'See anyone familiar?'

April smiled. 'Oh, yes. Just one.' She turned the screen of her laptop to face Meera. 'Xander Toth. Employed at ADAPT's corporate headquarters as a researcher four and a half years ago, fired for misappropriation of funds, taken to court, case dropped, no reason given. Scrubby beard and a body like a pipe cleaner. The picture's quite old, before he started working out.'

'Fired four and a half years ago? Long time to nurse a grudge. We have to get into his apartment.'

'It can wait for the moment,' said John May, coming in with Banbury. 'Giles just called. He's got a new ID on the other body. He's done his best work. I need everyone on this.'

'So who is he?' asked Meera.

'Adrian Jesson, thirty-four years of age. Giles found an operation scar over his left lung, and checked with the Royal Free Hospital's chest surgeons. They sent over nearly seventy pre-op photographs, and he matched one up.'

'Smart man. So Delaney wasn't in two places at once.'

'Jesson's an Old Etonian. He has no police record, no driving convictions, no bad debts, no prints on record – clean as a whistle. He was living alone in a run-down flat on Copenhagen Street, working at a Starbucks in Islington, ran a branch of Caffè Nero before that. No girlfriends to speak of, no friends at all. His family business was declared bankrupt and his father moved to Majorca seven years ago, leaving the family behind. Jesson worked in an Oxfam shop at the weekends and collected for Help the Aged, ran an Alpha Course at the church up the road. No one has much to say about him, just that he was very shy, got on with his life and minded his own business, visited his mother in Ealing every Sunday until she died of bowel cancer last year, collected tokens for the local special-needs school, and wouldn't say boo to a goose. Someone has to go to his current place of employment and interview his boss.'

Longbright slapped a coin on to her wrist. 'Call it.'

'Heads gets Starbucks, tails gets his flat,' said Meera. Longbright checked the coin. 'Damn.'

The Starbucks on Upper Street near Highbury Corner was a cluttered chaos of dirty crockery and baby buggies. Longbright located the harassed manager, and took her to the quiet office at the back of the shop.

The manager sat nervously jiggling her knees and playing with her braids as Longbright asked questions. Her name was Shirelle Marrero, and she had been running the branch for two years. Yes, Adrian Jesson had worked with her for the past year, but there was little she could add to the information about him that Longbright already had. With the unenlightening interview coming to a close, Shirelle rose to leave when a sliver of memory returned to her. 'It's probably nothing,' she said carefully, 'but you know he was a bit OCD?'

'In what way?'

'One of the baristas told me Adrian had been in trouble for stalking a girl; she tried to stick a restraining order on him. He was a collector.'

'What sort of collector?' *In a John Fowles sort of way?* Longbright caught herself wondering.

'Well, he went to those fairs where you get autographs of TV stars, pop memorabilia, comic conventions, lonely-guy stuff like that. He said some of the things he had were so valuable he had to keep them locked away. Adrian had this thing where he had to get the set of everything he collected, an OCD thing. His stuff was probably just valuable to him, like Batman toys and old records. He was always reading comics, talking to the customers about which was better, *Battlestar Galactica* or *Star Trek*, stuff like that.'

Meera had already phoned in from the flat, and had not reported seeing any collectable items. If they were really valuable, Jesson might have kept them off-site for insurance purposes, Longbright decided.

'He always came in with bags from Forbidden Planet,' said Shirelle, 'and that other shop on the Holloway Road. Rocketship.'

Drizzle continued to fall in the morning's half-light as Longbright searched the down-at-heel shop-fronts on Holloway Road. Sandwiched between the junk shops and takeaways was the Rocketship bookshop. A less appropriate name would have been hard to imagine. The rain-stained plastic sign above the door was missing half its letters. The outlet specialized in collectable toys and science-fiction books, but it looked shut. Longbright was surprised to find the door open when she leaned on it. The lights were off, half the shelves were empty and the old man behind the chipped wooden desk at the back of the shop seemed to be fast asleep. An overpowering smell of damp paper rose from the Dells, Pans, Arrows, Bantams and other yellowed paperbacks that lay in uncatalogued piles around the floor.

Longbright introduced herself. The bookseller looked as spine-broken and dog-eared as the novels that surrounded him. He blinked at her ID card, unimpressed, but recognized the photograph of Jesson that May had provided for her.

'Oh, *him*. He's always in here. A real nuisance. Never buys much.'

'Well, he won't be in any more – he's dead. How come you remember him?'

'He was always at the fan conventions. One of the really boring ones.'

'What do you mean?'

'I mean he took it all a bit too seriously. People like him get too cliquey, make a lot of enemies.'

'You think he had enemies?'

'I know it. I saw them arguing publicly at events. Everyone did.'

'Who exactly are we talking about?'

'Jesson's been having some kind of long-running feud with a guy called Richard Standover for years.'

'Who's he?'

'A very big memorabilia collector. One of the biggest. He's got a website he buys and sells from.'

'What were they arguing about?'

'I imagine they were both going after the same memorabilia, but Standover also lives with Jesson's sister.'

'Did Jesson ever talk to you about his collection?'

'He hardly ever talked about anything else,' said the old man wearily. 'He has a storage unit in King's Cross right next to St Pancras station where he keeps everything.'

'What sort of things?'

'He owns the first hundred issues of *Spider-Man* in mint condition, every Bob

Dylan single ever released, stuff like that. He specialises in original artwork from album sleeves, but he lives in a really run-down council flat. No furniture, nothing. I had to deliver some books to him once.'

Longbright wondered why Jesson had chosen to live in squalor when his collection was worth good money.

The man behind the desk seemed to read her mind. 'Blokes like him never sell their treasures,' he explained. 'They're not interested in investment value. They'd rather live like starving students, because they can never let go. It's the mark of a true collector. It becomes an unhealthy obsession.'

There were only a handful of storage places left in the King's Cross area, and it did not take long to track down the one used by Adrian Jesson. Longbright arrived to find rain sluicing from the brick arches of the undercroft beneath St Pancras station. The vaults had been constructed for storing beer, and were tailored precisely to fit the barrels. Once the area had been defined by these Victorian tunnels, which were eventually converted into everything from car washes to showrooms for antiques. One of the last surviving businesses was behind a pair of curved wooden doors marked *Rental Space Available At Cheap Rates*.

The manager was just about to leave for

the day. Longbright explained why she needed him to open Jesson's storage unit. For the next hour she dug through boxes filled with sealed and dated plastic bags of comics, albums, paperbacks and merchandizing ephemera from old movies, including screening tickets, invitations, drink coasters and VIP party tags. Without an expert, it was impossible to tell how much the collection was worth or which parts of it were valuable.

'When was the last time you saw him?' she asked the manager.

'About a week ago. He's got his own keys and can come by whenever he wants, but I happened to be on-site. He complained that the arch had a leak and was damaging his boxes. I said I'd try to get it fixed, and he told me he was going to come by the next morning to move his stuff out of the way, but he never showed up.'

'You remember the exact day?'

'It must have been Thursday.'

'Are you absolutely sure?'

'Positive. I only do a half-day on Thursday, and when he didn't show by lunchtime, I went home.'

'Did he ever come here with anyone else?'

'You're joking. He was far too scared of getting robbed.'

'Is this stuff valuable?'

'You could sell it piecemeal on eBay, but

312

it's worth more in sets.'

Longbright called the unit and spoke to May. 'Jesson definitely died after Delaney. He was last seen alive on the Wednesday, two days after Delaney was killed.'

'We mustn't get misled by the timing of the deaths, Janice, that's just muddying the waters. Jesson was a collector. Delaney had a habit of helping strangers. I can't help wondering if they had something valuable in their possession that had to be taken from them whether they were dead or alive.'

'What could they have had in common, John? They seem to have been complete opposites. Different backgrounds, different classes, different interests. The only thing they share–'

'–is the same location.' May completed her thought. 'What if Arthur is right and it's not who they were but where they *lived?*'

The arguments went back and forth, but nothing further was achieved that night. The rain continued to fall, the skies darkened, and King's Cross once more became a place of transience, somewhere to hurry through before reaching safe shelter.

The lights in the PCU's warehouse shone long after the bars had closed down and the streets had cleared. At night, the edges of the smart gentrified area frayed to reveal older incarnations; flyers for call girls and sex clubs filled the wet gutters, drunks and the homeless reappeared in the shadows. All would vanish with the coming of another dawn, but the central mystery refused to be dissolved.

33

DECAPITATION

Joseph was a devoutly religious man who had chosen to work in a cathedral of commerce. As the cleaner released his vacuum hose and guided the nozzle between the desks, he once more felt a sense of awe. The desk units were arranged like pews on either side of a central aisle, at the head of which was the boxed-off chancel where the Director of Operations received his clients.

It was not yet light outside, but here in the great nave of the open-plan office everything was sharp and bright from six a.m. onwards. Two walls of bare brick, two of glass, twenty desks, a conference area and the sacristy of the refreshment station, all intended to be maintained in immaculate condition throughout the day. Except that the workers here accumulated so much rubbish in their work spaces that Joseph could discern their individual personalities, forcing their way through like grass growing in concrete cracks. Each night they left something of themselves behind, as if anxious to leave evidence that they existed. When someone resigned from the company and was replaced, the space was cleared and inevitably filled again. To Joseph, even the photographs of families were interchangeable. He never met the people who sat on the chairs and hunched over these desks. For him, they existed only through their belongings, a draped cardigan, a gym bag, a sunlit photograph of smiling children.

However, this morning was different, because there was someone here. Joseph could see the shiny black shoes sticking out from the edge of the desk partition. As he walked forward, towing the vacuum cleaner behind him, he knew something was seriously wrong. The office cubicle was in chaos. The wastepaper bin had been overturned and a swivel chair lay on its side. Papers lay in sacrilegious disarray across the carpet tiles. Then he saw the dark, sticky patches gleaming in the light from the overhead panels.

Joseph took a step forward, and the victim was revealed to him.

The name on his cubicle wall was Maddox Cavendish, and he was one of the project's main architects, but Joseph had heard that he was Marianne Waters's hatchet man, and that presumably meant he fired people, and *that* meant there were a lot of people who really hated him.

Which probably explained why Maddox Cavendish had no head.

'Oh, God. Oh, Lord. Oh, Jesus.' Raymond Land sat clutching his head in his hands as Arthur Bryant looked on with interest.

'Isn't it funny how the most atheistic people start summoning gods when they're in a state of panic?' he mused. 'You could probably trace the birth of many religious cults to such moments of self-induced anxiety.'

'Oh shut up, Bryant. You're no help at all. What are we going to do? Maddox Cavendish, chief architect of the ADAPT Group's expansion plans, rendered headless in an office with a secure entry system. Murdered within a few hundred yards of two other men, one a builder, the other a manager of a sodding coffee shop! And you're telling me our only suspect is the clueless young leader of a local protest group. It's not going to stick. I can't go back to Faraday and tell him this. I can't contain it now. The story will be out and all over the networks by lunchtime. We can't have people fearful of going to work. Can you imagine the chaos? They'll be suing their employers. The publicity's going to backfire on everyone. I can't tell you how many times I've lied to Leslie Faraday this week. I keep telling him we're getting close to an arrest but he doesn't seem to believe me. He's not getting information from anywhere else, is he?'

'I can't imagine why you did that, old fruit. You should have told the truth and said that there's a mad killer roaming our streets and we have absolutely no clue about who he might be or what his motives are.'

'That's what you would have done, isn't it? Because you don't care what you say to your superiors; you never have. I remember the Brixton Prison breakout, when you called Faraday a time-wasting dung-beetle.'

'If I remember correctly, which is fairly unlikely, I accused him of behaving like Cardinal Richelieu or a rabid weasel, depending on whether he preferred to take his comparisons from history or the animal kingdom.'

'All very amusing, Bryant, but Faraday was a junior official then and he's your boss now, and that's exactly why we're in this fix. If you're mean to them on the way up, they'll knife you once they reach the top. We're all going to be thrown out on the streets any minute now.'

'Drink your tea, Raymondo, you'll feel better. It's got whisky in it.'

'It's half past eleven in the morning. I can't drink alcohol this early.'

'I only added a drop to buck you up. We're doing everything we can. Apparently the room was covered from every angle by cameras and very well lit, but he took the precaution of smashing up the CCTV's hard drive. There was a separate system in operation outside which he couldn't get at. April and Meera are going through the footage right now.'

'What about everyone else?'

'Renfield is with Kershaw at the morgue, John has gone with Janice and Dan Banbury to the ADAPT offices, Bimsley and DuCaine are getting interviews and I'm ploughing my lonely furrow here. In fact, you're the only one not doing anything useful.'

'Then tell me what I can do,' Land pleaded.

'Go over Faraday's head. Talk to Oskar Kasavian and tell him the truth. If you don't, I will.'

'I don't see what good it will do.'

'I want him to understand one thing,' said Bryant. 'He must realize that whether he likes it or not, we're his only hope. Tell him that we'll clear up the case. We need everyone on our side for this. And I think we can do it.'

'Do you really believe that?' Land asked.

'Yes, I do,' said Bryant. 'But if I told you why, you'd probably have a heart attack.'

'We know that he was here until nearly ten p.m. because he rang home from the office to collect his messages,' said John May.

'Where have you gone, Dan?'

Banbury appeared from behind the desk units. 'I'm trying to get the carpet tiles up,' he explained. 'There's an awful lot of blood underneath them.' The area surrounding Cavendish's desk had been taped off and photographed, and the floor closed to all members of staff, who periodically peered in through the glass with impassive faces. Occasionally one of them would discreetly record some footage on to a mobile phone.

'If the courtyard hadn't been closed outside, we might have had witnesses walking past. How the hell did the killer get in?'

'No forced entry. It must have been someone Cavendish knew.'

Longbright bagged the dead man's appointment book. 'I'll do the remaining coworkers,' she suggested. 'His suppliers and clients will take longer to sift through.'

'What happened, Dan?' asked May. 'You must have some idea.'

'This is only in the early stages, John. But I can tell you our man is starting to panic. The victim was killed here. The cuts are the same as before, but nastier, more ragged and careless. Once the bone was severed he tore through the remaining section of skin. There are bits of it all over the place. Looks like he's taken the head away. Hang on, here's something…' He raised a white rubber glove above the desk to show May.

Between Banbury's thumb and forefinger was a tangle of brownish-black hair. 'It's from a dead animal. The collar of a jacket?'

'No,' said May grimly. 'Too coarse. Looks to me as though it's from a deer or a stag. Mr Toth has every reason to panic. I think we've got him this time. OK, Janice, let's bring him in.'

34

EXORCISM

Liberty DuCaine had been the fastest runner in his school, but he had bulked up since then, and knew that the extra weight would slow him down. He had misjudged the height of the railing and was stuck halfway across it. The iron spearheads were digging into his upper thigh, and his quarry was getting away.

Xander Toth had decided to make a run for it.

DuCaine had been forced to kick in the front door but Toth had barricaded himself into the living room. Now there were crashes and slams coming from within the second-floor flat, so with Mangeshkar on guard at the front, DuCaine had run around the entire block to the courtyard at the rear. The morning light was unusually low, and although it had stopped raining the air was furred with damp. There were no lights on in the building. It sounded as if Toth had gained access to the apartment next door. Suddenly he appeared at the bathroom window. Toth was muscular and agile. A moment later he had jumped. His trainers skittered on the wet roof tiles, then he was pelting along the slope towards the end of the roof.

DuCaine ran up the concrete steps to the half-landing but knew he would not be able to reach his quarry from here. Toth was in navy tracksuit bottoms and a white T-shirt; it was almost as if he had been expecting to have to run. DuCaine tried to see which way he would move, but moments later Toth had passed the crest of the roof and leapt from sight.

Liberty pelted back down the stairs, wondering why Meera had not come down, then caught sight of Toth running across the dewy grass bank, heading towards the road. DuCaine raised the pace, pumping up the same slope, closing the distance, but Toth darted behind a row of parked vans. Toth was heading towards St Pancras Old Church. If he got inside the gates, DuCaine knew he would be able to reach the canalside and lose himself in the empty buildings awaiting demolition.

The silver coils of newly risen mist wreathed the churchyard like sheets of fragile silk. The effect was absurdly theatrical, something from a Hammer horror film, but Toth vanished into the mist as if passing back through the years into the past. The grounds were deserted except for some crazy-looking old hippy in a pin-striped suit who was shouting at Toth, warning him away. Toth ignored the commands and powered forward across the grassy graves, aiming for the far side of the churchyard. He had not got far when something tripped him and he fell. A green nylon tarpaulin closed about his legs and he vanished from view, into an open grave that had been covered to protect it from the rain. The gravedigger leaned on his shovel and watched from a safe distance, neither alarmed nor concerned.

'Bloody vandals!' Austin Potterton shouted at DuCaine. 'This is a site of archaeological importance and he's damaging it. Honestly, young people have no bloody respect for the past.'

John May looked at the watch Arthur Bryant had bought him. The second hand had never worked properly. Bryant's ability to infect every electronic device he touched had apparently spread to mechanical objects as well.

May wondered where his partner had disappeared to this time. It felt as if the pair of them hardly ever worked in tandem any more. Bryant was off sorting through arcane publications in an attempt to prove that London's criminals were influenced by myths from past centuries, while he was trying to cope with the exigencies of a modern metropolis.

Right, he decided, *I'm putting my foot down. It's time he learned that criminals aren't fingered by recourse to thousand-year-old ghosts. If the PCU is to have a future, I have to make Arthur understand how a modern police team works.*

But as he walked to the interview room a few minutes later, he thought, *Fat chance.*

'You can't hold me,' said Toth, sprawled out across a straight-back chair. 'You've got nothing.'

'Why did you run?' DuCaine asked.

'I don't want to talk to you. I'll talk to him, no one else.' He pointed at John May.

'I'll be happy to offer you advice after you've answered a few of PC DuCaine's questions,' said May.

'Then I have nothing to say. I've done no wrong. I'm not obliged to explain anything to anyone.'

'I think he might want to talk about this,' said Meera, carrying in a black plastic bin bag. Dropping it on the floor, she pulled out the stag-man's furry jacket and a handful of knife blades. Behind her, a nervous pregnant girl stepped forward into the room.

'Lizzi, what are you doing here?'

'I had to tell them, Xander. I know where you go at night. I saw you putting on that stupid outfit. I want to find out exactly how many lies you've told me.'

Toth pulled himself upright, and sat in stupefied silence. He was trying to come up with a fresh game plan, but realized there was no escape from the truth. 'Where do you want me to start?' he asked.

'Why don't you let me do it for you?' said Bryant, sauntering into the already over-crowded interview room. 'Can I have a chair? I'm knackered and it's only one o'clock. Is anyone on tea duty? Meera, would you ask April to fill up that huge teapot I saw in the hall? Make sure Crippen's not been near it first. Thank you so much.'

DuCaine dragged in a battered armchair and everyone waited while Bryant squirmed into it. 'The land, the land,' mused Bryant. 'You studied land rights when you worked at ADAPT, didn't you?'

'So what?'

'And the more you found out about the practice of coopting properties, the less you liked what they were asking you to do. Is offering someone money to leave their home a bribe? I'm sure ADAPT's lawyers would argue that no illegal acts were ever committed. But you saw the rules being bent, the meetings with councillors and property developers, and finally decided to complain. I found a pretty hefty file on you in Camden Council's planning department.'

'I tried the official channels but nobody would listen to me,' said Toth. 'So I switched to unofficial ones.'

'But all you could find were a few disgruntled householders who eventually caved in and sold out. After all, everyone wanted to see King's Cross restored to being a decent neighbourhood. That's why the ADAPT Group was offered so many sweeteners to start undoing the damage that the railway had done, clearing uninhabitable slums and unrentable factories. They're doing London a huge favour and making millions in the process. Marianne Waters will probably get an OBE.'

'She's a corrupt, thieving bitch.'

'I assume it was while you were digging into the land rights that you came across the area's extraordinary history. Everything you read made you angrier. Almost everyone who ever came to this site stole from it. The royals arrived and threw out the rightful owners of the land to build a spa. The railway destroyed the churchyard. Now ADAPT is paving it all over. And the final straw, of course – your own background. Your family descended from the great manor of Tothele, which was destroyed and sold off by an earlier generation of land speculators. I found an old photograph of you on your first protest march, dressed in a green suit—'

'The lord of the forest, Jack in the Green,' said Toth. 'I did it to attract a photographer from a local paper.'

'A nice traditional touch, but the novelty soon wears off, doesn't it? You needed to rekindle the fire of publicity for your cause. So you came up with a rather more elaborate outfit.'

'I couldn't think how to make the antlers. Real ones were too heavy.'

'So you riveted together some kitchen knives. Not such a smart move. Meera, how many are in the bag?'

She emptied the bin bag on to the interview desk and counted. 'Twelve.'

'But you still didn't attract enough attention. Did you enjoy going out on your late-night jaunts?'

'I was doing it for a reason.'

'But you started enjoying it, all the same. Who was the girl you abducted?'

'What girl?' asked Lizzi.

'She works at the club,' said Toth. 'I met her in the café. I was just mucking about with her. Call her if you don't believe me.'

'Have you been seeing a girl behind my back?' Lizzi fumed.

'That's why no one reported her missing,'

DuCaine explained. 'She wasn't a victim; she was a girl he fancied and picked up. When did you make the jump from faking kidnaps to committing murder?'

'He didn't,' said Meera. 'His girlfriend here can vouch for his whereabouts over the last few nights.'

'Mr Toth would have been quite happy to hitch a ride on the publicity,' Bryant added. 'Except that so far no journalist has bothered to link his appearance with the murders. A bit too clever for your own good, weren't you? The only person whose attention you managed to attract was me.'

'What about the hairs on Cavendish's trousers?' asked May.

'He was out at the site with us, remember?' said Bryant. 'He was there at the spot where they found Delaney's body. We all picked up mud and hair in the field. All it proves is that Cavendish and Shaggy here wandered over the same swampy ground, along with everyone else.'

'So what are you going to charge me with?' Toth demanded. 'It's not a crime to bring attention to injustice.'

'It is when it nearly results in a death,' said May. 'And we could do you for carrying an offensive weapon, or rather twelve of them. Go on then, Shaggy, you've had your Scooby-Doo moment; now bugger off before we beat you with sticks.'

'The outfit stays here,' DuCaine warned. 'We're still going to run some tests on those knife blades.'

'I'm surprised you're prepared to let him go,' said Meera, disappointed.

'He's going to get a roasting when he gets home,' said May. 'We have a bigger fish to catch. We've exorcized a ghost, that's all.'

'He could have killed someone.'

'I'm more interested in someone who *is* killing people, Meera. Keep your focus on that. It's a small recompense, but at least Marianne Waters and her team can inform their workforce that there's nothing super-natural to fear. The land doesn't throw up ancient spectres to stop the progress of the centuries, a myth which Mr Bryant has actually helped to dispel for once.'

'But the cause of these three deaths still lies in the past,' Bryant insisted, 'and there's the ritual element of the beheadings. I found some other old documents in the archives–'

'Arthur, there's no time left for this kind of – *excavation*. We need to know everything about Cavendish's movements – who he met, where he went, who his friends were, if there's anything missing from his desk or his home. Because it still looks like somebody is out to stop ADAPT from continuing with their project.'

'He lives in Brighton,' said Bryant. 'Commutes up every morning. We won't get any help from the Brighton police. We'll lose a day sending someone down.'

'DuCaine, handle this with Longbright,' said May. 'Hit Cavendish's office hard and work through all of his business contacts, then go to Brighton when you've finished and do the same there. Two of you will do it in half the time. I can't take Dan off the crime scene.'

'This is insane,' Meera protested. 'How are we supposed to make an arrest? We. Have. No. Suspects. Do. You. Understand?'

'Oh, we've done it before,' said Bryant cheerfully.

'With all due respect, sir, you've given us a bloke dressed as a deer—'

'A stag.'

'And bugger-all else.'

May held up a hand. 'Let him do it his way, Meera. At this stage it's not going to make a lot of difference.'

'Thank you,' said Bryant. 'You know, I think this is a very important case for us. The answer lies less in uncovering an identity and more about understanding why it has happened.'

'A man is going around beheading unconnected strangers and you're not interested in blaming anyone?' Meera was horrified. 'Tell that to Cavendish's family when they ask you where his ears are.' She turned to May. 'Honestly, the way you encourage him!'

'Listen, Meera,' said May softly, 'a week ago he was ready to give up and die. I'd rather have him back in the field investigating feudal rights and necromantic rituals than leave him at home to rot. It doesn't make any difference to the investigation. Show some respect, for once in your life.'

The makeshift interview room filled up with arguing members of staff. The rain which seemed to fall so frequently on King's Cross grew steadily heavier until it spilled from the blackened drainpipes and gutters of the warehouse, dampening the warren of rooms where once occultists and magicians had argued about spells and incantations.

35

A VIBRATION IN THE AIR

Arthur Bryant's chair creaked as he studied the damp patches on the ceiling. The rain ticked against the windows. The dusty bare bulb above them fizzled. 'What do you know about chaos theory?' he asked.

'A small change in initial conditions can drastically alter the long-term behaviour of a system,' said May without looking up. 'Invented in 1961.'

'You're probably wondering why I want to know.'

'Nothing you ever say or do surprises me any more, Arthur.'

'I'm thinking about the sheer number of people who pass through this area. Instead of asking ourselves why there's so much crime, why aren't we asking why there's so little? Every type of person, every walk of life, all brushing up against each other, everyone in a different mental state. Why aren't they all randomly slaughtering one another over trespassed territory and differences of creed?'

'They've been sedated by a steady diet of celebrity gossip, alcohol and junk food.' May looked up at his partner. Bryant was *thinking*. Always a worrying sign.

'Clearly social conventions prevail, but I think that each of their little butterfly movements, every flapping wing, disturbs the filthy air of King's Cross a little. Their lives touch each other faintly, but they carry the effect away with them to other places. Imagine – an embittered, lonely man passing through the station sees a beautiful young woman and feels a pang of sadness for the life he never had with her. That feeling contributes, in a tiny way, to his future actions. You see what I'm getting at?'

'No. Your every utterance is a mystery to

me, Arthur. Am I supposed to find relevance in this to our investigation, to see that in some indirect way it will help us locate a murderer?'

'You must agree that we resolve situations by understanding motivation.'

'And you think reading a book on chaos theory will help you do that?'

'Well, all crimes ultimately reduce down to cause and effect, and I've a feeling this will more than most.'

'You've a feeling? Is that it? A trembling in the air that will shape itself into a dirty great big arrow that points at a murderer? Can you find me something concrete? Preferably by lunchtime?'

Bryant looked at him very gravely. 'I'll do my best, of course,' he said, gathering his hat. 'I may have to take some very unusual steps to do so.'

'No, tell me,' said May. 'We've been partners for long enough; I should at least have some vague inkling of how your mind works.'

Bryant stopped and ruminated for a moment. Crippen was about to enter the room when he saw Bryant and thought better of it. 'Well, you remember the Highwayman? How we had no idea what his motive might be? In this case we have a company armed with a genetic determination to turn a massive profit, and the need to remove any obstacles in its way. But if the victims were obstacles, we are left with three seemingly random deaths using the same bizarre mutilation, so our first supposition must be modified. It's like mechanics versus technology. With something like, oh, let's say the engine of a 1959 Ford Popular, if something went wrong you worked out what was wrong and put it right, and then it would work. With a modern computer, if something's wrong you leave it for a minute and try again and then it works, for no known reason.'

'That is the least satisfactory explanation I've ever heard for anything,' said May, exasperated. 'Either we're looking at a case of sinister property dealings or we're hunting a monster – we can't both be right.'

'Well, that's where I think you're wrong. There are common factors to all three deaths. Look.' Bryant held up a Google Map printout with three sites ringed in red felt-tip pen. 'Here's where the bodies were found. Draw a line between them to get a rough triangle.' He tapped the sheet with his pen. 'What's in the middle of it?'

May squinted at the page. In the centre stood St Pancras Old Church. 'Oh, I get it. You're going to tell me they were murdered by a deranged pagan who still believes in an ancient head-severing sacrificial rite.'

'It would be tempting to believe so,

because of the date.'

'What do you mean?'

'Sacrificial ceremonies associated with the severing of the head traditionally climax at the end of the third week in May, so his timing is spot-on. But I certainly think it's someone who knows the churchyard well.'

'Why? What in Heaven's name has that got to do with it?'

'Simply this. Try to think of another place in central London so utterly desolate that you could dispose of the bodies of three grown men without being picked up on CCTV. There are a few cemeteries, I suppose, but they're nearly all locked at night. It has to be someone who's familiar with the churchyard and its immediate surroundings – the biggest construction site in the city. I just have to find a way to vibrate the air. I have to force him out.'

'Arthur, you may have a point there, but please, we need to present a united front on this. Go and hang out with your necromancers and astrologers, but come back with some tangible proof.'

'Jolly good. I shall do just that.'

'Fine. And call me if you get stuck.' May watched, shaking his head in wonder, as his old friend looped his scarf around his neck, took up his walking stick and stumped off along the corridor, into darkness.

36

ST PANCRAS DAY

Ed Tremble, Camden Council's land registry officer, seemed to be covered in more dust than ever. Bryant was starting to wonder if they stored the man in a broom cupboard overnight. There were fresh flecks of white in his hair. He caught Bryant staring and apologized.

'Oh, I was painting my kitchen ceiling last night. It's emulsion.'

Bryant threw him a disbelieving glance, then shifted Maggie Armitage into his line of vision. 'This is my friend Mrs Armitage,' he explained. 'She's going to help me go through the files.'

'Hello, Mrs Armitage. Are you an archivist?' asked Tremble.

'No, love, I'm a witch. A white one, so don't disturb yourself.'

'Ha-ha, very good.' Tremble looked unsure whether it was good or not. 'I've laid out all the documents you asked for.' On the plan chest before them a large-scale Ordnance Survey map had been constructed from dozens of separate overlapping pages, taped together. 'I'll just be in my cupboard when you need me.' *I knew it*, thought Bryant.

'That's mine, just down there.' Tremble pointed to a wooden cubicle filled with precarious stacks of folders and shambled off.

'I like him; he's come in useful to you, he has the aura for it. So – what are we looking for?' Maggie rubbed her hands together briskly, jangling her bracelets. It was freezing in the basement of the land records office.

'Mr Tremble has assembled copies of all of the land rights the ADAPT Group purchased before it could submit its plans to the Council for approval,' Bryant explained. 'The answer's here among these documents. This case is about ownership.'

'I don't understand why you're so sure.'

'Maddox Cavendish had helped to buy land for ADAPT, and Terry Delaney was hired to help clear it. That leaves Adrian Jesson, who has no connections with the company beyond the fact that his body was found near its offices. Jesson was an obsessive-compulsive, involved in a bitter feud with a rival collector of memorabilia named Richard Standover. It turns out that Standover lives with Jesson's sister in Spain, so Jesson has another reason to hate him.'

'Has anyone checked up on him?'

'Janice found out that Standover was in Majorca with the sister on the day his rival

336

was murdered, so that's a dead end.'

'It doesn't mean he wasn't involved. You should have him brought in.'

'Comic-book collector psychically slaughters three while holidaying abroad? Doesn't seem very likely.' He groped in his overcoat pocket and produced something that looked like a ball of brown modelling clay. 'Do you want some of this?'

Maggie examined the lump with suspicion. 'I don't know. What is it?'

'Carrot cake with yoghurt icing. It's come out of its packet.'

'No, thanks. I'm trying to lose weight.'

'I can't imagine why. It's not as if you make an effort to attract men.'

'I want to feel good about myself. Don't be so horrible. Your aura turns a very unhealthy shade of heliotrope when you're rude to people. Beneath the witch I'm a woman, you know. I do have feelings.'

'Well, can you not? We need to get back to the map. I want to see if ADAPT bought everything legally. I don't want to go back through the past property owners or check the original boundary lines – we'll be here for ever if I do that. What we do is place the last owner's deed details on top of each property and see if that turns up any anomalies.'

'This is such a boy's job,' Maggie complained. 'Making lists and rearranging the order of things.'

'You offered to help.'

'Only because Daphne is servicing my boiler this morning and I can't get in the kitchen. She wanted to cast a spell for it but I told her to use a wrench.'

They worked in quiet harmony for an hour, but Tremble had done most of the preparation for them. Soon they had filled the great triangular map with names, addresses, dates and purchase prices.

Bryant pointed at the map. 'So, this area to the east was entirely covered in factories and light industrial units... But on the other side of the canal there were five rows of terraced houses. The canal itself and the paths on either side of it are owned by British Waterways. That just leaves this bit, here.' He tapped a small oblong plot on the map. 'No name. Open space?'

'No, it was part of a street called – hang on, I saw it here a minute ago – Camley Lane. It should have an owner.'

'It's right at the middle of the company's plan for the extension to the shopping centre. They can't build on it without the transfer of title.'

'Look, there are three others in the same street that changed owners during the Second World War.'

'A typical bombing pattern,' Bryant pointed out. 'One house wasn't rebuilt, and it doesn't look as if the owner ever sold on the property deeds.' He summoned Ed Tremble from his cupboard. 'Ed, there are no property deeds for number eleven, Camley Lane.'

'Interesting that you picked this one. It was bombed flat during the War. The remains of the house were pulled down and the site was cleared. A small local jam factory occupied the site for five or six years in the fifties. After that it became a café and then a pub, the Tothele Manor Tavern, and eventually that also closed.'

'It's as if the ground itself was bad luck,' remarked Maggie.

'The company wanted permission to build on the land, but due to the property's tangled history there's no current deed of ownership on file.'

'What happens in that situation?' asked Bryant.

'According to British law an occupier must last for eleven years on a piece of property in this area before claiming the right to own it, so I imagine the land belonged not to the pub or the jam factory, but to the original owner of the bombed-out house.'

'Why?'

'Because most of the pre-war owners in this street were on their land for far longer than eleven years, and it would have been officially registered in the resident's name.'

'And if ADAPT can't locate the deeds?'

'They have to wait for the time limit to be reached.'

'But they're preparing to build on that section beside the canal right now. Are they acting illegally?'

'Not necessarily. They might have timed their work order to commence from the expiry date.'

'Is there any way of finding out the actual expiry date?'

'Give me a minute.' Tremble disappeared.

'Corporate skulduggery,' said Maggie while they waited for his return. 'You're thinking they turned to murder, aren't you, Arthur?'

'I'm sure of it. Thousands of people displaced and relocated, billions spent on contracts, funding raised and companies created for Europe's biggest railway project. Suppose one difficult man stood in the way of all this progress? Imagine how easy it might have seemed to simply get rid of him. What if something went wrong, resulting in the deaths of two others?'

'If you think captains of industry colluded to quietly remove one blockage in the system,' said Maggie, 'why would they draw attention to themselves by cutting off people's heads?'

'I have no answer for that.'

'I do. They're following this area's ancient tradition of severing the heads of sacrificial victims, in order to win themselves favour with the pagan gods of the forest who are the real owners of the land.'

'Dear Lord.' Bryant ran a hand over his face. 'I'm the first person to back you up when it comes to spiritual matters, Margaret, but I really can't see myself explaining that to the Home Office.'

'Fair point,' said Maggie with a shrug. 'Let's keep looking.'

'Here you are,' said Tremble, returning with a yellowed sheet of paper. 'It's unusual for such a deed to have a specific expiry date, but in this case it appears to be exactly one hundred and twenty years after the original land purchase.'

'That's in three days' time,' said Bryant, attempting to whistle through his false teeth.

'St Pancras Day,' said Maggie, awed. 'A day of great mystical significance. A time for the greatest sacrifice.'

37

HEALTH RESTOR'D AND PRESERV'D

Oliver Golifer, the unfortunately named owner of the Newman Street Picture Library, was digging the dirt from his dado rail with a golf tee when Arthur Bryant knocked on the window.

'It's open,' Golifer mouthed through the glass. 'I'm having a spring clean. Help me down, will you?' He leaned on Bryant's shoulder while lowering his massive bulk from the ladder. 'I've found what you're looking for. We have a lot of photographs taken in King's Cross because it was often used as a film location.' He pulled out a box of photographs from behind his counter. 'Here, the Guinness bottle-washing factory, the Tothele Manor Tavern, and further back, the house that was there in 1939.'

Bryant found himself looking at a sharp monochrome photograph of number 11, Camley Lane. He turned to the second picture, which showed a cellar surrounded by blackened timbers and smouldering bricks.

'They were unlucky. Read the back.'

***Daily Sketch*, 12 November 1940**

Mrs Irene Porter lost her husband Alf when her home suffered a direct hit from a Luftwaffe incendiary bomb last night. Her son was away on army manoeuvres at the time of the raid. She was taken in by Harold and Beatrice Barker, who live in the house opposite, at number 14, Camley Lane. The King's Cross community consists largely of railway workers, who were quick to pull together and rehouse Mrs Porter and the others who survived the attack.

Golifer took the picture in one meaty fist. 'There's a companion shot to this. I've seen it somewhere. I think it's filed under "King's Cross History". Your Mr May has been nagging at me to catalogue the library electronically, you know.'

'Why would you want to do that? This way you know where everything is.'

'Exactly,' Golifer agreed, rooting in a shoebox full of sepia snapshots. 'Here we go. The same *Daily Sketch* photographer.'

The photograph showed a brick circle with a dark centre. 'What am I looking at?' asked Bryant.

'Turn it over.'

12 November 1940

The bombing of Camley Lane reveals the remains of St Chad's Well. This ancient well stood on the once sacred 'River of Wells' at Battle Bridge in King's Cross. Valued for its healing properties, water was drawn up and heated in a great cauldron to restore the well-being of the many visitors to the pump room and elegant spa gardens constructed on the site. Beneath a sign reading 'Health Restor'd and Preserv'd' stood the Lady of the Well, dressed in her traditional black bonnet and gown.

It is said that the well appeared to spring from the ground at the bidding of Edmund Ironside's sword as he vanquished King Canute in 1016.

St Chad's Well was considered the oldest and most important well in all of London. St Chad became Bishop of Mercia in 669 and was ordained the Patron Saint of Springs & Wells. St Chad's Place is still to be found in King's Cross.

'Mrs Porter's house was built over a sacred well,' said Bryant, ruminatively chewing a piece of carrot cake. 'So what site was Delaney clearing just before he died?'

At five twenty on the same evening, Leslie Faraday put in a call to Jack Renfield's mobile phone.

Faraday: Ah, Mr Renfield. I'm glad I caught you.

Renfield: You rang my mobile. I always answer.

Faraday: Yes, well, be that as it may, I was rather hoping you were about to call me.

Renfield: I didn't see any point in ringing if I didn't have anything to tell you.

Faraday: Well, I thought you would, you see. A rather alarming report has reached my ears.

Renfield: (impatiently) What about?

Faraday: Somebody at Camden Council rang to tell me that Mr Bryant had been in questioning officials about building plans.

Renfield: Yes, he's conducting your investigation. He's following a lead.

Faraday: He had a witch with him.

Renfield: A what?

Faraday: A witch, Mr Renfield. Cauldron, pointy hat, talking cat, you know, a woman who consorts with the devil and believes she can cast spells.

Renfield: I have no information on that.

Faraday: Oh. I find that very disappointing. I recall specifically requesting that you keep an eye on Mr Bryant, something you've singularly failed to do.

Renfield: I've reported to you every night on the progress of the investigation.

Faraday: And you would have me believe that nothing unusual has happened?

Renfield: That's right.

Faraday: You don't call witchcraft unusual?

Renfield: Bryant takes friends along to help him sometimes.

Faraday: Friends, plural? Who else has he brought along to this private investigation? A wizard, perhaps? Some performing dwarfs? Are you laughing?

Renfield: (Coughing) No, sir.

Faraday: Do you understand that my report will go to Mr Kasavian, and if he finds anything untoward, he will take steps to bring prosecutions against everyone involved in this investigation?

Renfield: If that's the case, it's not in my interest to report to you, is it?

Faraday: But I've issued you with a formal request.

Renfield: Yeah, and I'm ignoring it.

Faraday: It's a command.

Renfield: Well, which is it – a request or a command?

Faraday: (Heatedly) It's a ... it doesn't matter what it is, you have to do what you're told.

Renfield: I've got a better idea. You can stick your request – and your command – up your arse.

Faraday: I find your attitude highly unsatisfactory, Mr Renfield, and what's more I fully intend– Hello? Hello?

Outside London, beyond the great grey saucepan lid of cloud that covered the metropolis, it was a raw, beautiful day. Ragged white scraps of cloud tumbled across the Sussex downs, and even Brighton's faded appeal was partially restored when viewed from the end of the Palace Pier. Fifty years earlier, the pink pavements and sky-blue railings had signified a town of civic heraldry in which a generation of vaguely lost spinsters and disappointed colonels had made their homes. Now the resort had been designated a city, with all of the ills that such status conferred. The burghers of Brighton had neglected the parts they disliked until those parts simply went away, and had added on bits that made them money, leaving windswept concourses filled with chain stores that

346

could be found in any town, anywhere.

Maddox Cavendish had lived in a new development overlooking the ruins of the collapsed West Pier. The porter refused to believe that DuCaine and Longbright were police officers, and it took several phone calls to get them inside the building. The apartment had been built to showcase its main feature, a wooden deck overlooking the sparkling sea. 'He was making good money,' DuCaine noted, thumping around the flat in his size-twelve boots.

'His employment record has him down as single. No photos anywhere, very impersonal.' Longbright stood in the centre of the living room and turned slowly. 'Very tidy. Gay, maybe.'

'Does it matter?'

'I'm just trying to get a mental picture.' She started opening drawers. 'I love snooping through other people's lives, don't you?'

'Not really,' DuCaine admitted. 'Not when they've just been murdered.'

'He's hardly a typical victim.' She riffled through a book of cheque stubs and turned out a pile of ATM receipts. 'He drew out two thousand pounds in cash just over two weeks ago.'

DuCaine searched the wardrobe and bookcases, but found only business suits and volumes on accounting, architecture and self-help.

Longbright opened a black leather diary and checked the pages. 'Oh, you're going to love this,' she said, reading. *"LUNCH T. DELANEY. One p.m."* Maddox Cavendish *had lunch* with Terry Delaney three days before Delaney died. Delaney was meeting him at the ADAPT Group headquarters, but it doesn't say where they ate, so presumably it wasn't somewhere that needed a reservation.'

'What the hell was an architect doing having lunch with a construction worker?'

'When two people of different social status break bread together, it's usually because one of them wants something.'

'Cynical.'

'No, pragmatic. What would Cavendish want from a day labourer? Did he fancy him?'

'I dunno. Maybe he was having some construction work done at home.'

Longbright called in their discovery to the team, who set about talking to restaurant staff in the building-site area. Meanwhile, the two detectives divided Cavendish's apartment into sections and searched every square on the grid, but turned up nothing else.

'If we catch the fast train back, we can give ourselves an extra hour,' Longbright told DuCaine.

'Why, is there something you wanted to do?'

'Yeah, I want to go on the pier.'

'It's a murder investigation, Janice.'

'I haven't been out of London in more than a year. I hardly ever get a good night's sleep in town. I'm knackered. I just want to get some sea air into my head. Can we do that?'

'Come on, then.'

DuCaine offered to buy her a candy floss but Longbright preferred a plate of whelks smothered in vinegar and white pepper. They leaned on the railings watching the seagulls screeching and wheeling over the remains of the fishermen's bait buckets.

'Do you ever get times when you feel really lonely?' DuCaine asked.

'Everyone in the force does.'

'You dated a copper, didn't you?'

'For eleven years. A bloody nightmare. I hardly ever saw him.'

'So you wouldn't do it again?'

'Meera said that the nurse who sutured her arm had gone into the profession because she heard doctors were good kissers. My mother used to say that people in the emergency services were more passionate lovers because they saw so much death that they needed to celebrate life. And that it also made them really untidy at home, because keeping things neat wasn't important.'

'You think that's true?'

'What is it with all the questions?'

'I want to go out with you.'

'What, on a date?' The idea caught her by surprise.

'On a boat. On a bike. Yes, on a date.'

Longbright narrowed her eyes, appraising him. 'Don't you think you're a little young for me? Besides, you don't know if I'm a good kisser.'

At the end of the pier, beside the rattling ghost train and beneath the diving white gulls, PC Liberty DuCaine found out.

38

SHADOW FIGURE

'Harry was my old man,' said Keith Barker. 'He lived in Camley Lane right to the end of his life. He was a station guard at St Pancras, and his wife worked in the ticket office. Not my mum, you understand, she died in 1964 – his second wife. You'll never guess what my grandfather's job was: he collected the holes from bus tickets. He used to box 'em up and sell 'em outside the church for confetti – at least that's what he told us.'

At five p.m. on Saturday, Arthur Bryant had arrived at the Barker household. That was twenty minutes ago, and Mr Barker had yet to pause for breath. The little flat off the Holloway Road was filled with trophies and awards for keeping tropical fish, but there was no room in the place to put an aquarium. Bryant decided that it would be a good idea to keep Barker away from the subject of fish, or he'd be there all day. There was a time when men like Mr Barker would have sat at home in a collarless shirt and braces. The old man seated before him was wearing trainers and a shiny blue tracksuit.

'I've got a heart condition so I don't get out now,' Mr Barker explained. 'All our family lived around Camley Lane, generations of us, which was handy 'cause you could keep an eye on the olduns. It turned into a rough area, though, 'cause a lot of traders moved into the arches after the War, and so many people were bombed out that the quickest way to make a bit of money was to open a lodging house. Every house in King's Cross had a dozen boarders in it, and naturally you got trouble, what with them all living on top of each other.'

'I'm particularly interested in the Porters' house,' said May, attempting to guide Barker back on track.

'Bombed to matchsticks, that place,' said Mr Barker. 'When Mrs Porter lost her husband and her home, she went to live with

Grandad. Later on, she came to live with us, 'cause she was like one of the family by then. There hadn't been a warning that night, see. Grandad said the air-raid wardens were quick enough to turn up if you had a light showing through your curtains, but they were so busy ticking things off in their little books that sometimes there was no one manning the sirens. The nearest siren to us was on the roof of the St Pancras Old Church, but half the time they kept the churchyard gates locked at night, 'cause they didn't want no one sleeping in the graveyard. Four flying bombs fell around here. Some streets were totally bombed out of existence.'

'Why didn't they rebuild Mrs Porter's house?' asked Bryant.

'There was nothing to rebuild. Plus, there was the problem of the well.'

'The house was built over St Chad's Well.'

'That's right. None of us knew it was there, although Auntie Rene – that's what we called her – she complained it had always been damp, and she swore that her husband had known it was there, because he'd talked to her about it but she didn't really listen. The authorities sent some bloke from the historical society down to look at it, but he didn't do nothing, then the rubble from the bombing was used to block it up and they put prefabs on top for the families who'd been bombed out. Trouble is, they was made of asbestos, so they had to come down. Then they extended the old jam factory over the land, but that wasn't successful, so finally they turned the extension into a pub, the Stag's Head. I moved here, but I still went back of course, 'cause all my old mates were around there. They hung on waiting to be bought out, 'cause there was talk of the railways buying the land.'

'Then it was finally sold to the ADAPT Group.'

'I figured that's why you're here, because of Terry Delaney.'

Bryant was brought up short. 'You know him?'

'He came to see me, 'cause ADAPT decided to go ahead and clear the site completely, and they brought him in, 'cause he knew the area. They brought the bull-dozers in but there was a question over who owned the land. Terry was hired to tear down the remains of the Stag's Head. He told me he was a bit of an amateur historian and knew a lot about the street. He tore up the foundations and found the well, but of course it had been filled in with bricks and then concrete had been poured over it, so there was nothing much left to see.'

'So how did he end up coming to you?'

'He found the deed. See, old Mr Porter never got around to putting his house deeds in the bank. A lot of people didn't, in them days. He kept his important documents in a tin box in the basement. Nobody ever went down there much 'cause it was too wet, and bad for the chest. I suppose when the house was bombed the box fell into the well. It couldn't have fallen very far, though, or Terry would never have found it. They've been turning up all sorts of things on those old properties, but apparently you only get a short time to dig up the site before they're covered by the new buildings.'

Bryant thought of the remains of London's Roman basilica, now only viewable from the basement of the hairdresser's off Gracechurch Street that had been built over it, and the sportswear shop that had housed the ancient and venerable London Stone for so many years. Notoriously, archaeologists had been given just six weeks to uncover treasures beneath a part of the London Wall before it was concreted into an office car park.

'You're telling me that Mr Delaney found the original freehold property deeds to number eleven Camley Lane and traced them to you?'

'He used a pile driver to break the well open, and there was the box. Terry thought it was a bomb at first. He told me there are over five thousand unexploded bombs still buried in London soil. He said he wanted to return the deeds to their rightful owner. Thought that way they'd have a chance to claim the land before the registration date passed, 'cause it was due soon.'

The deed expires on the day of the greatest sacrifice, thought Bryant. *I knew it. The city has plans for us all.*

'I explained that I wasn't the owner, that Mrs Porter had just lived with us until she died.'

'So who is the actual owner?' Bryant asked.

'I told him,' said Mr Barker, 'that would now be her granddaughter. But I didn't have her address.'

After Dan Banbury had visited her at Yield to the Night, Janice Longbright had reached a decision. She would no longer wear the obscure lingerie brands from the 1950s that were both uncomfortable and inappropriate for work. She would stop dressing like a post-war movie starlet. She had kept her signature look for many years, but you couldn't be young for ever, and it was time to start dressing like a woman in the full bloom of her middle years. Away would go the bleaches and lipsticks, as worn by Diana Dors and Jayne Mansfield. No more cleavage-revealing sweaters or strappy heels. She had not dressed for men, but to make herself feel good.

So she had bought herself jeans, trainers and a shirt, and started to look like everyone else.

Bad timing, Janice, she decided now. Because she was lying on Liberty DuCaine's sofa bed in his flat in Vauxhall, wishing she wasn't wearing her sensible Marks & Spencer underwear.

When you haven't touched anyone else's lips for a long time, Longbright thought, *it's a really weird sensation.* Her ex-boyfriend's kisses had lacked subtlety, consisting of either pecks or tongues. Liberty, however, had explored her mouth with gentle languor. For a brief moment she realized what she had been missing for so long.

He was a physically imposing man, and now he seemed to take up the entire room. He surrounded her with gentle warmth, his thighs touching her hips, his palms on either side of her face, his soft breathing a smile in the dark.

At some point – she could not later recall when – he tore off his shirt with thrilling enthusiasm; he threw the garment behind him and it settled over a lamp. His soft skin smelled of cinnamon but there was a faint, clean base-note of sweat that lingered on her hands. She heard herself say, 'Maybe we shouldn't do this,' but didn't believe her own words.

His chest hair formed a neat black trapezoid, a ladder of tight curls tracing to his navel and down into the waistband of his jeans. The wide, dry breadth of his hand covered her bare stomach. The shock of a man's cool touch on her was extraordinary; she could not recall the last time someone had cupped her so gently, unfolding her desires with such lightness and loving care.

She sank down deep into his IKEA cushions, her PCU uniform scratching against the blanket on the sofa bed. Suddenly it felt so tiring to be an English policewoman, to behave correctly wherever she went, to be strapped into a tight uniform and provide a role model for others all the time. She wanted him to tear at her clothes, to press her deep into the comforting night, the muscles in his thick brown arms lifting and widening as he raised his body over her. She felt him connecting with her at six or seven points, through toes and hips to mouths, and wondered if they could simply melt into each other, becoming one.

It was like a romance conducted backwards, starting with the fierce, hard culmination, his eyes never leaving hers, his body moving with increased connection, gentler and gentler, resolving to a faint and tender kiss.

She fought to stop herself from being sensible. She knew they had to work together. She knew that it could create problems if they decided not to be so close again. She knew she had to get rid of the IKEA cushions. Her eyes were fully open to all the attendant dangers.

But right now, on this cold, starry night in May, it seemed better to let them gently close.

After Longbright had called him from Brighton about the connection between two of the victims, Bryant had barely been able to contain his excitement. His interview with Keith Barker had lent further shape to the ideas that were developing in his head.

As the two detectives walked along the rainswept Caledonian Road that night, heading for John May's BMW, he started piecing together events. Old Mr Barker did not realize it, but he had just placed an international corporation at the heart of a conspiracy to murder.

'While Cavendish was clearing land rights for the ADAPT Group,' Bryant told May, 'he found that in the case of a few plots of land, ownership couldn't be verified – but the project has been in development for thirty years, so what's a few more months? All ADAPT had to do was wait for the rights to lapse, and that's what happened in most cases. I suppose if the worse came to the worst they could take a chance and quietly go ahead with construction, hoping that nobody would come forward. But then Terry Delaney threw a spanner in the works. He turned up a house deed, and went to Maddox Cavendish with news of his find. That was their first contact; Delaney rang Cavendish for advice. Then Cavendish took Delaney out to lunch and tried to obtain the deed. Whatever happened over that lunch, Delaney didn't feel comfortable about simply surrendering the deed to ADAPT, and told Cavendish that he was determined to trace the rightful owner. Cavendish needed the deed to stay hidden in order to prevent the blocking of the project, or he had to be able to purchase it. But now it had surfaced in the worst possible manner. He must have been having kittens.'

'How crucial is the property to the group's plans?' asked May, ushering Bryant into his car.

'Let me show you.' Bryant pulled a crumpled roll of paper from his pocket and spread it out on the dashboard. 'Most of the houses in Camley Street were subdivided before the War, except for number eleven. Porter's garden extended all the way to the edge of the canal and down both sides of the property. It's right in the middle of the shopping centre's main wing. This isn't a proposal that can simply be ditched and moved a few hundred feet to the left – it's taken years for the public hearings and for the Council to approve the plans. Worse still, any publicity could bring to light the fact that the house is constructed over one of Britain's oldest sacred sites, and although archaeologists usually get limited time frames to examine ancient remains, this one might be important enough to have a stay of execution granted.'

'So you think Delaney was trying to return the deeds to their rightful owner when he was killed? But if this is about property, why was it necessary to commit murder?'

'One scenario presents itself. Cavendish realized he had single-handedly screwed up Europe's biggest building project. He had failed to locate a key property ownership for the site, and knew that his future was on the line if he didn't resolve the situation. He went to Delaney's apartment and ransacked it, but Delaney returned home early and surprised him. In the ensuing struggle, Delaney died.'

'Come on, Arthur. Cavendish was a small, rather mousy executive. It seems highly un-likely that he would then decide to decapitate Delaney with all the professionalism of a hit man before dragging the rest of his victim's body to a chip shop in the Cally Road.'

'Banbury told me Cavendish wasn't well liked and didn't socialize with the rest of the department, rarely went for a drink with them even when it was someone's birthday.

When he wasn't in the office, he was in the company gym. And they all thought he was too ambitious.'

'But if his bosses got wind of what had happened, others at the ADAPT Group may be culpable to varying degrees. It could take years to prove anything.'

'Yes, that's a problem,' Bryant agreed. 'And derailing the project for a full investigation would be disastrous.'

'So, how would Cavendish have felt, presented with this do-gooder who, over the course of a lunch, decided he'd do the right thing and return the deed?'

'We can assume he panicked, and came to the conclusion that he had no other choice but to set about burgling Delaney's flat.'

'All right, let's say he did; why would he murder two people and remove their heads according to an ancient legend? Where does that leave Adrian Jesson, a coffee-shop manager with no connection to the other two?'

'There's something wrong with the theory,' Bryant admitted. 'Who killed Cavendish? Right now we need to find the woman to whom Delaney passed the property document.'

'What about the rest of the project's key leaders?' asked May. 'Are they suspects? Or are they in need of protection?'

'The only way we'll be able to answer that is by finding out exactly what Cavendish did when Delaney told him he couldn't have that deed.' Bryant shook his head gloomily. 'I have to know what happened, but I don't know how to access the information. I can't turn back time.'

39

THE FIND

A little more than two weeks earlier, the city had been a slightly different place. The PCU had still been in limbo, and Terry Delaney had still been alive.

Delaney watched as the canary-yellow bulldozer roared into reverse, trying to pull itself free from the remaining wall. His work boots found traction in the viscous mud and he quickly moved out of range as the brick slab toppled backwards and crashed over, lifting its concrete base out of the earth, spraying rocks and clumps of soil everywhere.

While the driver of the bulldozer concentrated on shoving the last chunks of rubble back into a pile, Delaney went over to the ragged crater and climbed in. He should have been working in a team today, but the other guy had called in sick, said he had food poisoning. *Alcohol poisoning, more like*, thought Terry as he checked the base of the hole.

Nobody was sure whether there were any foundations to the remains of the building they had just pulled down. The plans didn't show a basement, but they were often wrong. The worst job Terry had ever undertaken was digging out the lower ground floor of a warehouse in Wapping. The buildings on the docks were built without foundations, so their stability was provided by making them pyramid-shaped, with the thickest layers of bricks at the bottom. They had run weeks over schedule on that one.

He checked the perimeter but found no sign of another floor. He was just about to climb out of the hole when he noticed the faint circle of bricks in the very centre of the pit. He knew at once that it was a well; the whole area was peppered with them. Most old factories had drawn up their water from boreholes sunk into the River Fleet. Terry knew a lot about King's Cross. His family on his father's side had come from the area, and he enjoyed studying historical documents, matching what he read with what he had been told by his grandparents. The wells usually ran deep, and upon discovery would have to be reported, studied, then filled in – all in a short space of time, if the work schedule was to be kept to.

He pulled out a couple of the loosened bricks and then shovelled off a layer of earth, but found ragged stumps of concrete poured over broken brickwork; someone had filled it in, probably during the War. But something else had been exposed by the bulldozer, a flattened black box that at first glance appeared to be some kind of land mine. But now he saw that it was made of cheap tin, and had been cemented inside the well wall like a letter box, someone's homemade safe. The lid had been crushed and twisted when the bulldozer had pushed down the wall. He punched it with his gloved hand and it popped off, clattering to the ground. Terry looked up to see if anyone else had noticed.

Inside was just a brown manila envelope, nothing else, but it had once been considered valuable enough to hide. He stuck it inside his jacket and climbed back out of the crater.

The day dragged by. He could feel the heat of the envelope in his pocket. At home later that afternoon, disappointment set in as he opened it and tipped out the contents. A couple of insurance policies, three birth certificates, for Thomas Porter, Irene Porter, and their son, William, and some house deeds to a building long gone. He read the typed print. Number 11, Camley Lane, freehold and valid in perpetuity. Did it mean that whoever held the deeds owned the land?

The next morning, he went to Camden Council on his lunch break and did some research. The ownership of the plot in Camley Lane continued according to the original registration, providing that no other sole tenant had occupied the land for eleven years. Which meant, by his reckoning, that the Porter family still owned it.

Terry Delaney was broke. He was behind on his child support, and hadn't taken his little girl anywhere nice in months. He did not want to go through life getting into a financial hole every time his van's insurance came up for renewal. But it would not be right to claim the land for himself. It wouldn't hurt to check up and see if the Porters were still in the area. Terry knew what was going on to the site of number 11, Camley Lane, and how much it was costing. The deed might be worth a fortune. Better, he thought, that the Porters should have what was rightfully theirs than let some faceless corporation get away with stealing it. Perhaps they would even reward him for bringing the document to light. And if they didn't want it, or he couldn't trace them, maybe the ADAPT Group would pay for the find.

The casual phone call left Maddox Cavendish in a cold sweat.

Ever since he had realized that the documentation for Plot BL827 was missing, he'd been praying that no one would pick up on his mistake. He'd been working on the project for almost thirteen years, and still couldn't believe he had managed to overlook the plot of land, despite all the tabulating and cross-referencing he had painstakingly carried out. The system was so complex that Sammi, his assistant, left him with all the data inputting.

And now this call, from a moronic bloody workman of all people, saying that he was in possession of a valuable property deed, and was having trouble returning it to the rightful owner.

Cavendish had managed to talk him into a meeting. He would go in with an offer and strike a simple deal in hard cash. Workmen wanted everything off the books, didn't they? The deed could then be filed and forgotten, and he would trim the cash payment from the accounts system.

He would take Delaney to lunch – that was it. Buy him a fancy meal and a couple of bottles of wine, loosen his tongue, put him at ease. Cavendish pushed back in his office chair and started to relax. The worst was over. The mistake could be rectified. All he had to do was stay cool and treat Delaney like any other client who needed winning over.

He booked Plateau, on the fourth floor of Canada Square in Canary Wharf – glamorous white furnishings, floor-to-ceiling glass, fabulous food, what could go wrong?

The lunch was disastrous. Cavendish had appeared arrogant and dismissive, and Delaney wasn't impressed by the restaurant's good taste. Cavendish realized that he had underestimated Delaney, who had clearly done his research. He had left the deed at home, but had written down the wording to prove it was in his possession. When asked about the expiry date, he cheerfully informed Cavendish that there wasn't one, and that the property rights would pass to whoever held the deed in perpetuity. The only good thing was that Delaney didn't seem to know about the eleven-year rule. He wouldn't lie to an executive, surely?

So, how much was ADAPT willing to pay for it?

When Cavendish named the figure of £2,500, Delaney laughed in his face. No deal, he said, swigging back his wine with a vulgarity that made Cavendish wince. Not unless the amount could be quadrupled. But to do that, Cavendish knew he would need to seek permission from the company accountant, and that meant telling Marianne Waters what had happened. It was bad enough that his assistant might already know about the problem; he had foolishly left the planning-permission files open on his computer.

'You'll have to give me a few days,' Cavendish warned him. 'I can't get that kind of money together overnight.'

'I don't care if you have to draw it out of your personal savings,' Delaney countered. 'If you don't come through in the next couple of days I'll find a way to pass the deed to the owners, and the entire project will come to a halt.'

'You'll get nothing that way.'

'I don't care,' said Delaney. 'Two years ago you called me in to carry out a demolition, and fired me halfway through the job. I couldn't get compensation because you'd kept the job off the books. I'll be happy enough just repaying the compliment.'

Cavendish returned to the office and went to see the accountant, who referred him to Marianne Waters. No money could be authorized without her signature. He paused outside her door, but could not bring himself to go in. His entire future was at stake. He looked down at the contact number Delaney had given him, and realized that the construction worker wasn't so smart after all.

He had scribbled it on the back of his business card. Which meant that Cavendish could get his home address.

Stopping by his office to grab his coat, he

headed out into the streets of King's Cross, to find someone, anyone, who would be prepared to commit a burglary.

40

COMPLICATIONS

Longbright was awakened by the sound of rain in a bedroom that was clearly not hers. She raised her head and looked across the pillows. Liberty DuCaine was lying on his back snoring faintly. *Oh, my God,* she thought, *I didn't,* and knew at once that she had because her underpants were hanging on the bedside-table lamp. Her next thoughts were, in swift succession: *We have to work together, he'll be so embarrassed he won't even be able to look me in the eye, I'm not going to get into a blame spiral, best just to leave before he wakes up and never mention it again because men hate women who want to talk about it.* And something else stirred at the back of her mind, something dark as molasses, mysterious as night, faint as a ghost. *You must hold on to this,* said the ghost. *This will not happen again. He will soon be gone. Remember the good.*

How can I save him? she asked the ghost.

You cannot, came the reply.

How will I know when he is in danger?

It will happen when you call his name.

Then DuCaine woke up and saw her looking back. He raised himself on to an elbow and studied her slowly, carefully. 'What time is it?' he asked with a thick voice, pausing to clear his throat.

'Seven fifteen.'

'We have to be at the unit by eight.'

'Yes, I know.' She nodded.

'Let's save time by showering together,' he grinned, reaching for her.

At seven thirty a.m. on Sunday, Banbury was still collecting evidence at the closed-off ground-floor offices of ADAPT. The story had now broken in the national press, and photographers were lurking in the courtyard outside, waiting to snap any further grisly discoveries.

'Somebody must have seen him,' insisted Renfield, watching as Banbury continued to painstakingly remove every item from the desk and examine it in infuriating detail. 'Old Bryant's theory is that Cavendish panicked and went over to burgle Delaney's apartment, attacking him in a frenzy when he got home.'

'You're supposed to be giving me a hand,' said Banbury, annoyed.

'You're only bagging and tagging; that

doesn't take two of us. I'm thinking this through. Isn't that what you blokes are supposed to do? Have you finished with this chair?' Renfield dropped into it and swivelled himself around. 'So, Cavendish lays out everything in the apartment carefully, searching for the document. He knows exactly what it looks like; he's seen hundreds of them. He hears the front door open and realizes he's trapped. There's an argument and maybe Delaney takes a swing at him.'

'The carpet scuffs would bear that out,' Banbury agreed. 'Cavendish must have been carrying a knife – he didn't pick up anything in the flat. And he must have stabbed Delaney through his clothes; there were no arterial sprays.'

Renfield swivelled back and forth. 'He drags the body down the stairs of the empty house to the front door. The street is empty, so he shoves Delaney in the boot of his own car.'

'There's no evidence of that. I've been over the car.'

'Maybe you missed something.' Renfield jumped to his feet. 'Wait. There were no blood creases on the body so he used his own vehicle, a van. You don't need me here to hold your hand. I'm going to do another door-to-door.' He pocketed Cavendish's security ID. '*Someone* must have seen it. Then I'm going over to that bloody church.'

'Why there?' asked Banbury, dropping a stapler into a plastic pouch.

'Because Bryant keeps mentioning it. He's got an idea about the place, and I want to know what it is.'

'Is this case complicated or am I getting old?' asked Arthur Bryant wearily.

'Well, you're getting old whether it's complicated or not.' Longbright smiled sweetly, touching her hair.

'Is there something going on that I should know about? You look eerily radiant today. And you only wear that tortoiseshell comb when you're really happy. You've had a disconcerting smile on your face ever since you returned from Brighton.'

Longbright refused to be drawn. She thrust out her imposing bosom and delivered her news. 'I came in to tell you that Richard Standover is here to see you.'

'Ah,' said Bryant, 'the collector. Show him in.'

Standover was almost as wide as he was tall, and wouldn't have stood over many people at all. He had made up for the loss of a neck with an exorbitant goatee, and stared angrily at the detective through shrunken eyes. 'This is absurd,' he said testily. 'I don't know what I'm doing here.'

'No, but we do. I'm Arthur Bryant. Do find something to sit on. Your rival, Adrian

Jesson, turned up in two separate pieces while you were away sunning yourself with his sister in Majorca.'

'So this lady already told me.' He indicated Longbright.

'Not heartbroken, then?'

'Of course not. I barely knew Jesson.'

'Not what we've heard, old chum. Your mutual acquaintance at the Rocketship bookshop seems to think you were having a feud with him. He said you'd been rivals for many years.'

'Our business relationship was common knowledge. The collecting world is a small one, and highly competitive. We all know each other, and we all love to gossip. Collecting is a disease, Mr Bryant. Start collecting something professionally, whether it's china frogs or British beer mats from the 1930s, and you'll soon find out who else is doing the same thing.'

'You don't help each other, then? Say, if you're collecting a set and need a particular item, you don't trade?'

'God, no. The idea is to push up the value of your own collection, not someone else's.'

'And briefly, what's in your collection?'

'It's taken me a lifetime to build up. I can hardly be expected to quantify it in a few minutes. People collect anything of limited availability that's likely to increase in value. Tastes change all the time. You wouldn't believe what fetches money these days. There are a lot of amateurs in the business, too many TV shows explaining how to do it.'

'All right, what's your speciality?'

'If I had to pick one thing? Music, mainly. Original artwork and photography. Western pop memorabilia is highly prized in countries like Japan. The Rolling Stones, The Beatles, The Doors. Anyone who has died tragically – Kurt Cobain, Jimi Hendrix, Jim Morrison.'

'What were you fighting with Adrian Jesson about?'

'Oh, lobby cards. You know, the hand-inked cinema stills that used to decorate the exteriors of old movie houses. They were always produced in sets of six and came in sealed packets, which makes them highly attractive acquisitions. When the Rank film studio closed down, the new buyers sold off everything in the vaults. I had a set of stills Jesson was desperate to purchase, one of the old Ealing comedies, extremely desirable. He was missing one, and I wouldn't sell him mine.'

'So the argument wasn't about his sister?'

'Marie and I have been together for years now,' said Standover. 'Jesson's had time to get used to the idea.'

'But he wasn't happy about it?'

'Not particularly. He was very competitive in every part of his life. That's why he annoyed people so much.'

'And he annoyed you?'

'I wouldn't say that; I just know what collectors are like.'

'Mr Standover, I understand you were out of the country when Adrian Jesson died, but at the moment I'm not concerned with him. Have you ever seen either of these two people?' Bryant showed him the photographs of Cavendish and Delaney.

'No,' said Standover, clearly puzzled. 'At least, they're not in my business.'

Bryant switched tack. 'Know anything about St Pancras Old Church?'

'I've never heard of it. I'm surprised to hear there are any churches at all in an area as godless as St Pancras.' The answer felt glib and prepared. Bryant made a mental note.

'Tell me, are there collectors who specialize in murder memorabilia?'

'Of course. Jack the Ripper, Crippen, Christie, the American killers like Gacey and Gein. There are a few sick individuals out there collecting more recent stuff, but a lot of it is black market. You can find Internet links for that kind of thing. Professionals would shun such material. Is that all? Can I get out of here now?'

Bryant's early optimism waned through the day. He had sensed they were close to a breakthrough, but the solution remained tantalizingly out of reach. The PCU worked on in isolation, without equipment or data, doggedly backing up each step with the requisite paperwork, writing out reports by hand. At the end of the afternoon everyone was tired and bad-tempered. Renfield went out without telling anyone where he was going, and failed to report back in. A little after six o'clock May realized they could go no further. Obviously the killer had moved Delaney's body in a vehicle, but no one had seen it parked outside his flat, or outside the shop on the Caledonian Road. Vans were rendered invisible by their ubiquity. Kershaw had found no new evidence on the corpses. No new witnesses had come forward. Their leads were all played out.

'We'll give it another couple of hours and then adjourn until the morning,' May said. 'There's no point in staying late tonight. I want everyone in by eight a.m. tomorrow for a briefing session.' He rubbed his eyes wearily. 'Arthur, when we finish I'll run you back to Alma's.'

'If my home is still there,' said Bryant gloomily. 'We're being kicked out.'

'Then perhaps I'll buy you a beer instead. Hell, I'll buy everyone a beer.'

'Not me, chief,' said Liberty DuCaine. 'I said I'd run Janice home later.'

'You didn't come back to the unit after

Brighton,' said Bryant. 'What did you two get up to? You didn't stay down there, Janice, did you? Together?'

'*Oooooooh.*' Everyone turned to look at the pair of them.

'What?' said DS Longbright. 'What? I have a private life, you know.'

'You never had one before,' said Bryant grumpily. 'I don't know why you have to start now. It's very inconvenient.'

But she knew he was secretly pleased for her.

41

HAYWIRE

Maddox Cavendish took off his tie, rolled it up and put it in his pocket. He opened his collar, trying not to look like an executive. The afternoon was cold, but he was sweating. He drank half a pint of beer in each bar he visited. After the fourth, he had built up enough courage to start conversations.

In the Ruby Lounge he met a former boxer who offered to buy him amphetamines. Wandering in the gloomy depths of the Big Chill House he was offered drugs and a woman for the night. It took nerve to enter the

Flying Scotsman, considered by many to be the worst pub in London. He stood in a crowd of overweight skinheads watching as a bony crack-addled girl performed a dead-eyed bump-and-grind on the tiny raised stage. The more coins that were thrown into her pint pot, the more she took off. How desperate did a man have to be, Cavendish wondered, to watch a drug addict strip? This was not his world. He belonged in the Thames Valley, where the houses were lost behind hedges and every family had three cars. How had he been reduced to this?

Think of what will happen if you don't do it, he told himself. *You'll be unemployable.*

He struck up conversations and got strange looks. Finally, in one of the more brightly lit and respectable bars, a pub called the Golden Lion, he found what he had been looking for. Seated on a tiny verandah with the smokers, he joined a promising conversation and realized that he was talking to a burglar with a string of convictions. The boy's name was Mac. He was pale and ratty, with a scrawny tattooed neck and faux-Russian gang tattoos entwined over both arms. This was no good – Cavendish wanted someone who did not look guilty and would not get caught – but at least the subject was raised. Soon they were joined by others who boasted of TWOCing neighbourhood cars. 'Taking Without Owner's Consent' had to be explained to him, but a few minutes and several beers later, Mac had agreed to introduce him to a man who had never been caught, even though Mac was sure he was insane and deserved to be locked up.

Mac gave Cavendish a joint, which was mixed with dark rolling tobacco and nearly choked him, and after Mac had held several sly conversations on his mobile phone, they went off to the Thornhill Arms, to meet up with Mr Fox.

Cavendish felt the skin on his neck tingle as Mr Fox entered the pub. He was small-boned, sandy-haired, pale and inconsequential, and yet there was something terrifying about him. He nodded politely as he was introduced to Cavendish, but there was no life in his deep black eyes, nothing at all except the hungry prospect of taking something from another. He commanded the space; the others fell silent out of respect. Cavendish skipped the small talk. There was no point in wasting time. He explained what he wanted, but was careful to play down the importance of the item to be stolen from Delaney's apartment. He did not want Mr Fox to understand its value.

Mr Fox listened to the proposal as if it was the most normal thing in the world, as if it was almost beneath his attention. Then he nodded imperceptibly and asked for half the money up front.

'No,' said Cavendish. 'You get it when you deliver.'

Mr Fox rose to his feet. He seemed to have grown in stature somehow. Mac was clearly annoyed. 'You got to pay him,' the burglar whined.

'One third up front,' Cavendish offered.

Mr Fox hovered for a moment, and for that terrifying moment Cavendish feared he might lash out at him, but then he sat back down, grudgingly indicating that they had a deal.

Cavendish withdrew the cash from his personal account, knowing it was better not to involve the company. Nothing happened the next day. He sat at his desk, shuffling papers, biting his nails. Sammi, his assistant, kept looking at him strangely. When the phone finally rang, Cavendish found himself talking to Mac.

'Meet me back at the pub tonight, same as last time.' The line went dead.

Mac was skittering about at the bar, manically chewing gum, drinking beer, nervously tapping skull-ringed hands on the counter. The moment he saw Cavendish in the mirror he spun around. 'You didn't say nothing about him coming back from work early, didja?'

'Where's Mr Fox?' Cavendish asked, sensing trouble. 'What happened?'

'I'll tell you what happened. Your pal came back and caught him in the act. So Mr Fox had to deal with it.'

'Where's my package?'

'Don't know, mate. Don't know anything. He never met you and you never met him, all right?'

'We had a deal. I gave him money–'

'Don't know what you're talking about.'

'Don't try to scam me, you little weasel,' Cavendish hissed. 'Who the hell do you think you're dealing with?'

'It ain't me. Mr Fox knows where you work. It's him you have to worry about now. He's nuts; he'll do anything. You screwed him around. He's got nothing to lose. Nothing.'

Cavendish thought of Mr Fox's frozen dark eyes and the truth began to dawn on him. *'Oh God, Delaney's dead,'* he realized. He could see bony fingers digging into the construction worker's windpipe.

'Just get the rest of the money by tomorrow, all right?' Mac shoved past him and stormed out of the pub.

42

MAD DAY OUT

Before they left for the night, the PCU staff assembled at the front of the second floor in what had become the briefing room, simply because it was the room with the most floorboards. The last two hours of the evening had brought some leads, but hardly the breakthrough they had been hoping for.

'OK, everyone present and correct?' asked May. 'The good news is that we've managed to locate Mr Porter's granddaughter, Ellen. She lives just a few streets away, in Tiber Gardens. The bad news is that she doesn't know anything about a property deed. Looks like Delaney didn't have time to track her down. No one's been in contact with her.'

'But the deed wasn't in Delaney's flat,' said Bryant. 'So where on earth did it go?' He noticed that Jack Renfield had appeared in the doorway. 'Ah, Mr Renfield, glad to have you back amongst us. Where did you disappear to?'

'I decided to follow up one of your leads,' Renfield explained. 'You kept banging on about the St Pancras Old Church, pagans and such, so I went there and had a very interesting talk with the gravedigger. Seems you missed an obvious connection with one of the suspects.'

'I did?' Bryant sat forward, intrigued. 'And what did I miss, pray tell?'

'You missed the Mad Day Out.' Renfield looked around the room.

'What are you talking about?'

'The Beatles. Seems the old vicar remembers it well. In 1968, The Beatles were photographed all over London in what became known as their Mad Day Out. They were filmed in seven different London locations by a veteran war photographer named Don McCullin, but four other photographers came along as well. The fifth location was a big series of shots taken in the grounds of the old St Pancras churchyard. The photos were designed to promote their *White Album*. It's one of the most famous photo sets in pop history, after the shot of them crossing Abbey Road.

'In your report you say that Richard Standover denied ever having heard of St Pancras Old Church,' Renfield continued, 'but he specializes in Beatles memorabilia. He lied to you.'

Bryant looked as though he'd been hit with a brick. Besides, he hated being upstaged. 'You're telling me this is about *The*

Beatles?' he asked incredulously.

'No, I'm saying it's one element.' The sergeant threw the others a smug look. 'I did some further checking up last night while you lot were brushing your teeth and making cocoa. Adrian Jesson owned the original photographs from the Mad Day Out, signed by McCullin and all four Beatles. Standover was desperate to buy the shots because he owns the sets from the other six locations, meaning that he would have the complete photographic record of The Beatles' historic day. It would have sent the value of Standover's collection through the roof. You met him, so you know there's one problem: he's got the charm of an open grave. He failed to bargain the photographs away from his old rival after staging a very public argument with him. Everyone in the collecting community knew he was trying to get his hands on them, so when he got turned down he made himself a laughing stock.'

'But if he tried to steal from Jesson, surely everyone would suspect him?' Bryant argued. 'And even if he had done so, he wouldn't be able to sell the collection, because he could never reveal that he was in possession of Jesson's photographs.'

'That's right. You can see parallel situations rising between Maddox Cavendish and Richard Standover,' said Renfield. 'The connection between them is a desperate desire to

384

steal something. The architect Cavendish steals from Delaney, the collector Standover steals from Jesson, and now three of them are dead. Cavendish the workaholic screws up and kills Delaney, and the process changes him. He's a murderer now – he has nothing left to lose. Suppose Cavendish knew Standover? Did anyone think of that? Suppose he shows Standover how to get what he wants by killing his rival? And Standover does the job, but he's worried about Cavendish, who's nervous and fast becoming a liability. And now that Standover has killed, he's sure he can do it again. Out of the four, the only one left alive right now is Richard Standover.'

'No, no, no.' Bryant held up a wrinkled hand. 'It's all too complicated. There's a single, simple thread running through this and we haven't found it yet.'

'You'd better send someone round to bring Standover in, and quick,' said May. 'Renfield, if you're right, we'll have a lot to thank you for.'

As the unit mobilized into action, May followed Bryant back to his office. 'Don't take it badly, Arthur,' he consoled. 'You can't get it right every time.'

'Renfield is wrong,' Bryant said sadly. 'Everything was pointing to Xander Toth. The area's history, the fact that his family had been pushed off their land – all the pieces fitted together.'

'No, they didn't. You were trying to force them together. I'm not saying Renfield's one hundred per cent right, but you have to admit he's come up with a workable theory. Toth was dressing as a local character in order to bring publicity to his cause, that's all. The mistake has been thinking that the three deaths must be tidily connected. They occurred in the same place at around the same time, but it's exactly what you said about chaos theory. Tens of thousands of strangers, passing through here every day – so many of their lives intersect without them realizing it.'

'I think you may have hit upon a truth,' said Bryant. 'We're looking at a series of causes and effects rather than a single unified case. There are three distinct events that occurred here two weeks ago, and they triggered disastrous consequences. One, a protestor goes too far and makes himself a murder suspect. Two, a company man makes a mistake and tries to rectify it. Three, a collector gets a little too acquisitive. The city draws something out of them, especially here. It's the King's Cross effect – too many people brushing against temptation and losing sight of themselves.'

On the way out, Bimsley swung past Renfield. 'You missed a revelation, Jack,' he told the sergeant. 'It seems our Miss Longbright enjoyed carnal knowledge of PC Liberty DuCaine on the way back from Brighton. See what a bit of sea air does for you?'

Renfield stared at the handsome West Indian constable. 'You're bloody joking,' he muttered.

Bimsley knew he had made a mistake. Swallowing nervously, he quickly left Renfield alone with his fury.

43

DYING ALONE

At the age of eleven, Maddox Cavendish had switched his school satchel for the smart brown leather doctor's briefcase that he still carried to work. He treated his job as if he was permanently preparing to sit before an examination board. He went into the office seven days a week, although he allowed himself the luxury of spending Sunday afternoon at home, even though he was usually at a loss for something to do there. His spare time was spent seated at his laptop, surfing the net for news of rival companies. He knew that Marianne loved his corporate loyalty, but was also aware that she would not hesitate to fire him if he failed to deliver.

He couldn't go to her and tell her that he feared for his life, because it would mean admitting to his mistake. He had no friends, no lover with whom he could discuss his fears. His family idolized him for being a success, which meant that they could not be involved, either. Overnight, the shining path leading up the stairs of corporate success had become a dead end.

Cavendish worked hard but didn't play hard, partly because he didn't drink. In the past eighteen months he had started gambling online, and now his bank account was flickering on empty. To get the money to pay off Mr Fox, he knew he would have to borrow or embezzle. When the staff left that night, he remained at his desk trying to think of a way out.

After she'd shut down her computer, Sammi came back into his office with her coat on, and asked if he was all right.

'I'm fine,' he told her. 'Just a bit tired.'

He knew something was on her mind when she unbuttoned her coat and sat down on the other side of his desk. 'You've been on edge for the last few days,' she said, hesitant and anxious not to cause offence. 'I just wondered if there was something, you know, that you wanted to talk about with me.'

'What do you mean?' His question was a

little too sharp.

Sammi had been his assistant for eight years, and had never once questioned his judgement. Now she looked on the verge of saying something that could change their relationship for ever. She studied his eyes, waiting for him to speak first, then realized he would never open up to her. 'Maddox, I know about Camley Lane.'

He played with the ballpoint pen on his desk, unable to speak.

'If you're in any trouble you should talk to me, because I might be able to help.'

'I don't know what you're talking about.'

'Please, Maddox. I saw you talking with that awful man, the one with the tattoos. I saw you through the window of the pub. I'm not an idiot; I know when something's wrong. And I know that anything you've done is for the good of the company. You're trying to get hold of the property rights before Marianne finds out. Is that man blackmailing you?'

'No, nothing like that.'

'Then what?'

'Suppose I told you? What do you think you could do? You're a secretary, for God's sake.'

The only way to get rid of her was to hurt her. She studied him a moment longer, unconvinced that he meant what he said. 'Are you sure there isn't anything I can do?'

He decided not to answer her, to pretend she had left the office.

'It's not worth it, Maddox. All this ... paranoia. It's just a job.'

'No, to you it's just a job. This is my career.'

This time she really was hurt. Rising, she rebuttoned her coat, avoiding his gaze. 'I'll say good night,' she said softly, and although he wanted her to leave, part of him was willing her to stay.

When she had gone he sat with his head in his hands, and for the first time in his life he knew how it felt to be truly alone.

An hour later the door buzzer sounded, and he recognized the shape behind the glass, and knew that his time had run out.

44

SOMEONE IN THE SHADOWS

Arthur Bryant was not happy. He paced across the cluttered lounge, peered from the windows into the rainy night, clapped his arms about himself, muttered under his breath, paced back again.

'Could you stop walking about?' asked Alma Sorrowbridge. 'You're going to wear out my Persian rug.'

'The closest this threadbare runner has been to the East is the East End,' said Bryant testily. 'Where is he? He said he'd be here by now.'

'He only dropped you off a few hours ago. You see enough of each other during the day. I don't know why you have to spend your evenings together as well. It's nearly midnight. Most respectable people are in bed.'

'I told you, I'm awaiting news of a development. Besides, compared to a great many people I meet these days, I'm positively respectable. John May is the other half of my brain. I have to try my ideas out on someone.'

'You should be more worried about the compulsory purchase order on this place. We're about to be made homeless and you're going on about murderers. There's always going to be murderers, but we might not find another place to live.'

'I knew I couldn't expect you to understand. I've spent nearly an hour explaining my thought processes to you tonight.'

Alma didn't like to admit that she had been concentrating on her knitting. 'I tried to follow what you were saying. It would help if you made a jot of sense.'

The doorbell rang. 'I don't know why you don't give him a key,' Alma complained. 'You're like an old married couple.'

'Oh, go and make yourself useful. Boil something. And bring us food. We'll be working late.'

Alma let John May in. 'He's over-exciting himself,' she warned. 'He won't take his blue pills. Says he's worried they'll make him sleepy. Can you do something?'

'I'll try,' said May, hanging up his wet coat. 'I thought you'd prefer him like this to when he's not working.'

'Well, I do,' Alma insisted, 'but he's scaring me with all this talk of a murderer. I have my faith, but there's a limit to how much Jesus can do when Mr Bryant starts talking about chopping heads off.'

'Well, you can both rest easy now. We're bringing in his man. I've come to pick Arthur up.'

'What's that?' asked Bryant. 'You've got someone?' He seemed suddenly confused.

'You know we have. Our boys have gone to arrest Richard Standover for the murder of Adrian Jesson. I thought you might like to be there for the interview.'

'No, no, that's wrong.'

'What are you talking about? You were there when Jack put forward his theory and you didn't say anything.'

'I didn't want to demolish Renfield in front of everyone without a theory to put in its place. The idea that one man might teach another to kill would be feasible if they were

392

gang members, but we're talking about two middle-class businessmen here, not a pair of disenfranchised kids.'

'Don't tell me you're jealous of Jack,' said May, 'just because he came up with a solution you couldn't reach.'

'That's just the point,' replied Bryant. 'I do have a solution, or at least part of one. What I don't have is a way of catching him.'

May seated himself on the arm of the sofa. 'All right, go on. Explain. I'm listening.'

'Renfield's theory has been bothering me. It leaves too many loose ends, and we have no scrap of proof that Cavendish and Standover even knew each other. I think there's someone else still in the shadows, a connection we haven't been able to draw out. Maddox Cavendish would have been too scared to do his own dirty work. I know his type. He had to save his career by getting the deed back fast, but he wouldn't have been able to do it himself. People like Cavendish always hire others to handle the heavy lifting.'

'Where was he going to find a burglar?'

'I don't know. There are plenty of workmen on the site; maybe one of them knew somebody. But he wouldn't want the risk of involving anyone from his own company. Besides, the workmen would see him as management, and I don't suppose he found it easy talking to them. I think he went out on the street to look for someone who didn't know him, someone who would steal that deed from Delaney and melt away into the crowd. It had to be done the hard way, by discreetly asking around. He wouldn't have used the office phone or his mobile, and anyway, who would he have called, Rent-A-Thug?'

'You really think it's likely that he just went out on the street?'

'He was working in King's Cross,' said Bryant. 'How hard could it be? You can get drugs easily enough there just by talking to a few people in a pub. It wouldn't be much more difficult to find a burglar. What else was Cavendish going to do, a nice white-collar worker with no known criminal connections? Follow me on this.'

'All right, I'm listening.'

'Having found someone, Cavendish had to have a way of contacting his man, be-cause he needed to make sure the job got done and the deed would be delivered back to him. Presumably he then also had to pay him, unless he gave him the money up front, which would make him a complete idiot. We know Cavendish withdrew an unusually large amount of cash before he died. They could have had a pre-arranged meeting place. Probably somewhere in the station. God knows it's big enough. But he'd still need a number, an address. Without it how could he be sure that the guy wouldn't let him down?'

'We didn't find anything.'

'No, because his murderer destroyed the evidence. Think about it. Cavendish hires someone to steal the deed. What if Standover hired the same man to steal a packet of photographs? It would explain why he has an alibi for the night of Jesson's death.'

'So working with your theory, Cavendish and Standover don't know each other at all. The only connection is this Mr X.'

'Correct. What if the man they both hired is prone to violence, and didn't like being disturbed in the middle of a job? Delaney walked in on his attacker. Suppose Jesson did exactly the same thing? That's two of the three deaths accounted for.'

'But what about Cavendish?' asked May. 'You think he was killed by this phantom he hired?'

'Cavendish clearly knew his attacker; he let him into his office. Now you have one killer for all three victims, using the same MO.'

'It doesn't explain why the heads were severed.'

'I don't know. Cruelty, savagery. That part is still a mystery. You have to admit it makes more sense than Renfield's solution.'

'But if Cavendish's killer is cleaning up the mess he made, it would be logical to go after

the last of the group who knows his identity
– Richard Standover.'

'Exactly,' said Bryant. 'When a man
becomes involved in murder he opens himself to the same risks faced by his victim.
You're not bringing in a killer, John, you're
bringing in someone who's about to be
killed.'

45

COMPLETE

Richard Standover worried about his collection.

Now that it was finally complete, something indefinable had been lost. That
magical, mystical day in 1968 had been catalogued and pinned down, every last minute
accounted for. He had been there, at location number five, reading a *Beano* comic on
the park bench in the graveyard attached to
St Pancras Old Church, when the Fab Four
had turned up with their photographers.

They were rowdy and filled with laughter,
and he was seven years old. John Lennon
had insisted that he join them in the group
shot on the bench, and had even put his arm
around his shoulders. Passers-by had

stopped to gawp through the gates of the churchyard, but were too awed to come in. People were in those days. It was a working-class area; the olduns were dismissive of pop stars, and the young were shy.

The photographs were taken, then all four were off with a smile and a wave to be filmed in a flower bed of crimson hollyhocks beside the hospital buildings. Paul McCartney was in a pink suit, George Harrison wore a bright-blue shirt and orange striped trousers. The heat of the afternoon sun was starting to fade. Cool green shadows crept over the lawns as the watchers dispersed. Standover had remained on the park bench, touching the wooden slats where his heroes had sat, laughing and joking with him as if they were his older brothers.

It was the day his collecting habit had begun, and now the most important part of it was complete, sealing the faded memories of his childhood behind cardboard and clear plastic for ever.

Going online, he printed out a boarding pass for a seven twenty a.m. easyJet flight from Luton and threw a few clothes into a holdall. He would rent out the flat until it could be sold, but the slender envelope of photographs would remain in his hand until he arrived in Majorca, where it could take its place in the documented schedule of that extraordinary day.

His cleaning lady had promised to drop off her keys before he left. When the doorbell rang, he assumed it was her.

Renfield and Bimsley knew something was wrong as they approached the block of apartments in Bloomsbury where Standover lived. The lighting in the front-facing third-floor living room was askew; Renfield had seen enough rooms where fights had occurred. A lamp had been knocked to the floor, its shade displaced. A shadow stretched, the upturned beam passed across the opposite wall, then the ceiling, rolling fast.

'I know these flats,' said Bimsley. 'There are exits all over the bloody place.'

Renfield broke into a run, with Bimsley close behind him. He powered through the unlatched main door and up the stairs, through the open apartment door and into the dim hall. He could already see the bright scarlet smears in the room ahead. Standover was on his back, his right hand still frozen in a posture of defence, the left gripping his throat, ebbing rivulets of blood pouring between his fingers. He was already dead.

'Roof,' said Renfield. 'Come with me.'

There were smears and splashes on the staircase above, and on the landing over that. The exit door led to the lift mechanism and a shingled flat roof set in a hollow square, four apartment buildings with an internal garden at their centre. The low London night was yellow enough to see ahead, but they heard his crunching steps first. Renfield led by experience, with Bimsley hard on his heels.

At the far edge they saw him, a small figure in a knitted brown cap, moving with shocking agility. They saw him look back in panic, then brace, but could not believe he would actually jump. The noise of his landing was immense; a wide gap on to the next building, too wide for men as heavy as Renfield and Bimsley to chance, one floor down and on to an angled metal-skimmed awning that allowed little purchase.

Bimsley was calling in the description as Renfield searched for another way across. They ran back to the roof door, but four flights of stairs took them outside with no obvious way around to the next building. Even as they ran, they knew they were dealing with someone unusual, a man who knew exactly where he was going. They would search now, but their quarry had gone. Standover was dead, and somewhere in Bloomsbury's confusing maze of streets was a blood-smeared madman.

Renfield was always angry, and never more so than when a life which might have been saved was cut short. He had no way of knowing that, in one sense, Standover had died with his world completed at last.

46

PIECES

Marianne Waters was the kind of woman who only noticed members of staff when they made a mistake, and she regarded everyone of lower status as a member of staff, whether they worked for her or not. She handed her overcoat to the maître d' of the discreet Italian restaurant without engaging in eye contact and found her own way to Oskar Kasavian's table. She had no time for pleasantries and no facility for small talk.

'Oskar, don't ever try to palm me off with one of your juniors again, do you understand?' She poured herself a glass of wine but did not remove her jacket. She could unsettle anyone by confounding their expectations. 'I thought the Home Office had cleared out people like Faraday years ago.'

'He's a legacy.' Kasavian sighed. 'His father–'

'I know who his father was. The children of famous parents are nearly always less talented, which is why they make such messes of their lives. From now on, I'll deal only with you.'

'I don't know what more you want, Marianne.' Kasavian regarded her coldly. 'Your construction crews are all back at work.'

'I wanted Alexander Toth charged, not released. Your special unit let him go.'

Kasavian was shocked at the news. He had specifically asked Faraday to plant a spy at the PCU and get feedback every night.

'Now the press are crawling all over this multiple murder case. The media are desperate to suggest that it's the tip of a corruption scandal and they're sniffing around us, but so far, of course, they have no evidence. We can't be investigated now, not at this crucial juncture. Our investors are nervous enough as it is. One has already pulled out, and the others are keeping a close eye on developments. Nobody wants a spotlight shone on their finances or their internal policies, and they certainly don't want to attract the attention of the Inland Revenue. I'm not saying there are any irregularities, just that any audit would throw us off schedule. I need to know what you're doing for us, Oskar. I want your press officers to get something out by tomorrow morning at the latest.'

She knew – everyone knew – about Kasavian's affair with Janet Ramsey, the editor of *Hard News*. Strong women were Oskar's weakness. Marianne Waters was surprised and a little insulted that he hadn't made a pass at her – not that she would have given him encouragement; she was seeing a twenty-two-year-old Romanian barman from the Sanderson Hotel who made up in vigour what he lacked in experience.

'I'm not one of your suppliers, Marianne; I represent the state,' Kasavian pointed out. 'You all think you're above the law, but if we decide to investigate you, we will do so at our convenience and our leisure, without your permission.'

'I have the word of the Secretary for Trade on this,' warned Marianne. 'We have put mechanisms in place to ensure that the work is finished on time.'

'And I have the ear of the Prime Minister,' Kasavian reminded her. 'You need to remember who you're talking to. It's your job to make sure that your investors hold their nerve. Tell them the situation has been resolved.'

'Has it?'

'That's no concern of yours. The unit handling the investigation is being removed tomorrow evening. Islington and Camden will combine their CID departments and take over, and the whole thing will fall under the jurisdiction of the Commissioner of Police. He'll make the appropriate reassurances. The work must be completed on schedule.'

'But not at the expense of a financial scandal. I don't want your people–'

Kasavian leaned over the table and searched her face. The effect was unnerving. 'King's Cross is a dirty area, Marianne. I suggest you go back to your office and make sure everything is thoroughly *clean*.'

It was a good time to fish for eels. In the dark they swam nearer to the surface, and the boy did not have a proper fishing rod. He'd owned one when he was smaller, but his father had broken it. His father smashed up everything when he was drunk. Now the boy sat beside the canal beneath the bridge at York Way, dangling the string and waiting for a bite. It was cold and damp here, but better than being at home listening to his parents fight.

The minutes passed without any movement in the line. He was about to give up when the plastic Christmas tree ornament he had tied to the end of his line shivered and ducked. He pulled on the line. The weight was wrong for an eel, too heavy, too still. He had snagged the hook on something. Pulling harder with his left hand, he shone the flashlight down with his right, peering into the murky green water. Slowly a pale object began to surface.

At first the boy thought it was a shopping bag. Kneeling on the concrete lip of the basin, he tugged again and leaned closer. He could see the shape rising into view.

A pair of dark eyes stared back up at him.

47

BRIGHTENING DARKNESS

'Oh, something wicked this way comes,' said Bryant with a shiver. 'I can feel it in my bones.' It was still early in the morning, and the trees behind them were rattling in the rising wind. 'Do you believe that evil can grow inside a man? A brightening darkness, like a torch in reverse?'

'I don't think you should keep putting the willies up people, Bryant,' said Raymond Land. 'It's bad enough that we're having to work in some kind of satanic sorting office without you adding to the sinister atmosphere all the time.'

Land hovered uncomfortably in front of the door to the St Pancras Mortuary. The strange building unsettled him. He thought of heading back to the office, but that place was almost as bad.

'What's taking Kershaw so long?' he demanded. When he looked back, Rosa was standing in the open doorway staring up at him. Land recoiled in fright.

'He's waiting for you downstairs,' she answered, drifting back into the corridor.

'And she gives me the bloody heebie-jeebies too,' Land whispered. 'Creeping up like that. There's something extremely odd going on around here.'

'So you're finally allowing the dark history of Battlebridge to get to you,' said Bryant cheerfully. 'Good. You need shaking up a bit.'

'Why is it so gloomy in this place?' Land complained, searching the hall for the light switch. He hated being dragged out of his office, but May was over at the ADAPT headquarters and Bryant liked having someone to talk to.

'What have you got for us, Giles?' Bryant asked as they entered the morgue. 'You have Maddox Cavendish's head now. That's all the body parts accounted for.'

'I've still got a long day in front of me,' said Kershaw. 'I can't access any information. The system won't recognize my PCU status. I'm having to use my predecessor's tutorial notes – it's very primitive methodology. I feel like a Victorian coroner, operating from old medical textbooks. At least Professor Marshall was thorough when it came to keeping records.'

'Have you got anything fresh for us?'

'Not this head, for a start. The rats have

been at it. Let me show you.'

'Do you have to?'

'Perhaps you'd rather start with Mr Stand-over.' He crossed to the furthest autopsy table and rolled back the green plastic sheet on it. 'Looks like the same method: slender, flexible, long, four-sided. I'd go for a shar-pened meat skewer. He stabs behind the base of the ear and punches it hard up-wards, penetrating the brain to cause instant – and I mean *instant* – death.'

'Can you be absolutely sure that it's the same attacker?' asked Land.

'Well, I can't without referral to a national DNA database, can I? Dan is dying to pick up an LCN sweep from the items he removed from Delaney's flat, but he can't do that, either.' The Low Copy Number project could track DNA from tiny sources, but was expensive, time-consuming and only available through routes that were currently closed to the PCU.

Kershaw indicated the slashes across the victim's left palm. 'He's got a distinctive sweep from right to left, giving Standover a faint defence cut on his raised left hand. He's a little shorter than his victims, but his arms are long and strong. It's the same man all right, but now he's attacking more violently. This time he's gone a lot deeper. The earlier hits were nowhere near as deep. But I have to say that even in his anger he's got a steady, purposeful hand. He's a danger, this one, attacking in fury but always maintaining control. Very, very angry with himself.'

'Himself?' said Land in surprise. 'You mean with the victim.'

'No. Things have gone wrong for him. The first two victims were dismembered and hidden. Even if he hadn't planned to kill them, he certainly worked at hiding them. But the third and fourth were attacked with no thought of the consequences.'

'So now that his housekeeping has been completed, he can go to ground until something drives him to kill again.' Bryant was tapping an old pipe stem against his false teeth, thinking. The noise irritated everyone. 'That chap in the Midlands, former nightclub bouncer, just got convicted of murdering seventeen girls over a period of twenty years. That's what worries me.'

Silence followed as the others tried to figure out what he was talking about.

'Driven by an unstoppable anger, of course, but something else develops over time. An arrogance born of familiarity. This chap knows the area. He hides in plain sight. He's a lousy burglar, but he's accidentally become a good killer. He gets away with it; he kills again. He considers himself invulnerable. He thinks he's wiping away the traces that lead to him, but in doing so he's creating another path, one that we can follow.'

'You're a very annoying man, Bryant,' said Land suddenly. 'You're like a Blackpool fortune-teller, handing out bits of information without actually helping.'

'Well, you always have a go at me if I say what I really think.'

'Good God, if you've got any clue as to where we find this man, I think now's the time to tell us!'

'All right. First, I think the first two victims are connected by something more than the methodology. There's the area, for a start. All of the victims have been found within a tight radius. We've established that our killer lives right here, knows these streets, knows when they're busy and when they're deserted.'

'If we could access the CCTV cameras around the church and the station we might be able to pick him up,' suggested Land.

'He knows how to stay outside of their limits. Besides, it would take days to go through all the cameras and the hours of footage. What did we do before we became so reliant on technology?' Bryant asked them. 'We managed perfectly well before, and we can again. Second point, he severed the heads for a reason, even if it's a subconscious one. He knows the history of Pentonville, St Pancras, King's Cross and Battlebridge. It's too much of a coincidence that he picked the one place in the city where such specific rites were recorded.'

'Please don't suggest he's performing human sacrifices,' groaned Land.

'I didn't say that. He's interested merely in saving his own skin, which is why he threw Xander Toth in our path. He knows we're here.'

'What?' Land all but exploded. 'How do you work that one out?'

'Look at the map. Caledonian Road, King's Cross, York Way, the railway line. Islington Met handle the east side; Camden have control of the west and south. Remember Islington had to give Delaney's body to Camden because the boundary line runs down the middle of the Caledonian Road? I checked the maps at Camden Town Hall; it doesn't, not quite. The boundary line stops one road back. The two areas don't meet up. There's a small gap in the middle that neither of them covers – the west side of the Caledonian Road isn't patrolled by anyone. That's where he chose to leave the body, and that's exactly where we arrived a couple of weeks later. We've been asking around, walking the streets, conducting interviews. The local shopkeepers already know about the PCU moving in. If this is our man's patch, he'll know, too. The advantage to us is that others must know *him*. Beneath the commuter crowds this is still a village, with residents, shopkeepers, street vendors, neighbours who see each other every day. You can't operate here and not be seen.'

'We've been talking to people ever since we arrived,' Land pointed out.

'We haven't asked the right questions before,' Bryant replied. 'Who is the area's most vocal resident? Who knows everything that's going on?'

'Toth,' said Land.

'Precisely. Toth's a historian; he runs the local community website; he's made it his business to know about everyone who lives here. We were too busy treating him as a suspect to think of him as a lead. I'm sure Toth knows the identity of the man we're looking for. That means our killer knows Toth. And if he's really planning to clean up all of his loose ends, Toth's life could also be in danger.'

'We'd better not find this one dead,' Land warned. 'We'll take my car.'

48

ELEMENTS OF CHANCE

'You stay here,' warned Land as they pulled up. The block of flats looked miserable and forbidding in the dim rain. 'There's no point in you running up all those stairs. I'll be quicker.'

'You're no spring chicken yourself,' Bryant replied with indignation. 'I'll come with you.'

'What did I just say? Why must you always do exactly the opposite?' But Bryant was already out of the car and heading for the nearest staircase.

They reached the second-floor landing and moved along the balcony to the flat which Toth shared with his girlfriend. Lizzi opened the door at their knock, blinking sleepily at them. 'You again,' she complained. 'You know he's done nothing wrong. And anyway, he's not here.'

'Where is he?' asked Bryant.

'He got a phone call about an hour ago, and went out. I don't know when he'll be back.'

'Did he say where he was going? Or who he was going to meet?'

'I think he was seeing Mr Fox.'

Bryant looked blank. 'Who is Mr Fox?'

'Oh, you know – thingie.' She waggled her hand at them. 'From the church. He's a friend. So I imagine that's where Xander's gone.'

'How do you know this Mr Fox is a friend?'

'Xander met him some while ago. He's always talking to people he doesn't know. I think Fox is just his nickname, though. He works for the Diocese.'

'Leonid Kareshi,' snapped Bryant, annoyed with himself. 'The archivist. Why didn't I think of him earlier? It has to be someone who knows about the church's history. He met Toth and Delaney there, and Standover was always connected because of his obsession with The Beatles' photographic shoot. Call John. Tell him to run a check on Kareshi and meet us at the church.'

'We don't need him, I can handle this,' said Land, who was suddenly quite enjoying being back in the field.

'Then I'll call him,' said Bryant, giving Land the fish-eye.

Raymond Land was a careful driver. He had no desire to go racing down alleys, frightening old ladies and knocking over dustbins. It was impossible to do so in London anyway; the traffic was painfully slow, the roads doubled back on themselves, and any kind of vehicle pursuit was unthinkable. Even so, Bryant found his boss unnecessarily cautious. He self-consciously signalled and braked and waved pedestrians past when Bryant would simply have put down his foot and hoped for the best. Driving like a madman was one of the few perks of the job, as far as Bryant was concerned.

As they pulled up before the gilded gates of St Pancras Old Church, John May came running out to meet them. 'You may be right about the archivist, Arthur,' he said. 'I've just been talking to the vicar. Three years ago, Kareshi was brought up on corruption charges before the FSB, the domestic state security agency of the Russian Federation. There was talk of links to organized crime over the sale of rare artefacts, but the case was dropped after he cut a deal with them. Kareshi has diplomatic immunity now. The Reverend says that he's been growing worried about the number of dodgy-looking acquaintances Kareshi has been bringing here. He fears they're up to something.'

'It might have been a good idea if he'd told us that earlier,' muttered Bryant.

As they pushed back the vestry door, they found the vicar about to turn out the lights. 'Our verger just called in sick,' the Reverend Charles Barton explained. 'There's no service today, which is a good thing because someone stole our snuffer, and I have trouble reaching the candles without it. He has gout, can you believe it? I can't help feeling that it's an inappropriately excessive illness for a church worker. I think Dr Kareshi is downstairs. The lights are on in the crypt.'

'Is there anyone with him?'

'No, I don't think so. He held a meeting yesterday with three men – pretty un-savoury-looking types.'

'We'll take over, Reverend,' May suggested. 'Perhaps you'd be so kind as to lock the main doors.'

'There must be no violence here,' said Barton emphatically.

'Your church is built on a pagan sacrificial temple, for Christ's sake,' complained Bryant.

'That was a very long time ago,' the vicar bridled, 'and I'll appreciate it if you don't blaspheme.'

'Hopefully there won't be any trouble,' May assured Barton gently. The detectives headed to the worn stone steps leading into the crypt.

Beneath the arc lamps, Kareshi was working alone. He had sifted through what appeared to be a ton of dry grey dust, and had cleaned up more than a dozen small grey stone heads, which were arranged on the floor in groups according to type. The intrusion upon his work was clearly unwelcome.

'Is there something you want?' he asked them, standing upright and wiping his hands on a cloth.

'Did you receive a visit from a Mr Xander Toth?' asked Bryant.

'No, I don't allow visitors. This is like...' he gestured at the roped-off pit before him, 'one of your crime scenes. I have an extremely limited time to excavate this site before the Diocese requires it to be refilled,

414

and if the artefacts become contaminated I will not be able to verify their authenticity.'

'How long have you been down here?'

'Since seven. I've seen no one for days except the Reverend and your friend Mr Austin Potterton.'

'Reverend Barton says some men came to see you yesterday.'

'Oh, them,' Kareshi remembered, showing some awkwardness. 'Well, I am helping them.'

'Who are they?'

'They are Belarus exiles; their English is poor and they feel isolated here. They are trying to start a club for fellow expatriates, somewhere they can meet and discuss their problems. They want me to help them, but I cannot spare the time. I don't have much money, but I give them a little whenever I can.'

The detectives glanced at each other, thinking the same thing. Bryant voiced the thought. 'It's someone else.' Without explanation or apology, they headed out of the crypt.

'So much for your criminal mastermind,' said Land unnecessarily. 'A down-at-heel Russian archaeologist. Now what?'

'I could give Austin a call and get him to help us.' On the way out, Bryant collared the vicar. 'Unsavoury-looking types, Reverend?'

'Well, shabby, unshaven,' Barton admitted. 'Swarthy.'

'Trust a man of the cloth to think the worst of other people. Come on, John.'

Outside the church, Bryant stopped. He peered through the misty green gloom of the graveyard, as if expecting to find answers there. The Reverend Charles Barton appeared behind them with a bunch of keys. 'I have to let you out of the main gates,' he said sniffily. 'The usual team prefers to leave them open, but I'm taking no chances. I've started to keep them locked whenever I see the kids from the council flats hanging about.'

'No balm of sanctuary available here, then,' said Bryant, who could not help needling vicars he found to be pharisaical.

'Vandals, Mr Bryant. They urinate in my vestry; they desecrate the gravestones. Mr Fox has a hard enough job without–'

'Mr Fox?'

'Our interment supervisor.'

'You mean Fox is the *gravedigger?*'

'We don't use such archaisms any more; they upset the parishioners. Besides, there are no new graves here – it's as much as we can do to tend the old ones. Mr Fox looks after the grounds, and is currently engaged in removing some of the old coffins. This is a heritage site and standards must be maintained.'

'How long has he been here?'

416

'Well, he was here when I arrived. He was employed by the former coroner of the St Pancras Mortuary. There was some kind of scandal–'

'Where does he live?'

'On the Margery Street council estate, off King's Cross Road. Number seven, Spring House.'

Bryant's eyes widened. 'Spring House?'

'What's the matter?' asked May.

'Margery Street used to be called Spring Place. There was a woman called Black Mary – she belonged to a thirteenth-century Benedictine order that wore black robes.'

'Oh, I can't wait to hear where this one is going...'

'She presided over the subterranean spa room that became known as Black Mary's Hole. The spa was fed by a well bored into the Bagnigge River, which ran down from St Pancras Old Church. It was capped off into a conduit that lies right underneath Spring House. It's a chalybeate spring.'

'A what?'

'An iron-fed spring, with healing properties. People came from all over London to have their illnesses cured there. But when Spring Place was erected over the conduit in 1815, the local builder turned Black Mary's Hole into a cesspool, ruining it.'

'I don't understand,' said Land, unsurprisingly confused. 'What on earth has any of this got to do with our murderer?'

'I told you, he's a local man, and thanks to Xander Toth he now has an extensive knowledge of the area's history. He understands its mystical connections and knows how to exploit them. He lives on the site of London's most venerable spa, destroyed by a builder. I suppose it would be too much to hope that the builder's family name was Delaney.'

They were now outside the church gates, heading for Land's car. 'You'd love that, wouldn't you?' said May. 'It would really confirm your belief in psycho-geographical retribution.'

'You have to admit that certain areas keep the same properties through generations. The King's Cross delis and coffee shops were always Italian, and now hundreds of Italian students are moving back in. Is that just coincidence?'

'I don't know – is it just coincidence that all of this is happening on St Pancras Day, your time of sacrifice?'

'See, you're finally starting to think like me,' Bryant said smugly. 'Right now, we need to concentrate on finding Xander Toth before he forfeits his life and loses his head. I think elements of chance have led Mr Fox to reveal his true nature to us.'

49

THE WOMAN ON THE WALL

'I'd assumed he must be some kind of polymath,' mused Bryant unhappily as they drove, with Raymond Land cautiously following them in his BMW. 'He's not. He's feral and instinctive, the kind of criminal we see so much more of these days. Mind that old lady.'

'You always want to think they're twisted geniuses,' May chided him. 'You long to pit your wits against someone who hides clues in paintings and evades capture through their knowledge of ancient Greek. Forget it, Arthur; those days have gone.'

'Russian agents still get poisoned by radioactive pellets in restaurants. Read your daily papers.'

May was forced to admit his old partner had a point. 'It would be dangerous to underestimate this man,' he warned. 'He's clearly smart enough to use everyone he meets. I bet Toth never realized he was acting as the host to a parasite.'

'Precisely. Mr Fox has one formidable talent. He absorbs the knowledge of others.

419

He used Toth, and I'm sure we'll find he used Professor Marshall, the former coroner of the St Pancras Mortuary. That's how the heads were severed so perfectly. We assumed it was a professional hit because of the clean cuts to the neck. The decapitations were performed with surgical precision. I think our Mr Fox persuaded the disgraced coroner to do it for him, or at least to teach him how. You heard Giles – the cuts were virtually identical.'

May called Bimsley and Renfield, summoning them to the apartment building. Land's BMW turned into Margery Street. The council estate had been rebuilt and extended after being bombed during the Second World War. Flat Seven stood on the ground floor, beyond a neat concrete courtyard.

'Stay here,' May told Land. 'Wait for the others.'

'You can't tell me what to do,' Land complained as they left him alone. 'I'm your superior officer.'

'Oh, don't be ridiculous,' Bryant called back. 'That's just a title, like labelling a tin of peaches "Superior Quality". It doesn't mean anything.'

'We may have to kick the door in,' warned May. 'That'll be a challenge.'

Bryant pushed against the jamb. 'I doubt either of us has the strength to shift this. The kitchen window is unlocked.'

It was a simple matter to raise the bolt and swing the pane wide, but climbing inside proved trickier. A few minutes later May lowered himself carefully on to the kitchen counter and came around to open the door. 'There's no one here. Where else could he have gone?' The pair stood on the balcony, looking around.

'They went out,' called a girl in a lime-green tracksuit, leaning over the balcony. 'Him and his mate.'

'How long ago?'

'Just a few minutes ago. He had to hold the other guy up, he was so pissed.'

'Did you see where they went?'

'Through there.' She leaned further over and pointed down to a recessed door at the bottom of a flight of steps.

'Why is he keeping Toth alive?' May wondered as the detectives headed towards the basement.

'I think I know why, but I hope I'm wrong. They're going to Black Mary's Hole. It's directly underneath Spring House.'

May found a light switch and strip lights flickered on below them. Fourteen stone steps led to a damp cellar that housed the building's electrical circuit boxes and lift equipment.

'Look around,' said Bryant. 'There has to be something else down here.'

'I don't know what I'm looking for, Arthur.'

'Oh, you know.' Bryant waved his hand about with annoying vagueness. 'The tunnel.'

'What tunnel?'

'You don't listen to a word I say, do you? The Bagnigge River ran beneath the church to Spring Place, where it was capped off. Our Mr Fox was employed at the church as a grave-maintenance person, or whatever Barton called it. Fox used the tunnel underneath, the one leading from the spa, to get back here. Where else could he have taken Mr Toth?'

'All right,' May conceded. 'But what exactly are we hoping to find?' When Bryant failed to answer, but merely pointed, May slowly turned around. 'Oh.'

Behind him was a grey steel door studded with rivets the size of mushroom caps. 'Try it,' Bryant suggested. 'There's no lock that I can see. Put your shoulder to it.'

May did not have to push hard. The door's hinges were thickly greased, and it swung in easily.

'Do you have your Valiant on you?'

'Of course.' May pulled his cinema usherette's flashlight from his overcoat and switched it on. 'Mind your step. There's a lot of rubble on the floor. Hang on to my coat.' The pair made their way forward at a cautious pace. The floor was uneven, and followed a gentle upward slope. The tunnel smelled of standing water but was neat and square, cemented with lichen-covered terracotta tiles, most of them badly damaged. A channel in the floor indicated the former path of the healing spring. Clearly, nothing but rain had come through here in a very long time.

Bryant grabbed his colleague's arm and bade him listen. A soft fall of brick suggested movement far ahead.

'Are you sure you're up for this?' May whispered. 'We could go overland, back to the church. Land can watch this end.'

'No, we're too close now to risk losing them. I think he's drugged Toth and has brought him up the tunnel from Spring House because he couldn't go in through the church. The vicar and Kareshi would have seen them.' Bryant climbed around a pile of collapsed brickwork and moved ahead. 'Look.' He pointed his walking stick towards a bend in the tunnel. There was a faint glow of light beyond it.

'I don't like this, Arthur. Fox could be hiding anywhere, lying in wait for us.'

'I know exactly where he is,' declared Bryant. 'He's in the temple.'

'You mean the spa room Kareshi showed us beneath the church?'

'Yes, but it became a spa room precisely because it was a temple. There was a painting on the temple wall, worn and very faded but quite recognizable as Saint Helena. I knew at once it was her, because she was flanked by hunting hounds. Saint Helena is the oldest and most powerful of all the pagan goddesses ever to be worshipped on these shores. Saint Helena – or *Nouhelene*, who wore stag antlers, and who represented the force of natural regeneration.' He stopped to catch his breath, leaning against the tiled wall. 'St Pancras Old Church was founded by the Emperor Constantine's mother, Saint Helena herself. Over time her name was shortened to Nell, and she was depicted carrying a basket of fruit. And then Nell Gwynne moved into the neighbourhood. Nell and her basket of oranges. It's where all of this came from, where the whole plan began.'

'Arthur, you've lost me. Let's get our man first, then you can explain.' May shone the flashlight ahead. A glossy fat rat fell from the ceiling of the tunnel with a squeak, more alarmed than the detectives. They rounded the bend, picking their way over bricks and rubbish – others had been here before them – and the light ahead grew stronger.

A pale-yellow ellipse revealed the entrance to the temple. The edges of the circular room had been marked with fat stumps of candles. In the centre, blindfolded and gagged, his hands and ankles tied, Xander Toth waited like a terrorist's prisoner. The man who stood behind him was slight of build, but oddly nondescript in appearance, except that he was wearing a crimson papier-mâché fox's mask, like the ones sometimes worn on Bonfire Night. He turned to stare at the detectives as they appeared in the tunnel entrance.

'Why would you want to do this, Mr Fox?' called Bryant. 'Everything else you've done has made a sort of sense, but this is sheer madness. You're being somewhat overly theatrical, if you don't mind my saying so. Do you mind if I sit down? I'm beat.'

May was looking to his partner for a cue to act, but nobody seemed inclined to make the first move. He could feel the tension rising in the cold damp air.

'I thought Mr Toth told you about the temple, but I suppose it might have been Mr Kareshi,' Bryant continued cheerfully. 'But really – a *sacrifice?* Who do you think you will appease? You learned to steal knowledge from other people, but you really shouldn't start believing in too much of it, you know. You think it will come to an end and you can start all over again if you shed young Alexander's blood on this spot? You sold your case rather too well, Mr Toth.'

May had heard Bryant use this technique before, keeping up a soothing level of conversation with his adversary, gently disarming through the simple humanity of a caring voice. Except that Bryant sometimes got carried away and went for the Oscar.

'But I'm afraid you can't begin anew, because this is where it ends. We have officers here at the church and at Spring Place, too. All your exits are cut off. So you might as well let Mr Toth go. And it is my duty to arrest you for the murder of Terence Delaney.'

'I am here at the church from ten in the morning until ten at night.' Mr Fox's voice was surprisingly thin and light. 'I put in twelve-hour shifts. Barton will vouch for me.'

'I'll also be taking into account the murders of Adrian Jesson, Richard Stand-over and Maddox Cavendish.'

The crimson fox mask tilted slightly, regarding Bryant. Then it looked up into the darkness of the stairwell leading from the temple to the church above. Mr Fox seemed to have no fear. He was weighing up his options.

May saw the sharpened silver skewer glitter in his hand, and turned the flashlight directly into his eyes. He knew Mr Fox would expect to be attacked, so instead he kicked out at Xander Toth, knocking the bound man over on his side – in the process slamming Mr Fox against the temple wall.

The skewer swung out but missed its mark.

May's boot kicked again and he managed to trap Mr Fox's wrist, pinning him in place. Two of the candles were knocked out, then a third. Only one remained alight. The temple was flickering into darkness.

'Keep back, Arthur,' May warned as Mr Fox rose to his feet.

Now we're in trouble, Bryant thought, taking in the scene. *We're all trapped together here. His only way out is past us. He has the only weapon. And he's insane. My, it's nice to be back.*

'You're Arthur St John Bryant,' Fox said. 'You still blame yourself for the way your wife Nathalie died. Your partner's wife is in a mental home. Who are either of you to tell me what to do?'

Bryant was taken aback. How could he have known such things? *I've underestimated this fellow*, he thought. *We're for it now.*

But that was before DS Janice Longbright leaned over the stairwell and dropped a sizeable chunk of paving stone on Mr Fox's head.

In the light of the guttering candles, she bore a striking resemblance to Saint Helena.

50

THE LIE OF THE LAND

Events moved fast after Mr Fox was captured. The Home Office was informed that even in its etiolated state, the PCU had performed a service that no branch of the Metropolitan Police could have managed. Leslie Faraday hurried into his superior's office, and Oskar Kasavian sent word to the Prime Minister and the capital's news agencies. No one congratulated the men and women of the Peculiar Crimes Unit for their dedication to duty.

When Bryant and May arrived back at their headquarters, they spent the next three and a half hours talking with Mr Fox, who seemed surprisingly keen to unburden himself to them. Without resources, it was impossible to impound evidence yet, but the PCU team was prepared to work through the night if Bryant and May were satisfied that they had their man.

It was now late in the afternoon, and their suspect had been placed in the building's only lockable room until the staff could be debriefed and the suspect examination could be resumed. Time was of the essence in the initial interview process, and the detectives needed to bring everyone up to speed. On that point, it probably wasn't the best idea to let Bryant do the talking, but the old man relished explaining his thinking to others and would not be dissuaded, despite the fact that he was prone to lethologica, not to mention an annoying habit of wandering off-topic at the most crucial moments.

'The roots of this case go back almost as far as I do,' said Bryant, hovering uncertainly above the battered sofa Longbright had managed to dredge up for the briefing room. He failed to lower himself gracefully into the seat, so he simply fell backwards. Once he had settled, Longbright handed him a mug of murky tea. The others sat wherever they could find a space. Everyone was impatient to hear how the arrest had been made.

'It goes all the way to 1940, when a bomb fell on Mrs Porter's house.' Bryant took a sip of his tea, looked for a place to set it down and ended up cradling it in his lap. 'But in a broader sense, it began several thousand years before that.'

There was such a collective groan and rolling of the eyes from the rest of the gathered staff that he decided not to follow that particular avenue of investigation. 'All right, let's start in 1940. A bomb destroyed a house in King's Cross, the surviving member of the family moved away, and for over sixty years the deed to the property was not missed. That is, until the conglomerate entrusted with the regeneration of the area tried to identify the owners of every single parcel of land. And Maddox Cavendish, the architectural planner charged with this task, belatedly realized that a key piece was missing.

'It wasn't the end of the world; an occupier needed to last for eleven years in a property before claiming the right to own it, and the ADAPT Group had been registered there for nine years. So, in order to comply with the law, all Cavendish had to do was wait two more years for change of ownership to become available. Except that ADAPT didn't have two years to spare. Thanks to its agreement with the Prime Minister, it has to meet government targets on a very strict schedule, and is subject to a system of fines if this is not achieved. Cavendish's failure to notice the problem earlier suddenly looked like gross incompetence.

'Then, during the clearance of the ground, one of the construction workers, Terry Delaney, discovered the deed in the remains of the well. Delaney went to Cavendish to ask his advice about what to do. I think we can guess that Cavendish offered to take care of the matter, because we know from his assistant just how driven and paranoid he was about his career. The architect made a disastrous move: he invited the construction worker to lunch – was his plan to get him drunk? – and during the course of this charm offensive, Delaney grew suspicious, resisting offers and even threats from Cavendish about handing over the deed. Instead, he announced that he would find the rightful owner and return it himself.

'This is the point at which Cavendish had his hopes dashed; he realized that Delaney was smart, decent and determined to do the right thing.

'Of course, it was the worst possible outcome for the architect. Now Cavendish got himself into a panic. He set out to find someone who could burgle Delaney's flat. Of course, if there was a burglary, Delaney would have a certain amount of justified suspicion about who commissioned it. But it was a chance Cavendish was prepared to take; he'd already sailed close to the edge of the law on a number of previous occasions. And Mr Fox was fully prepared to go further than mere B&E. Cavendish emptied his bank account and paid his man some cash up front – perhaps he went through a go-between to do so – but he bought himself a far more serious criminal act: murder.

'Mr Fox broke into Delaney's flat, and meticulously searched for the deed. If he didn't find it, he would be able to offer photographic proof that he had been there and had ransacked the whole flat.

'But Delaney came back from work early. He was a gentle man, and before he knew what was happening – probably while he was still trying to reason with the intruder – Fox stabbed him in the neck with the skewer. Then he carried Delaney's body downstairs into an unmarked white van. Mr Fox says the vehicle wasn't his, but we've yet to find out who it did belong to.

'It was late afternoon, the locals were still at work; he timed it well and he knew how not to be noticed. Fox remembered the empty shop on Caledonian Road from a conversation he'd had with a local property agent. The shop was full of plastic sheeting and buckets, and even had a freezer. Using the surgical skill he'd been taught by Professor Marshall at the morgue annexed to the St Pancras Old Church graveyard, he severed Delaney's head. Then he shoved the body in the freezer, taking the head away with him. He rightly figured that the mutilation would delay the identification process.

'At this point we have to leave Delaney for a minute and backtrack a little, because by now another murderous situation had arisen. It's the sort of thing that could only happen in a place like King's Cross, where so many stories overlap simultaneously.

'A man on the wrong side of the law is

always on the lookout for work. Mr Fox had met a man named Richard Standover, who needed a similar task performed on his rival, Adrian Jesson; a robbery that had to take place *before* Jesson moved his collection of rare Beatles memorabilia to a more secure venue. Like Cavendish, Standover was disturbed by the thought that if a crime was committed, suspicion would fall on him. It was meant just to be a burglary, but perhaps Mr Fox was filled with the adrenaline of his earlier kill–'

'Oh, really,' May protested. 'Supposition, Arthur.'

'So what? We're not in a court of law. Anyway, Mr Fox visited Jesson and murdered him, taking away the precious packet of photographs. He drove the body to York Way and dumped it on the deserted wasteground in the early hours of the morning. Then he delivered the photographs to Standover. This time he was a little more circumspect about what he told his client. But he didn't realize that Standover and Jesson operated in a very small world, one rife with rumour and gossip, and that it wouldn't be long before Standover discovered that his rival was dead. Standover had no qualms about hiring someone for a little larceny, but he certainly hadn't agreed to murder. However, Mr Fox was nothing if not ingenious. He told Standover that he had bought his client some time, and encouraged the collector to leave the country fast.'

'What do you mean, he had bought him some time?' asked Longbright, bewildered.

'Mr Fox is no ordinary criminal. He's a networker. No knowledge goes to waste. He learned burglary skills by spending months with the local locksmith. He made friends with Alexander Toth and was taught to appreciate his home town's history. He found out about the empty shop from the estate agent. He investigated our own backgrounds. He was employed by the vicar of St Pancras Old Church, Charles Barton. He knew about boundary lines – which follow the ancient lines of the parish – as well as the area's mythology. And he discovered there was a strip of land running through the area not covered by either of the local police forces, which was why he left the bodies there. He wanted to provide Standover with some room to run or concoct an alibi before Jesson's body turned up. It made sense to put the coincidence of the two deaths to some use. So he severed Jesson's head as well, and switched it with Delaney's.'

'Wait a minute, you're saying Fox changed the identification expecting no one to *notice?*' Banbury gave a look of disbelief.

'It probably occurred to him when he took off Jesson's clothes to get rid of the evidence. Jesson and Delaney were very similar in body type and colouring. They were also alike in height and weight. Tanned, dark, minimal body hair. He was certain both bodies would be badly decomposed by the time they were discovered. He cut the second corpse in the exact same manner as the first, severing the head carefully between the cervical vertebrae; he'd been taught by a surgeon, after all. So when the body was dug up by workmen, we thought for a moment that we'd found Delaney, whereas in fact we'd found Jesson. Mr Fox didn't expect anyone to find the remains of Terry Delaney for a while, but unfortunately for him they were discovered first by Bimsley here, setting us on the right track. Thanks to the boundary line, even the police didn't know who would be in charge of the investigation. Mr Fox is the eyes and ears of the neighbourhood. He says he asked around and was told that some disgraced unit would be handling the case, that they had no forensic equipment, no legal powers. And then he probably watched and saw me doddering out of the building. He knew we were being forced to work from physical evidence without access to police databases.'

'How would he know that?'

'Because he talked to one of us. Didn't he, Meera?'

'Oh, my God.' Meera's hand went to her forehead. 'That was *him?* I was just having a cigarette outside. He started to tell me about the building, how it had once been owned by a Satanists' society, how he didn't think it was habitable. I didn't mean–'

'That's what he does. He ingratiates himself. He draws out the knowledge he needs from others.'

'I'm amazed he could get anything out of *her*,' said Bimsley grumpily. 'She won't even talk to her colleagues.'

'I imagine that if you compared your notes on him with everyone else who had undergone the same process, you would all describe him differently. He's colourless unless adopting a persona, like a character actor who only comes to life in his roles. So, now Mr Fox decided to clean house. First he took care of the complaining Cavendish.'

'Why did he cut off Cavendish's head?'

'Because of what Xander Toth had told him about the history of the area – the severed heads, the sacrifices. He saw how appropriate his behaviour had been to date. Was it accidental, or a subconsciously deliberate act? No matter; the more he kept to the same methodology, the more it placed Toth under suspicion.'

'He told you all this?' Banbury asked.

'For a multiple killer, he seems anxious to get everything off his chest,' said May.

Bryant glared. He hated interruptions. 'When he discovered that Richard Standover had been told that his rival was dead, Fox went after the remaining man who had hired him, before Standover decided to talk to anyone else. Which brings us to Toth. Mr Fox's relationship with Xander is a rather interesting one. Not only did he use Toth's detailed knowledge of the area, he was encouraged and inspired by him. But it still didn't stop him from making Toth a scapegoat. He planted fur from Toth's outfit on Cavendish's body and, all the while, continued to be his friend. Fox kept a mental note of the wasteland near the railway; it was an ideal place to leave a body. He persuaded Toth to continue dressing as the stag-man – not that I suppose he took much persuading – thinking it would keep workmen away from the site. Instead, Toth, ever the showman, attracted unwelcome attention, and finally had to be dealt with.'

'Why did he bother to take him to the temple? Why not just kill him?'

'As we were interviewing Mr Fox, I wondered if he might have come to trust in the power of the area's protective mythology. He had beheaded his victims in the time-honoured fashion. He had acted in accordance with the traditions of the region. And he had seen the figure of Saint Helena on the wall of the temple. Saint Helena, the British equivalent of the Roman goddess Diana, the huntress, upon whose temple St

Paul's itself now stands. But she was more than this. She was a symbol of the River Fleet, from whence came the Bagnigge well beneath the church. Mr Fox even lived above the site of the original spring. How could he not have felt the hand of destiny pressing heavily upon him? It seemed entirely appropriate to bring matters to an end by sacrificing Toth to Saint Helena. By returning Toth's spirit to the well, Fox would close this chain of bizarre and disastrous events. It makes me think of the Stockholm Syndrome, only in reverse; the felon came to believe his victim.'

'Bloody hell.' Renfield drained the rest of his tea in one gulp. If he had not believed in Bryant's powers before, he did now. 'What set you off in the right direction?'

'One question John had asked kept buzzing around inside my head. If Mr Fox had gone to the trouble of cutting off the heads, why would he then allow the first two to turn up? There had to be a purpose to such extravagant executions, and it could only be to misdirect us away from the commonplace issue of identification. But once he'd started following the pattern of the past, he couldn't stop. The third death had to be similar to the others in order to implicate Xander Toth. There was only one way to bring the cycle to an end: sacrifice the man who had accidentally encouraged him to initiate it. Such acts

438

are rare but not unknown.

'I must confess Mr Fox fascinates me. I've never encountered such a mentality before. He's psychotic, brazen and, in his own way, supremely rational. The thing I want to concentrate on in our next interrogation session is his real identity. On that subject he has so far refused to be forthcoming.'

'I have a question.' April timidly raised her hand. 'If Mr Fox found nothing in Delaney's flat, who has the deed to Camley Lane?'

'Come on,' said Bryant, pleased with himself. 'You can work this last part out for yourselves.'

Everyone looked at each other blankly.

'Delaney liked studying historical records at Camden Council. So naturally, he sent the deed to the one man who could trace its rightful owner – Ed Tremble, Camden's land purchase advisor. I spoke to him a few minutes ago. Thanks to our rubbish postal service the delivery was only made last night, but it's still in time to be registered in Ellen Porter's name. Now she can decide whether to sell it or not.'

'So you set out to catch a stag and ended up with a fox,' said Banbury lamely. Nobody laughed. 'What happens now?'

'After we've formally charged Mr Fox, it will fall upon me to make Mr Faraday's life a living hell. I'll demand a full reinstatement of our powers, our equipment and, most importantly of all, our salaries.'

'Did you torture Fox?' asked Longbright. 'I mean, how come he volunteered so much information? Why would he do that unless he knew he could get off?'

'Or get out,' said April suddenly. 'You said he studied with a locksmith. Who's guarding him?'

'Liberty,' Longbright found herself calling out. The back of her neck prickled with ice.

They all ran for the stairs, Longbright leading. The holding room was on the third floor. As Longbright climbed, the sense of dread deepened within her. They entered the dim corridor. She saw the dark, prostrate bulk and her stomach turned.

Liberty DuCaine was lying on his side across the hall floor. The boards were bisected by a single spray of arterial blood, as thin as a line of red ink from a fountain pen. DuCaine's right hand was clutched below his left ear. He had tried to staunch the flow from the puncture wound, but the skewer had been pushed deep in one thrust before being swiftly removed.

'No,' said Longbright, reaching out for the wall, 'not him.' She dropped down beside DuCaine and felt his neck for a carotid pulse, then began to massage his heart, but experience had taught her that it was already too late.

She tried to follow the path of the wound.

Could the skewer have pierced his brain? Mr Fox had received some form of medical training, hadn't Bryant told them that? A single centimetre would mean the difference between death and survival. The attack had been so sudden that DuCaine had fallen before he could call out for help.

She continued to press his chest, to ensure there was pressure to take the blood to his heart. *Death or brain damage,* she thought angrily. *One moment of lost concentration and this is what it causes.*

'I've got an ambulance coming,' May said. 'Leave him, Janice. He did a pretty good job of blocking the blood flow. Don't move him. Any extra movement now could disrupt the clotting.'

'I'll go with him,' said Longbright, numbly brushing her hair from her face. There was nothing more to be done, but she found it impossible to look away. As the medics arrived and took over, she rocked back on her heels, watching DuCaine's immobile face. She willed him to see her one more time, to register her presence before he was removed and placed out of her reach within the system, but there was no flicker of sentience.

May checked the holding room and found the door wide open. The lock was undamaged. It had been firmly closed, but Mr Fox had managed to spring it. He had jumped DuCaine as he left the room. May didn't understand; they had carefully searched their suspect for weapons upon arrival at the PCU. They had taken his shoes and most of his clothes, and checked his underwear; he had nothing on him. What the hell had they done wrong? What had they overlooked?

'My God.' With difficulty, Bryant knelt and held Longbright tight. 'I'm so sorry, Janice. This should not have been possible. We thought he'd be safe there. I'll never forgive myself—'

'You have to get that bastard,' whispered Longbright, pulling away and looking at Bryant with a ferocity he had never seen before. 'I don't care what you have to do. If you don't catch him, Arthur, I swear to you I will.'

Mr Fox slipped between the backpacking Italian students pouring out of King's Cross Tube station. He had perfected a way of insinuating himself through the tightest crowds without ever touching anyone. He paid cash for a ticket so that it would leave no record, and avoided the searching gaze of each hidden camera with ease.

He was glad his little trick had come in useful; it had been incredibly difficult to master. He had secreted the silver skewer in his throat by attaching a piece of fishing nylon to a tooth; an old trick used by drug smugglers to sneak their personal stash through Customs. He was surprised he had been able to hold it there for so long without gagging while they removed his clothing. Transferring it back into his armpit without anyone noticing had been the easy part.

He was disappointed with Bryant and May. He had expected to outwit them, but had thought they would at least be able to discern his purpose in taking Xander Toth through the tunnel to the church and dressing in the mask. He had been about to place the Fox's head on Toth when the detectives arrived.

The hunted had knelt before the huntress to take his own life. At least, that was how it would have looked. And who for a moment would have disbelieved the notion that Toth had become even more unbalanced, finally choosing to kill himself in accordance with the mythology he had so tirelessly promoted? The circle would have been perfectly closed upon itself.

Mr Fox looked different now. He kept emergency supplies hidden in alley bin bags around King's Cross, and had collected one from behind the Tesco supermarket on Caledonian Road.

Newly bald, bespectacled, dressed in a smart grey suit, white button-collar shirt and black tie, he headed down on to the Jubilee Line platform without a final destination in mind. He watched those standing on the escalators around him, the students and middle managers, the personal assistants, housewives, receptionists and computer salesmen, and saw only slack-stringed puppets, dozing creatures with the rudimentary qualities of animals, cows, dogs, mice, but mostly sheep.

If they ever woke up, he thought, *if just one of them could stop thinking about mortgages and sex and job prospects for a few hours, I might find myself faced with a challenger. But I know now it will never happen, not while everything conspires to keep them asleep.*

As he boarded the first train to arrive, he smiled to himself. All he knew was that wherever he was going, he would find his place in a corrupt new world.

All life, and all lives, were there for the taking.

Arthur Bryant stood with his hands pressed against the cold windowpane, watching dark rivulets of rain, and the smeary streets beyond. He was furious with his own stupidity and wilfulness.

You're a foolish old man who places lives at risk, he told himself angrily, *just because you refuse to give up outdated ideas. Liberty DuCaine is dead because you were too busy holding court with your staff. You were so pleased with the sound of your own voice that you didn't take time to secure your suspect properly. You forgot the first rules you ever learned: protect the innocent, and never lower your guard on duty. You don't deserve the people who work for you and trust you.*

Behind him on the desk was a note Mr Ed Tremble had sent through, the answer to a question he had asked about Battle Bridge, the site of Boudicca's last battle. Tremble had discovered that the legend was based on little more than a linguistic error. The name of the village was merely a corruption of Bradford Bridge, which in turn came from 'Broad Ford'. There had once been a bridge over the River Fleet.

So there had been no Roman battle here. No mystical link to ancient gods. No pagan retribution. Just human greed and cruelty.

You should have seen that, he thought bitterly. *You should have been an academic, not a detective. All that time spent attempting to convince everyone of the mythologies that surround you. How can we ever really know anything about the past? They talk about 'the lie of the land' – well, this land is filled with lies. Even our own memories can't be trusted.*

He wiped at a rheumy blue eye as the rain swam on the window. *I will never again make this mistake,* he swore. *I will spend the time I have left hunting you down, Mr Fox, and I will kill you.*

The publishers hope that this book has given you enjoyable reading. Large Print Books are especially designed to be as easy to see and hold as possible. If you wish a complete list of our books please ask at your local library or write directly to:

Magna Large Print Books
Magna House, Long Preston,
Skipton, North Yorkshire.
BD23 4ND

This Large Print Book, for people
who cannot read normal print,
is published under the auspices of

THE ULVERSCROFT FOUNDATION